Praise for
The Sandman: Book of Dreams

"Even if you don't care for the comic's hairstyles and attitudes, *The Sandman: Book of Dreams* is well worth picking up. It may not give you nightmares, but it will provoke enough deep thought to keep you awake for a few nights."

Thomas Deja
—*FANGORIA* magazine

"There isn't a dud in the lot. . . . A special delight is George Alec Effinger's crosshatching of Gaiman's *Dreaming* with the classic cartoon strip *Little Nemo in Slumberland*. . . . In *Each Damp Thing*, Barbara Hambly does a splendid comic-horrific romp featuring our favorite servants from Dream's court. . . . Caitlin R. Kiernan and Robert Rodi both write movingly about Alvin-Wanda. Each piece has its own introduction by Neil Gaiman. These introductions are definitely far too short."

—*SFX* magazine

"Though perhaps most interesting as an example of media-crossover, this collection presents some powerful writing about, and memorable images of, the other reality wherein we while away a third of our lives."
—*Publishers Weekly*

"Readers don't need a familiarity with the Sandman comic to appreciate these stories. Recommended."

—*Library Journal*

D1377547

The Sandman graphic novels,
written by Neil Gaiman and
published by DC Comics, are:

——————

Preludes and Nocturnes
The Doll's House
Dream Country
Season of Mists
A Game of You
Fables and Reflections
Brief Lives
Worlds' End
The Kindly Ones
The Wake
and
Death: The High Cost of Living

the SANDMAN™

book of dreams

EDITED BY

Neil Gaiman
and
Edward E. Kramer

HarperPrism
An Imprint of HarperPaperbacks

HarperPaperbacks
A Division of HarperCollins*Publishers*
10 East 53rd Street, New York, N.Y. 10022-5299

If you purchased this book without a cover, you should be aware
that this book is stolen property. It was reported as "unsold and
destroyed" to the publisher and neither the author nor the publisher
has received any payment for this "stripped book."

This is a work of fiction. The characters, incidents, and dialogues are
products of the author's imagination and are not to be construed as
real. Any resemblance to actual events or persons, living or dead, is
entirely coincidental.

Copyright © 1996 by DC Comics
All rights reserved. No part of this book may be used or reproduced
in any manner whatsoever without written permission of the publisher, except in the case of brief quotations embodied in critical articles and reviews. For information address HarperCollins*Publishers*,
10 East 53rd Street, New York, N.Y. 10022-5299.

ISBN 0-06-105354-6

HarperPrism is an imprint of HarperPaperbacks.

A hardcover edition of this book was published
in 1996 by HarperCollins*Publishers*.

HarperCollins®, ®, HarperPaperbacks™, and HarperPrism®
are trademarks of HarperCollins*Publishers* Inc.

Cover design by Dave McKean

First HarperPaperbacks printing: April 1997

Printed in the United States of America

Visit HarperPaperbacks on the World Wide Web at
http://www.harpercollins.com/paperbacks

❖ 10 9 8 7 6 5 4 3 2 1

This book is for Harlan Ellison,
Jane Yolen, Martha Soukup, and Charles de Lint.
With apologies—

Neil

table of
CONTENTS

the
SANDMAN™
book of
dreams

PREFACE

Frank McConnell

How do gods die? And when they do, what becomes of them *then*?

You might as well ask, how do gods get born? All three questions are, really, the same question. And they all have a common assumption: that humankind can no more live without gods than you can kill yourself by holding your breath.

(Of course, you just may be the kind of arrant rationalist who huffs that modern man has finally freed himself from ancient enslavement to superstition, fantasy, and awe. If so, return this book immediately to its place of purchase for a refund; and, by the by, don't bother trying to read Shakespeare, Homer, Faulkner, or, for that matter, Dr. Seuss.)

We need gods—Thor or Zeus or Krishna or Jesus or, well, God—not so much to worship or sacrifice to, but because they satisfy our need—distinctive from that of all the other animals—to imagine a meaning, a sense to our lives, to satisfy our hunger to believe that the muck and chaos of daily existence does, after all, *tend* somewhere. It's the origin of religion, and also of storytelling—or aren't they both the same thing? As Voltaire said of God: if he did not exist, it would have been necessary to invent him.

Listen to an expert on the matter.

"There are only two worlds—your world, which is the real world, and other worlds, the fantasy. Worlds like this are worlds of the human imagination: their reality, or lack of reality, is not important. What is important is that they are there. These worlds provide an alternative. Provide an escape. Provide a threat. Provide a dream, and power; provide refuge, and pain. They give your world meaning. They do not exist; and thus they are all that matters. Do you understand?"

The speaker is Titania, the beautiful and dangerous Queen of Faerie, in Neil Gaiman's graphic novel *The Books of Magic*, and I don't know a better summary explanation—from Plato to Sir Philip Sidney to Northrop Frye—of why we need, read, and write stories. Of why we, as a species, are godmakers. And spoken by a goddess *in* a story.

Books of Magic was written while Gaiman was also writing his master-piece—*so far* his masterpiece, for God or gods know what he'll do next—*The Sandman*. It is a comic book that changes your mind about what comics are and what they can do. It is a serial novel—like those of Dickens and Thack-eray—that, by any honest reckoning, is as stunning a piece of storytelling as any "mainstream" (read: academically respectable) fiction produced in the last decade. It is a true invention of an authentic, and richly satisfying, mythology for postmodern, postmythological man: a new way of making gods. And it is the brilliant inspiration for the brilliant stories in this book.

Like most extraordinary things, *The Sandman* had unextraordinary begin-nings (remember that Shakespeare, as far as we can tell, just set out to run a theater, make some cash, and move back to his hick hometown). In 1987, Gaiman was approached by Karen Berger of DC Comics to revive one of the characters from DC's WWII "golden age." After some haggling, they decided on "The Sandman." Now the original Sandman, in the late thirties and forties, was a kind of Batman Lite. Millionaire Wesley Dodds, at night, would put on gas mask, fedora, and cape, hunt down bad guys, and zap them with his gas gun, leaving them to sleep until the cops picked them up the next morning—hardly the stuff of legend.

So what Gaiman did was jettison virtually everything except the title. The Sandman—childhood's fairy who comes to put you to sleep, the bringer of dreams, the Lord of Dreams, the Prince of Stories—indisputably the stuff of legend.

Between 1988 and 1996, in seventy-five monthly issues, Gaiman crafted an intricate, funny, and profound tale *about* tales, a story about why there are stories. Dream—or Morpheus, or the Shaper—gaunt, pale, and clad in black, is the central figure. He is not a god; he is older than all gods, and is their cause. He is the human capacity to imagine meaning, to *tell stories*: an anthro-pomorphic projection of our thirst for mythology. And as such, he is both greater and less than the humans whose dreams he shapes, but whose thirst, after all, shapes *him*. As Titania would say, he does not exist; and thus he is all that matters. Do you understand?

Grand enough, you would think, to conceive a narrative whose central character *is* narrative. Among the few other writers who have dared that much is Joyce, whose *Finnegans Wake* is essentially one immense dream encompassing all the myths of the race ("wake"—"dream": get it?). And, though Gaiman would probably be too modest to invite the comparison, I am convinced that Joyce was much on his mind during the whole process of composition. The first words of the first issue of *The Sandman* are "Wake up"; the last words of the last major story arc of *The Sandman* are "Wake up"—the title of the last story arc being, naturally, "The Wake." (All of Gaiman's story titles, by the way, are versions of classic stories, from Aeschylus to Ibsen and beyond. A Brit, raised on British crosswords, he can't resist playing hide-and-seek with the reader—rather like Joyce.)

Grand enough, that. But having invented Dream, the personified human urge to make meaning, he went on to invent Dream's family, and *that* invention is absolutely original and, to paraphrase what Prince Hal says of Falstaff, witty in itself and the cause of wit in other men.

The family is called the Endless, seven siblings, in order of age—"birth," we'll see, is not an appropriate term—Destiny, Death, Dream, Destruction, Desire, Despair, and Delirium (whose name used to be Delight). They are the Endless because they are states of human consciousness itself, and cannot cease to exist until thought itself ceases to exist; they were not "born" because, like consciousness, nothing can be imagined *before* them: the Upanishads, earliest and most subtle of theologies, have a deal to say on this matter.

To be conscious at all is to be conscious of time, and of time's arrow: of destiny. And to know *that* is to know that time must have a stop: to imagine death. Faced with the certainty of death, we dream, imagine paradises where it might not be so: "Death is the mother of beauty," wrote Wallace Stevens. And all dreams, all myths, all the structures we throw up between ourselves and chaos, just because they are *built things*, must inevitably be destroyed. And we turn, desperate in our loss, to the perishable but delicious joy of the moment: we desire. All desire is, of course, the hope for a fulfillment impossible in the very nature of things, a boundless delight; so to desire is always already *to* despair, to realize that the wished-for delight is only, after all, the delirium of our mortal self-delusion that the world is large enough to fit the mind. And so we return to new stories—to dreams.

Now that's an overschematic version of the lineage of the Endless, almost a Medieval-style allegorization. For they're also real *characters*: as real as the humans with whom they are constantly interacting throughout *The Sandman*. Destiny is a monastic, hooded figure, almost without affect. Death—Gaiman's brilliant idea—is a heartbreakingly beautiful, witty young woman. Dream—is Dream, somber, a tad pretentious, and a tad neurotic. Destruction is a red-haired giant who loves to laugh and talks like a stage Irishman. Desire—another brilliant stroke—is androgynous, as sexy and as threatening as a Nagel dominatrix; and Despair, his/her twin, is a squat, fat, preternaturally ugly naked hag. Delirium, fittingly for her name, is almost never drawn the same way: all we can tell for sure is that she is a young girl, with multicolored or no hair, dressed in shreds and speaking in non sequiturs that sometimes achieve the surreal antiwisdom of, say, Rimbaud.

Nevertheless: the Endless *are* an allegory, and a splendid one, of the nature of consciousness, of being-in-the-world. And it can't be emphasized too much that these more-than, less-than gods matter only because of the everyday people with whose lives and passions they interact. The *Sandman* mythology, in other words, brings us full circle from all classical religions. "In the beginning God made man?" Quite—and quite precisely—the reverse.

And Dream, the Lord of Storytelling, is at the center of it all.

We begin and end with stories because we are the storytelling animal. *The Sandman* is at one with *Finnegans Wake*, and also with Nietzsche, C. G. Jung, and Joseph Campbell in insisting that all gods, all heroes and mythologies are the shadow-play of the human drama. The concept of the Endless— and particularly of Dream—is a splendid "*machine* for storytelling" (a phrase Gaiman is fond of). Characters from the limitless ocean of myth, and characters from the so-called "real" world—that's you and I when we're not dreaming—can mingle and interact in its universe: quite as they mingle and interact in you and me when we *are* dreaming. It's often been said by literary critics that our age is impoverished by its inability to believe in anything save the cold equations of science. (Hence Destruction, fourth of the siblings, left the Endless in the seventeenth century—the onset of the Age of Reason.) But our strongest writers, Gaiman included, have always found ways of reviving the vitality of the myths, even on the basis of their unreality. *Credo, quia impossibile est*, wrote Tertullian in the third century A.D., about the Christian mystery: "I believe it *because* it is impossible." Good theology, maybe; excellent theory of fiction, absolutely.

Now that *The Sandman* is over, and its creator has moved on, it continues to serve as a machine for storytelling. DC Comics provides *The Dreaming*, a series by various hands using the assumptions and the characters invented in *The Sandman*. And the volume you hold now, by gifted "mainstream" (i.e. non–comic book) writers, all of them expanding and elaborating the *Sandman* mythos, is perhaps only the first, rich fruit of Gaiman's new technique for godmaking.

De te fabula, runs the Latin tag: the story, whatever story, is always about *you*. That's the ancient wisdom *The Sandman* makes new: it's why, finally, we read at all. It is—and I know no higher praise—another realization of

Wallace Stevens's sublime vision of fiction in his great poem, "Esthétique du Mal":

> "And out of what one sees and hears and out
> Of what one feels, who could have thought to make
> So many selves, so many sensuous worlds,
> As if the air, the mid-day air, was swarming
> With the metaphysical changes that occur
> Merely in living as and where we live."

MASQUERADE AND HIGH WATER

Colin Greenland

I have known Colin Greenland (um, Ph.D.) at least three weeks longer than I have known anyone else in this book. That's about thirteen years. In that time he has written elegant fantasies, romping space operas, and wise works of nonfiction. He has also won many awards, including the Arthur C. Clarke Award for his novel *Take Back Plenty*. Oddly, he has not aged in any noticeable way, still looking a little like Gandalf's rock-and-rolling youngest brother would, if he were secretly a pirate.

It's a love story; which seemed like a good place to start.

Sherri stood in the doorway with a mug of iced tea, shading her eyes from the sun. "You missed the wedding!" she called.

Oliver shut the car door and went up the steps to the porch. "You had a wedding?" he said.

In fact Oliver had been aware of them all morning, the battered cars and bikes trailing up the road past his house. He had heard the laughter coming from up here, the distorted wail of old Jefferson Airplane albums. It was either a wedding or a wake. He kept away until the celebration all died down and everything went quiet. He didn't know why he had come up here now. Just being neighborly, he supposed.

Sherri was pottering inside and out, picking up. There was enough mess: paper plates smeared with guacamole, empty bottles, half-empty cans. There was always mess at Sherri's house, wedding or no wedding. Oliver kind of liked it. It helped confirm his resolve to keep his place down the road vacuumed and tidy, free of bachelor squalor.

"It was a great wedding," Sherri said. "I married Johnny and Turquoise."

She knew everybody in the hills for miles around, and always assumed he did, too. In fact in two years here she was the only one he had got to know at all. It was the solitude he liked—that, and the low property prices that meant he could own now instead of paying top dollar rent on some cracker box downtown. He liked living among the trees, in clean air, with the mountains in the distance. He sat on Sherri's broken-down porch and looked out into the soft dark green of spruce, the shivering yellow aspen. Above his head hung the sign, black letters charred into a slice of birchwood: CHURCH OF THE WILD ELK.

"Want some of this?" She put a big cold bowl in his lap.

"What is it?"

"Melon ginger ice cream."

Probably half an ounce of hash in there too, knowing Sherri. "No thanks."

Sherri half sat on the porch rail in her worn long tie-dye skirt, cradling the

8

bowl. Her arms were sun brown and strong. "You know, I had this amazing dream," she said, dipping her finger in the ice cream and licking it. "I dreamed I was sitting there where you're sitting, only there was this big white cat in my lap. And I stroked it, and it got up and went away, and I looked down in my lap and there were all these tiny little kittens! It was ama-a-zing," she said, drawing the word out into a whole drowsy musical phrase. "It was really amazing. Don't you think that was a good omen for Johnny and Turquoise?"

"I never have dreams," said Oliver.

In his black onyx boat in the form of a sphinx, Morpheus the Shaper and his sibling Desire float across the waters of the buried lake. The air is hot and gloomy. The sailors in their nightwear haul at the ropes, putting on more sail. Eyes closed, they trawl the darkness for the sluggish wind.

The two travelers lie upon cushions. They speak of responsibility. Desire says it is a tiresome illusion. Morpheus does not deny it, but claims it is inescapable in the human realm, inseparable from it as shadows from sunlight.

"People pursue things," says Morpheus. "As soon as they have them they run away from them. But what they run away from stays with them, dragging along behind them like an ever-lengthening cloak."

"Cloaks are nice." Bright-eyed Desire bites its finger. "You can wear a cloak and have nothing on under it at all. And you can go anywhere you want like that!"

The water is dark and murky, like an old painting. Desire makes water lilies in it, green and white and golden as egg yolk. Morpheus broods, as he does so often, his long chin resting in his wax-white hand.

Far away across the water, at the Pavilion of Recurrence, the summoning bell is ringing.

"Everybody dreams, Ollie," said Sherri, fetching him a beer. "They say you are what you dream. Did you ever hear that?"

"No," said Oliver. "I never did."

"You are what you dream," said Sherri again, nodding, and smiled her blissed-out smile. Her eyes were pretty. She picked up some butts, an empty corn chip box. She came across a shawl and draped it round her shoulders, despite the warmth of the afternoon.

Oliver glanced at her. She couldn't be much older than he, though she had a grown-up daughter somewhere running around. They always had dressed like grannies, the Earth Mother types, in long dresses and scarves and twenty pounds of beads. He did wish she wouldn't call him Ollie.

Sherri was a nice Jewish girl from New York, originally. She had come out here to clean out her headspace. Her house was a legally consecrated church, tax exempt. She had told Oliver she was figuring out a way to write off the hot tub as a baptismal font.

Oliver smiled and drank his beer. Sherri and her congregation. People who had crawled up in here when the sixties turned to shit and never crawled out again. But Sherri was okay. She had helped him the first winter, when he got sick, and when his Subaru went into that snowdrift she got somebody for him, somebody she knew who came with a tow truck and pulled it out and never even sent him a bill. Sherri was okay, when you had time for her. Sherri wouldn't do you harm.

Sometimes the Pavilion of Recurrence looks like an Arabian tent, a finespun marvel of white-and-scarlet cloth billowing in a place of sand and mirage. Sometimes it stands to one side of a grassy river meadow where swans glide beneath willows and great helms and targets with obscure devices hang amid the branches of bowed and ancient trees. Sometimes it is made of pellucid white marble, the Pavilion of Recurrence, with gilded balconies, and the sound of a piano tinkling lazily from an open window.

Sometimes, like today, the Pavilion of Recurrence has the aspect of an island monastery, with a bell tower and a thick coat of evergreen creeper. The bell tolls slowly, insistently, across the buried lake.

Inside the Pavilion of Recurrence, as anywhere else in the Dreaming to one extent or another, whatever is needed is provided. A morgue, where night after night forensic pathologists find members of their families stretched out on the slab, opened up for dissection, though still pleading to be released. A school where adults of all ages return again and again to face unprepared for and incomprehensible exams. A tram that takes commuters on an eternal journey to an ominous destination through unknown yet strangely haunting streets. A sepulchral secondhand shop, on whose shelves authors find dusty books with titles that are completely unreadable, but whose covers bear their own names.

Inside the Pavilion of Recurrence today they are assembling for a dream of masquerade and high water. The bell calls them in, the figments, the chimeras, the larval entities that make up the crowd. A raven perches on a sill above the jetty, inspecting them as they disembark. Beneath their long hair they are faceless. Smoke drifts from their unfinished fingers. One carries a tambourine. Others seem to be swirls of paisley and embroidered clothes with no bodies inside them at all.

A foreground character with the likeness of a placid child speaks to the librarian, who is consulting the index of a large book. "How many more times must we do this?"

The librarian answers, "Until he ceases to mourn."

Her voice was harsh, roughened by smoke and bad habits. "What are you doing the rest of the weekend?"

"I've got some stuff to sort out. Some projections."

"Astral projections?" she asked, teasing.

"Just the regular kind. Sales and budgets."

"Shit, Ollie, they really got your feet nailed to the floor, don't they."

Oliver drank beer, licked his lips. "The work don't do itself, Sherri," he said. "It don't go away." He found himself saying things like that, *don't* instead of *doesn't*, when he talked to Sherri. It was more appropriate, somehow, out here where people wore beer brand T-shirts and drove around with their dogs beside them in the front seat.

"Sure it does," she said. "When it goes away, that's when you start to worry."

He asked her: "What are you doing these days, Sherri?"

"I'm going into solar," she said. "You know that little place down on the mall? They got a sales training program and incentive scheme and everything. You sell enough systems, they fit you one for free." She braced her arms on the rail and beamed up at the sky as though she could already see the big glass panels erected on her roof, gathering heat from the benevolent sun.

"That would be good," said Oliver.

Sherri never told you what she was doing, always what she was going to do. She never seemed to do anything, unless it was some crazy scheme, charting horoscopes, designing children's clothes, selling tofu sandwiches out of the back of a truck. House painting, she did sometimes. There was a house across the valley she told him she had painted. It had a huge yellow sunflower on the side.

Sherri always made Oliver think of California, twenty years before. Nearer thirty now. She reminded him of when he had lived that way himself for a time, on the coast, in the days of Donna. It had been possible then. In the summer it was a gas—had they really said that? Something was a gas? The phrase seemed strange to him, as if it could not possibly have ever fit inside his mouth. In the summertime, anyhow, yes, the living was easy: plenty of work, warm nights, they slept on the beach.

In the winter it was different. Then there was no work, it was freezing cold and it rained all the time. You had to hole up in the empty tourist cabins, try to live on what you'd saved from the summer. The two of them had joined a commune, a bunch of psychedelic musicians and their "old ladies"— Jesus Christ, had he said that too, and called them chicks and talked about freaking out and scoring dope? Living on rice and beans, sleeping in bags on drafty floors, keeping watch for the Russian River to flood. Jesus Christ, he must have been crazy.

Oliver thought about Donna then, almost without knowing he did so; and as he always did, blanked out her features before consigning her to oblivion.

He drank his beer.

The figments troop into a small room. The room has walls and a floor of green jade. No matter how many of the figments come in, the room is always big enough to hold them.

In the green jade room the Continuity Girl checks their manifestations for them. The Continuity Girl wears gold bangles shaped like stirrups and a reassuring jacket of russet tweed. She tries to call the roll. "Parqua . . . Quarpa . . . Apquar . . . " The letters on her clipboard wriggle about.

"Minimum May . . . Dr. Scorpio Bongo . . . " The figments are ignoring her. Background characters settle into clusters, comfortably. Absentmindedly they start to merge.

The raven perches on the librarian's shoulder. It speaks. "What's the story here?" it asks.

Patiently the librarian adjusts his glasses, dislodged by the raven's landing, and turns over a page. He follows the line of an entry with his finger. "It looks like a dream about lost love . . . " he says.

"Yeah, well, typical," says the raven.

". . . and about a river rising."

The raven nuzzles its purple plumage. "I think maybe I've seen it."

The clustered figures are growing consolidated, like statuary groups. Their fringes are entwining, the patches on their denims running together. The Continuity Girl has not yet noticed. She is dealing with the thing that is Donna, helping it into a dress made of dried leaves and peacocks' eyes.

Over the years the foreground characters have become quite stable. Some of them are acquiring memories—personalities, almost. A little brown thing like an elongated cherub with bat wings and a screwed-up, miserable face speaks about the wonderful dress.

"His mother had a dress like that. He remembers her in it, dancing with his father in a state of high excitement. It was at his cousin Mona's wedding, but he has forgotten that. He was three. When they sat down after dancing he got under the table and put his head up his mother's dress."

A man with the beard of a lumberjack and the face of a turtle denies it. "She never had such a dress. No one ever had, not in the human realm. It is a piece of something else that has blown in from who knows where, and been caught between the teeth of the dream."

A grainy boy in a headband laughs. "Like getting your shorts stuck in your zipper."

"You ever seen Texas, Ollie? El Paso? I'm going down to El Paso, going to see Pepper."

Pepper was Sherri's daughter. Short for Chili Pepper, Sherri had told him. "Because she was so red and wrinkly!" Oliver had never met her, only seen photographs. The girl looked half-Indian; half-something, anyway. Sherri was always taking off somewhere or other to go see her.

"You ought to come along," said Sherri.

"How's Pepper?" he said.

"She's going to Mexico. She's driving a truck for this wildlife survey."

Sherri always made her daughter out to be a conscientious person—"really focused"—but Oliver had noticed that whenever she went to see her, each time Pepper was in some new place, doing some different thing. Once Sherri had come back from Wyoming in a beat-up Oldsmobile with a story about her and Pepper meeting two rodeo riders in Cheyenne and everybody swapping cars with each other. Pepper, Oliver suspected, might be a lot like her mom.

Oliver glanced down at his car. The transmission needed looking at. And there was that little bit of rust that needed fixing before it got any bigger. The little bit of rust had been there since last winter. He didn't want to think about it.

Sherri had left the porch and was doing something indoors behind him. Oliver pitched his voice to her.

"When are you going?"

There was a pause. Somewhere in the distance a dog barked; then another, and another. All along the valley, at all the houses hidden in the trees, dogs roused themselves on porches and in dustholes and under sheds. One after another they lifted their heads up and added their contribution to the neighborhood chorus. Whatever had woken them remained mysterious as always, remarkable only to canines.

Sherri reappeared. She was eating ice cream again. "Oh, I'm going real soon," she said.

The janitor sits down on the set and lights a cigarette. His team is setting up the redwood forest, giant trees that shoot up hundreds of feet to spread their branches. There are bits of twig all over the janitor's blue bib overalls. He says: "What I can't figure is, we're here luggin' these goddamn trees around, yeah? But the guy's got trees in the daytime, ya know? So what's he need the goddamn trees in his dreams for?"

The librarian turns a page. "I think it's other way round, Mervyn."

A black dog that has been hanging around has turned into a squat bird with a long beak. When it lifts its wings you can see it has legs underneath like a crab. There are several of the things. They run quickly among the shapeless furniture.

The Girl flicks back her hair. "What are those?" she calls. "I've never seen those before." Intently she searches her list. The list is getting longer. It slips between her fingers and drops to the floor, unrolling as it bounces away.

"No story is exactly the same twice," observes a figment with paper lips. "Even written down and printed in a book."

"Everything is the same as itself," says another in a dry, whiskery voice. "That's the way it is, man."

"It's not the same story because you're not the same person," says the first figment.

"I'm the same person, man," the second asserts. "I used to be in another dream," it recalls. "It was better than this one. It was all about flying and chocolate."

"You're not the same person because it's not the same dream."

Circling, the raven glides back to the librarian. "The Quapras are arguing, Lucien."

"Sort them out, Matthew, for goodness sake, before they start attracting Delirium," says the librarian. "Get everyone to their entrances." It is like looking after a tour party of forgetful old people, always squabbling and repeating themselves, telling each other the same things over and over.

Sitting on Sherri's porch, Oliver fell asleep.

Once again he is standing in the cabin in front of the enormous closet, watching the clown take out clothes and throw them to the people all around the room. The clothes fly over Oliver's head, very slowly. He is still in the cabin, but he can see gray sky beyond the floating Hawaiian shirts and party gowns, where the ceiling used to be. The people always catch the clothes with happy cries and put them on. They are dressing up as the summer visitors.

Some of the people are familiar. That boy with the snub nose and long curly hair, he is usually there. He called himself Dr. Scorpio. He used to take acid and play the bongos all night. Oliver had learned to sleep through the drumming. Dr. Scorpio puts on a pair of pajamas. For an instant the pajamas are a pair Oliver had when he was a little boy, with blue tugboats on, but he could not be expected to remember that. The clown has huge buckteeth. He is still throwing clothes. Oliver tries to catch some, but they seem to pass right through his hands.

He notices a man with a black beard who used to work at the funfair, and someone cooking food, and someone whose skin keeps changing color behind a pair of circular purple spectacles. "Fixing plumbing is Nixon cling," a face swims up and tells Oliver, who folds his hands in his sleeves and laughs desperately. Donna is there—Donna is always there—in red-and-green-striped trousers, playing the piano. In the cavernous closet a placid child sits, contemplatively stroking the jackets and dresses of the absent guests. "These clothes are not our clothes," it says. "That is why they suit us so well."

Oliver laughs and laughs and laughs.

On Sherri's porch, the sun sifted through the trees on Oliver's still face. Sherri was talking to him about Turquoise and Johnny, but he was very far away.

It is winter in the Pavilion of Recurrence. Oliver and a black woman he saw once on a street corner in Philadelphia are trying to warn everyone the river is going to flood. They are clambering up and down tiers of seats, like in a stadium, in and out of trapdoors, up and down ladders with just little stumps instead of rungs. Far below, the rest of the commune come running across the grass, fleeing from a huge wave of water. Oliver and the woman always slide down a chute in an upturned table with a placid child and a man with a fishing pole. Everyone passes around heavy packages wrapped in disintegrating paper. No matter how Oliver tries to hold on to the packages, the paper keeps tearing and the weight slides out of his fingers. The flood bears him away under the enormous trees. Oliver tries to hang on to the leg of the table, but there is no table anymore. Donna runs away between the trees, laughing. Oliver is not laughing now. He is always upset, or cross. Sometimes he tries to catch her, wading frantically through earth that has turned to water, or sometimes through the air. Sometimes she tries to catch him. They never catch each other, no matter what.

Sherri crumpled the last paper cup into the garbage sack. She looked at Oliver, wondering how long he could hold on to his beer without spilling it. He had the can propped on his belly. He was getting a little pot there, the years starting to pile up around his waist. Why were all the guys she knew getting fat? Sherri had the strongest urge suddenly to put her hands on Oliver's belly and feel the warm firm mass of it, to squeeze him awake and kiss him in his surprise. She snorted at herself and reeled back a ways on her heels. She was still a little stoned. Deliberately she went and got the cloth and wiped the tabletop, softly humming a tune that was going round her head, thinking about the wedding and the celebrations and all. Ollie was nice, Sherri thought, though he always seemed kind of sad, as if he was more alone, maybe, than he really wanted to be.

"Weddings always make me horny," she told the sleeping man.

In the buried lake at the bottom of the Dreaming the black onyx boat in the shape of a sphinx bumps against a shadowy jetty. Its somnambulant crew begin to reef the sails.

Desire inserts a ripe cherry into its own mouth, and one into its brother's. It draws its feet up and looks about. "I know this place," it says.

"The Pavilion of Recurrence," says Morpheus. This spot can be reached from any of their realms. All the Endless have sometimes been concerned in the ceremonies staged inside this gray secretive building, nightbound ceremonies of loss or discovery or consecration established and sanctified by repetition.

By the light of pale green torches Morpheus and his sibling climb the steps and walk directly through the wall into the flooded Pavilion. The wall grows vague and confused, admitting them.

Inside, enigmatic monumental furniture floats about, and vast trees seem to tower out of the thick brown water. A human man is being hounded this way and that by chuckling sprites. The Lord of Shapings points at him. "This is one encumbered by the cloak of his past," he tells his sibling. As he speaks you can almost see it, a dim integument of ragged moonlight that clings to the toiler's shoulders, holding him back like a spider's web. He tries to lunge forward through the liquid wood, but the phantasms baffle him easily, driving him astray this way and that.

Desire gathers up a handful of air. It seems to have caught the hem of the human's cloak, to be rubbing the unstable fabric between its fingers. With its free hand it points to a laughing woman hiding behind a tree.

"Who is that?"

"His first true love."

"How sweet."

Desire reaches into the dream, which seems to have become very small suddenly, like a toy theater, an enclosure of splashing, scampering little mammals. It does something to the face of the woman, turning her into someone else, someone older, with long dark red hair. "There," it says, straightening up again. "That's better, isn't it?"

At first, the flux of wood and water is so complete it is impossible to notice any change. Then it becomes apparent the endless recircling rhythm of the piece has been disrupted. Individual phantoms are shrinking, dwindling, turning into sparks that go whizzing away into nothingness. Agitated memories are being smoothed and quelled and laid to rest like ironed clothes folded in sheets of tissue paper. The Continuity Girl waves her arms like a scarecrow in a gale. Already she is coming apart, in a flurry of dark green underwear. An infinite number of golden bangles go shooting away in a cylindrical stream. Meanwhile Lucien is crossing something out in a big book, writing hurriedly in the margin with a long stout jet black feather.

Morpheus fingers his jaw. "I wish you would not interfere," he says mildly to his sibling, though anyone who knows his voice well might detect a touch of sardonic amusement.

Desire touches itself then in a way that makes even the Dream King inhale reflexively, narrowing his nostrils and hooding his fathomless eyes.

"Darling brother," Desire sighs yearningly. "I never do anything else."

Oliver started awake to a blare of sound, guitar and electric violin. Sherri had put "It's a Beautiful Day" on.

He sat blinking on the porch, entirely disoriented. The sun had gone down while he slept, and the sky was a rich thick wash of indigo. Soon it would be black, pricked and blazing, dripping cold silver fire from an inconceivable number of stars.

"Sherri?" he called. He could not hear or see her, and suddenly that seemed to matter.

He heard her footsteps inside the house and turned toward them from his chair, almost spilling the remains of his beer. "When you going to Texas?" he asked clumsily, before he could see whereabouts she was. It was hard to speak, sleep seemed to have gummed up his tongue.

"I don't know," her voice said, calm and easy as ever over the surging music. "Next week, maybe. You want to come?"

He saw her then, looking through the kitchen window at him. The smile on her face seemed to welcome him as though he had returned from a long absence, and not just woken from an unintended nap. Oliver had seen her naked one time, dropped in and found the door open and nobody home, he thought, until he came upon her sleeping out back in the yard in the sun. He had stood and looked at her curved and comfortable body, her lolling breasts with their broad dirt-brown nipples, her plump thighs drawn protectively up. He had stood looking at her a moment or two, and then he had returned to his car, got in, and parped the horn. He had sat and waited until Sherri had appeared with a dozy grin on the porch in her long gown of Laundromat gray, messing up her thick red hair with her hand.

"What about the solar job?" he asked, in a mischief-making drawl.

She caught his tone. Lifting a plate from a bowl full of suds she squinted at the sky. "I guess I missed the sun," she said. Sherri, Oliver thought, was not afraid of time; and that seemed suddenly very important.

"You want to come?" she was asking him again. "To El Paso?"

With Sherri driving, he thought cynically, probably they wouldn't ever get to El Paso. Like as not they wouldn't get to Texas at all. They would take her car and it would break down in New Mexico. Oliver could see it now, as clear as if it had been a memory, not a premonition. They would wind up waiting all day by the road in the middle of nowhere, comparing their childhoods, making lists of state capitals and singing all the songs they could think of, and finally a Navajo woman would stop in a truck full of paper flowers and take them fifty miles out of their way to go see some cave paintings and then on to a barbecue at the house of a professional hang glider, only the directions would be wrong, and they would wake up at noon the next day in the wrong town, still drunk, on somebody else's floor, and they would have to come home on the bus in each other's arms sharing a hangover and he would lie to his manager about the unprojected projections.

"Sure," Oliver heard himself say. "Why not."

Sherri paused, arrested over the dishes. Through the glass he saw her pretty eyes fill suddenly with hope and delight and not a trace of disbelief at all. "Really?" she said. It was like she was getting excited about something. "Really?"

"Sure," said Oliver, and yawned, and laughed. "Sure, why not."

CHAIN HOME, LOW

John M. Ford

John M. Ford is a genius, I think. He knows many things. He wrote about cyberspace before William Gibson; he won the World Fantasy Award for best novel with his alternate history *The Dragon Waiting*, and for best short story with his poem "Winter Solstice, Camelot Station"; he wrote *The Scholars of Night*, a modern spy thriller that circles and centers on a lost play by Kit Marlowe; and he wrote the only *Star Trek* novel without *Star Trek* characters (in *The Final Reflection)* and the only *Star Trek* novel with songs and me (in *How Much for Just the Planet?).*

Like Gene Wolfe, Ford writes stories that routinely function on a multitude of levels. This story takes place during the first episode of *Sandman (*in the first *Sandman* collection, *Preludes and Nocturnes).* On one level Dream and his family are conspicuous by their absence. On another level, they are all through it: Dream was a captive in Burgess's basement, remember; and here Ford concatenates a chain of events about that captivity, a chain of puppets and of strings.

After all, we each of us begin in desire, and we all end in death.

In 1916, three days before Christmas, Siegfried Sassoon wrote in his soldier's diary: "The year is dying of atrophy as far as I am concerned, bed-fast in its December fogs."

But he was writing about the war.

The town of Wych Cross sits on the Sussex weald, midway between London and the Channel. "Wych" refers to elm trees, and the town, having been rather overlooked by the Industrial Revolution, did not feed its stands of stout elm to the fires of change. Elm was the material that Arthur's knights used for their lances—at least, in legends. Wych is close to other words, of course.

The town was never large, and rates mention in Sir Nikolaus Pevsner's exhaustive *Buildings of England* only for the manor house nearby. The house, called Fawney Rig, was founded in the late 1500s as a residence for the local magistrate, a comfortable distance from the court hall in Serecombe. Fawney Rig was frequently rebuilt, so that by the twentieth century it was only an architectural oddity, a polyglot house. (Pevsner was dismissive.) On the manor grounds was the only other point of interest in Wych Cross, a raised ring of earth, some three yards high and twenty across. It was known as Wych Dyke, and was said to be Roman, or Druid, or a Roundhead artillery revetment.

In 1904, Fawney Rig was purchased by a man who called himself Roderick Burgess. His original name, his background, and his sources of wealth were all obscure, though he carried himself as an aristocrat and his cheques always proved good. Burgess made further additions to the house: externally, he added Gothic ironwork, gargoyles that vomited rain, coiling dragons along the ridgeline whose iron scales discouraged birds. Interior alterations were made by a firm from the Continent, odd, dark, silent men.

There was a great isolation around Wych Cross; whatever the maps might show, it was a long way from anywhere. So it took a few years for the first scandal to break, and that happened in London, with a police raid on a house in Belgravia. Several socially prominent members of Burgess's "Order of Ancient Mysteries" were involved, as was a naked woman. The papers were full of it for days.

Burgess went back to Wych Cross. That scandal, and those that followed, did not bother him. He swam in scandal, breathing and spouting it like Leviathan in the deeps. Burgess claimed to be a magus, a wizard of indefinably vast powers. People laughed at that. But not in Wych Cross.

In the summer of 1916, in a trench in Belgium, a German soldier named Gottfried Himmels received a letter from home that filled him with an unidentifiable fear. Himmels had been in the trenches for almost a year, and got frequent letters from his wife; they were mostly about his daughter Magdalen. A few months ago, Himmels had sent home some of his pay—he said, "It is a foolishly large sum, but in mad times one ought to be allowed foolishness"—to buy Magdalen a coveted doll for her eighth birthday. Frau Himmels's next letter had gone on for two full pages about the party, and the doll, and Magdalen's delight.

This letter said, "Magdalen is happy." Not a word more.

A few days after the terrible letter, there was a trench raid on Himmels's sector. Men carrying bayonets and Mills grenades wired to sticks as crude maces—weapons from half a millennium ago—tumbled through the mines and the wire in the wet dark. They fought in silence for a while, except to gasp or groan when a knife or a rifle butt or the odd bullet struck home, and then they began to shout to one another, because all of them were so covered in mud and slime and each other's blood that only the sound of a voice could separate friends from enemies. They yelled names, or "Kamerad" or "Ami" or "Kommen Sie an" or "Á bâs les Boches"; the sound counted more than the words. What Gottfried Himmels was shouting, over and over as he beat and stabbed and shot at faceless muddy men, was "Magdalen freut sich"— Magdalen is happy.

Trench fighting is desperate and fierce beyond even the imaginings of war. Of the forty-odd men involved in that particular action, Himmels was one of only three German survivors, and the only man not seriously wounded.

All three survivors received the Iron Cross First Class, and a period of home leave. When Himmels got home, he understood the letter. He understood why he had been afraid. He even understood, faintly, why it had seemed at the height of the battle that something greater than himself guided his hands, that the Angel of Death was standing apart from him and would not come near.

That same summer, with the lights of Europe dark for two years, sleeping people had begun to not quite wake up.

The victims of "sleepy sickness" were not inert. They would eat if fed, and responded, in a disconnected fashion, to voices and noises. They could and did move about by themselves, though the actions had no relation to the actual environment—walking purposefully into walls was common—and even if open-eyed they did not see.

Some people blamed the War; some thought it was a new manifestation of the terrible influenza that was affecting so many. But all the cases were isolated, and it struck in places the Great War had not touched. Missionaries and explorers brought reports of cases in the most isolated parts of the world. Sometimes the sleepers were called holy. Sometimes they were killed, or left to the elements. In the Western world they were kept in spare bedrooms, or hospitals, or nursing homes, or wherever seemed appropriate.

Sigmund Freud saw several cases, and wrote a careful but inconclusive monograph, *Beobachtungs des Wahrschlafssperrung*. The name was coined by Dr. Simon Rachlin, a young associate of Freud's; with the ungainly precision of German, it meant *Suspension of True Sleep*. One of the observed patients, identified as "Fräulein H.", was Magdalen Himmels, who had been found slumbering next to her dolls' house in August 1916, one of the very first cases. Once or twice in a month, Magdalen would act out a formal ball, waltzing an invisible doll around her hospital room.

Nine months after Gottfried's visit home, Peter Himmels was born. He slept in his mother's room until he was nearly two, but he slept no more deeply than any other baby, and woke as often and loudly as any of them. Peter would believe himself to be an only child until he was eleven years old.

In 1926 the last confirmed case of the sleepers' disorder was reported in Cape Town. It had been called sleepy sickness, sleepers' flu, *Wahrschlafssperrung*, midwar hypersomnia, Delambre's Disease (within the circle of Dr. Delambre), and the name that finally stuck, *Encephalitis Lethargica*. There were phantom reports for years afterward, other comas, other sleeps. None of them was quite *E. Lethe*, however: victims who could eat, could speak, could move, but were connected to life only by a heartbeat.

There were, at most, twenty thousand of the false sleepers worldwide, and perhaps that number again caught more shallowly, so they were never fully asleep or wakeful, still functional in a cruel way. Against the millions of casualties of the Great War, the influenza pandemic that followed on hard and killed twenty million, what were a quiet few, fading away? There was an entire war footnote to the Great War, an Allied invasion of Siberia to put down the filthy Bolsheviks, and it was entirely forgotten. The sleepers did not rave or suppurate or otherwise offend the wakeful; they needed no large amount of tending (indeed, many got no tending at all); they could hardly organize themselves, and no one in those days organized in their interest. Dopamine drugs were decades away. And so what had briefly been a great medical puzzle, a mysterious visitation, became a curiosity of medicine, a footnote, nothing.

In 1927 a man known as William B. Goodrich directed Louise Brooks in *Still Morning*, about an *E. Lethe* patient finally awakened through the efforts and love of a brilliant young doctor. *Photoplay* said: "It must have sounded like a natural: Brooks in bed for four reels. Who would have expected her to sleep the whole time?" The picture was quickly withdrawn, before the public found out that Goodrich was actually the disgraced comedian Roscoe "Fatty" Arbuckle.

Decades later, Louise Brooks said "The real sleepwalker on that picture was Arbuckle. He'd been dead with his eyes open ever since his friends hung him in public. He said the idea came to him in his sleep. Maybe it did."

A film critic who saw a "rediscovered" print half a century later said, "I know of no other film, even *Pandora's Box*, that makes such extraordinary use of Brooks's demonic innocence. If anybody but Arbuckle had made it, it would be in every film school in the world."

The management of the Ufa studio near Berlin saw the failure of *Still Morning* and quietly shelved their half-completed *Die Träumer*, starring Lil Dagover and almost identical to the American picture. Its scenarist had also dreamed the story.

In Serecombe, in 1928, a young couple named Martyn had their first child, a boy they named Theodore after a favorite uncle of the mother's.

Mrs. Martyn confided to her best friend that the couple had intended to wait for a year or two, putting money by, before starting a family. "But it really wasn't carelessness, Rose. It was desire, just plain desire, like neither of us had ever thought on."

Theodore Martyn was of course never told of this circumstance of his birth. He grew up fairly typical, fond of sweets, sports, adventure stories, and things forbidden to him. And since a boy like that couldn't very well be called "Theodore," he became "Tiger" at a very early age.

Of the forbidden things, there were two in particular. Tiger's best friend Willy Bates was the son of the local newsagent, and thus had access to "Yank magazines," the cheap American pulps with brightly colored covers that went to England as ballast in merchant ships. Willy's father sold a few of them and tossed the rest into the bin, whence they were rescued by the boys.

The other thing was Wych Cross, three miles down the Wych Road. Tiger and Willy knew this had something to do with the mysterious manor house—everyone knew about the mysterious manor house—but exactly what put Wych Cross beyond the pale was delightfully vague.

From the second decade of the century onward, Roderick Burgess was perpetually locked in a battle for fame and followers with Aleister Crowley and a Cornishman known as "Mocata," a sorcerers' duel conducted mostly in journals of strictly limited circulation. The received wisdom was that Mocata was the most urbane and by far the handsomest, Crowley the most voluble and spectacularly degenerate, and Burgess the most philosophical and ruthless. (That he was Oxford, while Crowley was Cambridge, delighted the papers.)

Mocata died of apparent heart failure in 1928. Burgess lacked Crowley's bizarre sense of humor (or any other sort) and eventually lost his taste for the spotlight. He was not seen outside of Fawney Rig after 1930, though there was a continual flow of visitors in Rolls-Royces and Bentleys and the occasional aeroplane.

It was said, though not closer than Serecombe, that Burgess had a devil, or *the* Devil, in the basement of Fawney Rig. It was said he had made a bargain with darkness and could not die. It was said that he had reached that curious state of wealthy old men, of being able to afford any pleasure and to appreciate none of them.

In 1930, James Richard Lee of Liverpool was eleven years old. He lived in a small coal black house with two other families, three couples and eight children all told. All the men were dockers, on different shifts, so that at any given time there was a man out working, one sleeping, one at the local or reading the *Daily Worker*, all interchangeably. There was the occasional raised voice, the good hiding for a proper infraction, but the three wives formed a unified front against tyranny of all sorts, and the small black house was happy, by the standards of the countless small black houses around it.

So there was nothing obvious that drove Dickie Lee down to the waterside in all his spare moments. He would sit, sometimes for hours, looking empty-eyed at the oily port water. This wasn't something boys did in Liverpool. Anyone disturbing Dickie Lee, however, was met first with a word, then a stone thrown close enough to whistle in the ear, and then another stone to prove that the first was not lucky.

Not that he ignored his extended family. Dickie understood that a family, no matter how odd its structure might be, hung together, helped out when one of the members was in trouble. He helped as he could, and got into remarkably little trouble for a boy of his age.

By the fall of 1930, when Dickie was eleven, this had been going on for nearly two years, and he was largely let alone. When someone came up, quietly, behind him this time, he turned, the stone invisible in his palm.

It was his father. Dickie waited a moment, then turned back to the sea.

His father crouched beside him in the gray air, great muscles poised without tension. At some length the man said, "Do you see that seagull yonder, on the post?"

Dickie nodded.

"Can you scare'm off, without 'urting'm?"

The boy's hand flicked back and out, as if it were the only living part of him. The flat rock skipped off the top of the post not half an inch from the seagull's feet, and it screamed and fluttered off.

"Someone you ought to meet," Dickie's father said, and they went off together.

The someone to be met was Davy Cale, who ran a corner shop. Every boy in the neighborhood, except Dickie Lee, knew that Cale had been a footballer of some note, and every boy but Dickie knew he was trying to put together a club for boys.

"He dun't seem to understand what a team's for," Dickie's father said, very mildly. "But trying 'im as goalie might bring him halfway out."

Dickie was asked again to show what he could do with a rock. Handed a football, he looked at it with vague interest, but demonstrated that he could put it anywhere it needed to go. So did the least likely boy in England become the starting goalkeeper for the Liverpool Junior Racers.

As a movement in James Richard Lee's life, it worked, as his father had said, halfway. He never became one of the lads, still didn't play with them, club football excepted, still did his time alone defended against all comers.

But he was supernatural on the field. He seemed to begin an interception before the goal attempt was fairly begun, and once blocked, the ball would infallibly go to the boy best placed to return it. The Racers were champions; and Deadeye Dick Lee was champion of champions. So, for a while at least, the rest of it didn't matter.

In 1933, the man who had designed the fastest aircraft on earth went to visit Germany. R. J. Mitchell was not a well man; he had undergone a lung operation during the testing of his latest plane, and the trip was supposed to be part of his convalescence.

Mitchell met with a number of young German pilots. They spoke about what airplanes could do, what they might do. Something happened inside the Englishman's mind.

Mitchell went back to England deeply troubled, with a vision of something to come. The design he had been working on was flying, awkwardly, by the end of the year. Mitchell saw that it would not do, and began to work at it obsessively, continuously, with no thought of his physical condition, possessed by a dream of shapely wings and destruction.

In 1934, when Peter Himmels was sixteen, he was aware that his sister existed and had a terrible sickness. It did not frighten him. He began to visit the hospital regularly, got to know the nurses and Simon Rachlin. Dr. Rachlin was delighted by Peter's visits; the other *Wahrschlafssperrung* patients seemed as forgotten by their families as the disorder had been by the world at large.

"Why do you think she dances?" Peter said.

Dr. Rachlin said, "I do not know, though I hope to someday. I have asked her, when she seems aware, but as I have told you, the *Schlafssperr'* patients almost never answer."

"Do you think I could dance with her?"

Dr. Rachlin smiled. "I cannot imagine any harm in it. Would you object to my watching you?"

Peter and the doctor cleared a space in the dining room. One of the nurses got some waltz music on the radio, and Dr. Rachlin sat by with a notebook as the young people danced.

Peter tried to look as if he were leading, but in fact Magdalen was pulling him around the floor. Nor, though it kept vaguely to the radio's waltz time, was the dance much of anything formal—perhaps, Rachlin wrote, an eight-year-old's imagining of a waltz.

"Do they not look lovely?" one of the nurses said.

When the dancers finished, Peter stepped back from his sister and bowed from the waist.

Magdalen curtsied in reply. She had never done that in her solo dancing.

"She wakes!" a nurse said.

"If she does, we shall all take dancing lessons," Dr. Rachlin said, and his hand was shaking as he scribbled the description; but a moment later Magdalen was standing still, unseeing, as ever.

At eighteen, James Richard Lee got a docker's button as his father and the other men in the black house wore. In an attempt to get the best out of his talents, he was made a crane operator, and after the first weeks' training, never dropped a pallet or missed a hold. His fellow dockers felt safe with Dick on the crane; management liked that, while he was certainly a union man, he didn't seem too Bolshie about it.

In early 1938 his old coach Davy Cale had another proposal: for a while now the Royal Air Force had been training a "Volunteer Reserve." Local flying schools would teach young men to fly, tuition paid by the government; in addition, the volunteers took night courses in gunnery and signals. They would be sergeants, if some other things happened: if a war broke out, if Britain entered it.

As usual, Lee did not oppose a reasonable suggestion. He joined the RAFVR.

Then some other things happened.

In 1940, not long after the fall of France, Dick Lee was posted to RAF Crowborough, in East Sussex, part of 11 Group of Fighter Command. It was farther from home than he had ever been, and for a few days he seemed dazed by the greenness of the fields, the clarity of the air, far from the Mersey quay. It was apparent soon enough that his quietness was not a response to anything, but an essential bit of Lee himself.

He was friendly without being convivial, well liked without any special likability. Once the German air attacks began in earnest, with the inescapable tensions and terrors, it was accepted that whatever kept a man sane and able in the cockpit was right. Lee got the squadron's second confirmed kill, and was a good man to have on your flight; that, for the second time in his life, paid for any other failings.

Lee's one actual friend in the squadron was a Lieutenant called Chips Wayborne, a wealthy young man, three years older than Lee, who had been in one of the Auxiliary Air Squadrons before the war. Wayborne had scored the squadron's first kill, on the same flight as Lee; it was the closest thing to a cause the friendship had. The two men seemed to have nothing else in common.

On a late night in August, after a long dogfight in which Wayborne had gotten his fifth German and Lee his seventh, they sat in the barracks with cold cigarettes and staling beer, talking.

"Do you sleep bad, after a fight?" Wayborne said. "I always do. When we're warming up, I think about the other chap, the one I'm trying to kill, but once the wheels come up I don't anymore. It's just our machines and their machines. But the night after, I see them again. In my dreams, I see them."

"People are always talking about dreams," Lee said. "There are songs about them, on the radio, all the time it seems."

Wayborne laughed through his tiredness, and sang a bit of a song about things never being as bad as they seemed, in the worst imitation of Vera Lynn ever heard by man.

Lee said, "People say they dream. When they're asleep. They say it's like the cinema."

"Well, yes, we dream," Chips said, trying to get the joke.

"I don't," Dickie said.

"What, never at all? I mean, you don't remember most of them, but—"

"I mean never. I fall asleep and that's it till I wake up again."

"Have you told any of the medical boys about this?"

"I hardly ever saw a doctor until I was in the service. I don't think the first one believed me. Since the shooting started, I've been afraid to say anything. I'm afraid they'll think I've cracked—"

"Not bloody probable."

"—or funked it."

"Balls to that."

"You won't say anything, Chipper?" Lee's voice was flat, as if it didn't really matter.

"Course not, Dickie. Nothing to say, is there?"

———

In September of 1940, a young man in Luftwaffe uniform arrived at a hospital near Munich. He was wearing the insignia of a *Staffelkapitän*, a bomber flight leader, and had the "double badge" showing that he was both a highly qualified pilot and an aircraft commander. He was promptly shown to the office of the hospital director, a doctor in a crisp white coat, his Party badge prominently displayed.

"Good afternoon, Captain. What may we do for you?"

"I am Peter Himmels. Where is Dr. Rachlin?"

"Dismissed," the doctor said. "It is of no importance. What brings you here, sir?"

"My sister is a patient here. I haven't been able to visit in some time." He gestured at his uniform, smiled and said, "You know. Now I should like to see her."

"We are trying to discourage visitation," the doctor said. "It tends to disturb the patients."

"If only!" Peter said.

The doctor looked puzzled, and said, "Of course, Captain, I shall see what can be arranged." He clicked his heels and went out of the room.

A few minutes later he returned, his expression oddly blank. "Your pardon, Captain. The old staff here have left the records in an atrocious state. I was not aware your sister was one of the encephalitis patients. They are, of course, quarantined."

"They are what?"

"*Encephalitis lethargica* is a very severe disease. We certainly do not wish to start an epidemic. Why, its effect on the war effort—you must understand this."

Himmels laughed. "I've been dancing with my sister for years, *Herr Doctor*."

"Excuse me?"

"I just want to see her. Please."

"That is not possible today, Captain. Perhaps another time. Now, it is almost time for afternoon medications; you must excuse me. *Heil Hitler*."

Peter Himmels returned the salute and was left alone in the office.

At about the same time, Sergeant James Richard Lee was being called into his squadron leader's office. The officer was turning a letter over in his hands.

"This is the bad part of the job, Dick. There's this message, from Liverpool. They were pretty badly blitzed two nights back, and, well—" He handed the letter over. Lee read it, without any change of expression.

The squadron leader said, "I am sorry, Dick."

"Hadn't been our house, would have been a neighbor's," Lee said. "If my dad had been out on the docks when it hit, one of the other men would have been there asleep. Or else it would have been one of the mums."

"If you want leave . . . "

"If it's all right, sir, I'd sooner stay. Here I've a chance of keeping a few of them out of the goal. That's more use than I'd be up there. Sir."

"As you wish."

"Thank you, sir."

A few days after his visit to Munich, Peter Himmels walked into the officers' bar, wearing a leather flying jacket. Men were drinking, idling, telling tales; one of the fighter captains, a man named Jost, was playing the piano.

Jost looked up, played a few measures of the *"Stukalied"*—a joke, parodying the rivalry between fighter and bomber fliers—and everyone laughed. Jost went to the bar with Himmels. "Good to have you back, Peter. Take your coat off, stay awhile."

"We're supposed to go on a raid shortly. Those radio towers again."

"They didn't tell me! No escorts?"

"Weather's supposed to be too bad for fighters. Besides, we're only going to the coast and back."

Jost said, "Well, before you go, we got some good cognac. Compliments of the *Reichsmarschall*. A small one for luck."

"A small one for luck," Himmels said. "And a bottle for my men, eh? With Göring's compliments."

"Just as the *Staffelkapitän* says!" Jost poured a glass, which Himmels drank with grace.

Himmels said, "I'd better go see that they've put the propellers on right way forward. See you for breakfast, Jossi."

"Surely, Peter."

When Himmels had gone, another fighter pilot came over to Jost. "Peter was rather quiet."

"They've given him a mission tonight, if you can believe it. And he just got back from leave."

"Oh. 'Good-bye, Johnny,' eh?"

"I think he went to see his sister. She's been in a hospital most of her life, I hear, and the parents are gone."

"That's a lot to carry."

"I suppose you learn how. Did you see what happened, just now? I offered him a drink and he said to make sure his *Staffel* got a bottle." Jost shook his head. "If anything could get a man out of fighters and into bombers, it would be an officer like that."

"Don't let the *Reichsmarschall* hear you say that."

"Oh, yes, Göring." Jost raised his glass. "Here's to him again. Until the brandy runs out."

The Dornier Do 17 was an older aircraft, designed for powerful engines that few planes received; slow therefore, with a small bomb capacity. They were called *Fliegende Bleistiften*, Flying Pencils, for their slender fuselages. They had four seats, closely placed; the cockpit was so small that the crew had to board in a particular order.

Still the crews liked the Dornier; it was stable in flight and very strongly built. One plane, badly shot up over England, limped home with over two hundred bullet holes, and the crew all survived to count them.

The radioman climbed into his seat, then the flight engineer; they each had a machine gun as well. The last two seats were for the pilot and observer, but Captain Himmels had both those jobs. He checked controls and communications, then gave the order to the *Staffel* to begin taking off.

"Radio towers and home for dinner, right, Captain?" the engineer said.

"The towers, yes," Himmels said, as if there were something else entirely on his mind.

The British had two kinds of air-defense radar, then known as Radio Direction Finding or RDF. The Chain Home antennas were tall, open structures, something like oil derricks; the Germans across the Channel could see them. Chain Home had a long range, at points reaching back to France, and looked only out to sea. It was also blind to low-flying aircraft.

The Chain Home Low radar used smaller, rotating antennas. Its reach was shorter, only about half the width of the Channel, but it could see inland and pick up planes near the ground.

Both systems produced blips: not clearly defined lights on a dark screen, but spikes and tremors in a wobbling line of light on a glass tube a few inches across. Young women, many in their teens, watched the tubes and waited for the flickers. Officers, as ever jealous of others' right to play the best of games, said they would panic, said they would faint.

The reports from the radar watchers went to a room that combined them, adding visual observations and pilots' reports, trying to assemble a picture of what was actually happening in the air; this was communicated to the flight controllers, and then to the pilots, who followed instructions to whatever degree they felt like following them.

Any student of organizations could tell you that this system could not work. All those separate people, threaded together by telephone wire or crackling radios, keeping count with wooden blocks pushed about on a map, could not possibly bind together into a workable model of fluid, chaotic, three-dimensional reality, any more than twenty thousand people separated by continents and oceans could all have the same dream in the same night.

At the 11 Group Filter room, the telephone was ringing. One of the operators answered, and waved to the flight controller.

"Sir, RDF Hollowell's reporting. Bomber flight, very low. They'll be over the coast in eight minutes."

"Assuming they're there," the controller said. *Bloody women,* he thought; *not even women. Girls. Girls on the telephone, ringing you up—*

"Shall I alert squadrons, sir?"

Oh, dear! Jerry's coming and my hair's a fright! Hitler's in Whitehall and I'm not dressed!

"On the coast in five minutes, sir."

"Anything from the observers?" *What was RDF anyway, a lot of wire, couldn't tell a bird from a bomber, a twitch on a piece of glass, a voice on a telephone—*

"Nothing yet."

"Then we don't send planes up, young lady. It is an X classification because there is *no confirmation.* That is the *procedure.*"

"Yes, sir . . . Oh, God."

Oh God indeed. *They were always hysterical, always not ready, always either dumb or delirious, on the telephone, the telephone, the bloody mad telephone telling you good-bye.* . . . "What are you cursing on an open line for, Corporal?"

"It's the RDF station, sir. They're saying—"

"What are they saying? *What* are they saying, by God?" He grabbed a handset, shouted in a voice hardly removed from delirium, "Hollowell, report. What's going on down there?"

The voice on the other end of the line was absolutely calm, though she was speaking loudly above a terrible racket. "Your X raid is bombing us, sir."

Then the line went dead.

"Good job, all crews," Peter Himmels told his *Staffel*. "All planes head for home, maximum speed. We'll be along."

"We haven't dropped our bombs," the radioman said.

"I'm certainly aware of that," Himmels said, and the way he said it made the other crewmen laugh. Then, quite seriously, he said, "I have special orders. Very secret. Radio silent, please."

"Yes, sir." The radio was switched off. The radioman gave a small smile to the engineer. Where were they going? London, perhaps? It didn't matter. They would go with Captain Himmels wherever he led.

In Serecombe, the air-raid warnings had sounded, the houses were blacked out, Tiger Martyn's father had put on his flat A.R.P. warden's helmet, slung his gas mask, and gone out on his rounds. The house was quiet.

Tiger was in his bed, entirely awake. He had been dreaming, but he was very sure he was not dreaming now. If there were going to be planes, he wanted to see them. He dressed, pulled on his jacket, slipped a torch into his pocket, and was down the stairs and out the back door with no sound at all.

It was very dark. The sky was all opaque cloud, and the town showed no lights. Tiger didn't dare use his torch until he was certain no one else would see it.

Somehow he didn't need it. The Wych Road glistened before him as if it were silvered over, and the elm trees arched above it like a cathedral ceiling. A spirit—possibly of Adventure—drew him on.

Over RAF Crowborough, the clouds were thick, and there were spatterings of rain. About nine o'clock, Dickie Lee was having a cigarette with Chips Wayborne. Lee had never smoked before his Crowborough posting, but it was something to do between scrambles that required no thought, and the mechanics of lending, borrowing, and lighting cigarettes were a fair substitute for idle conversation.

Wayborne was telling a story passed over from a neighboring squadron: "So the Ministry says, 'Nobody could have got that many in one sortie, and anyway we don't think there were any Germans in the sector in the first place. We'll call them probables.' Tom says balls to that, goes out and finds the wrecks, and brings home their serial numbers."

The squadron leader looked into the hut. "We've got an alert."

"In *this* stuff?" someone said.

"A flight of Dorniers bombed Hollowell radar station. Last message through said one of 'em broke off and headed our way. Could be lost."

"Or a pathfinder," Wayborne said.

"Or photo-recce. At any rate, he seems to be up there, and we're selected. You chaps drink up and get some sleep; I'll take it."

"I've had as much sleep as anyone, sir," Lee said. "If this muck clears tomorrow, there'll be more than one of them—well, the flight'll need you then."

"Do you really want this one, Sergeant?"

Lee's face was invisible in the dark. He said without inflection, "If he's up there, I'll get him, sir."

"Care for company?" Wayborne said.

"This is better for one, Chips. Wouldn't do to run into each other. Thanks for the offer, though."

The squadron leader said, "Very well then. Good hunting, Sergeant."

"Thank you, sir." Lee started to turn toward the hangars, then paused. "Sleep well, Chips."

When Lee had gone, the squadron leader said, "I'd lay eight to five he can't take off in this. That German's either lost, or mad."

"I believe Dickie, sir. If there's a plane up there, he'll get him."

"You're a better pilot. He's good, but you're better."

"Possibly, sir." Wayborne ground out his half-finished cigarette. Quietly, evenly, as if it were something he had been considering for a long time, Wayborne said, "Sometimes you have the best team, and the right wind, and the prettiest girls cheering you from the stands, everything on your side, but there's this chap at the other end of the field; maybe he's not as nice as you or your mates, but he knows what he's out there for, and he's there when you don't expect him. The best scheme in the world can't get past a man like that."

"Lee was a footballer, wasn't he?"

"Yes, sir, he was. If you think I'm the best pilot in this squadron, I'm honored to hear it. But Sergeant Lee's the best killer, God forgive me for saying so. And God help him for its being true."

An hour and a half after leaving his bedroom, Tiger Martyn stood at the gates of Fawney Rig. Beyond the rusty iron and the vines twisted around it, he could see lights, small and wavering, like candles or handheld torches. Were the people in the big house just careless, as the Martyns' neighbors were when the air raid wardens weren't looking? Or was the house full of spies, signaling to the German bombers?

The gate was closed, but the bars were quite far enough apart for Tiger to slip through, and he had learned from Simon Templar to test fences for electricity with a tossed twig.

So. He was through. He could hear no guard dogs, though a murmur did carry through the wind and the wet, from near the front of the house, where the lights were. The house was to Tiger's left; Wych Dyke was to the right, perfectly placed to cover a closer approach. The ground was soft, and the fallen leaves were wet; he made no sound as he moved to the ring of earth.

Dickie Lee opened his wireless link to ground control. While RDF Hollowell was being patched together, they were trying to stretch the neighboring CHL radars to cover.

"Crow Flight to Control, airborne and climbing. Can you give me a vector?"

"Roger, Crow Flight, vector one nine zero. Bandit at angels two."

"Say angels again, Control?"

"I say again, bandit at angels two."

Two thousand feet of altitude wasn't much room to work with. Not that there was much to work with for anyone tonight. Lee turned south-southwest as ordered and climbed to eight thousand. The weather was no better at that height; if he tried to get above the cloud, he might never find the bandit.

After twenty minutes and three new vectors, Lee had him. Just a smear of light; it could have been almost anything, that low. But it was moving too fast to be anything but a plane.

Lee let it pull a few hundred yards ahead, just to the limits of visibility. Then he dived on it. It didn't evade; they hadn't heard him, they surely hadn't seen him. If one of the gunners opened up, he could still get a burst off before veering aside—assuming there was enough space beneath them that a veer aside didn't auger the Spit straight into the ground.

There were only two ways to bring a plane down. You could pump bullets into the airframe, trying to bend enough tin to make the machine unflyable, or you could kill the men inside. There was no question which way was easier.

Lee brought his nose up, came to within a thousand feet of the Dornier, and pressed the trigger. Eight streams of half-inch slugs raked the plane. Lee pulled up, hearing his own airframe creak, putting as much load on the thin Mitchell wings as they would take.

Tiger Martyn crested the dyke. In front of him, halfway between the dyke and the house, he saw a man, standing bareheaded in the wet.

He was old, and ugly, and bald, with a huge bulb of a nose. He was wearing what looked like a long purple bathrobe, and heavy bracelets and pendants, like a pantomime King Herod. He was standing on the metaled drive before the manor, in a pattern of red-and-white-chalked lines that the mist didn't seem to smudge and a circle of candles that defied the wind.

Tiger's taste in villains ran to the air pirates hunted down by the indomitable Biggles, or (forbidden again) oily foreigners smartly dispatched by Captain Hugh Drummond, but he knew well enough what a wizard was. There were good wizards, like Merlin, and evil ones, like—well, the rest of them. It was as clear to Tiger as the shield of St. George, as plain as the luridly smudged covers of Willy's Yank mags, what heroes did when they met evil wizards.

Tiger stood on Wych Dyke, raised his arms, and shouted, "Hey, you, mister! *Put out those lights!*" He *felt* something then, from the earth. The elms of Arthur's lances supported the sky overhead. And though he never would know it, he illuminated the night, bright in that particular color as Dover Lighthouse.

The ugly old man's mouth dropped open. He crossed his arms, then held them out straight. His jaw waggled like a wooden dummy's. Two of his candles went out, bang like the White King's dreams. The man turned and ran, knocking over the rest of the candles, floundering barefoot over the wet grass, nearly tripping over his robe. Tiger could hear the door of the house slam shut from where he stood.

Suddenly he was cold, and very tired. He went back home, slipped inside miraculously unseen, got into bed, and was asleep at once.

A few days later, when the war news reached Serecombe, Tiger cursed himself for what he had missed, but he dared not speak of it, not even to Willy, and in time he would forget whether he had really climbed the dyke, or only dreamt it.

Peter Himmels was sick at heart. He had known, deeply, that he would not return from this mission, that he was flying into the holy twilight of the

Führer's favorite composer. But he had hoped his two crewmen, brave and loyal to a dream they had not shared, might have survived, at least as prisoners of the English. They were both dead, cut nearly in two, within seconds of each other. The *Spitfeuer* pilot was very good. Now Himmels was flying through weather thick as mud, carrying his bombs toward a target he had seen only in his dreams.

Suddenly, like a candle going out, the mist seemed to part before him, and he saw the house with an unreal, impossible, bomber's-moon clarity. Nothing could stop him now; the Spitfire was behind him, out of ammunition or fuel or simply lost in the clouds.

Peter Himmels had no doubt then of the truth of his dream. He would see his sister, awake and laughing and calling his name. They would both see their parents. And they would all dance together, as long as a dream could last.

Dickie Lee had made two long firing passes at the Dornier, which was still flying level and constant speed, like a flying sleepwalker. It hadn't even fired back at him. Lee knew he had used up most of his ammunition, and he was dead certain he had hit the plane. It was just possible that she had a dead crew and a jammed stick, though it hardly seemed likely.

There was one way to find out, and that was to take a look.

Lee sped past the Dornier, which continued to ignore him. He came around in the easiest turn he could manage without losing close sight of the German.

Then he flew head-on at the bomber.

At one hundred yards range, even in the weather and the dark, it was possible to read the identification on the Dornier; it was possible to see the cockpit as a clear white-faceted crystal, fragile glass with men inside.

At eighty yards, four-tenths of a second from midair collision, it seemed that Lee was looking into the lamped mouth of Despair itself. His consciousness froze up, just for a fraction, just enough for him to have missed firing on that pass.

But Lee's consciousness had never been in control at times like this. His instinct had sent the order a long time ago. Stuttering lines of red light reached out from the Spitfire. Tracer rounds, the last handful of ammo in the bottom of the box. The guns were clicking dry even as Lee pulled up; he felt the wake of the Dornier suck at him as they passed.

Lee came around, wings almost vertical. He had no clear idea why; he was out of ammo, and at this range one of the Do 17's side gunners could cut him apart with one burst.

He saw the bomber at once. It was descending, wings dead level, as if it were making a practice landing on a sunny afternoon. With a start Lee realized that the bomber was lower than the trees. Two seconds later the flash came. Lee called it in, got a decent amount of space under his own backside, and turned for Crowborough.

A few days later Lee and Chips Wayborne borrowed a staff car and drove to Wych Cross. They were directed, with some hesitation, toward Fawney Rig.

"Chap at the Post Office said no one's been out to it," Wayborne said. "Can't say I blame him. Look at this place. Looks like bloody Dracula's castle, doesn't it?"

Lee said, "I see the wreck."

"Yes," Wayborne said softly, "Yes, I should say so." They drove on, past the PRIVATE PROPERTY TRESPASSERS WILL BE SHOT signs, away from the silent house.

They parked the car and approached the plane. It had belly-landed, and half of the right wing had sheared off on a tree trunk, but the fuselage was quite intact. It looked like a bad, but survivable, landing. Chips hallooed, then called out all the German he knew ("Would you like to dance, madame?") but there was no sound.

They climbed up to the cockpit and looked in. There wasn't much to be said then.

"Dorniers have a crew of four. That's one short."

"I was on her until she was scraping the trees. Nobody bailed out."

Wayborne looked again into the small cockpit. "Fellow could have lived through this. If he were damned lucky."

"Yes, I suppose so," Lee said. "We'll report it. No hurry."

"No. No hurry. I tell you, Dickie, if the pilot's out there somewhere, I'd gladly buy him a pint."

Lee nodded. He was looking directly at the man in the pilot's seat, dead with his hands on the yoke. The two side gunners had been torn by several bullets each, but there was only one wound visible on the pilot's body. A shard of the Perspex canopy, as long as Lee's hand and three inches wide at the base, was embedded in his throat. It had severed an artery, and the man had bled to death. That must have taken several seconds at least. He had, at a fair guess, been alive when the plane had touched ground.

There was no other way to explain how the Dornier, after losing half a wing in the trees, had made a belly landing as straight as a ruler, aimed with draftsman's precision at the manor with the gargoyles. Another six hundred yards—six seconds, a dozen or so last heartbeats—and the plane would have been through the house's front door.

"They had better not call this one a probable," Wayborne said as Lee climbed down from the plane. "Shall I write down her markings, Dickie?"

"I saw them," Lee said.

Dickie Lee offered to fly Peter Himmel's flying helmet and decorations across the Channel and drop them on an enemy airfield—a chivalric gesture left over from the last war. It was vetoed, of course. The bodies of the Dornier crew were supposed to be dispatched to a military graveyard, but the order was lost—in an air raid, as it happened—and rather than let them sit above ground, the people of Wych Cross buried them, without ceremony or markers, in their own churchyard.

A year later, roses bloomed on Peter Himmels's grave, enormous blossoms of a curious iridescent gray, the petals edged with crimson. The vicar, who was historically minded, called them "gules-and-argents." Someone of a different background might have described them as like fresh blood on torn aluminium. A man from Kew was supposed to come out and examine the flowers, but never did, and the only visitors Wych Cross ever saw went directly to Fawney Rig, going nowhere near the churchyard.

Lee brought down eight more aircraft. In one engagement he scored two kills, then damaged a third, a Bf 110, and guided it to a safe landing at Crowborough. He bought each of the crewmen a pint. He ended the war as a squadron leader, with the Distinguished Flying Cross. He bought a modest, bright house not far from the Mersey for the survivors of the small black one, but he never went there for more than a short visit. When Crowborough was closed, he bought a bit of it and settled there, alone. In his forty-third year he surprised his neighbors by offering to help coach a junior football team. It was a group of the boys who found him quietly dead of a stroke; he had been sitting in a deck chair, by one of the rotting old hangars, looking through the trees toward the Channel, just as if he were waiting for a scramble. Chips Wayborne was head pallbearer, and bought the stone. It read:

SQUADRON LEADER
JAMES RICHARD LEE
DFC MC
1919–1967
SLEEP WELL, DICKIE.

———

In June of 1942, as part of Nazi Germany's T4 Program of forcible euthanasia of the mentally ill, Magdalen Himmels was given a lethal injection. No one involved with the program knew the nature of her disorder, and all German copies of Freud's paper on *Wahrschlafssperrung* had been destroyed, as merely another lump of "faulty Jewish science." Dr. Rachlin survived the war as a camp doctor in Theriesenstadt, became a professor of psychiatry in Israel, and lived to see the sleepers awaken in 1988.

In his ninety-sixth year, he wrote: "I have come to think it a great sin to lack hope, but I may say I have little expectation that we shall ever understand this phenomenon. I believe (and I believe also that Freud would forgive me for sounding like Jung) that we have seen only the surface ripples of something very deep . . . a rustling, if you like, of the Great Chain of Being.

"The Lord does not jest; but I wish I better took his meaning."

Memory as ever is short. Most people thought he was writing of the camps.

STRONGER THAN DESIRE

Lisa Goldstein

Lisa Goldstein is the winner of many literary awards. Lisa is a small, dark lady with a fine smile and a sharp mind. She wrote *Strange Devices of the Sun and Moon*, a novel about the fairies leaving England in Shakespeare's day, and about the death of Marlowe, and about books.

This is a story about Desire, and a wager. Historically, it is, of course, the only explanation for the whole business.

It is said that nowadays Desire rarely takes a human lover.
For Desire, who is male and female, fair and dark, old and young, anything and everything you have ever wished for, or coveted, or needed, is irresistible. And so what would be the point, after all? Love is not a game to Desire, as it is to so many mortals, or if it is, it is a game with a foregone conclusion: Desire always wins. And Desire hates more than anything to be bored.

In the year 1108 Desire saw a young lord and his retinue leave his castle to go hunting. They rode through the village, the early morning sun glinting on their banners and finery, on their spears and the tips of their arrows. The hounds, red and gray and spotted, sensed the presence of the forest ahead of them and grew excited.

Desire had not seen anyone as beautiful as this lord in many years. He was tall, with high cheekbones, full red lips, a cap of black hair. His clothes were made of fine wool and colored with costly dyes, and he wore them with a flair that none of his vassals could match.

And so Desire followed as the party came to the forest and passed under the great trees, the hounds coursing before them. Desire heard the hounds bay loudly as they flushed a deer, watched as the hunters gave chase through the dark and light corridors of the forest, heard the horns ringing, saw the moment of triumph as the bowman brought down the deer.

The hunters stopped to cut a branch and lash it to the deer's feet, and then rode on. The sun rose up over the forest, shortening the shadows of the trees. Everything was quiet now; the birds had stopped singing, and the hounds sniffed the trail silently, lagging behind a little. The young lord, whose name was Raimon, urged his vassals deeper into the forest.

Desire surprised a deer. The deer bounded in front of the lord, passing only a few feet from his horse before it disappeared into the shadows.

Startled, Raimon gave chase. He rode hard down the narrow forest path, then followed as the deer plunged off the path and through the trees. Leaves and light flashed overhead. The sounds of his party faded behind him. The deer twisted and feinted, moving now left, now right as it tried to lose its pursuer.

The deer began to slow. Raimon urged his horse forward, followed as the deer leapt farther into the forest. Desire stood among the shadows of the trees in the aspect of a woman.

Lord Raimon saw her and pulled hard on the reins of his horse. The deer hurried away, unnoticed. "Who are you?" he asked.

"I am Alais," Desire said.

"I would like to take you back with me, to my castle," Raimon said. "No—I am sorry, I am being discourteous. Will you come back with me? I will make you my wife, will give you everything that is in my power to give. I am lord of this land, of all this forest and everything around it for many miles. You are the most beautiful woman I have ever seen."

Desire laughed. "I will go with you," she said. "But I will not be your wife."

Raimon helped her mount behind him. He rode slowly back through the forest, and when he heard the barking of the hounds and the laughter of his men he did not hurry to join them.

At last he saw his party in a clearing of the forest. The sun was setting, darkening the trees against the sky. He rode into the clearing.

His men turned toward him, and one or two called out. But when they saw Desire they fell silent, and some stirred uneasily. "This is Alais," Raimon said. "She is returning with us to the castle."

"Where—Where does she come from, my lord?" one of the men asked.

"Where?" Raimon said. "Why, she comes from—It does not matter where she comes from. Come—we must hurry. It grows late."

Raimon and his retinue left the forest and rode through the village. Darkness had fallen; only the moon and stars and the distant lights of the castle remained to show them their way.

The men stayed a little behind their lord and his new woman, watching them with suspicion in their eyes. They had urged Raimon to marry, to beget heirs to secure his lands. Many had put forward favorites, an unwed sister or cousin. Now, with the coming of this strange woman, all their plans were thrown into confusion. Who was she? Who were her parents, what was her lineage? The men whispered among themselves, careful not to let their lord overhear them; one was even bold enough to speak the word "witchcraft."

In the days that followed it seemed that their worst fears had been realized. Raimon kept to his apartments. Orders came to the servants for meals, for a priest to say Mass on Sundays. And everyone who saw him in his rooms reported that the strange woman, the witch woman, was still there; some had even seen them sharing the bed.

Finally one of the men had had enough. Ignoring the entreaties of his fellows, he climbed the stairs that led to his lord's apartments and knocked on the door.

Someone giggled. "Who is it?" Raimon asked.

"It is I, my lord."

"Come."

The man entered. Raimon and Alais lay in the bed, the bedclothes around them disheveled and filthy. Raimon sat; the movement caused a blanket to slip and reveal his naked shoulders and one of Alais's white breasts.

The man stared at her. "What do you want?" Raimon asked, smiling.

"I—" The man looked away with an effort. "This is not right, my lord. All of your men say so. You must marry. You must have sons, legitimate heirs."

"I have asked Alais to marry me," Raimon said. "She refuses."

"Alais?"

"Yes. Is that so surprising?"

"My lord, you know nothing of this woman. Who is she? Where does she come from?"

"I know all I need to know about her," Raimon said. He looked at her fondly and she smiled, amused.

"My lord, you must—"

"I must? Are my vassals to give me orders now? Is the order of this castle to be overturned?"

"If it is, it is you who overturned it. You and this woman—"

"Leave me," Raimon said. "I grow weary of this discussion."

The man went to the door, hesitated as if about to say something, and then hurried down the stairs.

Raimon looked at the woman beside him in the bed and laughed. "He's right, you know," he said. "Sooner or later I must marry. Why will you not marry me?"

"I cannot."

"I don't care about dowry. I'll give you everything you want. Is that what you're concerned about?"

"No."

"Are you contracted to someone else?"

"No."

"I will go mad," Raimon said, laughing a little. "I will go mad, and it will be your fault. Why won't you marry me?"

"I cannot," Desire said again.

It seemed to Raimon that she shifted slightly on the bed, that her hair grew shorter, her features coarser. He jerked away, alarmed. Her face returned to what it had been, all its strange beauty restored.

"Who are you?" Raimon said.

"I am not what you think."

"No. No, that is quite clear. You are no mortal, I see that now. Who are you?"

Desire laughed. "I am the most powerful being, man or woman, that you will ever meet. I am the most important thing in the world."

"You are not God," Raimon said. His heart beat loudly in his chest but he forced himself to speak evenly. "And God is the most important thing in the world."

"I am even stronger than your God. I am one of the Endless. I am Desire."

"Desire. Yes, I see." Raimon fell silent. Suddenly he turned to her and pinned her to the bed as he had so many times before. "And if I can prove to you that you are not the most powerful thing in the world, prove that there are those who can resist you, then will you marry me?"

"No one can resist me," Desire said scornfully. "Not even you, and you are a great lord."

"Will you hazard your future on that? Will you wager marriage?"

"It is not given to the Endless to marry with mortals."

"What? Not given? Surely a being as powerful as you can make your own laws."

"Very well," Desire said slowly. "Show me two people, any two, and I will make them paw at each other like animals in rut."

"And if they will not?"

"If they will not, then you have won the wager. I will marry you."

The next day Lord Raimon and Desire came down from his apartments. He attended to business he had neglected, rode through his estate, received petitions. In the evening, after supper, he waved to his steward to join him at the head of the banquet table. "I would like to hold a feast," he said. "And to invite Count Bertran, our neighbor to the east. See that you send him an invitation."

"Yes, my lord."

When the steward had gone, Raimon turned to Desire. "I have begun the wager, my lady," he said.

A week later Count Bertran and his retinue came to dine at the castle of Lord Raimon. Raimon was lavish in his hospitality, sparing neither meat nor drink. At the end of the meal the lord clapped, and a troupe of jugglers came out to perform.

The jugglers threw knives and caps and apples. They grabbed the hat of one of Raimon's men and threw it back and forth over his head as he tried vainly to catch it. The men and women at the banquet laughed and applauded. One man, however, sat apart; he frowned and studied the jugglers as though presented with a difficult problem in Latin grammar. He had brown hair to his shoulders, brown eyes, a long narrow nose, and a small mouth. He would have been handsome if he had not looked so serious.

"That man," Raimon said, pointing him out to Desire. "He is clerk to Lord Bertran. His name is Aimeric. I want him to desire the countess."

Desire looked at him, and then at Carenza, Count Bertran's wife. She was old, in her forties at least, and worn out from childbearing. Her cheeks had the hollow look of someone with several teeth missing, and there were brown pouches under her eyes.

Desire smiled. "It is done," she said.

Slowly Aimeric looked away from the jugglers, toward the countess Carenza. His face still wore its studious expression, but as Raimon watched it changed, became softer. Once he frowned, as if returning to his senses, but then Carenza laughed and Aimeric surrendered wholly to his enchantment. For the rest of the evening he did not take his eyes off the countess, and when Bertran's party rose to leave he followed her closely, and once he even reached out his hand to touch her cloak.

"I think I have won the wager," Desire said.

"Wait, my lady," Raimon said.

Raimon and Desire became frequent visitors to Bertran's castle. They watched as Aimeric gazed after the countess, as he looked up in delight when she entered the banqueting hall. Raimon sought him out and spoke to him, and he noticed that the clerk took every opportunity to mention his beloved's name in conversation.

But Aimeric made no move to speak to her. At supper he kept to his place at a lower table. When he saw her coming toward him in one of the drafty corridors of the castle he hurried out of her way, and she and her ladies would pass by without glancing in his direction.

"I have won the wager, my lady," Raimon said when they had retired to the rooms Bertran had given them for the night. "His fear of the count, and his habit of obedience, are stronger than desire. He will never speak to her, let alone take her to his bed."

Desire said nothing, but went to the pitcher of water Bertran's servants had left for them. She poured water into a goblet, then breathed softly on the water.

"What are you doing?" Raimon asked.

"Hush," Desire said.

Raimon moved closer to her and looked into the goblet. As he watched a picture formed on the surface of the water. Aimeric sat at his desk, writing. Yellow candles burned profligately around him.

"Is he working on Bertran's accounts?" Raimon asked. "At this hour?"

"Hush," Desire said again.

The picture on the water changed. Now Raimon could read the words written on the page. "Poetry," he said, astonished.

"He has never written poetry before," Desire said. "Now it is all he does, even when he should be working for the count."

"Poetry is one thing. He will never approach her—he is too fearful."

"Do you think so?" Desire asked. She looked up at him, her eyes veiled by her lashes.

"Yes." Raimon laughed, delighted with her beyond words. "Why is it that I think you are planning something? Why do I imagine the game isn't over yet?"

"Wait," Desire said. "You'll see."

The next day, as they sat feasting at the banquet table, Desire pointed to Countess Carenza. Raimon watched, fascinated, as the countess looked up from her goblet of wine. Her eyes sought Aimeric's. She smiled at him, and brushed a lock of hair from her forehead.

"Unfair, my lady!" Raimon said, whispering so that the others could not overhear.

"Not at all," Desire said. She held out a piece of venison to one of Bertran's dogs, lifted it higher as the dog jumped for it. She laughed. "The wager was that desire is stronger than anything in the world. She will make excuses to her lord tonight and share his bed."

"And if she does not? Then will you marry me?"

"It will happen, tonight or some other night. You will have to look elsewhere for a wife."

"There is no one else I want, my lady. You know that."

"Nonetheless—"

"Look! Look there, my lady! Aimeric is leaving."

Desire frowned. The clerk had stood up from his place at a lower table and was leaving the banquet hall. "Why?" she asked.

"It is as I said, my lady. Fear and habit are stronger than desire."

"No. No, he will have her. You'll see."

"And if not? Will you marry me?"

But Desire frowned again and did not answer.

Over the next few weeks, as Raimon and Desire watched, the countess and Aimeric danced a complex measure. She would approach him, smiling, and he would find an excuse to leave. He would gaze at her in chapel or in the banqueting hall, but when she glanced up he would quickly look elsewhere. Raimon was amused to see that the countess Carenza grew more beautiful by the day: her expression had softened and the pouches under her eyes had disappeared. She carried herself confidently, secure in the knowledge that she was fascinating to one pair of eyes at least.

"You see," Desire said to Raimon when they were alone in their rooms. "Desire can turn foul women into fair ones. Tell me one other force in the world that can do that."

"He still has not come to her bed, my lady."

In answer Desire poured water into her goblet, breathed on it. Aimeric's room looked the same as it had the other nights they had observed him: the candles, the paper, the inkhorns and pens. The picture changed, and Raimon saw the page before Aimeric.

"'Although I should be sad I am joyful,'" Aimeric wrote. "'For my love loves me as I love her. And although we cannot be together—'"

A knock came at his door. Raimon and Desire, staring at the pictures in the goblet, heard it as clearly as Aimeric did. The clerk stood, began to pace back and forth. The knock came again.

Suddenly Aimeric seemed to make up his mind. He went toward the door and opened it. The countess Carenza stood there, wearing her finest dress.

"Now," Desire said. "Now it happens."

"My friend," Carenza said to Aimeric. "Something tells me that you feel for me as I feel for you. Please, please do not run from me anymore. It has taken all my courage to come to your room, to speak to you—"

"My lady," Aimeric said. "I love you more than I love my life. When I close my eyes at night it's your face that comes before me. When I see another woman I'm disappointed because she's not you. But I cannot—I cannot dishonor my lord this way—"

"Your lord! Your lord cares nothing for me. His parents and mine arranged our marriage in order to form an alliance between our families. There is nothing between us but policy."

"Even so, my lady—"

"Bertran used me to bear his children, his heirs. Now that my childbearing days are over, he has cast me aside. You have shown me that there is something more—something higher—"

"My lady." Aimeric reached out and took Carenza's hand. Raimon felt Desire grow tense beside him. Now it happens, he thought. "My dear lady, these things you tell me wound me deeply. It seems to me that Lord Bertran has thrown away the most precious jewel in his possession. Even so, I cannot dishonor your wedding vows, nor the oaths I swore to him when I entered his service."

"Why not? He has dishonored our vows twenty times over. We sleep apart, he takes a serving-woman into his bed—"

"I'm sorry, my love."

"So you will send me away," Carenza said. A tear fell down her cheek. "Send me away with nothing, not even my pride."

"Not at all," Aimeric said. For the first time Raimon saw him smile. "I will sing to you, my lady."

Aimeric took a lute from the corner of the room. He strummed it once or twice, tuning it, and then began to sing.

As Raimon and Desire listened, Aimeric sang of Carenza's beauty. He sang of the oaths he had given to his lord, the count Bertran, and of another oath, one that he had sworn to Countess Carenza in his heart. He would keep her at the forefront of his thoughts, he would cherish her forever. They would never satisfy their desire, never even kiss one another, but he would be faithful to her until he died.

As Aimeric sang, Raimon saw that his yearning for Carenza had become something different, something wholly new. He spoke of her as the priests spoke of God, or of the Virgin. He had transformed his love for God into his love for Carenza. Raimon nearly gasped at the daring of it.

"Love," he said. "Love is stronger than desire."

Desire laughed scornfully. "They are the same thing," she said.

In the days that followed Aimeric sang in the banquet hall after supper. He performed the song Raimon had heard and others as well. All had the same theme: constant love, love stronger than desire.

Several times Raimon looked at Bertran, but the count seemed unaware that it was his wife who was being addressed. But something of Aimeric's seriousness and passion communicated itself to the court; Bertran's vassals began to linger around Carenza, to flatter her, to vie for her attention. To Raimon's eyes she grew even lovelier, worthy of all of Aimeric's metaphors: she was a flower, a gazelle, a bird.

"I have won the wager," Raimon said. "Love is stronger than desire."

But Desire shook her head. "They are the same thing," she said.

No one knows how the concept of romantic love began in western Europe. There are those who say that the Crusaders brought back Arabic songs and poetry from the East; those who argue, more prosaically, that the invention of the chimney allowed for more privacy and so created an atmosphere in which love could flourish. What is true is that before this time men and women, like Bertran and Carenza, were given in marriage by their families, and for reasons that had nothing to do with love: territory, titles, money.

It was Aimeric who changed everything; after he sang nothing could be the same again. Love became the fashion: men and women vied with each other to create songs like Aimeric's, extolling the virtues and graces of their loved ones. To keep the structure of their civilization intact, their love had to be adulterous, to have as its object someone not chosen by the family but by the lover, and therefore almost always unconsummated. They lived in a world of incredible tension. Love never faded because it went unresolved for years, sometimes even for life.

Some of the authors of these songs, the troubadours, traveled through the south of France and beyond, spreading their songs south into Spain and east into Italy. Other wandering performers, like the jugglers who entertained Lord Raimon and his court, picked up the songs of the troubadours and carried them even farther; they became known as jongleurs.

The tales grew longer, more elaborate. Every story of love in the Western world was called into being by the wager of Desire and her lover: Tristan and Iseult, Romeo and Juliet, Prince Charming and Sleeping Beauty, Hollywood tearjerkers and Gothic novels. Lives were ennobled, and lives were ruined, because people tried to live up to an ideal that was invented hundreds of years before they were born. And for all this, too, Desire must bear the credit, or the blame.

Raimon was one of the few who understood how the world had changed. He saw that Aimeric, through his music, had transcended desire, had turned it into something completely new. He insisted that he had won the wager; daily he asked Desire to marry him, and daily she refused him. His arguments grew more cunning, more philosophical, but Desire remained unconvinced. "Desire and love," she said, "are the same thing."

As he listened to the songs of the troubadours and jongleurs Raimon became convinced that what he felt for Desire was love. He wondered how he and Desire could come together in passion every night without her feeling at least a little of what he felt for her, wondered how she could allow him every intimacy but that one.

A year after he and Desire had made their wager, he woke and saw that she had gone. He searched the castle for her, rode through the forest, sent out riders to every city and town within a hundred miles. No one ever found her.

His vassals were relieved. Now, at last, Lord Raimon would forget the strange woman who had obsessed him; he would marry and beget heirs. But Raimon never married. He hunted within the forest; he visited Count Bertran and his wife. People noticed that he spoke a great deal to Bertran's clerk, the man who sang such beautiful songs, but no one made anything of it. When he attended to the business of his household it seemed that his mind was elsewhere. His vassals whispered that late at night he wrote poetry.

Forty years after he met Desire in the forest Raimon lay dying. His vassals gathered around the bed he had once shared with Desire. "He should have married and had children," one of them said softly. "They say now that the castle and lands will go to a son of Count Bertran."

"No," Raimon said weakly.

His men looked at him in surprise; they had not thought that he could hear them, or that he was alert enough to speak. "What is it, my lord?"

"I could not have married. I stayed faithful to her all my life, even if she was not faithful to me. Love is the strongest thing in the world. You see," he said, closing his eyes, "I won the wager."

EACH DAMP THING

Barbara Hambly

Barbara Hambly bustles from place to place, like a hurricane with a sense of purpose. She is a fine and funny novelist, and I met her when we were Guests of Honor together at the British Easter Convention, some years ago. I kept introducing her to people. She returned the favor by naming a planet in a *Star Wars* book after me; as a result of which my twelve-year-old son Michael now thinks I may, possibly, be cool (although not as cool as I would be if I were to write a *Star Wars* novel myself).

Barbara was one of the few authors to write a *Sandman* story set mostly in the Dreaming. Sweet and sour it is, funny and scary too.

"I dreamt I dwelt in marble halls,
And each damp thing that creeps and crawls
Went wobble-wobble on the walls."
—*Lewis Carroll, "The Palace of Humbug"*

It was Cain's fault, really.

After all the shouting was over, and the mess cleaned up, there was never any question about that.

Part of Cain's problem was that he was genuinely the cleverer of the two brothers. His mind was more complicated, and he was better at seeing beneath the surface of lies. Thus he knew that his mother had always cared for his younger brother more than him—and how not, when he had been her first experience of the humiliating sickness of pregnancy, the agony and travail of childbearing, and the pesky, persistent labor of looking after infant, toddler, *No* and *Why*? By the time Abel was born, she had gotten somewhat used to it, and was able to relax, and love.

Cain never forgave either of them.

Every time he killed his brother, reenacting that first glorious, furious, sickening rage, Cain was aware that whatever he did, even in death their mother would still love Abel best.

Thus in his heart, Cain was always looking for ways to manipulate the world around him, to gain an advantage, to hold an edge.

And thus in the long dun-colored chaos season when the Lord of Dreams was held prisoner by those who knew not what they did, and the palace of the Dreaming crumbled and withered in the winds of Otherwhere, Cain could not forbear a cautious investigation of the ruins.

He moved warily through the dense blocks of shadows, the fallen stone doorways, and miles of lightless stair and corridor, for he knew some, at least, of the things imprisoned in the crypts. It is true that the King of Dreams invents nightmares. But it is also true that he was put in charge of the Dreaming to control the nightmares that arise into being from human minds, nightmares so powerful that should they drink of the souls of their creators, and the souls of those with whom those creators share them, they would grow until they devoured the world.

They say that King Morpheus is overconscientious, a workaholic, sacrificing all things to the proper performance of his duty.

He has to be.

It is why he, and not any of his brothers or sisters, was chosen for this particular job.

There was a doorway that had not only been locked, but bricked across, so that only its marble jambs and lintels stood out from the stone of the wall. But the brick and plaster that covered the door were crumbling, as the Dream King's strength was crumbling, ebbing, in his crystal prison. Bricks had fallen out, revealing hinges, and Cain found that if he thrust a lever—the world's most perfect cricket bat that one Humbert Knowlseley had dreamed about in 1881, lying stored for some reason in a nearby room full of the echoes of monstrous fish—if he thrust this behind the bricks, they fell out easily enough.

The wood around the hinges and lock had rotted away with the damp. Cain's foot made short work of it.

And for all that, there was nothing much in the room. A good deal of dust. Patches of something black on the plaster. A doorway in the opposite wall, likewise bricked over between marble lintels and jambs that had once been gilded—though the masonry held strong this time despite all Cain with his cricket bat could do.

And a mirror, lying on a table.

The mirror's glass was painted over black.

Cain took it home with him.

"Cuh-Cain, I think you should take it back."

"If you're trying to get credit for thinking, sponge-wit, you're not succeeding." The razor blade Cain was using made a horrible noise as he scraped at the paint. "Take it back and tell *him* what? That I just happen to have this hanging about, five years after his return? You know how he is about his crummy little bits of things."

"B-But he's away from home right now." Abel wrung his plump hands. Sweat stood out on his round face, not only because Cain's dark little basement workshop was hot with the flame of the gaslights Cain preferred. There were a lot of sharp objects down there. "I wuh-was talking to Matthew this afternoon up at the cave . . . "

Cain slewed in his chair, pale hazel eyes glittering behind his spectacles as he looked up at his brother, and Abel stumbled back a pace, hand to his mouth in guilt. Cain knew Abel spent a good deal of time at the Raven Lady's cave, and didn't like it one bit. But he only said, "Why the hell do you think I'm cleaning this thing up *now*? Instead of last week when I dug it out when I was cleaning the attic? By the time he comes back I'll have finished with it. There."

He sat back, and held the mirror up. There was still black paint around the edges of the plain silver frame, but the circle of glass, a handspan broad, was clear.

It reflected only Cain's thin face, the aggressive jut of the reddish beard, the maniac spectacle-gleam.

"Hmf," sniffed the Son of Adam. "Now what the hell is it supposed to do?"

"Um," said Abel hesitantly. "Uh . . . Look behind you. Not in *this* room," he added, as his brother started to glance over his shoulder. "In *that* one."

Cain angled the mirror. Behind him, reflected in the glass, was not the damp confines of his workroom, with its glittery tools grinning from the rough-cast walls, but the dark little chamber in the forgotten crypt of Dream's palace, faded gilt gleaming on the worn marble lintels of the bricked-up door.

"Fascinating." Cain dug around in his workbox for another mirror. "I wonder how much of the room we can see?"

"Cuh-Cuh-Cain, I think . . . "

"You *think*?" Cain's voice scaled shrill as he turned on his brother in fury. "You haven't had a thought in your life, you microcephalic cretin! Now shut up and hold this."

Trembling, Abel obeyed, backing to the opposite wall with a large shaving mirror in his hands while his elder brother moved and shifted the silver dream-mirror back and forth, to see every corner of the hidden room.

"Fascinating," whispered Cain again. "Do you see it?"

Abel saw. Sweat was rolling down his plump cheeks. "Cuh-Cain, I don't think you should . . . "

Reflected in the second mirror, there were no bricks in the gilded doorway. Only darkness, and the suggestion of a corridor leading back.

"Shut up!" screamed Cain. "Let's see if we can see anything down that hall."

"No." Abel set the shaving mirror on a nearby bench. "We shouldn't be . . . "

"*Don't you tell me what I should or shouldn't do!*" Cain whirled on him, face white with rage. "How *dare* you . . . ?"

Abel fell back against the wall, raising his hands to protect his head, knowing what was coming. "Cain . . . "

A crowbar seemed to spring of itself from the rack into Cain's hand.

"Cain, no . . . !"

Cain kicked aside Abel's body as he came back down the cellar steps. Even dead, he reflected, his brother was a nuisance, an unwieldy lump of suet always in his way. . . .

He carried the large, camel-backed mirror from the dining room buffet. This he set up on his workbench—carefully wiping the blood off his hands—and placed a branch of candles where the light would fall clearly on it. Then he arranged the shaving mirror, and finally picked up the dream-mirror, holding it by the frame in both hands as he moved it in relation to the other two, trying to cast the light of the candles down the corridor that stretched beyond that narrow door.

He stopped. A trick of the light?

The movement of the candle flame in the draft of the door.

Had to be.

He went over and shut the door. The candle flames burned straight up. He picked up the mirror again.

No. There was something moving in the dark of the corridor. Trickling along the floor.

Water? He squinted, moved carefully—so as not to disturb the alignment of the reflections—closer. Thicker than water. It glistened with a queer vileness on the stone floor as it trickled out into the bricked-up room where the mirror had been, glimmered a little in the dark.

Cain stepped back quickly, almost tripping over his brother's corpse, and set the camel-backed mirror down. He went and turned the shaving mirror to the wall, then picked up the dream-mirror and looked into it directly.

Over his shoulder, he saw the shadowed doorway still open . . . and something oozing in a thick pus-colored stream along the wall and out into the center of the room, where it gathered into a faintly shining pool.

The pool began to stir.

"Get up!" Cain knelt beside Abel's body, slapped the waxen cheeks.

Painfully, agonizingly, in the sagging mess of a broken socket, one brown eye pried itself open.

"We're going to the palace."

Though his jaw was broken and most of his teeth knocked out, Abel managed to say, *"Now?"*

Oskar Dreyer jolted out of sleep sweating. It wasn't so very late; outside he could hear the buzz of traffic along the Mariahilferstrasse, and the dim, tinny voices of the television in the next apartment. Not so very late at all.

He had had the most peculiar dream. An American film, he thought— *Dracula*, wasn't that absurd? *Dracula*, and that little man sitting in his madhouse cell, eating flies and begging for a bird to eat, a bird or a kitten. *The blood is the life*, he'd said. *The blood is the life.*

But that wasn't true.

All life was the life.

Oskar Dreyer was suddenly, desperately hungry.

Upon his return from his imprisonment, Dream had remade his palace, the center and heart of the Dreaming, but it was a long process. Much was re-created as it had been—as it had always been—but there were halls and towers that never came back from the dust, and gardens where weed and vine continued to devour, unchecked, the old statues and archways that had once decorated them, much as certain conversations, unremembered for thirty years, return to consciousness embellished with unexpected ramifications upon the rediscovery of old letters, old ticket stubs, old jewelry or scarves. Dream had been very tired upon his return, and later, had had other matters to which to attend.

The library was one of those places that had been refound, after being lost for decades. Even years later, Lucien, the librarian, was still counting and recataloging the books, making sure they still said what they had said before Dream's disappearance and making note of the ones that didn't. When a knock sounded on the library door he was lecturing the shade of a stout white-haired woman whom he had encountered in the stacks—

"Disappeared, sir?" she was saying. "When disappeared? I've been coming here reading every night for the past sixty-two years. You're not going to send me away?" Her bright blue eyes filled with tears. "I haven't finished Plato's comedies!"

"No," said Lucien soothingly. "No, of course not, Mrs. Norton. Er—You don't happen to remember where Lennon's novels are shelved, do you? I can't seem to find . . . Yes?"

"It's me, sir," said a voice from down the long aisles of shelves. "Cain."

He had Abel with him in a wheelbarrow. Abel showed every sign of having been recently dead, but was slowly reviving and trying to sit up. In the wheelbarrow also were Goldie, the daffodil yellow baby gargoyle, and a silver-backed mirror.

"I think—er—I'm afraid there might be some trouble, sir." Cain jerked a nervous little half bow. "You see, I found this mirror—uh—on the road between my house and the Shifting Zones, and when I looked in it I saw a room here in the palace and—well, I thought you ought to know about this."

He handed Lucien the mirror. The whitish, gleaming pool had widened until it touched the feet of the small table on which the mirror had originally lain, and the table now lay, half-melted, in its midst. The patches of black mildew on the wall had changed, swollen and thick, their dark bristles beaded with what looked, in the shadows, like blood. The ooze had trickled out among the broken bricks in the corridor, and a tiny night-fright—of the kind that ran squeaking through the bottommost foundations of Dream's realm—had become trapped in it, struggling frenziedly as the flesh was eaten from its odd-shaped bones.

It took a lot to scare Cain. He was scared now.

The tall librarian's pale eyes skewered him from behind the round spectacle lenses. "And how do you know this room is here in the palace?"

"Uh . . . " explained Cain.

"Do you know where it is? How to get there?"

Abel was looking up at him pleadingly but didn't say a word, possibly because his jaw hadn't healed yet.

"I've seen it on maps," said Cain. "I think I can locate it again."

"Awrp?" said Goldie.

There are, of course, no maps of the palace of the Dream King. This is because the vast halls, the colonnades of porcelain and glass, the gardens where it is always sunset, or summer night, or the eighteenth century, move around. Dream never gets lost. If others do, it is not his concern. Sometimes new halls, new chambers, new gardens appear. In the vaults of the palace it is worse.

Reptile dreams. Hindbrain dreams. Eyes-in-the-darkness dreams.

"Didn't we come here before?" whispered Cain, as Lucien held his torch high. Pillars radiated in all directions, pillars of different marbles, different stones, their time-eroded capitals cut in different patterns where they supported the brickwork of the vaults. Silty dust stifled their footfalls, and the darkness was like a miser's greed, all-encompassing, swallowing even the torch's red light. The sound of feet, frenziedly running; a thin giggle dying away in the dark.

"We came down those stairs before," said the librarian in his chilly voice. "Not the same thing at all. We . . . "

"Lucien!"

The girl's voice sounded terrified. Lucien turned, a very tall thin man in prim blue livery, spectacles shining like moons in the dark. Between the pillars in the direction in which they had come the doorway was just visible, a narrow slit high in the darkness of the wall, and like a firefly a seed of light bobbed and shivered down the long steep drop of the railless stair. Lucien, Cain, and Abel—now on his feet and carrying Goldie on one still-dislocated shoulder—were at the bottom of the stair when the little brown elf-girl reached it.

"Lucien, it's—there's something terrible happening in the Hall of the Warriors!"

"The Hall of the Warriors!" cried Cain in alarm.

Lucien said a word Cain hadn't thought Lucien knew.

After you've had a fight-dream, pounding or clubbing Them—usually with maddening impotence, or weapons that break, or blows that don't connect . . . Ever wonder where They go?

The lights were quenched in that big, smelly barroom when Lucien threw open the door. The only illumination came, hideously, from the walls themselves, from the tables that were sinking already into the appalling softness that was the floor; even the paneling on the walls was beginning to run, trickling sickeningly from beneath the bare-breasted pinups and old motorcycle shop calendars.

The screaming was hellish, the smell beyond belief.

They must have been watching one of the dancers on the narrow mirrored walkway behind the bar, and not seen the walls begin to bleed, and shift, and change. They were, mostly, half-drunk. The suddenly mollient floor gripped their boots, tripping them if they tried to flee, holding them when they tried to rise, drinking them, drinking them, pulling the flesh off their bones as they tried to rip clear their arms and legs. . . .

Someone at the bar who hadn't checked his weapon was firing a semiauto wildly, bullets spattering everywhere; a Crusader was hacking at the gelatinous bands that held him to the wall and shrieking as they bled and he realized it was his own flesh, his own veins, he was cutting. . . .

Under Lucien's hand, the doorknob turned suddenly soft and warm. Lucien jerked free and leaped back, palm bloody—the whole wall on the outside of the Hall of the Warriors was starting to drip, shapes bulging and blistering from it.

"Where's the Master?" cried the elf-girl Nuala. "Earth?"

"Worse. The Realm of Order . . . "

"I hope he packed a sandwich," said Cain. "Even Hell has better food."

"*MOTHERFUCKING NAZI PIGS!*" shrieked a voice from within the Hall, and there was another spattering of gunfire.

A thousand tiny pockmarks puffed in the wet gorp that had been the corridor wall, and in unison they shifted, moved. . . . "We'll all be one. We'll all be one. The time will come and we'll all be one. . . ."

Near them the wall bulged out suddenly into a huge shape, like one of the ugly little dust-bunny frights that hide under children's beds, but blown up to almost man-size: squid, roach, orchid of one of the more repellent varieties. . . .

"All life," it said, from a woman's red lips in its belly. "All life is really one great continuum."

Lucien and the others backed hastily away. "Matthew," said Lucien. "Matthew will be able to reach him." Nuala ran across the hall to the long window, leaned out, and cried the raven's name. "In the meantime we must . . . we must take steps to isolate this wing of the palace. . . ."

"And just exactly what steps are those?" demanded Cain sarcastically.

Jamilla Beyaz wondered what in the name of all Creation she was doing dreaming about going to the mosque. Since she'd moved up to Istanbul from Ankara and gotten a job in the Postal Ministry she'd visited a mosque maybe half a dozen times—she tried to be a good Moslem, of course, but she considered it possible without wearing veils and letting some imam tell her how to run her life. This was the twentieth century, after all.

But here she was, kneeling in the women's section of the Blue Mosque, crowded shoulder to shoulder with those veiled women in the black polyester chaddurs she saw in the markets in the old part of the city. . . .

And the place was jammed. Filled, as if it were Ramadan . . .

She couldn't see who was reading, up in the mimber, under the rings of low-hanging lamps. But she could hear him, hear what he was saying, his voice filling the tiled swell of the domes.

"We are all a part of one another," he was saying. "All life is all life, one great continuum. We are all of one another. We must become one another if anyone is to be happy."

And to her horror, all the men packed, kneeling, on the carpets before her turned to one another and began to bite one another—*eat* one another—tearing off bleeding hunks of flesh. Jamilla sprang to her feet, sickened, appalled; the women in the little boxlike alcove were falling on one another, tearing with their teeth, their hands. . . . Bloody mouths, bloody fingers. One man a few feet from the railing twisted, ripped the head off another. Blood fountained forth and the head said, "We are all one. We are all one. . . ."

Jamilla woke, gasping, trembling in the dark. Beside her, her husband Pierre rolled over, blinked at her. "What?" he asked.

She didn't know why she had the words on her lips as she'd come out of her dream, but she repeated them now. "We are all one," she said.

"Can you muh-move the rooms?" asked Abel. "Puh-put the bad ones all in one place?"

"The bad ones are *already* all in one place, fatwit!" Cain backed another few hasty steps down the hall as the softening wall bulged and blistered again, birthing in a kind of obscene bas-relief more frights, big ones, this time: closet-mutterers, cellar-groaners, attic-knockers. The first fright, still whispering about all life, all life, was slowly drawing out from the wall, veins bulging in the bands of flesh that still held it to the wood of the paneling.

"What the firetruckin' hell . . . ?" Matthew the raven swept in through the window Nuala had opened, saw the things—the movement, the shifting farther down the hall—and veered to land on Lucien's shoulder. Lucien and his party had backed a considerable distance from the door of the Hall of the Warriors. The door itself was melting now, flowing down to join the squishy, flocculent mass of the floor, and from the putrid-glowing dark within came only the mutter of men's voices, "We are all one. We are all one. . . ."

"Get Lord Morpheus. Quickly."

Feet thundered past them—no bodies, just running pairs of feet. Those dreams about footsteps in the dark have to live somewhere, too. With them fled the Lightswitch Thing, pausing only long enough to extinguish the torch Lucien still carried in his hand.

Matthew flapped for the window again. With a wet snap and a spattering of blood, the roach/squid fright pulled free of the walls, manifested a pair of rubbery wings, and sprang in pursuit, far faster than one would have thought such a thing could move.

The other frights pulled free a moment later. Eyeless, they turned as one and lunged at the little group in the hallway.

"This way!" yelled Cain suddenly, turning and plunging down the hall.

Of course the Lightswitch Thing had locked most of the doors.

The frights were boneless, amorphous, but they moved fast, with the veering scuttle of mice and roaches across bedroom floors, the juddering bounce of enormous crickets, and they muttered and squeaked and hissed as they came. Cain and the others veered through a bank of school lockers, where the gym clothes and books and final exams sealed in those combinationless cubbyholes were melting, flowing out under the cracks, to form pulpy white spiders that crawled in a devouring mass over the screaming archetype of a math teacher, and even as they fled past, Cain heard the man's screaming change . . . *"OH GOD OH GOD OH GOD WE ARE ONE LIFE IS ONE. . . ."*

"The Salt Garden!" cried Lucien, understanding.

The squeaking, grasping frights were on their heels as they plunged through the cold white rock of the colonnade that surrounded the place. The fugitives' shoes keened thinly on the combed crystalline waves of the salt, the dunes shaped around the bare black bones of coal. It was always day in the Salt Garden, hard and cruel and hot, and the ground smelled of bitter sterility, of the death locked up in every necessity of life.

The frights fell, wailing, to the ground, and began to shrivel.

"Fill your pockets!" yelled Cain, ripping off his coat and throwing it down. "Fill your clothes, damn it . . . !" He knelt to scrape the bitter crystals in piles onto the cloth. "Take off that stupid scarf of yours, bitch. . . ."

Nuala looked up, startled, as shadows crossed the burning noon sun and Matthew plunged down toward them, shrieking, "Get under cover!"

Flabby, flapping, dripping as they flew, the dirty-colored things followed him in a clumsy, deadly swift horde.

Cain tried to spring to his feet and tripped on his coat; Abel caught him by the arm, dragged him after them as the foul, pinkish creatures dropped out of the air toward them. Cain hurled the whole coatful of salt at them, but they parted like a flock of bats to let it through, regathering to strike . . .

The frights hit the door of the hall on the far side of the garden with a soggy splat as Lucien slammed it, shot the bolt. The heavy oak panels immediately began to soften.

"Organic," panted Lucien. It was night here in the rest of the palace. He produced a match to rekindle his torch. "They—it—can absorb anything organic."

"That's what they've been *saying*, isn't it?" demanded Cain, brushing the salt from his knees. "And let go of me, birdbrain." He pulled his arm free of Abel's steadying grasp. "So what's your story?" He cocked an eye at Matthew.

"Too many," panted the raven. "Coming out of every window—Jesus, take a look at the palace! It looks like the whole southern side of it's caving in. . . ."

"The Stone Tower," said Lucien. "We can go through the stables. . . ." He turned toward a door at the far end of the Painted Chamber, but even as he spoke it was opened, and the Fashion Thing came through, panting and scared, with old Mrs. Norton from the library, still clutching a book, in her wake.

"It's in the stables," said the Fashion Thing, shaking all over at what she had seen there. She was into neo-sixties these days, a Cardinoid ripoff made of clear vinyl and slabs of brushed steel, probably the only thing that had saved her, black hair (this week, anyway) brushed slick against her skull, lipstick now no whiter than her frightened face. "It's . . . the things from the Hall of the Warriors . . . They're tearing up the horses. Eating them. Eating each other." She shuddered, and pressed her hand to her mouth. "They caught . . . some of the other servants. . . ."

"Is there another way through?" asked Abel.

Mrs. Norton pulled her pink quilted housecoat more closely around her throat. "Perhaps Lord Raven saw from the air which way is safest?"

"Not 'Lord,'" corrected Matthew modestly, preening at his breast feathers. "And yeah. Through the Sunset Terrace still looked safe."

"And with all the trees and plants along there, won't we be in fine shape if it's not?" retorted Cain savagely.

"You wanna stay here?"

The wet door manifested a small intestine and a number of hands, and a woman's face that smiled and said, "But all life is one. We are all really elements of the same thing. It's only natural—it's only *right*—that we all come together. . . ."

"His helmet," said Abel, as Lucien opened the door that led through Teddy Bear Hell and thus to the Sunset Terrace.

The others looked at him.

"If Duh-Dream went to the Realm of Order, he won't have his helmet. When he cuh-comes back here, thuh-thuh-they'll be waiting for him."

"Let's discuss this in the next room," suggested the Fashion Thing. The walls of the Painted Chamber were plastered adobe, but the massive window shutters and sills were wood, and had begun to pulse and bleed and put forth tongues that wagged drippily, trying to form words. Thick streams of pinkish matter were beginning to creep in under the shutters and beneath the door.

Lucien bolted the door behind them—wood also. The teddy bears had fled. The room held only darkness within its line of candy cane pillars; darkness and a thick smell of peppermint, kapok, and unicorn piss.

"His quarters are on the other side of the library this week," said Lucien quietly. They all looked at each other. The library was, at present, very close to the Hall of the Warriors.

"It has to be done," said Nuala hesitantly. "I mean he . . . he won't stand a chance."

"Whoever goes after it won't stand a chance, either," retorted Cain.

"This is serious," said Lucien. "Quite apart from the danger to ourselves, *what is going to happen when this thing breaks out of the Dreaming?* When it enters human consciousness? At the moment, Dream is the only one who can stop it . . . *if* it does not destroy him."

"I . . . I'll go," offered Mrs. Norton hesitantly. "If you'll tell me what it is that I'm looking for and how to get there."

The tall man turned to her. "It is a helmet wrought of the bones of forgotten gods," he said. "Long, narrow, covering the whole head . . . But we would not ask that of you, Madame. You are a guest in this house." He glared at Cain and Abel. "I am manifestly against asking it of either of the two young ladies, for that matter."

Cain said, "We'll draw straws."

Abel got the short one. Abel always got the short one, when Cain was holding the straws.

"Will you cuh-care for Goldie?" he asked Cain timidly, handing him the tiny gargoyle that had clung, all this time, to his shoulder. "Will you muh-make sure nothing happens to her?"

"Sure, sure," said Cain, not liking the look of the bolted door behind them. "Now we'd better get going. . . ."

"Awrk?" Goldie struggled in Cain's grip as Abel cautiously unbolted the door back into the Painted Chamber, peered into the heaving dark. There still seemed to be a way across one corner of the slime-coated terra-cotta floor to the door that led back to the colonnade around the Salt Garden. . . .

"No, honey, you stay with us," said Mrs. Norton, catching the tiny creature as Goldie leaped from Cain's grip, tried to follow Abel through the door. Cain and Lucien were hurrying them along, horribly aware of how quickly the threat was moving through the palace. "Oh . . . !"

Goldie sprang down from Mrs. Norton's hands, raced at a fleeting toddle through the half-open door. "Oh, no, come back, sweetheart . . . !"

Cain grabbed the woman by the wrist and dragged her after him.

Bert Blaine walked the alleys around Leicester Square in the darkness, looking at the girls. Dirty slits, the lot of them; ten pounds and they treat you like they're doin' you a great bloody favor—wasn't a woman in the world who didn't think she had a solid gold wazoo, as the Yanks at the yard said. Well, he'd been paid and he had ten quid, and some was better than another night with Five-Finger Mary. . . .

Thought they were so hot. Well, one night he'd show 'em. Generally he did slap 'em around a little, just to let 'em know who was the boss, but it crossed his mind now that it would be finer—it would be more fun—if . . . if . . .

Jesus, what in hell was he thinking! He shoved the thought aside, but it came creeping back.

There was a chap he'd met inside once, a merc in Africa, nobody had messed with him. Big bloke with the devil's own smile. "Ever eat 'long pig'?" he'd asked him once. "Holed up in the bush, or under fire . . . it ain't bad."

"What," Bert had asked, "you . . . what? Draw straws?"

And the big bloke had grinned. "Not while you got the ladies of the regiment around, you don't," he'd said, and winked. In a whisper he'd added, "Gets your money back, you does."

Why did he think of that?

And why didn't it bother him?

"Dear God." Lucien pressed his hand to his mouth in horror.

The Dream King has many servants. Some he has taken from unremembered dreams of humankind, or has wrought to serve in those dreams; others have been given to him, like the elf Nuala, as gifts by the monarchs of Realms other than his own. Others yet, no one has the slightest idea how they came into his service—perhaps not even they.

Driven from the palace, they had fled to the long terrace that forms its western edge, where the sunset had failed and the sky above lay hard and starless and utterly black as the night at the bottom of the sea. And there they were devoured.

Whitish, glowing, flaccid as dirty mushrooms, the frights birthed by the thing within the palace had taken the forms of that which it had already eaten, but changed and shifting, amoebalike. Rats' heads formed like buboes out of the gelid bodies of spiders, or parts of spiders; skulls bled out of their ears and nostrils as they tore mouthfuls of Morpheus's warriors, serving-women, grooms. Caught in the sticky muck to which all grass, all wood, all fabric had been transformed, the servants could only scream for help as their flesh was torn from their bones, and all the while the dripping tongues, the gaping pock-pits, the open esophagi and veins of the thing around them kept saying, "We eat, and we become one. You are becoming one of us. You'll thank us for this; you'll thank us. . . ."

Like filthy rubber squids, or the gross spawn of the unspeakable deep, the flying frights came sweeping out of the sky.

"Run for it!" screamed Matthew, and Cain, and Lucien, and the women ran.

They reached the door of the Stone Tower at the terrace's far end barely ahead of their pursuers, slammed it, bolted it, only to realize that the door was made of dragon bone and gargoyle tooth . . . harder than forged steel, but organic as the wood. "Dream, you pea-brained idiot!" screamed Cain, as they climbed the twisting stair, heard the soft, nasty drip of the door trans-muting, the thick trickles of matter seeping under it and flowing, one step at a time, up the stone stairs.

"Slate shingles," Lucien was enumerating as they climbed, "iron bars on the windows . . . " The orange light of his torch jolting grimly over the walls, cast huge drunken shadows on the curve of the walls, the spiral of the low ceiling curling ever upward. "Narrow mesh . . . "

The window bars were close-set, but the frights that clung to them, gib-bering, thrust greedy, probing tentacles through, like tongues, or grasping gargoyle hands. The faint light of them was a dirty phosphorescence in the dark chamber, and glowing slime dripped from them, running in thin streams down the stone of the wall. Lucien strode from window to window, thrusting with his torch, and the smell of roasted flesh, of the charred drops of matter that fell to the stone floor, filled the room with a choking stench. Cain and Nuala kindled other torches from the holders around the walls and helped him, while Mrs. Norton and the Fashion Thing clung together near the dragon horn door of the upper chamber, listening to the sea-surge of voices crying in chorus below.

We are one. We will be one. All life is one with us, with you. . . .

Then the things fell away from the windows. Outside there was a horrible cacophony of wet flopping, a vast stench, and the faint, sickly glow of them shifted over the faces of those within as hundreds of them circled the tower. . .

And flew away.

Cautiously, Lucien stepped close to the window.

They had merged into a single, monstrous, filthily shimmering cloud, heading in the direction of the Shifting Zones.

Lucien said softly, "He's coming."

"I won't let you take her!" Charlotte van der Berg screamed. "I won't!" She seized her daughter from her crib, clutched her close to her breast, and Boetie—scum, pig, Boer chauvinist that he'd turned out to be under that modern Jo'berg businessman front—grabbed the baby's feet and pulled, trying to drag Renata from her arms. Charlotte clung tighter, the baby screaming in shrill uncomprehending pain.

Charlotte finally ripped her away from Boetie, ran . . . ran through the house, which like all houses in nightmare was dark, with impossible numbers of rooms, halls, doorways. Boetie's footfalls thundered on the wooden floors behind her; she heard him blundering against walls, cursing in Afrikaans, "Hoor! Swine! Kaffir-lover!"

She threw herself into a closet, the little girl clutched to her breast. "I won't let you take her," she whispered frantically. "I won't let him take you from me, my darling, my darling. You're mine, all mine. . . . You'll forever be mine. . . ."

And slowly, deliberately, she pulled the arm off her child, and began to eat.

"NO!" Charlotte van der Berg convulsed, sitting up, gasping as she fumbled at the bedside lamp. Damn him, she thought, damn Boetie for invading even her sleep with his damn divorce settlement, his damn custody battle. She sank back on the pillows, trembling. She couldn't—she *couldn't* let him take Renata. Not her daughter. Not and bring her up to be as closed-minded, bigoted, vicious as he.

The child was hers. *Hers.*

She got to her feet, stumbled across the hot, stuffy little apartment bedroom to where the infant lay sleeping.

Before I'd let him take her, I'd . . . I'd . . .

Mad thoughts flitted through her mind. Insane thoughts that made sense. She'd keep her. Always. They would always be one.

She stayed standing by the crib, staring down at the child inside, for a long time.

In the dark of the Shifting Zones, Dream floated like a rag of midnight borne by the winds.

He was tired. Kilderkin, the Manifestation of Supreme Order, was predictable and ostensibly not to be feared, but the endless intensive legalism, the meticulous *pilpul* of splitting rules into finer rules, definitions into yet more exacting definitions, exhausted him, and in his heart he understood intuitively that the Manifestation of Supreme Order did not approve of him. Kilderkin would not, on its own, attempt to imprison or destroy Dream. But he was aware that the Manifestation—or any of its numerous sub-Manifestations or sub-sub-Manifestations—might at any time be manipulated in some complex game played by one of the younger Endless, by Desire or Despair.

And then he would have to beware.

He let the night carry him on its back.

A glow in the sky, a swirling lift, like the Milky Way surrounding him.

Far ahead of him he saw the Gates of Horn and Ivory, the boundaries of his realm, and knew, suddenly, that something was amiss there. Amiss in the Dreaming . . . voices crying his name . . .

And he was enfolded in the stench of a thousand deaths.

He made one dropping plunge through the air to avoid them, but for all their—its—many-bodied clumsiness, it was fast. It was all over him, clinging, sticky, vile, burning his robes, chewing the flesh of his bare arms—acid, ants, rats. The weight of it fell about him, smote him out of the air and they plunged together, it mouthing him as they fell, and they smashed into the dry rock of the Shifting Zones with a force that would have crushed a human's bones.

It was huge, bearing him down when he tried to rise. He clawed the stuff out of his eyes when it gnawed, digging, at the sockets, tore it from his mouth and nose as it covered him in a suffocating wave. He saw the bones of his own hand, his own arm as he tried to thrash free of it, tried to summon his power to him through the hissing yammer that clogged his mind. *We are one, we are one, all life will be one.* . . . It seemed to him that he was being buried under half a mountainside of maggots, each maggot opening its little brown-red mouth and whispering, *We are one* . . . and the next second he was ripping the half-rotted, chewing skull of one of his own dream-warriors off his hand.

It wasn't his flesh it wanted but his mind, his being—the mind that was ripped, scattered, invaded by the sea-surge of the voices. . . .

"My lord!"

A voice that was not one with those others. A shape in the crowding chaos of shapes, a fleshless skull in which one eye still remained, blood streaming down the eaten bones . . .

"My lord!"

Torn hands falling apart held out to him his helmet.

Abel had had a lot of practice being dead.

A squeak like the note of a high-pitched bell. As he put on the helmet, through the curved cabochon eyes Dream saw Abel—what was left of Abel—turn, hold out one hand, cry despairingly "Goldie!" as the tiny speck of brightness fluttered awkwardly toward him. . . .

Then a gluey skeleton fist shot from the muck, caught the flying speck of gold, and crushed it like a ripe strawberry in a crunching of bone.

"Goldie!"

"THAT IS ENOUGH!"

With the helmet on his head, the hard cool curving bones of gods who had been worshiped by the races preceding humankind protecting his mind, the hellish charivari of the attacker ceased. Dream's mind focused, his power focused, to cold laser light, sloughing all that had been done to his flesh . . . gathering to him the immense and terrifying power of the Dreaming. He rose up among the glowing slime, the clawing tentacles and talons, and cried again in the voice of power, *"THAT IS ENOUGH!"*

He raised his hands, fleshless to the elbows, and the stars flashed through the bones of them. The alien power swirled around him, tearing at him, a whirlpool of shining mist, and through the eyes of the helmet he was able to see how much of its substance had been taken from his servants, his realm, his creation. They had been turned against him. Reaching out, he called forth his strength, to wrest them back.

Very quiet, he said, "Cease."

The glowing muck surged as if with the release of gas, then fell still. He stood for a long time, brown ooze clinging, dark and dirty as old blood, to the rags of his robe, to his body, to his hands which hung now whole and healed at his sides.

The entire world was silent.

Dream reached up, took off his helm, and shook the slime-dripping hair out of his eyes. Under starlight the hard earth of the Shifting Zones looked like a place upthrust from the floor of the sea, inches deep in a layer of primordial filth through which rocks and dead trees projected like broken bones. There was no movement anywhere. No howling voices. No greedy, all-absorbing pseudolife.

Dream walked over to where a tiny chip of white lay. The bones of a baby gargoyle, broken, the flesh stripped away.

Dream took them up in his hand, stroked with his forefinger the curve of the little skull. Then for a time he stood, a tall pale man robed in torn rags of black, looking down at the perfect, golden creature sleeping in his hand.

He went to kneel by the gummed wreck of Abel's bones, passed his hand across them, and said, "Abel?"

"Muh-My lord?"

"Meep?" said Goldie.

"Profanity is *not* going to help us, young man!"

It had been so long since anybody had called Cain "young man" that he only stared at Mrs. Norton in furious shock, unable to reply. Pressed to the stone of the wall between the two windows, Lucien, Cain, and Nuala had alternated in stepping forward and thrusting with their torches at the ever-thickening tentacles of glowing ooze that crept in under the slowly dissolving door. Twice they'd had to burn out the pools that were forming, taking shape into knots of things that might have been serpents or entrails, and the room was thick with smoke. Wet, heavy, like filthy curtains, the frights clung to the window bars again, reaching in with glowing tendrils, and Nuala slashed at a groping tube with a mouth and eyes that wriggled toward her along the stone of the wall.

"Any suggestions as to what to do when these brands are exhausted?" The torches had burned short; the flame on Lucien's was almost touching his hand, and his sleeve was charred. Sweat plastered the librarian's gingery hair to his face; he pushed up his spectacles more firmly onto his nose, and added, "Technically speaking, Mr. Cain, I might point out to you that the mark you bear on your forehead protects you from any *man's* hand raised against you. . . . I doubt it will save you from this."

"I think I want to wake up," said Mrs. Norton unsteadily, as a glowing spider leg the length of a man's arm groped inches from her face. "This is the most extraordinary going-to-the-library dream I've ever had in my life, but I think I'd like to go home now."

"Will it . . . er . . . " Nuala gulped. "If that thing were to . . . to devour Cain . . . would *it* then be Protected? From everyone?"

The door softened, shifted. Running with blood, a woman's face appeared, smiling, and a hundred tongues lolled out from the puckering surface around her. "We will all be one," she said, and smiled. The flesh ran down off her face; her eyes fell out and turned into thin creepers of fluid trickling toward Lucien's feet. "We will all be one."

Lucien bent and seared the creepers into stinking worms of ash, gasped and tried to maneuver the few inches of burning wood in his hand to something that wouldn't scorch him every time he bent down.

"I fear, Miss Nuala," he said, "that we are about to find that out."

The door dropped off its hinges in sodden chunks. A great ground swell of pus heaved through, then spent itself, flaccid, on the floor only half a yard from their feet.

It lay still. It was already turning dark, rotting and settling into a wet residue of harmless slime. With an indescribable sound, the frights plastered over the windows released their hold, and fell.

Silence filled the room. The stench was unbelievable.

"I trust," said Dream's voice from the doorway, "that there is an explanation for all of this?"

His boots made no sound in the rotting muck of the floor. His robe hung damp and torn on his thin frame, and under the filth-streaked black tousle of his hair his eyes were very angry indeed.

"Boss!" croaked Matthew's voice from the window. "Damn, I'm glad to see you—"

Dream snapped his fingers. Matthew fell silent at once.

From the folds of his robe, Dream produced a silver-framed mirror. "I found this downstairs," he said. "In Cain's wheelbarrow."

"I—er—" stammered Cain. "I came across it . . . "

"I know *exactly* where you must have come across it." His voice was like iron pipe in winter, that tears the skin off a human hand. Eyes dark as the slag of failed stars turned on Cain, who sank to his knees, his face pressed to the floor.

"Eight hundred years ago I came close to being destroyed, binding that thing, chaining it when a stupid and irresponsible wizard first summoned that particular variety of solipsistic nightmare into material form." When Dream was angry his voice became terrifyingly quiet. "I bricked it up in the bottommost crypts of my palace so that it could never wreak its havoc on humanity again. There its heart, its essence, is imprisoned once more."

He held up the mirror, and in it could be seen the gilded lintels, the bricks between them not only whole, but layered as they had always been with cobweb and dust.

"I will not have my secrets meddled with."

"No," whispered Cain, clenched hands pressed together. "No, my lord. I swear, my lord, I . . . "

"Silence." He turned to the others: Lucien, Nuala, Mrs. Norton, the Fashion Thing. "You all may go." As they filed past him he laid a hand on the librarian's arm, looked up into the sweat-streaked face. "Thank you, Lucien."

"I'm only glad to see you survived, my lord."

Alone, he turned back to Cain. "Son of Adam," he said, and held out his hand palm down, "for that which you have done, I condemn you . . . "

"Muh-my lord?" Abel's chubby face appeared around what was left of the door. "Puh-please . . . Cuh-Cuh-Cain didn't mean any harm."

"What he meant," said Dream, each word cold and separate, "is no concern of mine. Leave us. And bid your brother good-bye."

Abel took a step back, cradling the tiny gargoyle in his hands, then inhaled, stiffened his shoulders, and came forward again. In his own way the Dream King, in his anger, was much more dangerous than Cain to cross.

"Muh-my lord . . . I ask a . . . a boon. A g-gift. I did . . . I did save you. Puh-Please. D-Don't . . . D-Don't . . . " His voice failed him, tongue-tied, and he stood biting his lip and gazing up at the thin, pale master of the Dreaming.

Dream looked from Abel to the wretched man groveling at his feet, then back at that round, earnest face. He lowered his hand, and though there was no change in his countenance, he sounded almost sad. "Is this truly what you want, out of all that it is in my gift to give?"

"Y—Y—Y . . . " He couldn't speak, but nodded so that his dark thinning curls bounced on his head.

Dream's eyes returned to Cain. "Get up," he said quietly. "Get a mop. Have this palace clean by morning."

"Yes, my lord. Certainly, my lord." Cain scampered for the door, pausing beside Abel only long enough to hiss viciously at him, "And I don't need you to fight my battles for me, nitwit!"

And he was gone.

"Cuh-Cain . . . !"

Dream caught Abel's arm, staying him as he would have gone through the ruined doorway after him. "He will only kill you again," he said, in a voice like the dark beyond the stars. "You know that."

"He muh-might change," said Abel. "One day."

He broke free, and hurried down the twisting stairs after his brother, his yellow gargoyle in his arms.

THE BIRTH DAY

B. W. Clough

I met Brenda Clough in Washington at a signing, and it was a very long signing, and she had waited with an astonishingly patient infant son for hours to get her books signed.

This story arrived unsolicited, and is chronologically the earliest of the tales in here. It's science fiction, I think. Or maybe romance.

It was quite a new thing the band was planning, a thing so new there was no name for it yet. "I will think of a name," Ikat promised her uncles. "It will be here ready when you all come back, triumphant."

Her words were deliberately well-omened. Uncle Rav winked at her—there were no flies on him. Everyone else murmured approvingly and fingered their pebble bags or sticks to rub the luck onto where it would do the most good. "Now remember," Uncle Oren fussily repeated, "don't kill! We're just scaring them along. You remember where the dead-end canyon is. And you, Ree, keep your paws off that sling of yours, it's deadly!"

The boy grinned happily at this slanted compliment. People moved off in twos and threes down the hill to find their places. Everyone except Ikat went, old and young, even the nursing mothers, who were supposed to wait at the canyon and keep the captured goats inside by yelling and whistling until the woven wicker barriers could be tied into place.

Though it was autumn, the day was too hot for garments. Ikat wore nothing but the clay bead around her neck. She reclined on her folded deerskin skirt, with the dogs for an armrest, in the shade of the big cedar tree overlooking the river valley. The yellow dust of the band's descent rose up into the blue sky, higher and higher, to join the bigger yellow stain up there, the one stirred up by a thousand thousand cloven hooves.

"Do you wish to go, too?" a voice asked quietly behind her.

Startled, Ikat half turned. A stranger, lurking in the brush? "Flint! Thunder!" The dozing dogs leaped up, alert in an eyeblink. Flint and Thunder knew something exciting was happening down the hill, and felt left out. Now they were delighted to discover an enemy. Flint's lionlike mane rippled and bristled, and his eyes got red. Thunder's savage low growl hung like smoke in the air. They loomed on either side of Ikat, waiting only for her word to tear the intruder apart like a buck. "Come round the tree, stranger, to where I can see you," Ikat ordered.

"This is not the way a New Meeter should greet people," the visitor said reprovingly. His feet made no noise at all on the coarse grass. He loomed very tall over Ikat, but then she was sitting down. A black antelope hide was knotted around his thin brown body, and his bead was smooth-polished red agate, cunningly bored through to take a neck thong.

"You are not quite a stranger, then, if you know my job," Ikat said sunnily. "If I have offended against hospitality, let me make amends. Flint, back! Please, sit in the shade here—I will move over to give you the coolest spot. Lie down, Thunder! When you are thirsty there is a skin of water in the tree hollow there. I regret, sir, that I have forgotten your name, if I ever knew it."

"You have long known it, Ikat, but we have never met," the visitor said. "You call me Shaper, and you have served me all your life."

"Oh!" Quickly Ikat averted her gaze in respect and touched her forehead to her sitting knees. "You honor me, lord!"

"You are not afraid," the god noticed in mild surprise.

"I have never met a god before, but what sort of a New Meeter should I be, if meeting someone new frightened me?" She would have said that anyway, but was pleased to feel only a slight flutter in her stomach, no worse than when Uncle Rav called on her to tell a story after supper to guests. "And as to your first question, lord, if you know me so long, you know why I do not go with my band today." She stretched out her legs, so that the sunshine fell on her club foot.

"Are you sorry for that?"

She frowned. If anyone else asked, she twisted her answer, but it's unwise to lie to a god. "Well, it's horrid not to be able to run. I dislike that a lot. But I can walk fast enough to keep up, when we move to the winter camp. The cousins take turns carrying my bundle. I might never have become the New Meeter if my foot was well. It's fun to tell the stories, and put names to new things. And this year I've found something truly new, something really useful and exciting if it all works out. So I'm a helpful member of the band; what more could anyone want?"

She glanced sideways at him to see if she was rambling on too much, for that was a fault she was often subject to. But he was gazing out over the heat-hazed valley at the wild goat herds on their journey. The oncoming winter drove them out of the northern mountains, south and west to where summer lingered all year. Ikat imagined the summer place as green and well watered, buzzing with bees. "We should follow the goats someday, and see," she said out loud, and then covered her mouth to show she meant nothing by it. "I'm sorry, I will make a story out of that one. I shoot out these things like sparks from a flint. It's my job."

"You do it well," the god said. "What is this new spark of yours?" He pointed to where some band members were just visible down below trotting through the tall grass.

"Oh, it is my best one so far! It came to me when I went with Aunt Ama to draw water from the river. We use baskets lined with clay because these goatskins are too hard to come by." She dragged the waterskin out and took a drink, first politely offering it to her guest. "It was last spring, right after the goats passed by on their way north. We had eaten all the meat, and were living on nothing but wild grain and roots. You don't get berries around here till mid-summer. And, I thought, the animals are a lot like the river, flowing by us. We can dip out the water and save it in baskets and skins. Wouldn't it be great to dip out some goats and keep them a little while? Then instead of eating meat until we fall down, twice a year, we could spread out the food for a longer time."

"Very clever," the god said.

"It's not me that's going to make it work," Ikat admitted. "The band will do all the work—Uncle Rav had the idea about tying basketry panels to pen the goats in, for instance. I'm the New Meeter—I had the thought, like the way the father begets the baby in the womb. The band has to actually go into labor to birth the child, and today is the birth day. That's why it's really all right, that I'm not there. Fathers aren't allowed in the birthing tent." She knew it sounded silly, a girl referring to herself as a father, but Shaper, of all gods, would surely understand.

Then she sat up straight, digging her elbow in so suddenly that Thunder whined protestingly beside her. "And that spark came from you, lord! For you are master of the Uncreated. You must be come to bless the occasion and receive our thanks! Do you prefer blood sacrifice, or sex, or—"

Her own unheeding chatter suddenly made her blush right down to her breasts. The other big problem with her foot, which she hadn't mentioned to the god, was that no other band would accept a limping bride, however clever. And she couldn't marry any boy here, they were all her cousins. Up to this point her best hope had been to captivate some visiting hunter. But now—she looked full at him, as a girl should when assessing a possible sex partner, and her heart sank. So far as she could read his strange face, he looked acutely embarrassed! "Libations," she blurted. "Some gods prefer drink offerings; that's good, too. Just indicate your wishes, lord."

The god fingered his neck stone, staring down at it. "To speak the truth, Ikat, I come because I am of two minds about your 'new thing.' You might call it 'herding,' by the way. The goats are already in their herds, you are merely moving them to your own design."

"It shall be named as you say, lord, thank you," Ikat said, delighted.

"But think carefully about it. You press forward to embrace new things. As you say, it is your job. But is every new thing a good thing?"

Ikat stared. "How could this be other than good? You are a god, lord, and know no hunger, but for us it is very different! Do you know what I dreamed yesterday night?" The god nodded, but Ikat, absorbed in her words, didn't notice. "I dreamed that the little canyon was brimful of imprisoned goats, so full that we ate meat once a day!" She sighed with pleasure at the memory.

"Ikat, listen to me. Your band, all of humanity, is like a fish in the river, at a place where the stream splits into two channels. The choice the fish makes will change its life, its world, forever, and should not be taken lightly."

Ikat clapped her hands in delight. "You can talk in word pictures, too! But I shouldn't be surprised, the thought skills are yours. It is the best fun! Do you warn the fish, then, against the river channel ahead? What is it like?"

Suddenly, though he did not stir, the god seemed to be very tall. "I could show you," he said quietly. Thunder the dog shivered beside her, and Ikat noticed for the first time how very shady the cedar was, how its broad cool boughs cast the deepest and most clinging shadows around the god. They were shadows of the uncreated, of things that were not now and might never be. And the chief horror was their namelessness. Ikat, the namer, could not name them, though she could see that some were big and some were little in the hand, and others were thought skills while yet others were arts of finger and leg and arm. There were literally no words yet, for the things that stirred there in the shadow of the god. The New Meeters who would name those things were themselves yet to be born.

Dizzy and sick, Ikat turned and hid her eyes against Thunder's flank. "Forgive me, lord, I am not strong enough to see!"

"No—I should not have done that. It is not weakness, Ikat. It is your strength that prevents you from seeing, the strength of simplicity and innocence. . . . Tell me, what is the name of that river?"

Ikat swallowed her nausea. The god had actually apologized, and was trying to soothe her—amazing! It was up to her to respond. She seized on the plainness of his question with relief. "It—we have no special name for it, lord. It is just the river. Is it your will that I should find it a name?"

"I will name it for you," the god said. "Call it Euphrates."

More important issues distracted Ikat from this pronouncement. What about the "herding"? He had said he was in two minds about it. She thought about pleading for mercy, but discarded the idea. Too late to be humble, and anyhow it was her way to be bold. "Oh, Lord Shaper, if one wishes to prevent the birth of a child, it is far easier at the beginning. Perhaps the pregnancy has already come too far to abort it."

He looked down at her, wrapping the antelope skin more firmly around himself. "Even the birth day is not too late. A child may die of its birthing. Have you no stillborns in the birthing tent?"

We will conceive again, she wanted to retort. Instead she said, "But you've already named the baby, lord, named it yourself!"

"So I did," the god said, disconcerted.

Mistake, Ikat thought to herself, wincing. Even kindly Uncle Oren didn't appreciate having his inconsistencies pointed out. No man did—how much less a god? She bowed her head to her knees again. "We are the grass under your feet, lord. Do to us as you will."

For a moment, bent over, she knew he was still there, maybe thinking it over. Then Thunder gave a half whine, and Flint sneezed. She sat up and saw the deity was gone, evaporated like a puddle in the sun. "That was scary," she told Flint, pulling his ears. "And, oh dear, what's happening down at that canyon?" She couldn't stand waiting anymore—suppose the god was down there right now, tossing goats over the wicker barriers like Ree slinging pebbles?

She hung the waterskin over her shoulder and hauled herself to her feet. Tying her skirt on, she began limping down the rocky slope. The dogs ran ahead, but she called them sharply to heel. Trained to chase and kill, the dogs might never learn the art of "herding." "Heck, we haven't learnt it ourselves," Ikat sighed. "And it was such a good idea. . . ."

She paused, listening. They were coming; she could hear the voices! As soon as the first people came in sight she shrieked, "What happened?"

The children ran up the hill to her, seizing the waterskin and talking all together at the tops of their voices. More tired, the adults came on in a tight clot, arguing all the way. "Only a partial triumph, niece," Uncle Rav said. "Half a dozen goats caught alive, no more. And all because of this beanballed, wisp-brained, snot-arsed, misborn—" He shoved someone forward, someone entirely new.

"I'm sorry," the strange young man said miserably, hanging his head. "But I really didn't know. I still don't."

Ree said, "I keep trying to tell you!"

"We need that limber tongue of yours, Ikat," Uncle Oren grumped, "to get it through his thick head. This is Neem, from a band up the river. A hunter, and thought *we* were hunting. Jumped in and speared half the goats before we could stop him!"

Ikat assessed the newcomer with one piercing glance. His beautifully flaked spear showed there was a clever flint-knapper in his band. And the tiger skin he wore—wow, if he killed that animal himself, he was a superb hunter indeed! "I'm Ikat, the New Meeter," she said to him. "Since you killed, you should eat of the kill with us, that would only be fair."

Neem's face lightened at her words. "How kind you are," he said. "I thought you'd hand me my head, for spoiling your trick, whatever it was!"

"Lend me your arm up this hill, for you see I have a limp, and I'll forgive you." Close beside him like this, Ikat could smell Neem's strange and attractive odor, a whiff of male sweat and tiger leather. *Aha, I see your plan, Lord Shaper,* she said to herself, smiling. *Admirably subtle! You will distract me with pleasures, perhaps even children, and count on my other child, the child of thought born this day, to die of neglect. But I am not so poor a parent as that!*

SPLATTER

Will Shetterly

Will Shetterly is one of those people I feel like I've known forever. Will is a fine writer who, inexplicably, keeps doing other things instead, like nearly becoming governor of Minnesota, and nearly directing and releasing an independent film. He has had a beard long enough that I cannot remember what he looked like without one. He is also a nice man, gentle and perceptive. This is not a story I would have expected him to write, but then, nasty tales lurk in the nicest of us.

He sets his story during *Sandman* #14, the story I called "Collectors," in *The Doll's House* collection. (It's also a pretty accurate portrait of the whole signing tour thing.)

Sometimes he suspected his publisher called each city before a signing tour to order, "Fans, assorted, at least two geeks in every batch." Today, the geeks seemed to be a Demented Duo, a young man and woman dressed in black who placed a stack of his books before him and asked for an autograph doodle on the woman's thigh that could be turned into a tattoo. He obliged them, pleased for just that moment that this last-minute appearance was so poorly publicized that no photographers were present. He knew he was grateful that they wanted his signature sketched on her skin with a felt-tip rather than a razor blade.

He drew a cartoon cat's head with vampire teeth and a knowing wink, then added an indecipherable scrawl that might be *Peter Confry* or *Please Crucify.* They both thanked him profusely. He felt old as he realized he had miscategorized them. They were actually a Nice Young Couple who would not embarrass him with offers of obscure drugs or inventive sex that he would have to politely decline. This realization saddened him. It was always nice to be asked.

He inscribed their books and instantly forgot their names (Teri and Jon?), though he wrote thirteen times "To (her name) and (his name)—Best wishes! P-scrawl C-scrawl." While he scribbled in the worn paperback copies of every novel of his except the new one, the hardcover that they'd bought here, they told him they had driven from Alabama just for this. Before they drove home, they would eat cheeseburgers side by side at McDonald's with their copy of *Hunting Butterflies* open between them. Grandma liked to take care of the baby, and besides, their autographed copies of Confry's complete works weren't just to make them happy—those signed books were investments in their baby's future.

He nodded and grinned, and told them he hoped they'd like the new one, and wondered when his driver would arrive to take him away. He glanced at the wall clock four times while the Nice Young Couple hugged their books and repeated that he'd have a place to stay if he ever came through Mobile, that their long drive home would seem to fly by 'cause she (Kathi with an *i*?) had brought a flashlight to read to him (Rod? Todd?) while they drove, or maybe they would splurge on a cheap motel room and finally have their honeymoon, alone for the weekend, reading chapters to each other. She added, "Except when, well, we *are* married, you know," and they looked at each other and smiled. He told Confry, "I wouldn't share her with anyone but you," and she swatted him with a freshly autographed copy of *I Hear the Heart of the Night*, saying, "Dream on, Mr. In Control." After a last awkward laugh, the Nice Young Couple that looked like a Demented Duo left.

Two fans from the standard selection remained in the mall bookstore: a balding Thirty-Something Exec and an overweight Commando–Wanna-be. Both had waited quietly for everyone else to leave, which put them into the subset of Shy Hoverers. The Thirty-Something Hoverer shook his head, smiled, and said, a little mockingly and yet sympathetically, "Fans."

Confry's stomach contracted at the word. Before he could select the right response from (a) Smile, say understandingly, "It's a privilege to make others happy," (b) Laugh, say seriously, "And thank God for them; they pay my bills," or (c) Sneer, say mockingly, "So what don't *you* like about my work?", the Commando–Wanna-be thrust forward an often-handled first printing of *Banshee's Need*.

"Sure." Confry took the book and glanced up. "Who for?"

The Commando–Wanna-be looked over Confry's head, as if there were something more interesting on the shelves behind him, then glanced out into the mall and mumbled, "Karl. With a *k*."

"Karl, with a *k*." Confry scribbled: "For Karl—Best wishes! P-scrawl C-scrawl."

"Uh, thanks." The Commando–Wanna-be looked at the books piled on the cloth-covered card table in front of Confry. "'S good." He looked at the door at the back of the store. "Bye." He looked at the manager by the cash register, turned on the heel of a polished army boot, and walked quickly into the mall.

"Glad you liked it!" Confry called to the man's back. It was easy to sound sincere, though *Banshee's Need* was his only book that made him feel defensive. It was his grimmest novel, and his first popular one. He had written it just after he lost his teaching job, while Jan, pregnant with Lisa, had supported them as a travel agent. He had written it more quickly than anything before or since. It was his only book told entirely from the point of view of a mass murderer.

He turned to the Thirty-Something. The man held out a hand without a book. "John Hunter."

"Ah." Confry smiled, stood, and shook the hand. "The convention?"

Hunter glanced to either side, though Confry had spoken quietly. "Didn't want to say anything until your fans had gone. Be embarrassing if one tried to crash a private affair. For them, I mean, of course."

Confry nodded. "A sold-out con is a sold-out con."

"Yes. And, frankly, our collectors wouldn't mingle well with most of your fans. People in my trade tend to be, well, conservative."

"Eh. It's refreshing to be invited to a convention where I'm not a star."

"To me, you are."

Confry laughed self-deprecatingly. "Critics complain about my fondness for trademarks, but I never had anyone drown in a bowl of Wheaties. Still, if a cereal convention wants to pay me to show up and sell more copies of my books, I won't complain."

Hunter set a pale leather briefcase on the card table and unsnapped it. The lid rose between them. Hunter reached in with the satisfaction of a Hollywood hit man about to display an automatic pistol or a former U.S. vice president about to display an anatomically correct doll. "I have everything you wrote, of course, but I thought you might be getting writer's cramp after a long signing, so I restricted myself to two." He held out a copy of *Hunting Butterflies*.

Practice made Confry's smile perfectly sincere. "I wouldn't do signings if I didn't enjoy them." With one exception, he hated everything about signings and conventions: nights in bland hotels, flights at awkward hours, meals in restaurants that were convenient rather than good, meetings with journalists and store managers who would never read his books but who needed him for an interview or a signing to make themselves a little more money. The exception? He was neither so selfless nor so selfish that he could be annoyed when people told him they loved his work.

"And this." Hunter took back the signed *Hunting* and offered a pristine copy of *Buzzard Love*.

"My God." Confry held the book in both hands. "I thought it had a negative print run."

"Two thousand five hundred copies."

"Almost all remaindered." Confry turned the book carefully and looked for a mark across the edge of the pages. "Not this one." He opened it, quickly enough that some collectors would have winced, but this book had been open before. "You read it?"

Hunter smiled. "No point in having something without enjoying it."

Confry smiled too, a heartfelt smile that made him realize he was no longer looking at another Thirty-Something. He was looking at a man in blue chinos, a white short-sleeved shirt with an orange tie, and wire-framed glasses. He was looking at a man with watery brown eyes, receding dark hair, a bushy moustache, and a small scar on one cheek. He was looking at a man who had asked himself late at night what the good things in life could be, and had answered that among them were the writings of Peter Confry.

Confry flipped to the title page and poised his pen above it. "Deface it?"

"Please."

He wrote, "For John Hunter, with the greatest pleasure, Peter Confry." Each letter of his signature could be seen, or at least, inferred. "You know, I didn't kill a single person in this."

Hunter nodded. "It's a young man's book. But it's very promising. When Quinn talked about his rage after Janet left, I felt it here." Hunter placed his open hand over his heart.

"I—Thank you."

"It seemed like a first draft for the scene in *Banshee's Need* when Christopher's in the baby-sitter's basement."

"Well." Confry's signature would add hundreds of dollars to the value of this book. He flipped toward the end, found the scene Hunter had mentioned, and opened the book wide, cracking its spine. After a glance at the words, he handed the book back and, feeling guilty for hurting it, said, "Writers always cannibalize themselves. I hadn't realized the bits were so similar."

Hunter smiled. "Not *that* similar. Quinn gets drunk and vomits. Christopher kills seventeen people with each tool of a Swiss Army knife."

Confry laughed. "It's the difference between a quiet academic novel and a book that pays for a Manhattan town house."

Hunter shook his head. "You shouldn't belittle your work. You're too good."

"Hey, the only reason you find my books near Joseph Conrad's is we're both filed under Fiction *and* Literature."

"No. You understand the heart of darkness."

Confry gave a loud laugh that made a teenager in the Human Sexuality section turn to stare. "Come on! You can't compare my little hack-fests—"

"Of course not. Conrad looked from the outside and saw—" Hunter grinned. "*The horror! The horror!* But you look from the inside, and see—"

"Royalties without end."

"Beauty. Love. Power. The attempt to remake the universe as it should be, even when we don't know what it should be. The courage to act without regard for anyone's opinion."

Confry, still grinning, shook his head. "I try to show the effects on the little people—"

"Exactly! The *little* people. They suffer. But compare their suffering to that of Christopher or Big Red or everyone in the Dogmeat Gang. Little people can only suffer, but those who see—" Hunter stopped. "I shouldn't embarrass you with my pet theories."

"Well. I just write the stuff. How can I know what it means?"

"You know. Your work proves it."

"Eh." Confry glanced at the clock for the first time since the Nice Young Couple had left. "Hadn't we better be going?"

In Hunter's car, Confry answered the usual question about his next book with the usual answer: "I never know what it's about until I'm into the final draft." The truth was that he had not begun anything for almost a year. He kept thinking about a serious novel concerning a writer of fantasy instead of horror going through a divorce instead of a separation involving a blonde and a son instead of a brunette and two daughters while trying to decide why he was commercially successful and artistically unhappy. It would be a supernatural horror story, but the ghosts haunting him would be the ghosts of complex, ambitious novels that he had never written. Confry thought the conceit might be sufficiently self-referential to win the respect of the reviewers. And if he could figure out a way to have those phantom novels kill a critic or two of the sort who skewered work that bore no resemblance to what the writers had written, Confry might keep enough of his fans to keep his career.

As they drove, he thought about Jan and Lisa and Meg. Meg still saw him as Daddy, and she leaped into his arms whenever he came home. He could not remember the last time Jan or Lisa had hurried to him. Lisa seemed unable to talk to him without sounding exasperated. And Jan said something was wrong, but she couldn't tell him what had changed. The closest she had come to saying something meaningful about their marriage was that perhaps nothing had changed in sixteen years. Shouldn't that be good?

A dead German shepherd lay by the highway. Confry stared, not wanting to see its strewn guts and not wanting to look away.

"I hate seeing an animal like that," said Hunter. "Killed so carelessly."

Confry glanced at him. "I saw my dog hit when I was a kid."

"They catch the guy that did it?"

"No." He had never told Jan or the girls about Buster. Maybe telling a stranger was proof that he could change. "We were running across the highway. I made it in time, but my dog didn't." He thought he should add the rest, that he had been eight, and he had seen the truck coming, but he had run for the thrill of winning a forbidden race and had not thought about Buster at his heels.

"Another of life's lessons."

"Yeah." He decided to say no more. He had read that confessions were never the full truth, that something was always withheld. That had seemed profound. Now he thought it stupidly self-evident. Who would have the patience to listen to anyone's complete confession?

"We're here." Hunter turned at a sign announcing the Empire Hotel and WELCOME CEREAL CONVENTION.

"Great." Confry forced enough enthusiasm to be polite. He had visited too many conventions at similar places, motels twenty years past their prime on the outskirts of small towns near enough to a city to attract truckers, salespeople, adulterers, swap meets, and fan conventions. He had hoped to be bathed for three days in breakfast food profits. Now he suspected that the World Cereal Society was only a letterhead in John Hunter's computer. He wished he had asked for a check in advance.

Hunter insisted on carrying his suitcase. Holding open the hotel door, he said, "Enter freely, and of your own will." He laughed, and Confry smiled in spite of himself. If this was only a gathering of poor but avid fans, he would be bathed in adulation instead of money. Someone would undoubtedly buy his drinks, and someone would probably sleep with him. Jan had often told him that if he'd just take part in the things around him, he could be happy anywhere.

In the lobby, perhaps fifteen attendees sat on the sofas or spoke quietly with the desk clerk. Most were white men, a few were women, several were people of ambiguous sex and race. Their clothing tended toward working-class: jeans and feed caps, T-shirts and baseball jackets, running shoes and wide leather belts with heavy buckles. A few wore black leather, and a few wore tailored suits, but this was not a flamboyant or a wealthy crowd.

He hesitated inside the door, then answered Hunter's glance. "I'd kind of hoped to be met by Tony the Tiger or Captain Crunch. Don't the companies give you posters or T-shirts or free samples or anything?"

Hunter smiled. "We're a very self-sufficient bunch."

At the registration desk, while Hunter signed him in, Confry listened to a gray-haired black man in a cheap suit tell a young Asian woman in a leather jacket, "I don't keep no mementos, girl. It's all up here." He tapped his head. "Safer, that way."

"Cheaper on insurance, too," Confry said. The two gave him looks that asked him to explain his interruption. "I'm Pete Confry. This is my first cereal con."

The black man smiled. "Oh, yes. The writer."

"Ah," said the Asian woman. "You collect?"

"Just books, now," Confry said. "Butterflies, coins, and comics, when I was a kid. I've been wondering. Do cereal collectors eat the stuff they collect, or isn't that the point?"

The Asian woman smiled. "Some eat nothing else."

Confry shook his head. "Fandom is a way of life, I guess. I think I'd keep the packages and dump the contents."

The black man shrugged. "Some do that, too. We best be gettin' ready for opening ceremonies. See you there?"

Confry nodded and watched them go. As Hunter turned from the registration desk, a thin young man in a Bugs Bunny T-shirt hurried toward them. "Nimrod! Hi! Is this—"

Hunter nodded without pleasure. "Peter Confry. Yes."

The man thrust out a moist hand that Confry accepted. "Hi! I love your work. I really do! I'm—"

Confry released the hand as he read the young man's name badge. "Fan Man?"

Fan Man grinned. "Yeah. It's a silly handle, but—"

"Fan Man?" Confry repeated, hearing a sharp, brittle emphasis in his voice and not caring.

"This is unfortunate." Hunter took Confry's arm to lead him away.

Confry jerked his arm away and jabbed a stiff finger into Bugs Bunny's eye. The thin man winced, then blinked as Confry said, "What the hell kind of joke—"

"C'mon." Hunter slapped a room key into Confry's hand, picked up his suitcase, and led him into a hallway of numbered doors.

"I love your stuff," Fan Man yelled. "I really do!"

"Then get a goddamn clue!" Confry called back. "Get two; they're cheap!"

"Kids," Hunter said. "You've got to expect a certain amount of excess from the young."

"Excess. Right." Confry swallowed, then nodded. Two families had been killed in ways that seemed like intentional recreations of the first mutilation scene in *Banshee's Need*. The press had called the killer Fan Boy. Then a third family had been killed in the same way, and a signature had been left in blood: Fan Man.

"I should've told you," Hunter said. "For the weekend, we've all got the handles of serial killers. Seemed like a fun idea for Halloween." He took a badge from his pocket and pinned it to his shirt. "See? I'm Nimrod." Hunter shook his head. "I forgot about the Fan Man until I saw him heading toward you."

"Fun. Yeah. I guess." Confry tried to smile, failed, then said calmly, "You think he believed using the name was funny?"

Hunter shrugged. "It bothers you?"

Confry shook his head as though shuddering. "No way. It's not my fault I have more imagination than a nut with a knife. The real Fan Man would use the Bible for inspiration if he had nothing else."

"And he'd be continuing a fine old tradition."

"Yeah." Confry breathed deeply, then laughed. "So, who'll I be? The Ripper? The Corinthian? The Boston Strangler?"

"You're our author guest. Everyone should know that." Hunter drew another badge from his pocket and handed it to Confry. The others in the lobby had been white, but Confry's was the red of drying blood.

Alone in his room, he picked up the phone to call Jan and ask about Meg's cough. After three rings, a male Southerner said, "May I he'p you?" His voice suggested the task was hopeless.

"I want to call—"

"Sorry. Line's down."

Confry heard a disconnecting tick. He listened to the empty song of the telephone for several seconds, then punched "O" again.

"May I—"

"What's this about the phone line?"

"Can't make no outside calls. Ever' phone in the place is out. Sorry."

"For how long?"

"Monday aft'noon, most like."

"Monday. Thanks." Confry dropped the receiver into its cradle. He had often said he wanted privacy. Now he had a weekend's worth. He missed his office at the house he still called home. There, privacy had been a choice, enforced by the occasional yell at the girls to be quiet 'cause Dad was working. Writers wrote, right? No one resented fire fighters for putting out fires. He had thought himself one of the lucky ones, because Jan had encouraged him to write.

He whispered, "No matter how you choose, you lose." Then he smiled. A good line always pleased him, no matter how bad the circumstances. Jan hadn't understood that, either.

Feeling as though his hotel room had been cut adrift from the world, he clicked on the television. The world promised beaches, bikinied blondes, and beer. He clicked off the set. The world always made promises. Maybe he should see what the world delivered.

In the lobby, eyes turned toward his red badge, then away. Conversations grew quieter. He did not fit in here, but he was used to that. He did not fit in anywhere. Perhaps he should have stayed in his room until Hunter returned to take him to dinner. Perhaps he should have opened his notebook computer and begun creating a world in which purpose was defined by plot and a pure heart always prevailed, where love held true if you persevered and every path could lead to redemption, so long as you watched the signs.

He walked toward the convention area. A posterboard placard on one door identified the art show, so he stepped inside. A bearded man filling out forms at a table looked up in surprise, then shrugged and kept working. On his badge was written, "Fuck you."

Confry pointed at the badge. "Never heard of him."

The bearded man grinned. "No one knows the fuckin' best. Everybody's heard of fuckin' McDonald's."

Seven oil paintings had been hung in the place of honor before the door. "Who's the artist guest?"

"Haven't got a fuckin' one. We fuckin' got a fuckin' honored artist instead, 'cause he fuckin' couldn't get the fuck away."

Confry turned toward the seven paintings. The first showed a sleeping man writhing on a bed. A chalk white man leaned over the sleeper, whispering into his ear. In the dark room, furniture and shadow coupled like beasts.

In the second, the man who had been asleep sat on a park bench, watching two teenage girls pass with schoolbooks pressed to their chests. The man stared at them, though they did not see him. His hands pressed into the flesh above his knees, bunching the cloth. Beside him, a pale and beautiful androgyne looked at his face and smiled.

In the third, only the man's face could be seen. Beside him, a white-skinned woman with skeins of multicolored hair pressed her cheek against his. They wore identical unfocused smiles. Around them, toads flew with butterfly wings, and the two schoolgirls scampered hand in hand through fields where van Gogh sunflowers grew with petals larger than the girls' heads.

In the fourth, the man sawed wood in a basement while a red-bearded giant watched him. Four steel manacles sat on top of a stack of lumber.

In the fifth, the man drove his car behind the two schoolgirls, who walked down the sidewalk without seeing him. In the car's backseat, a hooded man sat, chained by the wrist to a heavy book.

In the sixth, the man stood in the basement. Beside him, two crucified forms on a wall might have been shadows or stains. Before him, a wall opened on a green field. The schoolgirls, clad in white robes, ran through the grass toward a black-garbed smiling woman whose skin was the color of bone.

In the seventh and last, the man stood in a courtroom with his hands cuffed together before him. The lawyers, jury, and audience were all faceless manikins. The judge, a naked obese woman, raised an iron hook like a gavel, perhaps to strike the desk, perhaps to strike the accused man in the heart. He looked up at her, expecting the blow with something like resignation or hope.

"Hey!" said Confry. "This's whatsisname's, that death row guy's work, right?"

The bearded man glanced up. "Brilliant fuckin' deduction, dude. Fuckin' everybody's heard o' that fucker."

"Well. I like this better than Gacy's clowns."

"Fuckin' amateurs."

"Well, you have to admire the effort."

"Fuck," said the bearded man. "You'll see fuckin' shit in here by fuckin' pros you fuckin' never heard of—" He sighed. "Fuckin' amateurs."

Confry studied a jar that appeared to be filled with eyeballs, and decided he didn't get it. He almost respected a painting of a nude man sitting in a car seat with his decapitated head facedown in his lap, but he only liked it for the title, *Auto-fellatio*. There were a number of grotesque human-sized dolls made of leather, and an assortment of realistic body parts embedded in Lucite. His favorite effort was a group of forgettable portraits made strange by being framed in long bones tied together with hair, but he hesitated longest before a large skull and several smaller ones, displayed on red velvet with a sign saying, FAMILY GATHERING, BY NIMROD. He stared at that, thinking of Fan Man, then of Jan and the girls. How did three people you loved become an enemy and two strangers?

In the back of the room sat a large wooden crate labeled "Work in progress." Muffled moans came from within it. Confry jerked his thumb toward it and told the bearded man, "You guys should sponsor a haunted house. Kids'd love it."

"Yeah." The bearded man grinned. "It'd fuckin' slay 'em."

Confry was looking at a series of photographs when Hunter hurried into the art show. Confry said, "I studied this case when I was researching *Dreams in Darkness*. I thought I'd seen all the photos, but this—"

Hunter said, "We should get some supper before opening ceremonies."

"Oh. Sure." Confry followed.

Hunter said, "So, what do you think?"

"Your piece had a certain black charm."

"Thanks. Your overall impression?"

"Eh. Some interesting stuff."

"But?"

Confry shrugged. "Well, as usual with fannish shows, I can't say I'm impressed by the level of execution."

The bearded man at the door said, "Fuck. Most o' this shit's only worth lookin' at for the fuckin' quality of execution."

The hotel restaurant surprised him. The menu had a small selection of Hungarian specialties, and Hunter insisted on ordering the best red wine in the cellar. While they waited for their orders of chicken paprikas, a stout older man in a hunting vest approached their table. "Hey, Nimrod, bag anything good?"

Hunter nodded. "A big buck standing right by the side of the highway like God put him there for me. Smokey, this is Peter Confry, the writer."

"Oh, yeah. You write them killin' books."

Confry shrugged.

"They scare my ma, but she keeps on readin' 'em." Smokey peered at him. "You ain't eatin' here?"

Confry said, "Well, uh—"

Hunter said patiently, "The food's very good, as you well know."

"Could be any ol' thing." Smokey pulled a plastic baggie from his vest and unzipped the seal. "But I can vouch for this. Meat an' smoke, nothin' else, jus' like the good Lord intended."

Confry glanced at Hunter, who nodded as he took a bit of jerky. "Smokey's got a way with pork."

Confry accepted a piece and bit into it. "Good."

"Meat keeps you healthy," Smokey said. "Only kill your own, though. They put all kinds o' chemicals in livestock nowadays. I don't know what the world's comin' to."

"I hear you," Hunter said.

As Smokey walked away, Confry said, "I take it he doesn't eat from his collection."

Hunter shook his head. "Smokey's a natural cereal sort. We get all kinds."

Following a sip of his after-dinner Tokay, Confry said, "I should get to a phone to call my wife. Ex-wife. Ex-wife-to-be." He smiled. "God, separating's the shits."

"Anything urgent?" Hunter asked.

"Not really. Just wanted to hear my kids' voices."

"We'll have some time after opening ceremonies."

"All right."

"I know how you feel. My divorce was hell."

"Still bother you?"

"Not really. I see my family whenever I wish."

"I wish Jan was as understanding. The lawyers are still working out visiting rights."

Hunter aimed his fork at Confry's chest. "Sometimes you can't compromise without compromising yourself. I saw you understood that in *Nicky's Pleasure*."

"Well," said Confry. "She *was* crazy."

Hunter shook his head. "Driven. If her husband had understood that, he wouldn't have had to die. What did she want? A room of her own in which to pursue her own concerns? Is that so much?"

"But she was still crazy. I wanted to suggest they were both right and both wrong."

Hunter turned his fork toward his *polecinta*. "Who were your sympathies with? Really? The whining husband and the nagging kids? Or Nicky, who wanted to make something that was hers alone?"

"Well—"

"Be honest."

"Hey, Nicky wanted to make art out of dead things." As Confry finished the sentence, he thought of the art show and realized what had disturbed him. The concepts and techniques of construction might have been crude, but the materials were as perfect as Hollywood could demand.

Hunter said, "Something wrong?"

"Just a crazy idea. Maybe it'll turn into a story."

"Really?"

"You never know."

"Ah." Hunter cut into his dessert. "What you said about art out of dead things. That's a metaphor, right? So it's not relevant. Who do you feel for when you write? Honestly?"

Confry finished his Tokay, then smiled. "Honestly? Okay. I admit it, I love my monsters."

"I knew it!" Hunter slapped the table, rattling glassware.

"The monsters can do anything," said Confry, his meal and his suspicions forgotten. "Which means I, in turn, can do nothing at all. It's the greatest freedom, having characters act for you."

"Oh? Which is greater, the shadow or the substance?"

Confry laughed. "The shadow. The police don't get you for fiction, no matter how badly written."

"You're never tempted to act out the things you imagine?"

"Imagining them *is* the acting out."

After a sip of coffee, Hunter said, "You do a lot of research."

"Some."

"Ever interview a killer?"

Confry shook his head. "I read a lot. And I know enough about my own impulses to extrapolate, I like to think. Besides, real killers are pathetic."

"Oh?"

"Sure." He had made this argument before, so it came easily. "Your average killer's someone who's drunk or high who kills a friend, a neighbor, or a family member. Nothing interesting there. Hired killers tend to be simple people with little education. They don't have any real sense of the humanity of anyone who isn't part of their family, clan, business group, or"—he smiled at his cleverness—"in the case of armies, nation. That's not very interesting either. Mass murderers and serial killers are the sorriest of the lot. They're stupid or ignorant and usually both, and they only succeed for as long as they do because they're so pathetic that no one suspects them. Usually they've been abused as kids. Look at the Wisconsin boys, Ed Gein and Jeffrey Dahmer. Once you learn a little about them, they're pitiful, not horrible." Confry sighed. "That's why I write about brilliant sociopaths and wealthy megalomaniacs. Dracula's heirs. The stuff of fiction. Of fairly popular fiction, if you'll forgive a bit of immodesty."

Hunter sipped his wine. "You don't think people like that exist?"

"About the best you get is Ted Bundy. And he was a lying little weasel compensating for a failed personal life."

"Which is the failed life? The life in a world that couldn't understand him? Or the life that he made for himself in private with his prey?"

Confry set down his glass. "Hey, I can entertain that argument, but it really doesn't amuse me."

"Fine." Hunter smiled. "Bundy was a failure. He was caught. But what about the ones who aren't? Who knows how many they are, or how clever they may be?"

"How many miles of unexplored caves in Carlsbad?" Confry laughed.

"Seriously."

"Seriously? Well, sure, there are some who're never caught, but that's because they quit before the police get close. They get frightened, or find religion, or kill themselves. It doesn't change the profile."

"They must get caught?"

"They tend to get caught. You kill a few people, you're going to leave a trail."

"Really?" said Hunter. "This country expects to find people killed. Forty thousand automobile victims a year. Thirty thousand suicides. Twenty thousand fatal home accidents. How many of those were faked? Then there's missing people. How many of them—" Hunter's eyes narrowed. "Does this bother you?"

"What?"

"Talking about killing with a fan you don't know."

Confry made himself laugh. "Isn't that what most of my books are?"

Hunter smiled. "I knew you understood."

Confry knew then that he understood, too. If his understanding was wrong, he might look foolish. If his understanding was right, he could not stay in this hotel. "I should make that call before opening ceremonies. I noticed a gas station down the block."

"Damn, I wish there was more time. We start in a couple minutes."

Confry stood. "Tell you what. You get the bill. I'll run to the corner. Won't take five minutes." He looked around the room. Only a few attendees were still in the restaurant, and none of them were paying attention to him.

"You're determined?"

Confry began walking away. "It's important. Jan's expecting it. I'll be right back."

He felt as though every eye in the hotel rode upon his shoulders. That made him think about the jar of eyes, and the sounds from the crate, and the jerky he had eaten. He kept his face still. He had no idea whether he was walking too fast or too slowly or perfectly normally, but he knew he wasn't running, and, more importantly, no one was running after him.

At the front door, he felt something like hope and something like embarrassment. He wanted to turn and agree that the call could wait. An active imagination was an occupational hazard. Would he really go to the nearest phone, call the police, and tell them that most of the country's serial killers had gathered for a convention? The idea was insane, but when he thought about what he had seen and heard, he knew he would rather be paranoid than dead.

The night air, cool and moist, drove his doubts away. He strode across the well-lit sidewalk and headed for the parking lot. Someone walked toward the hotel, undoubtedly another member of the convention. Confry continued on, keeping his eyes averted, planning to run only when he was out of the parking lot lights and close to the street.

Something about the man's silhouette seemed familiar, familiar enough to draw Confry's gaze until he recognized Karl-with-a-K, the Commando–Wanna-be from the signing.

Karl-with-a-K said, "I came to hear you talk."

"That's great! I got to make a call, 'cause the phones are out here, but—"

Karl-with-a-K seized his arm, spinning him toward the hotel. Fan Man ran silently toward them, and Hunter walked behind him at a comfortable pace.

Confry said, "Please. Let me go. I don't know any of your names."

Karl-with-a-K said, "You know mine, Mr. Confry."

"I sign thousands of books, I—I don't remember anything that the police could use. I thought—" Confry swallowed. "I thought you liked my work."

Fan Man nodded several times. "That's why you're here."

Confry screamed, "Police! Help me! Police!" He stopped when he heard the others join in like a chorus of drunks or madmen. Karl-with-a-K shouted, "Eee-hah!" and Fan Man shouted, "Listen to this!" then screeched even louder than Confry had.

In the following silence, Hunter said, "Smokey's a state trooper. Even if someone came to investigate, they'd leave after he said a few of the boys had had a li'l too much to drink."

Confry said, "This is, ah, a joke. Some kind of hidden video show, right? Scare the scaremeister, am I right?"

Fan Man drew a Swiss Army knife from his pocket and opened one of its shorter blades. "I'll cut something off you if it'll make you feel better. I collect Peter Confry mementos."

Confry shook his head. "You—" He bit back the impulse to say, "—can't let me live," and finished, "—won't hurt me?"

Hunter said, "We don't want to hurt you."

Fan Man, pocketing his knife, said, "And we don't want anyone else to hurt you. We all agreed."

Hunter tapped Confry's chest. "We want you to write about us." He smiled. "Because no one will believe you. Isn't that right?"

Confry nodded, pursed his lips, then nodded again more slowly to show them he thought that was reasonable. "I'd do that. I'd love to do that. It'd be a great book. Sure. It's a deal."

"Good. Let's go inside."

"Oh. Sure." He looked at them, wondered how far he would get if he ran, and began to walk toward the hotel.

In front of the door, though he knew it was too late, he stopped. The others looked at him with something like kindness, and Hunter said, "Yes?"

"How do I know? That you know. That you can trust me?"

Hunter nodded. "It's simple, really."

"Simple," Karl-with-a-K agreed.

Hunter put a hand on Confry's shoulder, propelling him into the hotel. "When we disperse at the end of the convention, and you get left at the airport, you could go to the police and describe some of us well enough to catch us."

Confry said, "I wouldn't."

Hunter smiled. "But you couldn't hope to find all of us. And you know that any of us could find you, now, don't you?"

His throat was so dry that his tongue felt like a dead toad. He would remember that the next time he needed to describe a nagging awareness of an unconfirmed fear. He sat on a metal folding chair in the front row of the Rhett Butler Room and listened as Hunter took the stage. Fan Man sat on one side of him, and Karl-with-a-K, wearing a badge naming him "The Neat Freak," sat on the other. The guards were not necessary. A hundred people or more filled the room. All of them knew he was not one of them.

Hunter told a joke. For Confry, the sentences did not parse. At the punch line, "He used a scythe," he laughed with the audience. That seemed better than vomiting. When Hunter told the second rule of the convention, that no one was to do any collecting until the convention was over and everyone was at least two hundred miles away, he winked at Confry, and Confry grew calmer. He felt like a reporter on the front lines of battle. When this was over, he would go home, and though he would never tell anyone what had happened this weekend, he would tell Jan that he would do anything for her and the girls, even if that meant learning how he had failed them.

Hunter introduced a man in sunglasses as the guest of honor. Fan Man whispered, "Whoa, the Corinthian!" Several seats away, someone whispered loudly, "Fuckin' injury to fuckin' eye fetishist."

The man in sunglasses grinned and waved. He spoke briefly about opportunity, self-expression, and the satisfaction of pursuing a dream. As Confry tried not to wonder what someone would do to win the admiration of this crowd, Hunter took the stage again and introduced his favorite author, and America's, Peter Confry.

Fan Man chanted, "Speech, speech, speech, speech!"

Karl-with-a-K nudged Confry. "Go on, Mr. Confry. This is what I came for."

He walked awkwardly to the podium, clenched it in both hands, then waved to the crowd. Hunter indicated the microphone and whispered, "Say something. We'd appreciate it."

The crowd looked much like any other crowd, and his fear was much like his usual fear of speaking before any crowd. "Hi. Er. This is, er, an honor. I didn't, ah, prepare a speech, but, er, I'd like to say, ah, thank you." As the applause began, he added, "I'd also like to say, ah, I appreciate your trust. And, um, I won't let you down. I'll write a book about this weekend, but I know how to disguise people in fiction. Um, it'll be the best thing I've done. And it'll all be for you. It'll inspire me to keep writing better and better books, and that'll be our secret. Ah, thanks again."

As he turned toward his seat, Hunter spoke into the microphone. "Don't sit yet, Pete. A few of us got together to get you a present."

Half of the crowd smiled. The rest merely watched. Confry did not know which disturbed him more. He said, "You didn't have to."

"Oh, yes, we did."

An obese man in a skull cap topped with Batman ears wheeled the crate marked "Work in Progress" onto the stage. Whistling "Hi Ho, Hi Ho, It's Off to Work We Go," he and Karl-with-a-K pulled nails with a hammer and a crowbar.

As the side of the crate came away, a set of black-jeaned legs and another set in torn fishnets, both bound at the ankles with silver tape, kicked outward. Continued thrashing told Confry that the people were alive, and so did their muffled, desperate grunts. High on one of the stockinged legs, a gap in the netting revealed an inked cat's head caught in an eternal wink.

"Don't be shy," said Hunter. "You remember Ron and Keri from the bookstore?"

Karl and the man in the Batman cap dragged the Nice Young Couple out of the crate. They stared at Confry over wide bands of silver tape that sealed their mouths.

In the audience, several people shouted, "Hi, Ron and Keri!"

Hunter said, "Ron and Keri are from Mobile. They're big Confry fans. They told Grandma they'd be back by Sunday. Come Monday, someone'll start looking for them, and they'll find their car far from here, by a river at a roadside rest that's on their route home."

"Please," Confry whispered. "Let them go."

Hunter shook his head. "There's something I didn't tell you. The threat about never being safe from all of us, well, that's an appeal to logic, and people simply aren't logical. You might get a notion that your life is worth risking to capture a few of us, or you might think the government could hide you under a new identity. You might even decide we could do for your sales what the Ayatollah did for Rushdie's."

"I wouldn't. Honest."

"I know that. But the rest of the folks here don't. Neat Freak?"

Karl-with-a-K came back with a plastic box. Hunter said, "Battery recharger, jumper cables, miscellaneous clamps. Glue. A hacksaw. Dishwashing gloves and condoms for those who like to play safe. It's wonderful how much fun can be had in the average home."

Fan Man spread a plastic tarp on stage, then rolled the Nice Young Couple onto it.

Karl-with-a-K reached his free hand into the trousers of his fatigue pants and drew out a black commando knife. As he handed it to Confry, he said, "Careful, Mr. Confry. It's sharp."

Confry glanced at Hunter, who nodded. "Okay. First I'll cut them free, then—"

Hunter shook his head.

The breathing of a hundred or more people seemed very loud in the absence of other sound. The Nice Young Couple breathed loudest of all. What was the sound of a dog's breath as it ran before an oncoming car?

Confry could not remember. He looked at the couple, and then at the dark blade in his hand, and then at Hunter. "What do you want?"

Hunter smiled. "You get to choose. Be one of us." He shrugged and jerked a finger at the Nice Young Couple. "Or one of them."

Karl-with-a-K drew a Luger and pointed it at Confry's knee. "I'll always think you're the very best writer, no matter what."

SEVEN NIGHTS IN SLUMBERLAND

George Alec Effinger

George Alec Effinger lives in New Orleans. He has written many novels and many short stories and won many awards, and he can recommend a strange-but-wonderful restaurant with the very best of them.

Winsor McCay has been dead for many years. He was drawing comics ninety years ago that are stranger, more inventive, and more innovative than anything you'll see today.

Effinger builds something more than a simple pastiche. It's the literary equivalent of a Winsor McCay comic. But, as you'll see, it's more than that.

THE FIRST NIGHT:

The year was 1905. Little Nemo was six years old, and he was having trouble falling asleep. He wore a long white nightshirt, and he lay between stiffly starched and ironed muslin sheets in his wooden bed with the high headboard. He said, "I hope I can get to the palace in Slumberland tonight. I do so want to meet the Princess again. Yes! I hope I don't wake up before I get there."

The lonesome Princess had sent many of her servants and subjects to lead Nemo to the royal palace of her father, the King of Slumberland, but almost every night some accident or adventure caused the boy to waken before he arrived. Every night Nemo's papa and mama were roused by the sound of his tumbling from his bed in the throes of his dream struggles. Every morning they wondered what ailed the boy, and determined that he should never again be allowed to eat cheese toast at bedtime.

On this night, the Princess of Slumberland had sent a special courier with wonderful news to Nemo. The courier's name was Lopopo, and he was a tall, thin man with a tuft of red hair and a wide, friendly grin. He was wearing a fine purple coat with wide lapels, green tights, and green boots, and he had a very high green hat that came to a point. "Oh, Nemo," he said politely, "the Princess herself has sent me with this invitation. It is for you, yes!"

Nemo took an envelope from Lopopo and opened it. Inside were a pasteboard ticket and a brief note from the Royal Box Office of Slumberland. "This is for me?" the boy asked.

"Yes, yes. There is to be a special base-ball game played for the entertainment of the Princess. That ticket is for you. You will join the Princess at the stadium, and after the game I will present you to His Majesty."

"A base-ball game! Oh, I am excited!"

Lopopo led Nemo down a flight of stairs that had never before existed in the boy's bedroom. "Yes, it will be a thrilling contest, I have no doubt, a game between the New York Giants and the Pittsburgh Pirates. They are the two best teams in the National League."

Nemo was so pleased that he clapped his hands. "The New York Giants are Papa's favorite! He will wish that he had come with me. Oh!"

At the bottom of the stairs, Nemo discovered that they were in a low-ceilinged tunnel. Torches mounted along the sides of the tunnel gave a smoky light, and it glittered on the facets of many colored gems that decorated the walls.

"This cavern will lead us to Slumberland, all right," Lopopo said. "It is only about a thousand miles long. Then it is but another five hundred miles through the King's realm to the Slumberland Stadium. We will be there soon, ha!"

They walked for a very long time, and Nemo was surprised by all the bizarre and wonderful sights to be seen in Slumberland and its outlying reaches. He was beginning to grow tired, though, and he stopped and stretched. "Will we ever get there?" he asked.

Lopopo laughed. "Come along, Nemo! You do not wish to disappoint the Princess, no! Everyone in Slumberland knows how much she has missed her playmate."

They walked another hundred miles, and then another. At last they climbed a very long, very broad set of marble stairs, from the underground cavern up into the fresh, flower-scented air of Slumberland.

"Hurry, Nemo!" Lopopo urged. "We have five hundred miles more to walk, and we have only a few minutes!"

"Oh, I am walking as fast as I can!" Nemo said.

They hurried through wide, tree-lined boulevards, where crowds of Slumberland's citizens cheered the boy who had become their beloved Princess's new friend. They passed by grand, imposing buildings in which the affairs of Slumberland were debated and ordered. After a while, Lopopo pointed. "There! Nemo! The Slumberland Stadium!"

"Good," Nemo said. "I do not think I could walk another hundred miles."

"Now, you have not lost your ticket, have you, Nemo?"

The boy held up the envelope. "I have it right here."

"Then give it to the man in the blue uniform and we will go right in. It is almost time for the base-ball game to start!"

The Slumberland Stadium was the biggest Nemo had ever seen. He and Lopopo began walking up the marble ramps toward the special box of seats reserved for the King of Slumberland, his daughter, and their guests. At last they emerged, and Nemo could look down at the base-ball diamond laid out below.

"Oh! It is so beautiful!" he said. "I have never seen grass so green!"

"This way, Nemo," Lopopo said, directing him to his seat beside the Princess.

"Oh, come to me!" the Princess said. "I have missed you! You will enjoy the base-ball game. It will be grand!"

Nemo bowed to the Princess, then sat beside her. He looked down at the field again, where the game was about to begin. "Oh, it is 'Matty'!" he said. "Mathewson is pitching for the Giants! 'Matty' is Papa's favorite player. He will wish he'd come, gracious!"

The Princess looked through her field glasses. "And now it is Honus Wagner batting for the Pittsburgh fellows," she said.

"He is a very good hitter," Nemo said. "'Matty' will have to be careful."

Mathewson pitched a hard fast ball and Wagner swung at it. He hit a foul ball that sped like a rocket toward Nemo and the Princess.

"Aha," Nemo said. "'Dutch' Wagner is sending us a souvenir!"

"Oh, I'm afraid it will hit us!" the Princess said.

"I will catch it," Nemo said. The ball began as a little white speck down on the playing field, and as it came nearer it grew larger and larger and larger. Soon the ball seemed the size of a melon, then it was as big as a house, and then Nemo could see nothing at all except the gigantic base-ball that was screaming toward him.

"Oh!" he said. "It will crush us! Help!"

And the next thing Nemo knew, he was tangled up in his bedclothes on the floor of his room. His papa had come to see what was making the boy shout aloud in his sleep.

"Pshaw!" Nemo said. "I wish I'd seen the rest of that game!"

"Go back to sleep, Nemo," his papa said. "And stop that dreaming!"

THE SECOND NIGHT:

Nemo was fast asleep in his bed when a noise made him sit up in astonishment. Once again he saw a strange man in his room. This fellow was dressed as a clown, with a white face and a broad red grin painted around his mouth. He wore a tiny cone-shaped hat on his smooth white head, and a baggy clown suit decorated with purple, yellow, and green circles. He held his right hand out before him, and a small bird perched on his forefinger.

"Have you come from Slumberland?" Nemo asked.

"Yes," the clown said. "I am Doopsie the Chief of Clowns. The Princess sent me to fetch you. She has a special surprise planned, you see! You will meet the Spirit of Heart's Desire."

"It is such a long walk," Nemo said, yawning. "I am always so tired before I get there."

"Do not worry, no!" Doopsie said. "We will not need to walk tonight." He knelt down and let the bird hop onto the floor of the bedroom.

"Oh!" Nemo said. "It is Budgie, Mama's pet!"

"Yes, and he will carry us both quite safely to Slumberland."

As Nemo watched, the little bird began to grow. In a moment he was so big that his feathered head brushed the room's ceiling.

"Oh, mercy!" Nemo said. "He will never get back into his cage now! I hope Mama will not be too unhappy, no!"

Doopsie mounted the giant bird's back and held out a hand for Nemo. The boy climbed up behind the clown, and Budgie spread his huge wings. Then they soared upward, smashing through the ceiling, flying through the upstairs room where Angelus the Negro maid slept, and then breaking through the roof of the house into the cool, sweet, moonlit sky.

"Papa will not be pleased with the hole in the roof, I guess," Nemo said. He clutched Doopsie around the waist.

"It is a long way down, but don't be afraid, Nemo," the clown said.

They circled over Nemo's house, then flew away across the city. Nemo laughed when he recognized his school, the church, and his friends' houses far below. "Wheeo! This is much better than walking, yes!" he said.

"Hold on tight," Doopsie said. "We will be in Slumberland soon."

As good as his word, the clown steered Budgie up into the clouds, toward the shining spires of Slumberland. In a few minutes the bird descended, and at last came to a gentle landing in the courtyard of the Princess of Slumberland's palace.

"Yes, we are here, Nemo," Doopsie said. He jumped down and lifted the boy from Budgie's back. The bird began to shrink again immediately. When it was its normal size once more, it flew back into the air and disappeared.

"I hope he goes back to Mama," Nemo said.

"Look, Nemo," Doopsie said. "It is your dear friend, the Princess."

"Yes," Nemo said, "but oh! who is that with her?"

Doopsie said, "That is the Spirit of Heart's Desire. I am sure the Princess will introduce you." The clown made a low bow to the Princess and another to Nemo, and then he backed quickly away.

The Princess smiled. "I am so happy to see you again, Nemo!" she said.

"I am glad I did not fall off that bird's back."

"I want you to meet the Spirit of Heart's Desire," the Princess said. "Desire is the most beautiful of all in Slumberland. Don't you think so, Nemo? Yes?"

The dark-haired Princess was herself very beautiful, and Nemo was about to tell her so when he was interrupted by a sudden commotion. Someone had burst into the very palace of the Princess. "Heart's Desire, pshaw!" the ill-mannered intruder said. "I can not even tell if it's a beautiful girl or a beautiful boy! What sort of a game is that?"

"Oh!" the Princess cried. "It's Flip! If my father hears of this, he will be very angry!"

Flip was a sour, unhappy person with a green face and a huge cigar stuck in a corner of his mouth. He wore a long black tailcoat, green trousers, and a very high stovepipe hat with a broad hatband. Written on it were the words "Wake up!" He was jealous of Nemo; he always did his best to interfere with anything the boy and the Princess had planned.

"If you cause trouble, Flip," Nemo said, "then you and I are for it, and you will have to take a lickin'!"

Flip glared at Nemo. "I don't care two shucks for that. I may call my uncle, the Dawn Guard, to bring on the sun and melt all of Slumberland into daylight! Just see if I won't."

The Princess looked unhappy. "Oh, Nemo, we will pretend he is not even here. Now listen, because the Spirit of Heart's Desire must ask something of you."

Desire gave Nemo a charming smile. "You see, Nemo, it is this. I have lost something very valuable to me, and the Princess said only you could find it. Will you help me? Yes?"

Looking into Desire's golden eyes, Nemo was glad to be of service. "I will do anything I can for you," he said.

Desire smiled again. "Yes, I know you will." The Spirit's voice was sweet and melodious.

"So what are we looking for?" Flip asked. "I am coming along, too. It is no use leaving me out of this."

Desire glanced at Flip, then turned again to Nemo. "I hope you will find my golden bottle. It has a stopper carved from a beautiful diamond. It is a small thing, and Slumberland is a very big place."

"I will search everywhere," Nemo said. "What is in the bottle?"

"It is dream dust," Desire said. "King Morpheus himself gave it to me."

"Come along then, Flip," Nemo said. "We won't come back until we have found it."

"Oh, Nemo, good luck! Yes!" the Princess said.

"You will have a special reward when you find it," Desire said.

Nemo and Flip left the palace and began their quest for the golden bottle of dream dust. "I guess I am stumped, kiddo," Flip said. "Where will we look first? The jungle? The desert? The frozen north?"

They turned down a narrow street between two great domed buildings. "Gracious," Nemo said, "this may take all the rest of the night."

"Well, ehem, what is this?" Flip said. He had lifted the lid of a metal trash can and was peering inside.

"Come along, we don't have much time, no!"

Flip reached down and lifted something from the trash can. "I guess it is a golden bottle with a diamond stopper! I guess it is!"

"Oh my!" Nemo said, astonished.

Flip was very pleased with himself. "They say it is always in the last place you look, but not this time, eh?"

"Now we can take it back to the Spirit of Heart's Desire. We will get our reward, sure!"

"Oh," Flip said, "I will keep this for myself. I found it. Yes."

Nemo tried to pull the golden bottle away from the green-faced rascal. Flip would not let go, and they wrestled for a while until Flip called out to his uncle. "Uncle Aurora, help me! Bring on the sun and send this kid back where he belongs!"

Suddenly, all of Slumberland was flooded with bright sunlight. "Oh no!" Nemo cried. "I am falling sound awake!"

And then he turned over in his bed. His mama had come into the room and was shaking him by the shoulder. "Come along, Nemo," she said. "It is nearly time for Sunday school, yes!"

THE THIRD NIGHT:

Dressed now in a pale blue coat with brass buttons, blue breeches, shiny black leather boots, and a peaked military cap with a black visor, Little Nemo wondered where the Princess of Slumberland's city had gone.

The palace had completely vanished. The maze of streets, the carefully tended parks, the vaulting marble edifices had all disappeared like the cool morning haze. Nemo stared in astonishment. There was nothing to see except a grass-covered plain. Not even a tree stood between him and the distant horizon.

"Oh, dear!" Nemo said. "This is all Flip's doing! When I find him, I will make him sorry! Yes!"

"You know," a young woman's voice said, "what happens sometimes is there are just some people you can't make sorry. Um, like my brother. One of my brothers. At least one."

Nemo turned and saw her. She was not much taller than he, and she looked a little bewildered, and he decided that he liked her even though she was the most unusual-looking person he had ever seen, even in Slumberland. She had skin as white as bone, and wild hair that was long in places and cropped short in others; sometimes the hair was blond and sometimes it was pink or purple or orange. She wore earrings—little white skulls—but she also had a ring through one nostril and another in her upper lip, like savages in Mama's picture-books. She didn't look like a savage, though; she looked nice. She wore a jacket made of heavy black leather, and a short black skirt. She had one blue eye and one green eye and she was staring over Nemo's head at absolutely nothing.

"Excuse me, ma'am," Nemo said, "but I am looking—"

"He called me 'ma'am'," the young woman said. "The last time anyone called me that—um, I forget."

Nemo tried again. "I am looking—"

"You're looking for a golden bottle with a diamond stopper."

Nemo raised his hat and scratched his head. "How did you know that?"

"I don't know how I know, I just know," she said. "Don't you know when you know?"

"Don't I know what?" Nemo asked.

The young woman gazed at him for a moment. "Here," she said at last. "I can help you find what you're looking for. We'll use my cards."

"Mama and Papa like to play cards."

"Let's sit down on this nice red grass," she said. "Now, shuffle."

Nemo sat beside her, but he didn't say anything, because there was only one single card, and he didn't know how to shuffle one card.

"That's good enough," she said. "Now turn it over." She touched the grass, and tiny fire-breathing dragons in many bright colors began to crawl around.

Nemo watched for a moment, then he turned the card. It was the four of hearts.

"Ah," she said. She smiled. "The six of pentacles. A nice card. Um."

"What does it say?" Nemo asked.

"How can a card say? I can tell you what it means. A card can mean. Um, wait a minute. It means that this is a really, really good time to help somebody. So that's why I'm helping you."

"Thank you, yes!" Nemo said. "I must find that bottle!"

"Now shuffle again."

Nemo turned the four of hearts over so the back of the card faced up—it was from a deck of Delta Airlines playing cards. Then he turned it over again. Now, somehow, it was the jack of spades.

"Oh, wow," she said. "It's the Little Nell card. That's a *horrible* card. It means lots of grief and suffering and sometimes as much as you want to help someone, you just *can't*, you know?" She stared over Nemo's head again. "Well, um," she said, standing up, "in that case, good-bye."

"Oh! Oh!" Nemo cried. "Please don't leave! No!"

The young woman sat down beside him again. "Okay, we'll try it again. Turn the card over; but if it comes up Hiroshima or the King of Anchors or something, I'm gone."

Nemo nodded and turned the card: the deuce of diamonds.

"I'll bet that even felt better, didn't it?" she said. "It's all about freedom and happiness and, well, goldfish, I guess, if you want goldfish. I like them until they're, you know, dead. You're going to have a wonderful future and you're going to have a good friend, a tall, pale man who lives far away from the city. Oh. *Oh.* I'll bet I know who that is!"

"Who is it?" Nemo asked. "Tell me, do!"

"Um," she said.

"Shall I turn over another card?"

The young woman raised her eyebrows. "There *aren't* any more cards," she said.

"Then how will I find the golden bottle?"

She sighed. "All right. Take this string." She lifted the end of a long piece of white string and gave it to Nemo. "The other end is tied around your golden bottle. All you have to do is follow it."

"Thank—"

"And, um, hope that somebody bad doesn't untie it before you get there."

"Thank you, ma'am," Nemo said.

"He called me 'ma'am'," she said happily, as she vanished.

Nemo opened his eyes and found himself back in his bedroom. He heard his papa calling him: "Nemo! Sleepyheads don't get breakfast in this house! No!"

THE FOURTH NIGHT:

Little Nemo realized suddenly that the healthy grass of Slumberland was gone. Swirling patches of fog had appeared while he'd followed the string, and now he could barely see the ground.

"Oh, gracious!" Nemo said. "Where am I now? What is happening, eh?" He wasn't out under the bright blue sky any longer. He was in some dimly lighted, dank and echoing room. He still held the string, and he walked and walked and walked, but he didn't seem to be getting anywhere. He couldn't see walls on any side of him; he couldn't see the ceiling or the floor. There was just the fog, getting thicker and thicker.

And there was a rat, a huge gray rat the size of a large dog. "Oh my!" Nemo said. "Maybe that awful rat won't see me in all this fog. I hope!"

"I do see you there," the rat said. It had a rough, rasping voice.

"Oh! Oh! It is a talking rat!"

"What are you doing in my realm, Nemo? I don't get many visitors, and they're usually sorry they came here."

Nemo felt a cold emptiness within him. "I must wake up!" he said. "I must go home to Mama and Papa!"

The rat made an unpleasant growling sound; it may have been laughter. "You won't ever go home, Nemo. Look at your string."

Nemo glanced down at the string in his hand. It had been chewed off, and the end of it dangled uselessly from his fingers. He became even more frightened. He sank to his knees, searching in the impossibly thick fog for the other end of the string.

"You won't find it, you know," the rat said. Its voice was barely above a whisper, but it was compelling nonetheless. "You'll never go back to your home or your family again. Just this easily, hope turns to despair."

Hot tears ran down Nemo's cheeks. He stood again and looked wildly around himself; he saw only the fog and the rat. "Mama!" he cried.

"She can't hear you."

"Why is this happening? Why am I here? Eh?"

The rat showed its long, crooked fangs. "Your task, Nemo. You haven't found the golden bottle with the diamond stopper. Desire is waiting for you, and you haven't even begun to look."

"I have looked for it, yes," Nemo said hopelessly. "I would look some more, but how can I find it here?"

"There's an important lesson, then: Yearning may lead only to unhappiness. A wise person knows when to stop searching. It's time to quit, Nemo; it's time to give up."

Little Nemo blinked and the rat became an ugly old woman. She had skin like a cold dead thing and eyes the color of a bitter morning in December. Her short black hair was caught together with a dirty piece of cord, and she had on no clothes at all. On her left hand, where Nemo's mother wore her wedding ring, this woman had a ring with a barbed hook, and with it she ripped at the flesh of her own face. Nemo watched the blood trickle downward toward her chin. He shuddered, and then he shuddered again.

She reached for him. "Come, boy," she said in her low, disquieting voice, "I will show you how you'll end."

Little Nemo ran. He could hear the blood roaring in his ears. He felt prickly and hot. He ran through the fog; it twirled and twisted around him, but it could not hold him. There were many window frames suspended in the air. Nemo wondered what he might see if he stopped by one, but he was too afraid to look.

"Oh, why can I not wake up now?" he said. He ran some more. He had run a thousand miles, and he had not gained a single step on the ugly woman, who was still chasing him.

He ran along a narrow muddy path where, here and there, someone had set down wooden planks. "I am in a deep ditch," Nemo said. Now there were walls made of dirt, and they reached a few feet higher than his head. There were sandbags piled on top of them, and ladders going up. He could not see where he was, and he could not see where he was going, but he did not stop running. The way turned and crossed itself, and Nemo quickly became confused in a maze of intersecting channels.

"A dozen years from now," the ugly woman said, "you'll die here in the trenches."

Nemo heard her as if she were beside him, whispering into his ear. "The trenches?" he said.

"The next twelve years—the rest of your life—mean *nothing*. You'll end here in the cold, in the mud, with all the others. The sound of the maggots will be like winter wind rustling the dead straw, except there will be no one alive to hear it. Why do you even—"

Nemo felt a sharp pain in his side just beneath his ribs. It hurt too much to run, so he continued walking as fast as he could. He turned into a trench that crossed to the left, and then into another leading back to the right. After a while he no longer heard the voice of the ugly woman, but he did not stop hurrying away.

At last, a long time later, he needed to rest and catch his breath. He looked behind him and saw two bright points of red. "Oh, I can see the eyes of the giant rat," he said. "I must get away, that's all!"

He had gone only a few more steps when he tripped over a rock embedded in the muck. "Oh!" he cried. "That did hurt my toe, oh!"

Nemo discovered that he was home again, but that he'd fallen out of bed and now lay on the floor twisted up in the sheets. "I guess I was dreaming again, Papa," he said.

His father shook his head. "Dreaming, eh? I wonder what you do dream about!"

THE FIFTH NIGHT:

"I hope the Princess sends another messenger for me tonight," Nemo said, sitting up in bed. "He will help me find the golden bottle with the diamond stopper, I know! It is lost somewhere in Slumberland, and I must return it to the Spirit of Heart's Desire."

"Then you must look for it in Slumberland, Nemo."

"Who said that, eh?" Nemo looked around his bedchamber and saw a young girl somewhat taller than he. She was dressed like the older school-maids he knew except that her sailor-dress was black rather than blue, and she wore black cotton stockings, black high-button shoes, and a sort of silver cross around her neck. "Oh, you are very pretty! You are as pretty as King Morpheus's daughter, the Princess, yes! You are almost as pretty as my mama!"

The girl smiled. "You're sweet, Nemo."

"Do you go to my school? I think I have seen you there."

She shook her head, laughing. "No, we haven't met before. For most people, one visit from me is more than enough. Now, if you like, I can show you the way to Slumberland. It's just through that door."

"But there is no door there! Oh, oh, now there *is* a door!"

The girl opened the door that had just appeared in the wall. Little Nemo stepped through, still dressed in his nightshirt and slippers. He was outdoors again, beneath a bright blue sky. He was unhappy to see that he'd returned to the awful trenches.

"What's the matter, Nemo?" the girl asked.

"I don't like it here. The ugly woman said to me—"

His amiable companion smiled again. "I know what she said to you, and now *I'll* tell you something: She doesn't always know what she's talking about."

Little Nemo shivered even though the sun was warm overhead. "Who is she?"

"She's my sister. My younger sister."

Nemo was confused. He didn't believe she could possibly be the sister of the ugly woman who'd chased him—and it was even more unlikely that she was the older of the two. "Why did she bring me here?" Nemo asked.

"She thinks if people get a look at how they're gonna die, it'll tip them over the edge into despair. She doesn't realize that there are worse things around than death. *Lots* of worse things."

Nemo felt afraid. "How does she know what will happen to me?"

"She *thinks* she knows."

"Will I really die here in twelve years?"

"Maybe," said the girl. She looked more closely at Little Nemo and shrugged. "And maybe not. I think my sister could use a good lesson."

She took Nemo by the hand, and they walked a little farther. He thought she had the palest complexion and the blackest, most disheveled hair he'd ever seen. "What is that, eh?" he asked after a while. Nemo pointed to the heavy silver pendant the girl wore on a chain around her neck.

"It's an ankh."

"An ankh, is it, eh?"

She smiled and lifted it up. "I have a brother who insists on calling it an ansate cross. Ansate means having a handle, like a long-haul driver on the CB."

"What—"

"Never mind. Now, I want you to look up there." She pointed to a wooden ladder raised against the wall of the trench.

"Shall I go up that?"

"Yes, Nemo, and tell me what you see."

He was glad to climb the ladder and look out of the trench. "Oh, it is a lovely garden!" he cried. "Have we found our way back to Slumberland? Is the palace of King Morpheus near? I do hope it is!"

"Just follow the path through the hedges," she said. "And give the Princess a kiss for me when you see her."

"If I never do anything more as long as I live," Nemo said, "I *must* find that golden bottle. I would do *anything* to please the Spirit of Heart's Desire."

The girl frowned. "I know," she said. "Almost everyone would. I hate the way people are punished for the crime of falling in love with Desire. Now, get yourself up that ladder—and be careful up there."

Nemo scrambled over the top of the ladder. In his haste and excitement he caught his feet in the coils of barbed wire, and he fell sprawling to the muddy ground.

"Nemo!" said his mother, shaking him by the shoulder. "If you kick off the covers every night, you will soon catch your death of cold!"

THE SIXTH NIGHT:

There were hedges and gravel paths, a sundial and an iron bench. The garden—if it was a garden—went on and on.

"Now where am I, eh?" Little Nemo said. "Is this Slumberland?"

Just as he'd been lost in the maze of trenches, Nemo was now lost in a labyrinth of tall hedges. The shrubbery towered over him; as before, it was impossible to see where he had been or where he was going. Every twist and turn in the maze brought him to a place that looked exactly like all the other places Nemo had seen there: There was the carefully groomed lawn and the trimmed hedges and a green-painted bench.

And the statues—Nemo had never seen so many statues, of men in overcoats or business suits, women in gowns or servants' uniforms, even children sitting at desks or at play. The statues weren't particularly heroic or even memorable. Then Nemo followed an avenue of the maze and came upon a statue that looked familiar. "Oh gracious!" he said. "It is my uncle Alexander! I wonder why there is a statue of Uncle Alexander in this place."

He walked along some more, beginning to feel both tired and hungry. He said, "I do hope the Princess will send someone soon to find me. Yes!"

A moment later—a dream moment that may have lasted seconds or hours or years—a man appeared from beyond a turning of the way, perhaps in answer to Little Nemo's wish. The man wore a long brown robe and his face was hidden within its cowl. He walked along the path, studying a large book. Nemo saw that there was a chain around the man's wrist, and the book was attached to the other end of the chain.

Nemo didn't want to disturb the man in the brown robe, but he was very curious. "What is that great book you are reading, eh?"

The man gazed at Little Nemo for a moment. "It is a book that contains everything that ever happened, and everything that *will* ever happen." He had a calm voice, like a churchman or a librarian.

Nemo was astonished. "Does it tell how the world was made?"

"Yes, it does." He turned to a page about a quarter of the way from the beginning. "Here it is, in this chapter."

Nemo was puzzled. "If this is when the world was made, what is in all those pages that come before it?"

"Things that happened before there was a world," the man said.

"If there wasn't a world," Nemo said, "where did they happen?"

"You may read it if you wish."

Nemo looked at the book, and although the words were in English, the pages didn't make a particle of sense to him. He shook his head. "And does it tell how the world will end?"

The man nodded his cowled head. "Here," he said, indicating a page about three-quarters of the way through the book.

"What will happen after the end of the world?" Nemo asked.

"You may read it if you wish."

"Thank you, sir," Nemo said, "but if that book tells about everything that will happen, does it say if I find the golden bottle with the diamond stopper?"

Without a word, the man opened the book to a certain page and showed it to the boy.

"Now I must find my way to the palace of King Morpheus," Nemo said. "Can you tell me—"

The man didn't even look up from his reading. He just pointed to a path.

"Thank you, sir!" Nemo said. He turned to hurry away, and stumbled into a wall of hedges. "Oh, pshaw! I will be tangled in these bushes now!"

He fought with the branches for a moment, until he realized that he was fighting with the sheets and his pillow. "Oh, Mama!" said Nemo. "I was only dreaming again!"

THE SEVENTH NIGHT:

Little Nemo woke and sat up in his wooden bed with the high headboard. He'd heard a noise in the room, but he saw nothing out of the ordinary. "Was that you, Leo?" he asked the family's cat. "Did you meow?"

"Yes, Nemo," the cat said. "The Princess is eagerly waiting for you. Do hurry!"

"Oh, now you can talk, Leo!"

Leo stopped a moment to lick his paw. Then he went on: "The Spirit of Heart's Desire wishes to have the golden bottle with the diamond stopper returned. Nemo, you are to rush to the palace as quickly as you can. All of King Morpheus's loyal subjects are expecting you, yes!"

"Will you come to Slumberland with me?" Little Nemo asked.

"Yes, I will go with you. And Captain Jack the Soldier will go to protect us, and Bobby Bear, too!"

Nemo took off his nightshirt and put on his clothes. "How will we get to Slumberland, Leo?" he asked.

"Hobbyhorse will take us easily, you will see!"

Little Nemo climbed onto Hobbyhorse's wooden saddle. He carried Captain Jack in one arm and Bobby Bear in the other.

"Oh my!" said Leo. "Is there enough room for me?"

"Yes, yes! Jump up here, Leo!" The small gray cat leaped onto Nemo's lap, and the boy began rocking back and forth on his Hobbyhorse. Soon, as if by magic, they were racing across meadows and fields, leaving the town far behind.

"Gracious!" said Leo. "I have never ridden so fast! It is making my head spin!"

"We will be in Slumberland in no time," said Captain Jack the Soldier.

"I can see the domes of King Morpheus's palace!" said Bobby Bear.

"Tell me when we get there, for I will shut my eyes until then," said Leo.

In less than a minute, Hobbyhorse came to a stop at the bottom of the grand marble staircase that led up to the palace gates. "We will come back soon," said Little Nemo, "and then we will go home again."

"I will be here, yes!" said Hobbyhorse.

Still carrying Captain Jack and Bobby Bear and with Leo following behind him, Nemo began mounting the marble stairs. From his previous visits he knew there were exactly 1,234,567,890 steps; he had counted them often. It took a long time to climb the staircase, but when they arrived at the top, the Princess's special courier, Lopopo, was waiting for them.

"I see you have brought your friends to Slumberland, Nemo!" Lopopo said, grinning. He took off his pointed green hat and bowed. "The Princess asks you to wait for her in the Ice Cream Chamber. You may have as much ice cream as you wish!" Lopopo bowed again, and then he went to tell the Princess of Nemo's arrival.

The Ice Cream Chamber was a room as big as a castle, and in the middle of it was a mountain of ice cream. "Oh, that is grand!" said Nemo.

"There is enough ice cream to freeze an ocean!" said Bobby Bear. "This has got me winging!"

"I will have some," said Captain Jack the Soldier. "All that riding made me hungry!"

"Oh, what kind of ice cream is it?" asked Nemo.

"Ah! Ha! It is rum raisin!" said Captain Jack.

Before Nemo could eat even a tiny bit of the ice cream, the bad-tempered, green-faced Flip threw open a door and strutted into the chamber. "Huh!" he said. "You thought you could have a party without me!"

"It is that Mr. Flip," Leo said.

"Flip," said Nemo, "you may leave now! We don't care if you do!"

"I'll show you something," said Flip. "I'll fill this flubadub with ice cream and have some all day and all night!" He held up the golden bottle with the diamond stopper.

"Oh! I have been searching for that!" said Nemo.

"I know it, kiddo! I guess if I give it to the Princess, she'll like me and forget about you anyway!"

Little Nemo felt a terrible fury, a passion greater than anything he'd ever known before. "I guess you will give it to me!" he said fiercely.

"Wait, Nemo!" Flip said, astonished by the boy's grim expression. "For mercy's sake!"

"Let it go, or you'll be worrying!"

Nemo tore the golden bottle with the diamond stopper from Flip's grasp. As soon as he touched it, Nemo was filled with a profound happiness. "Gracious!" he said in a quiet voice. "This must be the most wonderful thing in the whole world!"

Captain Jack the Soldier said, "Now you must take it to the Princess and the Spirit of Heart's Desire."

"I . . . oh!" Nemo said. He didn't want to give it to anyone. He ran out of the Ice Cream Chamber, chased by Captain Jack, Bobby Bear, Leo, and Flip. They shouted at him to stop, but he just ran and ran. He didn't know what was inside the golden bottle with the diamond stopper; he just knew that it was *his* Heart's Desire as much as anyone's.

"Come back, Nemo!" called Captain Jack. "That does not belong to you! No!"

"I will not let them have this," Nemo told himself. He dashed out of King Morpheus's palace and began running down the 1,234,567,890 steps; halfway down, he came upon two people. "Mama! Papa!" he exclaimed. "You are here in Slumberland!"

His papa reached for the boy's treasure. "I'll take that now, Nemo," he said.

Nemo woke suddenly in his bed. "Um! Ooh!" he said. "I was dreaming! You weren't really chasing me, Leo!"

The gray cat did not reply.

"I'll take that now," said the Spirit of Heart's Desire.

"Hurrah! Look!" said Little Nemo. "I still have the golden bottle with the diamond stopper!"

"Yes," said the Spirit, "and now you must return it to me."

Nemo felt his heart beating faster. He didn't want to surrender his prize.

The Spirit of Heart's Desire sat on the bed beside Nemo, holding out one hand. "Don't you love me, Nemo? I won't love you anymore if you don't give it to me."

Nemo felt like crying. He wanted the Spirit to love him, but he didn't want to give up the golden bottle.

Someone else came into Nemo's bedroom. He was tall and very thin, and he was dressed all in black. "I will take that now," he said.

As soon as the gaunt man took the golden bottle from him, Nemo felt a great relief. "I must still be dreaming!" he said.

The man in black turned to the Spirit of Heart's Desire. "How *dare* you use one of my dreamers to steal the illusion of Heart's Desire!"

Desire gave Dream a mocking laugh. "His desires are under *my* jurisdiction—or have you forgotten about that?"

"It is not right for a child to desire something that strongly. Get out." In an instant, Desire vanished.

Dream stood beside Little Nemo's bed. He put a hand on the boy's forehead and looked into Nemo's eyes. Then, like Desire, Dream also disappeared. Later, Nemo could never quite recall what the King of Dreams had said to him that night. Nemo didn't wake up because he was already awake. He lay in his bed and watched as the sunrise flooded his room with soft, golden light. Soon his papa and mama would call him to breakfast.

ESCAPE ARTIST

Caitlín R. Kiernan

Wanda, née Alvin, Mann, was my favorite character in *A Game of You*, the fourth *Sandman* story arc, the fifth book.

The story went through a couple of name changes before it got its final title. I originally wanted to call it "Inside of Your Heart," and then I wanted to call it "The Bimbos of Night," but eventually, the ghost of an old Robert Sheckley spy novel rattling around in my head (my then-editor, Alisa Kwitney, is Sheckley's daughter), it became "A Game of You," and there it stayed.

Two writers took Wanda on. The first of them is Cait Kiernan, a tall, elegantly gothic lady, who looks good in dark green velvet, and how many of us could dare to make that claim?

The big black bird, unkindness of one, rarely leaves the smelly little cave he shares with her, the woman who has chosen to live in nightmares, rarely shakes the sifting, rust-colored dust she dreams from his feathers. Except, sometimes, when she opens her eyes and leans close, lips crackling like winter twigs and parchment and the bones of things much too small to make a raven's meal, her voice dry as a salt flat breeze, and she whispers, one word, or two, never more than that, "Desire, Raven," or "Delirium," or "Despair, Raven."

And he stretches his wings, stiff, arthritic pop, and always he wonders if maybe this time it hasn't finally been so long that he's forgotten how, if maybe this time he'll simply go tumbling down the hill, ass over beak, lie bloody and broken in the slate and bramble until someone or something kindly comes along and eats him.

But that never happens, and the wings that still feel impossible carry him out into the twilight, bear him high above the frontiers, across neglected dreamspace and blight and finally, far below, the gates of horn and ivory and the palace, like a chandelier smashed to cloudy crystal shards. And he circles, circles and descends, wheels nervous between the needle spires and shattered arches, until the ruins close away the sky. Sometimes the librarian's there, patching diamond walls with spit and putty and Krazy Glue, or sweeping away the glittering rubble of a collapsed arcade or flying buttress; more often, there is no one and he is alone. Comes alone, at last, to the gallery, *His* gallery, the frames dangling crooked on their crooked nails or fallen to the floor.

And he lights, claws click-clacking, on some piece of rubble or the marble floor, the cracked and pitted flagstones, his black eyes shifting warily from one frame to the next. Wishing he were back inside his drippy damp cave, nestled warm against her, wishing he were a crow instead, a lying, shit-for-brains crow that could just flap around a bit and go back and lie, tell her he's done the deed, done his best, and what difference would it make, anyhow?

Their answers are always the same. When they even bother to answer.

And this time, this particular time, it's not the heart or the book or the frame that swirls like a flickering, liquid kaleidoscope; this particular time it's the barb, the fishhooked ring, tarnish and patina green, but still so sharp, and if that's not the worst, it's surely bad enough. He hesitates, buys himself another second, but *Jeez, there ain't no use in draggin' this thing out*, so he hops, leaps back into the air, wings fluttering. And at just the precise moment when he's always sure he'll bash his brains out, and the perfect image of the bright Rothko smear down the canvas, sticky blood and maybe a little gray speck of bird smarts for contrast, something shifts, or slips, or wrinkles, and he's through, moving fast between the steel gray void and the roiling mist, viscous, meat locker–cold here, and the windows hanging in the nowhere on their taut wires and chains and glossy jute twine. A hundred million windows, for starters; Victorian casements of polished oak, granite arches, snazzy, modern louvered affairs, and enormous rose windows of lead and stained glass. Windows to everywhere and everywhen and every*one* stretching into the flat, horizonless distance.

And he sees her almost at once, hunched thing, paler than the rat-filled mists that writhe like insubstantial tentacles about her legs. Palms and stubby fingers braced flat against a punky-looking sill, flaking paint and dry rot, and if she even notices as he perches on one of the window's sagging shutters, she makes no sign, does not acknowledge the intrusion. Her eyes are the color of jaundice and ocher and she stares, past intent, through filth-smeared glass at the murky shapes moving about on the other side. She grinds her teeth, and although she does not smile, she isn't frowning either. She wears her ring on the left hand, and he shivers in his feathers when he sees it. From the sill, a fat black rat, sleek coat and twitching whiskers, watches him cautiously.

"Ah-hem," but she doesn't move, doesn't so much as flinch or even blink, and so he tries again, much louder this time—"*AH-HEM,*" and sends the rat squeaking and scurrying into the gloom.

And she turns her head, slowly, shaggy hair knotted, and he can see the scars now, puckered white traced on white, and he swears to himself that *next* time he'll at least argue with her before flying off to . . .

For a moment he can't even think, padlocked inside his head with those bottomless eyes, and then she speaks, and her words are sandpaper scritched slowly across raw meat, gristle sighs and murmurs, hardly as loud as the mist slinking around her. But it's better than the eyes.

"What do you want, raven."

"Uh, um, you know. It's that time of the month again," he says, and shifts uneasily from foot to foot. "Same shit, different day, if you get my meaning."

"*I don't know where he is,*" she says. And slowly, she turns back to the window, absently raises her ring finger, and digs the hook deep into the soft flesh of her cheek.

"Yeah, well, you see, that's just exactly what I *tell* her every time, *honest.* But, hey, I just go where . . . "

"*I said, I do not know where he is,*" and she twists the ring, pulls it free, flaying skin and dark muscle, spattering blood.

"Right! Yes, *ab-so-lutely,*" and he springs from the shutter, frantic wings slapping the cold, still air, darting between the windows and wires, between faces framed in ornate, gilded wood and stone and agony. And when he comes to one that opens into sunlight, and fields, and cloudless, blue sky, the raven spreads his wings and sails through.

Five-thirty-seven in the morning by the plastic Pepsi-Cola clock over the door, and at least the rain had stopped, but he was still sitting in the booth, worn and duct-taped Naugahyde the color of strawberry licorice, waiting, and Buck Owens was still wailing from the jukebox; still so dark outside that the diner's plate glass window may as well have been a mirror.

Alvin Mann's face stared back at itself, transparent, but solid enough to see the bruisy red gathered beneath his eyes, puffy from crying, and he was no longer sure how long it'd been now since he'd slept, really slept. He stared through himself, but there was nothing out there. Dregs of the Kansas night like an oil stain and the handful of pickups, a rust and bondo Mustang, the pumps alone on their crumbly island of concrete and light. At the edge of the mud and gravel lot, a portable sign flashed wearily, half its bulbs blown and nobody'd bothered to replace them, half its plastic letters plucked away by autumn storms, an epileptic's word game left behind. KORA'S KOUNTRY KITCHEN, OPEN 24 HRS, BREAKFAST ANYTIME, DAY OR NITE—if you knew how to play.

He turned away from the window and tried hard not to notice that there were other people in the diner—the handful of men in their overalls and John Deere caps, scattered along the counter, filling other booths—tried not to feel their eyes or hear their conversations. The diner was too warm and smelled like grease, coffee and cigarettes, frying eggs and thick pink slices of ham.

"You sure you don't want nothing to eat?" He looked up and the waitress was already pouring more of the bitter coffee into his cup. "That bus ain't due in here for another hour, and it's usually late."

Her name was Laurleen, Laurleen printed on her name tag in black, and he shook his head no, no thank you; she shrugged, have it your way, wandered off to refill other cups and scribble orders for pancakes and sausage and hash browns smothering in lumpy melted cheddar. He tore open a packet of sugar and dumped it into the cup, stirred briefly, and then added another two and cream from the little pitcher shaped like a cartoon cow, until the liquid was the muddy color of almonds and most of the acid taste was hidden beneath syrupy sweetness.

Elvis coffee, Charlotte would have said, because she'd read somewhere, in one of her mother's supermarket tabloids, *The Star* or *Weekly World News* maybe, that Elvis Presley had drunk his coffee the same way. Charlotte, who'd drunk hers black.

Alvin sipped, scalded his tongue and set the cup back down, wondered if it was always going to be like that, Charlotte everywhere he looked, Charlotte sneaking herself into whatever he did. And the tears were still very close, hot and heavy behind his bloodshot eyes. He marveled that there could still be a drop left inside him to spare.

"Hey, you're Zeke Mann's boy, ain't you?"

And this time when he looked up, it wasn't the waitress, this time it was one of the men, turning away from the cash register, toothpick staked firmly between tobacco-yellowed teeth. The man stuffed his change and an unopened pack of Doublemint gum into an already-bulging denim pocket.

"I'm Alvin Mann," he answered, eyes immediately back to his cup and the thin white foam still swirling there like a lazy galaxy winding down, prayed a silent, faithless prayer that the guy wouldn't say anything else, that the next thing he'd hear would be the brass bell above the door, beneath the Pepsi clock, clanging exit and release, telling him he could breathe again.

"Yeah, I thought you looked familiar."

And the adrenaline, then, playground hair trigger response, hammering through his veins, heartdrum in his ears. Alvin wrapped his hands, his mother's long, delicate fingers, tight around the cup, too hot to hold, but the pain calmed, almost as soothing as the little white pills he and Charlotte had sometimes stolen from her mother's medicine cabinet.

"Damned shame," the man said, "about your friend, I mean. The Williams girl. She *was* your friend, right?"

"Yes sir, she was my friend," and now the coffee cup wasn't enough, and he bit down hard on the tip end of his tongue, *but don't let them see it, Alvin-baby,* and it was as much Charlotte's voice as his own, *'cause that's just what they want, and Jesus, you're almost out'a here.*

"Yeah, a damned shame," and the man was still standing there, and Alvin could taste his own blood, blood and coffee spit, rich and faintly metallic. "But lots'a folks seen it coming, I guess. Kid that weird is bound to come to no good. Gotta pay the fiddler, you know, sooner or later."

Pause, and he could hear the clock, ticking insect sound, and someone chewing loudly.

"You headed somewhere?" the man asked, pointing to the small, blue suitcase tucked underneath the table.

"Away," and his voice wavered, "just *away*," faintest tremble, but in another second he knew there'd be tears, salty wet stigmata, and they'd all be pointing, pointing and laughing their growling, throaty man laughter, and *that's just what they want, that's just exactly what they want*, Charlotte said.

Then, Laurleen, harpy-voiced, "Hey, Billy. You left your car keys laying over here."

Billy patted his jeans, his coat pocket, frowned.

"*Shit.* Thanks, Laurleen. Guess I wouldn't'a gone very far without those."

Billy went back for his keys, and Alvin was up, up and moving, past Laurleen swabbing at the countertop with her soppy gray rag, past the pay phone and the jukebox (Buck Owens having surrendered unnoticed to Ricky Skaggs) and the gumball machine with the faded March of Dimes sign stuck on top. Past the cigarette machine with "out of order" Scotch-taped to its face; two doors, each painted the same hospital puke green, sexed with varnished cedar plaques nailed up like horseshoes, GUYS and GALS wood-burned in ropy, lariat script.

Alvin pushed one open and slipped inside.

November, one day and a week since Halloween. Bonfires and pumpkin grins finished now and the dead month, autumn's gourdhusk heart, and nothing else, stood between them and winter. They lay together in the brown sea of soybeans, listening to the whisper and rustle of leaves, the shriveled bones of leaves. The soil was damp and smelled faintly of earthworms and the tiny white mushrooms that grew between the rows, and above them, the sky thought it was still October, brilliant electric blue showing through the waist-high canopy.

For a long time Alvin had lain with his eyes shut, feeling the shadow-dappled sunlight, dull warmth on his face, his hands, and Charlotte talking,

Charlotte almost always talking, reciting the KERC New Wave show out of Lawrence; Missing Persons and Devo and Gary Newman, and then she'd gotten around to the new Kate Bush album, a song about Houdini and Beatrice Houdini. Last Wednesday, she'd skipped school, out more than in this fall, had hitched all the way into Junction City and pocketed the cassette at Kmart.

While she talked, Alvin watched the sky and an enormous black bird circling low overhead, a crow, maybe the biggest crow he'd ever seen. It passed between them and the sun, fleeting eclipse of flesh and feathers, dazzling corona, and wheeled away, cawing like a hoarse old woman.

Charlotte took his hand, then, hers so much harder, callused, the nails chewed down to nothing, and he held on tight as the ground began to vibrate, to thrum and thump like a hundred thousand pissed and bottled bees. And he knew that he'd been hearing it for some time now, the huge combine harvester dragging itself slowly, inevitably, across the field. That he'd been trying not to think about it; Charlotte was still talking, almost singing, *with a kiss*, her voice thin and raspy from cigarettes and talking all morning long, *I'd pass the key*.

Alvin squeezed her hand tighter, didn't dare let go or close his eyes again, didn't dare so much as blink. Dug the fingers of his free hand as far into the soft skin of the field as he could. Charlotte was staring into the sun, her hazel-green eyes beginning to tear, seeming almost to melt, vitreous trickle leaking across her temples into her red hair, hair the same vivid cinnamon as his, *this is no trick* as the thrum became a grinding thump, and finally, the thunderous rattle and clamor of steel on steel. She turned to him, her lips still moving, but the words lost, simply swallowed by the combine, and the water streaking her cheeks glistened, and she wasn't smiling, but she wasn't frowning either.

One summer afternoon, when Alvin had been seven, his mother had caught him sitting at her dressing table, painting his mouth the color of pink carnations with her lipstick. For a moment pulled so long and brittle it had seemed a small forever, she'd stood behind him, staring in horror and disgust at her son's reflection, and he'd stared back at hers, the lipstick frozen halfway across his lower lip.

Finally, she'd taken it away from him, had wrestled the tube from fingers too frightened to turn it loose, and slapped him so hard that his ears had rung and the pink had smeared across his chin like candy blood. Had slapped him again and ordered him down onto his knees, bare knees against the bare pineboard floor, and by then he'd been crying and she'd threatened to hit him again, twice as hard this time, if he didn't stop his bawling, bawling like a baby, not the little man he was.

She'd made him pray with her for God and Sweet Baby Jesus nailed up on Calvary to forgive him. Had made him recite the books of the Bible, Old and New Testament, frontwards, then backwards, and the Lord's Prayer, and part of the Pledge of Allegiance, both of them speaking through hitching sobs and tears and strangling snot.

And she would have made him stay right there until his father and Uncle Lonnie had come in from the fields, if his aunt Dora hadn't found them first. Hadn't led him to the bathroom and scrubbed his face with a washrag and Dial soap, scrubbed at his mouth until his lips had burned. Then she'd sent him to his room and Alvin had listened through the wall to his mother crying, her sister comforting her, praying with her, telling her that it didn't mean anything, that he was just a child and didn't know what he'd done.

That nothing like this would ever happen again.

And he'd understood.

Tip? and always it was his mother's voice in *this* dream, or just that terrible once, his father's, but when he turned away from the mirror and all the pretty things in the old steamer trunk, there was never anyone standing in the attic except the Woggle-Bug and Jack Pumpkinhead, the Tin Woodman and the Walrus, waiting for him in the musty half-light jumble of cardboard boxes and produce crates. Downstairs, the pot 'n' pans silverware sounds of his mother setting the table for Sunday dinner, and then the thunder that rattled the roof and made Mr. H. M. Woggle-Bug, T.E., mutter and rub his antennae together anxiously. The Tin Woodman counted backwards, *four mississippi, three mississippi*, waiting for the lightning that never came.

"That's the jackdaws, mind you," muttered the Walrus, and Jack crossed his wooden legs like he had to pee.

Alvin turned back to the mirror, to rose-scented powder, the rouge and mascara, but someone had taken an eyebrow pencil and written *adnaWadnaWadnaWadnaW*, over and over again until the letters filled up the entire looking glass, row after row, top to bottom, and he couldn't see his face through the sloppy scrawl. And when he reached out to wipe it, to smear away the greasy black with his fingertips, the mirror was always smooth and clean and squeaked. But the letters were still there, indelible nonsense, unreachable, and the Walrus leaned down over his shoulder to see, tuna breath and his mustache scratching against Alvin's cheek like a wire scrub brush.

The Tin Woodman, who'd tired of counting after lightning that was never coming, cleared his throat impatiently.

"Don't think she'll wait forever, Tip," he said.

And that was true, what with Charlotte tap-tapping her tennis shoes somewhere in the shadows and the thunder rolling off the tin roof like bowling balls. Alvin hurriedly picked out a hat, a velvet red cloche, something Clara Bow or Lillian Gish might have worn, tugged down the narrow brim.

"One day, lady, one day you're gonna learn," Charlotte said, and her fingers brushed the nape of his neck, trailed up to the zipper's dangling tab just below his hairline. She tugged gently and it felt like a loose tooth or an old scab pulling free as the metal teeth parted the tiniest bit.

Before he slapped her hand away.

She laughed as he closed the trunk, hiding the mirror, all the old clothes and the stolen makeup, his silverfish-chewed notebooks and comics, checked the latches twice and carefully replaced the camouflage of paint-splattered drop cloths and the moldering rolls of calico wallpaper.

"Oh, so careful, box girl, trunk secret girl, *shhhhh* . . . " whispered Charlotte. "Watch your skinny ass, box girl."

And the Tin Woodman and Jack Pumpkinhead and the Woggle-Bug and the Walrus made a circle around him, naked Alvin, face drawn and eyes shaded perfect and the hat on his head, and together they walked slow, in stately, measured step, between the attic country trees of discard and throwaway. Charlotte's warnings grew faint, and then fainter, and finally were lost completely in the distance and dust and the clanking jangle of the Woodman's footsteps.

Past the tiny window, glass gone to milky cataracts with cobwebs and cloudy age, the world out there blown and buffeted beneath the storm-feathered wings of the birds, and *phantomwise, Alice moving under crow black skies*.

"Pay *that* no mind, Father," said Jack. "She went through and there's hardly ever any coming back."

And before he could answer, they had already stepped over the ladder and the trapdoor, past forgotten bundles of *Reader's Digest* and *Progressive Farmer* trussed in shiny baling wire. *Off of the white and onto the red*, and here was the crimson king, bleeding quietly to himself; he watched them pass in silence.

Behind them, the jackdaws had found the attic window and slammed themselves furiously against the glass. Thunder and blackbirds falling like the hail before a twister and his aunt Dora, calling him down for dinner. Alvin tried looking back, caught a mad blur of pecking beaks, birdshitty smear, *and it won't hold them all out, it'll break*, before the Walrus seized his head roughly in both blubbery fists and twisted it back around.

"*That's* what she wants," the Walrus snorted between his nicotine-stained tusks. "That's *exactly* what she wants."

And then the wardrobe. His mother's oak and cherry wardrobe, and before that, his grandmother's; treebone cut and carved, stained rich and dark as menstrual tea. And wrapped selfish in chains that slithered and scarred the varnish skin, that knotted themselves tighter as Alvin approached, so tight finally that the wood began to pop and splinter.

Alvin tried to push between Jack Pumpkinhead and the Walrus, hurled himself at the wardrobe.

"Make it stop," he wailed, and "*Please*, before they hear," but already there were voices downstairs, concern and anger, his aunt demanding to know what was going on up there, demanding to *know* right this minute.

"*No*, Mother," Jack whispered urgently. "That's what she wants."

And behind them, as the Tin Woodman lifted his ax high above his head, glass shattered, and the world filled with the howling whoosh of wind and the roar of a thousand charcoal wings.

And one gray winter morning, when Alvin had been thirteen and away at school, his mother had gone looking for a misplaced box of Ball Mason jars in the attic and instead, she'd found the trunk. She had almost forgotten about it, hidden away up there for so many decades, since sometime just after the war and her grandmother's death. She'd been feeling low all morning, her usual bout with the January blues, but suddenly she'd felt a little better, had begun to quietly hum "Bringing in the Sheaves" as she'd cleared away all the junk and clutter piled on top of the trunk. It hadn't been locked, just the two latches that had creaked loud like barn doors in wet weather.

And hours later, when Alvin had come home, he'd seen the smoke all the way from the road, wisp thin, almost white against the sky, rising up from behind the house. The bus ride home from school had been especially bad that day. When he hadn't been looking, when he'd been busy trying to keep Dewayne Snubbs from grabbing his lunch box, one of the Harrigan boys had taken his social studies book, *Our Foreign Friends Around the World*, and drawn pictures, dirty pictures in ballpoint ink, so that he'd have to rip out five whole pages of the chapter on South America.

And as he'd trudged toward the house through the wind and ice-scabbed snow, the smoke had seemed anything but important; so many things to burn on the farm, empty Purina feed bags or the old papers his father let pile up for weeks on end until they buried the back porch beneath a sprawling drift of newsprint.

Inside, the house had been very dark, no lights on and only the dimmest anemic day filtered through the drawn curtains. Dark and empty and almost as cold as the walk from the road. Alvin had wandered from room to shadowy room, still carrying his books and lunch box, until he'd found his aunt Dora sitting alone at the kitchen table, smoking, tapping ashes into a saucer.

"Auntie Dora?" he'd whispered, setting his school things down on a countertop, suddenly very much afraid; the cold had found its way inside him, had slipped past his teeth and down his throat, had pooled in his bowels like molasses sludge.

"What's happened? Where's Momma?"

She'd said nothing at first, had seemed to watch him from somewhere outside of herself, high up and far away, and then, "She's out there, boy," and she'd motioned toward the back door with the softly glowing tip of her cigarette. "But maybe this time you'd better just consider turning around and . . . " but she'd stopped, sighed smoke, and crushed her cigarette out in the saucer.

"She's out back, child."

Alvin had stepped past as she'd fished another Marlboro Red from the pack lying on the gingham tablecloth. Had opened the back door and the screen storm door, and stood shivering on the porch.

His mother and the black circle of earth, scorched and muddy where the snow and frost had melted from the heat. And almost everything already laid inside, already gone to unrecognizable cinder, all the gifts from Charlotte, the thrift store dresses and plastic pearls. The five-and-dime cosmetics and a yellow-green bottle of tea rose. And what little remained, the books and magazines, his comics, a single, burgundy evening glove like flayed velvet skin, in a careless pile at her feet.

A sudden gust had ruffled pages and the fake fur collar of her overcoat, had caused the fire to flare and gutter. She'd turned, fierce eyes loathing him, loathing herself for having made him. Her lips had chapped and cracked open in the cold, and blood flecked her mouth and chin.

"*YOU,*" she'd howled over the prairie wind, "YOU ARE AN ABOMINATION, ALVIN ROBERT CALEB MANN, IN THE BENEVOLENT EYES OF THE LORD YOUR GOD AND THE HOLY HOST OF

ANGELS, YOU ARE FILTH AND CORRUPTION AND AN OBSCENITY!"

The paperback dangling in her brightly mittened fingers, *The Land of Oz*, had fallen onto the fire, and he'd watched its cover blister and darken around the edges, curling back on itself, exposing dog-eared pages, vulnerable words. And Alvin had said nothing, had not cried this time or begged her to stop, had only stood silent and watched.

And when she'd finally dropped to her knees in the slush and turned her face up to the sky, praying for his immortal soul to merciless clouds the color of frostbite and lead, Alvin had knelt on the porch, his hands pressed into the same penitent steeple as hers.

But his eyes had never left the fire.

Charlotte, who'd lain laughing on railroad tracks until the train was so close that Alvin could see the panic in the engineer's eyes, and the ties and rails and limestone ballast had danced in time to the spinning razor wheels. Charlotte, who wore black lipstick and everyone at school called a witch because she carried an old pack of tarot cards in her purse.

Charlotte, who'd learned to handle rattlesnakes and to drink strychnine mixed with tap water from hanging out at tent revivals, who'd been born two hours and a day and three weeks before him. Who lived with her crazy mother in a lopsided avocado house trailer in the middle of another soybean field, a few miles away from the one where they were lying now, listening to the grind and diesel rumble of the combine harvester, feeling the ground shudder and spasm as the pickup wheel turned and drove row after dirt-clotted row of steel teeth forward.

And it wasn't his life that was rewinding itself behind Alvin's eyes, it was Charlotte, Charlotte, who knew everything, all the writhing, twisted secret things he'd kept shackled inside, because he'd *told* her and afterward, she'd held him while he'd cried, had cried until he'd thrown up on her bedroom floor, and still she'd held him even after that.

Charlotte, who knew.

She smiled, tear-streaky smile, raised the hand mirror, her cracked Woolworth's looking glass held together by its shell of tawdry, pink plastic, held it like a periscope up above the beans. Inside, there was room for nothing but the red machine's reflection, metal the color of fire trucks and fresh blood.

This is no trick, Alvin screamed, screamed for her to move her ass, to run, pried his fingers free from hers. Above them, the big crow was back, shrieking, and his mind was trying to make words of its noise, imagined desperate, absurd warnings. She dropped the mirror, arms spreading wide, and Charlotte only shook her head *no, not yet*, something sad and relieved flashing hot across her face, settling in her eyes.

And he let her go, rolled, and was scrambling on all fours, still screaming her name, crushing row after row of the dead, brown plants flat beneath him, until he was somehow up and on his feet, running. Running, and running through fields and pastures, crossing empty highway and dirt back roads, through autumn-leafed stands of cottonwood and sycamore and dry creek beds.

Until at last he tripped, foot snagged by a root or a furrow or a gopher hole and tumbled, landed hard and the air knocked out of him, and lay, choking on the nothing filling his lungs, his lips still forming screams his voice was no longer able to follow through.

Alone in the diner rest room, alone with the stink of Lysol and piss and little blue cakes of toilet cleanser, Alvin leaned over the sink again and splashed his face with the icy cold water gurgling halfheartedly from the tap.

"C'mon, bubullah, you gotta pull this show together now," and he groped blindly for a paper towel, but there was nothing within reach but a tampon dispenser. And that was funny, so he laughed and let his face and soggy red hair drip into the sink.

And behind him, the softest sigh and rustle, frantic, caged flutter of wings, and the slow scrape of something sharp across the tiled walls or floor. He did not turn around, looked slowly up and into the big mirror bolted above the sink. And there was no one and nothing else, just the row of empty stalls, his too-thin sixteen reflection, acne and cadaver greenish skin in the unforgiving fluorescence. Faint hints of stubble shadow and the jutting Adam's apple like a tumor.

But not his parents, come to drag him back, and not Laurleen, come to tell him to get his fag butt out of the ladies' room or she'd call the cops.

And no ghosts, no zombie Charlotte dripping last-minute wisdom like maggots and formaldehyde.

All the ghosts you're ever gonna need, Alviekins, and he made a pistol of index finger and thumb and pressed it firmly against his right temple. *Crammed right in there.*

Alvin dried his face on his sleeve, ignored the homesick smell of fabric softener and flannel, and went back out into the diner to wait for the bus.

"'A slow sort of country!' said the Queen. 'Now, *here,* you see, it takes all the running *you* can do, to keep in the same place. If you want to get somewhere else, you must run at least twice as fast as that.'"
—Through the Looking Glass *by Lewis Carroll*

———

In memory of Elizabeth Aldridge (1971–1995), who must have known Despair better than me.

AN EXTRA SMIDGEN OF ETERNITY

Robert Rodi

Bob Rodi wrote a book called *What They Did to Princess Paragon*, which was a hilarious satire on the world of comics—Stephen King's *Misery* meets the Chicago Comics Convention. It's a very funny book. It has a minor British-writer character in it who dresses a lot like me, but thinks more like Alan Moore circa 1984, and behaves like Grant Morrison (two other strange British people who write fine comics).

This is a beautiful story, technically delightful, and funny, and sad. Darren isn't the only one who would like to hear how the story ends.

The room was still and quite dark when Wanda stuck her head through the door, so she softly called out, "Knock, knock."

Something stirred against the far wall; she could just make out a silhouette as it traversed a murky blob of window.

"Just a sec," said a voice—Ray's voice. A heartbeat later a thin white light hummed into the room, and Wanda caught Ray fingering the light switch that was draped over one arm of Darren's bed.

"That's better," he said, and he scooted around the bedside to greet her with a kiss.

She pecked him on the lips in return, then dropped her import car–sized purse behind the door and followed him into the room. "How's he doing?" she whispered as she gave Darren the once-over.

"Some bad patches," said Ray, running his fingers through his mass of dirty blond hair. "I've just been sitting, holding his hand. Hours. Didn't notice the sun go down." He plopped back into the hideous, off-beige chair. "Actually thought he'd have gone by now. Yesterday, even. We've taken him off everything but morphine. He's running on stubbornness alone." He smiled, somewhat unconvincingly.

Wanda made a move to sit on a corner of the bed, then thought better of it and remained standing. "He looks—peaceful," she said. She'd almost said "good," but that would've been too gross a lie. Darren's arms and legs were twiglike and gray. His mouth was hanging open like a broken latch. His eye sockets were as deep as billiard pockets. The onslaught of one disease after another had winnowed away bits of him till this was all that was left.

Wanda held her hair from her face and leaned over to kiss him on the forehead. When she did so, he emitted a watery, ancient-sounding sigh.

"Didn't hurt him, did I?" she asked, straightening up quickly.

Ray shook his head. "Course not."

She took a good, hard look at Ray. He wasn't looking so hot, himself. Eyes teary and crimson from lack of sleep. Cheeks hollow from worry. Bit of crusted food at the corner of his mouth. A sour milk body odor.

Wanda had evidently arrived just in time. She went to him and rubbed his shoulders. "When was the last time you ate?" she asked maternally.

He wobbled beneath her ministrations, as though he were made of cloth. "Dunno," he said. "What time's it now?"

"Nearly eleven." She squeezed his neck affectionately. "Off you go, then. Commissary's closed, of course, but there's a pancake house two blocks down. Open all night. I highly recommend the peach cobbler. Tasty, and almost nontoxic."

"Not hungry," he said, rubbing his eyes.

She lifted him by the armpits and put him on his feet; she was so much taller and bulkier than he that it wasn't even an effort. "I don't *care* if you're not hungry," she said in a mock-stern manner. "I have a right to feel needed and validated, too, and I'm not about to let you deny me that by not letting me watch Darren while you go grab some grub."

He smiled and rubbed his smarting armpits. "Ow. You're a tough bitch."

"Sorry if I hurt you. Better go before I do it again." She settled into the chair while Ray donned his black leather jacket. "Should I read to him, or what?"

"Up to you." He flipped up his collar. "Doubt if he hears a word."

She tsked. "I can't believe that. I have to believe he understands what we're saying. On *some* level."

He sighed. "Hope you're right."

She brightened. "I'll tell him a story! Everybody loves a good story."

"You got one?"

"With *my* sordid past? Dozens. Hundreds, even."

He gave her a thumbs-up. "You're a good guy, Wanda."

"*Girl*, please," she said sharply. "I *am* in preoperative therapy, you know. And even if I weren't!"

He threw his hands in the air. "Mea fucking culpa!" Then be blew her a kiss and shambled out.

Darren heaved another sigh—this one significantly more bone-rattling than the last. Wanda placed her hand on his (so hot!) and cooed, "Oh, hon, you miss him already? He'll be back in a flash. Meantime, how's about I tell you a nice story?"

She waited for a response, then fancied she saw a twinkle in his eye, and continued. "Got a good one, too. A nice, dishy, scandalous one that has the distinct advantage of being true. What'll I call it? How about—um—'Wanda and the Apparent Errant.'" She paused for a reaction, in vain. "Well, I'm sure you're excited, deep down. Now." She crossed her legs and folded her hands in her lap. "It starts about two years ago. In that old rat trap I had on Avenue A. 'Member?"

No response. Darren stared toward the ceiling, a film over his eyes.

"Wiped it from your memory, huh? Wish I could say the same. Anyway, this pair moves in just around Halloween. Remember the date 'cause there was a smashed pumpkin on the doorstep, all the movers kept having to scoot around it—this big choreographed ordeal while they're carrying, you know, dressers and stuff. I kept thinking, why don't they just spend two minutes sweeping it away? Anyway. Distractions.

"The woman—now, she's the dramatic type. You know? Failed actress. Hell—probably failed *acting* teacher. Kaftans with big prints. Peacocks. Water lilies. Wearing lots of makeup. Hair pulled back so tight, her lips are cracking. Sees me in the hallway and throws her hands in the air. At first I think she's gonna hit me." She paused, grimaced. "Well, with my history, you blame me?"

She recrossed her legs and continued. "So, anyway, she rushes up to me and with both hands takes one of my arms, and she leans way, *way* too deep into my personal space, and says, 'I am your new neighbor, Countess Protopsilka, but you must call me Deirdre.' Because, see, the count was long dead, and anyway he lost his title when Greece stopped being a monarchy after the war. And the more she protests that she's not a countess anymore, the more I realize I'd better *call* her Countess or she'll hate me. So she tells me she's moving to town with her new husband, who ran an orange juice bottling plant in Jupiter, Florida, till his brother bought him out behind his back and ruined him.

"And it's then that I see this little guy behind her, struggling with four suitcases, one in each hand, another one under each arm. A dapper little man with a pencil-thin mustache and ruby red lips. Lips I'd kill for. I smile at him and he winks at me. Which, you know—being the kind of girl I am—I accept winks from *anybody*. They're *gifts*, Darren."

She paused, as if waiting for him to chuckle. His soft, quick, shallow breaths were all she got; she shrugged, as if they'd have to do.

"Then the countess turns and says, 'Hurry up, Cary.' And I can't really continue down the stairs with the big old countess and pack mule Cary on their way up. So I back up two flights and then I'm at their apartment, which is above mine and one over. Filthy. Family of nine had lived there just before. Least, I'm assuming they *were* a family. Anyway, the countess professes herself enchanted by the place and asks me to stay for tea. And I tell her I can't because I have an appointment, not to mention she can't possibly have any tea things unpacked anyway, and she laughs this crazy laugh and kisses me.

"Now, this is where I get the impression that maybe she's seen better days, and maybe not so long ago, and maybe the sudden change has made her a little crazy. Desperate-friendly, you know the type. I mean—okay, I'm not saying I'm not *convincing*, or anything. As me, I mean. My hair's my own. I've had electrolysis. But this countess babe is, like, nose to nose with me, and I mean, come *on*. She doesn't even give me a hard look. Instead she tells me, I'm a beautiful girl, and of *course* all beautiful girls are always rushing off to some romantic rendezvous or other, but I must agree to come and have tea with her and Cary very soon. I say, sure.

"Then I turn and smile politely at Cary, who gives me this look like he'd ravish me right there if the countess weren't around to stay his impeccably manicured hand. I kind of swallow my disbelief at this whole Merchant-and-Ivory-on-the-skids scene, and bolt.

"I don't even remember where I went. But that night, when I get home, I'm on my way up the stairs, right? And who do I run into but Cary. Gives me this silent-movie leer and asks why I'm unescorted. I put on my best Lewis Carroll and say, 'Because I do not have an escort.' He laughs, laughs, laughs. Then he insists on walking me up the stairs, and when we get to the door to my place, Darren, I swear to God, I have to *fight* the bastard off. He's, like, got one shoulder in the door, and he's pushing, telling me he understands me, he wants to 'comfort' me. I tell him he better go, I have a yeast infection, and that confuses him for just long enough for me to give him one big shove and get the door bolted on him.

"Next morning, there's a knock, and I think, *Christ*, and start foraging around for my Mace, but while I'm looking I hear someone sing out my name so that it's, like, seven syllables, and I think, Gotta be the countess. So I open the door, and there she is in a turban and a big apron that says KISS ME, I'M WELSH. And she's got a tray of muffins in her hand, because she's sorry she couldn't offer me tea yesterday and this is to make up for it and aren't we going to be the *best* of friends.

"Well, can I tell you? First of all, the muffins are wonderful. Cranberry or something. Little bursts of tang. And second, there's something kind of grand about old Deirdre—I mean, something romantic and indomitable. Something no queen can resist. I just looked at that face and kind of fell a little in love. So I'm like, yes, aren't we going to be the *best* of friends. And she starts telling me about the time she and Princess Grace had to share open toilets at an arms dealer's villa in Rangoon, and I'm going, no *way* am I talk-ing to someone who saw Princess Grace take a dump, which till now I was quite certain she never did. And then in walks Cary."

At this point, Wanda was interrupted by a knock at the door. She turned and found a youngish, gap-toothed duty nurse leaning into the room. "Just come to check the morphine feed," the nurse said in hushed nurse tones.

Wanda got up and moved the chair to give the nurse access to the buzzing, squidlike monitor. She gave it the once-over, then said, "How *is* our golden boy tonight?"

Wanda looked at him; he was fidgeting now, moaning faintly. "Little restless."

The nurse hit a button that sent the LED indicator whirling into the numerical stratosphere. "Well, that ought to make it easier on him." She made a little notation onto a clipboard, and said, without looking up, "Keep-ing him amused, are we?"

"That's the idea."

She looked up, slipped her pen through the silver clamp, and smiled. "Doubt if he can hear you. Still, worth a try."

I can hear you, thought Darren as the extra shot of morphine flowed through him like a potent, fiery steak sauce. *I can hear you fine. I can* see *you fine. Stop talking about me like I'm in utero or something.*

Wanda looked at him fondly and said, "Yeah, worth a try," and Darren could see that her eyebrows were really strips of anchovy. *I hate anchovies*, he told her.

The nurse left the room, and Wanda swam over to the chair and climbed back into it. She had a tail like a Shetland sheepdog that she had to shake dry. Then she said, "Where was I?"

Cary just walked in, he told her.

"Oh, yeah, Cary just walked in," she said as her hair began to grow and fill the room like time-lapse ivy. "So, I see him, and I get a sick feeling in my stomach."

Darren sighed and leaned back into his pillow, and gave himself up to the story. "How," Wanda continued, "can I possibly tell the countess that her husband was raining on my lawnmower? Obviously, I can't. So I ask her to please die because I have to redistribute gravel for my morning appointment. And she smiles and says, 'Clandestine,' and leaves."

Darren watched the countess depart Wanda's apartment, and as he did so he became increasingly aware that her turban was really an egg, and that it was broken and spilling yoke all over the carpet. *Oh, no*, he said, and he told Wanda he'd clean it up. And while he looked for rags, Wanda kept talking to him.

"Darren, what can I say, I had to fight with Cary *again* to get him to matriculate. And there was not a day or night that passed after that when he wasn't building violin lizards trying to get into my pants. It got to the point where I couldn't open the nirvana slip of fluoride without him being there ready to pounce. Now, I'm a normal, healthy girl—no comments, please—and it just so happens that at this abbatoir of my aquatic filament, I was suffering a decided lack of love."

Darren's heart broke for Wanda, whom he watched from across her apartment, where she languished at a window that was made up entirely of coloring book pages. As she poked holes in the paper panes with a lit cigar and listlessly peered through to the streets below, her right leg swung slowly back and forth. She was wearing metal swim fins, and as she moved her foot she was carelessly scraping the scales off an upturned alligator's belly.

Stop hurting that alligator, he tried to cry at her, but he found that was a chair.

"So," she continued, "much as I hate to admit it, I began to consider perhaps giving a dromedary to Cary's stucco mueslix lust. Especially since girls of my sort—well, we can't exactly be too reflective napalm about a man who knows what's what with us, and still wants us, you know what I cinched arpeggio? But my prismatic envelope with the countess was worth a lot to me, too. What was I to slate?

"Well, you can guess. I did it. Lost all my lyric longitude. Said yes. Let him in one evening, and he spent the whole night winking my demotic charnels, and don't even ask what else."

Darren was shocked and dismayed by this development. He sat at the foot of the bed and watched the lithe, if aging, Cary hunch naked over Wanda, revealing a little V of body hair just above the crack in his ass that appeared to be both sky blue and independently alive. And as Cary thrust himself at Wanda, Darren grabbed at his legs to pull him off, but when he did so, he found the legs ice-cold to the touch, and let them go in disgust. *Wanda*, he called out, *push him away!* But it turned out not to be Wanda lying beneath Cary's weight—it was Ray! Darren was overcome with love and gratitude, that Ray would selflessly take Wanda's place to save her.

"The next morning, of course," said Wanda, "I was tubered with shame. Swore right window-thin lair that I'd tell the countess everything. But when she came down that evening with her mule filled with iconics and silvered actuary, I couldn't. And Cary saw that as permission to keep log tiling. And I let him. That night, and the one after, and the farm oscillator."

Darren placed himself before Wanda's door and held it in place, but it was buckling between the hinges; someone on the other side—Cary, surely—was pushing, pushing to get in, and Darren couldn't stop him. There was a buzzing, too, loud and disorienting, like a fire drill on Mars.

"Finally," said Wanda with a sigh, as she crawled beneath the carpeting and hid, "I nimbled to my senses. Not just like that, I admit. I was worm-rolling a pimento down at Penn Station one coffeespoon and I saw him. Cary. With another dolmen. A redhead. Nuzzling and dyslexing like they were head-over-heels in scuba nucleus. And I figured, okay, time to stint aorta. So I went to the countess."

Now the door wasn't a door, it was something alive, alive and buzzing, and Darren's eyes were filled with bees that broke off from it like paint chips. But still he pushed against it, because he sensed that it was the only way to save poor Wanda from utter humiliation before the countess.

"And guess what?" Wanda said, with a hint of wonder and delight in her voice. "I tell the old broad, 'I'm sorry, to the snack of my *fawn* I'm sorry, but I have to confess I've been dickin' your laminate for almost Croatian spray now.' And she near faints. Garlands her forehead and says, 'Wanda, that's not hoover den! You can't be shellacking ill tents with my dear cilantro, Nestor! He's still lowering *nub* dale in *Jupiter.*'"

Who's Nestor? Darren asked. The door-thing gave way, broke over him like a wave.

"'Who's Nestor?' I ask her. And she says, 'My husband.' I say, 'Countess, what gives? I came to dim quotient that I've been ladling Cary for weeks now—' And she cuts me right off. 'Cary?' she says, and she starts to fibrillate. 'You thought I was married to *Cary*?' And she's *shaking*, she's buxom so gland. And I say, 'If Cary's not your tipping, then *who is he?*'"

Then Darren found he couldn't hear Wanda, couldn't see her anymore. Through the buzzing and the stinging he called out to her, *Stop, I can't hear.* He tried waving the bees away, as though they were nothing more than cigarette smoke or a bad smell, but they felt more like water—flowing right back into the places his hands had cut through.

He gasped from the effort and some of them flew into his mouth. He tried to spit them out, but they lodged under his tongue and between his teeth and cheeks. He curled up and tried to dislodge them, but more bees got in, and soon, in a blind panic, he found himself eating them just to be rid of them. And the taste, while unusual, wasn't unpleasant. Like blue corn chips and CoffeeMate. He reached out and shoveled some more into his mouth. Mmm. How long since he'd actually eaten anything, anything at all?

He reached out for more, and—and there weren't any. Oh, the swarm of bees was still there, thick as ever, but he couldn't reach them. And then someone parted them—parted them just like a curtain!—and stuck her head out, and glared at him with eyes of two different colors, neither of which he could name. A girl—no, a woman—no, a girl. With a shock of red hair. No— she was piebald. No—she was—well, it was hard to say; even as he looked at her, she was receding, falling away.

"wHAt's goINg oN?" she asked. She sounded like a radio not quite tuned in to a station. "We wEre HAviNG So mUCH fuN!"

And someone from Darren's right—and his left—answered, in a voice like amber. *He is but passing from your realm, to mine. That is all, my sister.*

"oH," said the girl-woman-girl. "i fOrGOT tbAT SOmeTiMes bAPPens."

And will happen again, alas, added the newcomer, just as the girl-woman-girl fell out of sight. *He is to be my own guest but briefly.*

Darren closed his eyes, then, and found him: a tall, thin, emaciated man wrapped in black—looking just enough like Daniel Day Lewis to get Darren's heart gallumphing in his breast.

The stranger put his pale face close to Darren's, and Darren waited to feel his breath, but he felt no breath. *Little man,* the stranger said softly, *One foot in your own kingdom, another in mine, and ever resisting the inevitable pull of the next. What a dogged creature you are!*

And his face moved closer, and closer still, and then even closer, until it seemed to wash right over Darren, like a wave of milk, and then he was in his hospital room again, and Wanda was there by the bed, looking at him with great intensity, her hand clasped over her mouth.

"Darren?" she said.

He sat up. "I'm all right. It was just a bad spell. Finish the story. Who was Cary?"

She leaned toward him and lay a hand on his leg. "Darren?" She shook him. "*Darren.*"

"Right *here,*" he said, growing a little annoyed. "Finish the goddamn *story,* okay?"

"Never mind the story," said yet another newcomer, whom Darren now saw seated on the windowsill. She was as pale as his last visitor, and evidently as fond of the Gothic look; a thin thing, waiflike, in a black halter top, black jeans, and black boots. Around her neck she wore a chain with some kind of amulet—an ankh, if Darren recalled the name correctly from his college explorations into the occult (which he only undertook because he was hot for that dreamy shaman lecturer).

Then the newcomer smiled brilliantly, and Darren knew who she was.

"I know who you are," he said.

She smiled even more widely, slipped off the windowsill, and approached him. Wanda didn't notice their new distinguished guest, but instead kept shaking Darren's leg and mumbling, "Darren! Oh, God, *Darren*!"

"You're here for me, aren't you?" he asked, as he realized exactly what her presence meant.

She nodded. "Mm-hmm. Come on, hon," she said, extending her hand, "time to hit the road."

Darren was surprised to find that he *liked* her; he really did. If he'd known all along that she was what awaited him at the end, he might not have minded so much, fought so hard. Even so, he folded his arms, slumped into the pillow, and said, "No."

Her eyebrows arched, and she puckered her lips. "*No?*" she said, in a kind of amused disbelief.

He shook his head. "Sorry—but I'm not going anywhere till I hear the end of that story."

"Well, it doesn't look like Wanda's going to tell it." And sure enough, Wanda was right beside him now, holding his arm as if checking for a pulse, and saying, "Oh God, oh God, oh God."

His heart sank, but he refused to submit. "Listen," he said, "you look like a nice pers—well, you look nice. Try to see this from my point of view. Stories are *important*. They're all that we've got, really. Growing up, I was spat on, ridiculed, beaten, ostracized—and the only thing that kept me going was stories. Stories are *hope*. They take you out of yourself for a bit, and when you get dropped back in, you're different—you're stronger, you've seen more, you've *felt* more. Stories are like spiritual *currency*."

She shrugged. "I know some who would agree with you."

He almost jumped out of the bed. "Well, then! This is my last story! It may not be much of one, but it's still my last ever, before you take me off to get my wings, or whatever it is you do."

She giggled and sat cross-legged on the bed. "I don't do that!"

"Like I said, whatever. Just let Wanda finish, please? Then I'll go quietly."

She sighed, and ran her fingers through her hair. "Listen. First of all. Um—how should I put this? The best part of stories—that's the part that comes between the beginning and the end. Right?"

He was wary of a trap, so thought carefully before answering. "Rrrright."

"Because that's like eternity, isn't it? It's like being held aloft, or something. So, you should probably look at this as kind of like being in that story forever. Like a little extra smidgen of eternity for you. How 'bout that?"

He drew a breath (or at least that's how it felt) and said, "Well, eternity is supposedly infinite, isn't it?"

It was her turn to be wary. "Uh-huh."

"Okay, then, if eternity is infinite, how can I have a 'little extra smidgen' of it? You can't get *more* of something that has no limits."

She glared at him a moment, then stuck out her tongue. "Oh, pooh on you!" she said. "Don't be so darn literal. You know what I mean. Being in the middle of a story is like being suspended in time—it's a kind of blessed existence. A charmed state. And you're lucky, because you get to be in that state forever. Right? And really, you might as well get used to it, because Wanda's the only one who can tell you how the story ends, and she's just not going to. Not now."

As if to illustrate this, Wanda got up and walked dolefully to the door, then stuck her head out and said, "Excuse me. Please. I think—I think—" And then she burst into wracking sobs.

A flurry of nurses rushed in, like a flock of swallows descending on Capistrano, and examined Darren—or rather Darren's body, because by some means or other, the essential Darren now found himself sitting in a chair opposite his visitor, watching the activity.

"Damn," he said, turning to her. "Don't *you* know how it ends?"

She shrugged her shoulders and grimaced.

"So," he said, as two of the nurses drew a sheet over his remains and the others left the room to console Wanda. "That's it. I go through the rest of timeless time, on a new, higher plane of existence, and as I float godlike among the insubstantial void, all I'll ever be thinking is, *Who the fuck was Cary?*"

She giggled again and took his hand. "For what it's worth," she said, "floating godlike among the insubstantial void is probably not something you'll be doing a lot of." An orderly in plastic gloves and a filter mask arrived with a stretcher on rollers. "You'll get used to this, you know. Where you're going, there's lots more to occupy you than the ending to a gossipy little story."

He pouted and wouldn't look at her. "It's the principle. It's my last one." He took a studied look at his fingernails. "And I haven't had the easiest life, you know. *Or* the easiest death."

She narrowed her eyes. "Others have had worse." Immediately, she softened. "Oh, darn. Don't know why I let you get to me, you old fussbudget! But, listen, you're a sweet guy. I hate to break the rules like this, but, shoot, what are rules for?"

"For breaking," he said, growing excited. "Precisely for breaking! What are you going to do?"

"Overstep my bounds just a tad," she said, getting to her feet and helping him to his. "I'm gonna make you a promise that in a little under two months' time, I'll see to it that you personally get to ask Wanda how the story ends."

"You *swear*?" he said, as the orderly started rolling his body out the door. "You'll bring me back to the world just for that?"

"That's not what I said. Just trust me. And in the meantime, *try* to enjoy that extra smidgen, will you?"

He gave it a mere moment's thought, then said, "Okay. I'll trust you."

And he did.

And she brought him closer to her.

THE WRITER'S CHILD

Tad Williams

Tad Williams bounded to prominence by writing huge, bestselling novels. When I moved to America, he moved to England, as a counterweight. When he moved back to the USA, I immediately crossed the Atlantic to work on my television series *Neverwhere*. Possibly, like a Chestertonian villain, we could in fact be the same person. After all, you've never seen us together, have you?

You have? Well, scratch that hypothesis.

Here the spirits of Byron and Pound conspire to give us a cheerfully nasty little horror story with some sweet dreams glinting through it....

This is a story I made up. Its about Jessica. She is the Princess and she lives in the Glass Castle. Listen! It is really important.

Jessica knows she is supposed to like it in the Glass Castle. Because there are lots of things to do there. Theres Nintendo, and television—Jessica likes Rescue Rangers because it would be really neat to go around and have adventures and go to far away places—and a bunch of other stuff to do. And she has dolls that are really old that she had when she was a little girl.

But she is a princess so she doesnt need stupid dolls. And they never say anything. Thats why they are stupid. Sometimes she used to twist their arms and take off their clothes and rip them but they still never said anything.

A lot of other people live in the castle. Jessicas mother is the Queen of Flowers. She spends a bunch of time in the garden. The peeyonees, she always says, are so damed difficult. Nobody really cares about the peeyonees but me, she says. She is very beautiful, much more beautiful than Jessica, and she always smells like flowers. She talks very slow and quiet and tired.

Theres a special helper named Mister George, who is sort of a bear. The Queen of Flowers gave him to Jessica when she was really little and said Mister George will be your friend. But its okay because Mister George likes it. He is very good at listening and he is not like one of the dumb dolls, because he says things. He only talks at night, and he has a really little skwinchy voice but he says really smart things.

It is hard to hide in the Glass Castle, he says sometimes. So make sure that nothing bad happens so you dont have to hide. Mister George is all brown and has funny raggy ears and one leg is crooked. Jessica the princess used to laugh at him sometimes, but he said that hurt his feelings so she doesnt laugh at him any more.

Jessicas grandmother lives in the Glass Castle too. She is the Duchess and she doesnt come out of her room very much. She has a television in there, she likes to watch Jeopardy. How do they know those things, she says all the time. Jessica honey could you bring me a little more hot water is another thing she says. The Duchess likes to drink Oh Long tea, which is a weird name but real. She has funny hair, all white and curly but with pink skin showing a little where the hair is thin.

The King of Glass is in charge of the castle. He is Jessicas father and he is very handsome. Sometimes he picks Jessica up and swings her up in the air until her head almost touches the ceiling and says helicopter, helicopter. This used to make Jessica laugh. He still does it but it is too much of a dumb kid thing now.

The King of Glass likes to write things. He goes into his room, the only one in the Glass Castle that you can not see into and he writes things. Sometimes he doesnt come out for a long time. The Queen of Flowers says he is working really hard but sometimes he just comes out and says nothing nothing nothing. His eyes are really sad when he says it. Then he goes back in the room and makes those glass noises.

Here is something the King of Glass wrote.

THE WRITER'S CHILD, OR, THE SECRET MURDERER OF TIME

Let's make a baby.

Wait, don't turn the page! I know this seems forward, even—to those of delicate sensibilities—dramatically rude. Let me explain. It's a sort of game.

First off, I'm going to pretend I'm a writer, so please pretend you're a reader. Please. It's important that we get these roles straight. Have you found your character, yet? Have you—in the old Method acting parlance—got your motivation? Good. Then we can begin.

I hope my first sentence didn't shock you. (Well, that's not true. I wanted at least to catch you off-balance. Most good romances begin that way. Stability and trust should be a late addition to surprise, I think, rather than the other way around. That's just my opinion; I'm sure you have your own.) I meant, of course, that we were going to make an imaginary baby—a writer's child. But the hint of an unexpected (and certainly unasked-for) sexual relationship between you and me, between reader and writer, was not at all spurious. Whether a writer is a man or woman, there is something masculine in the crafting of a story—a casting-out of seed, a hunger that results in a brief spasm of generation. The reader—again, your real gender is unimportant—has a more feminine part to play. You must receive the kernel of procreation and give it a fertile resting place. If it does not please—more importantly, if it does not effect—then it passes out again, unaccepted, and the union is barren. But if it takes hold, it may grow into something greater by far than either of its parents.

In ancient civilizations, it was sometimes believed that the lightning was the generative force of heaven—that when it struck the waiting earth, life came forth. Let me be as a bolt of fierce lightning. Let me burn for a brief moment, flashing above your green hills. Then I will be gone, and you can accept or reject my gift. The choice will be yours.

But surely, you ask, a book, a story, the things that writers make—aren't these complete births unto themselves, read or not? Don't some writers speak of their works as children? A little thought will tell you that they are wrong, or at least incomplete. Without you, I am lightning flickering in the eyeless void. A story unread is a zen conundrum, a shout in an empty universe. Unread, unheard, a writer is a dying thing.

Let me show you. Let's make a baby: a writer's child, the one I often think about during the early hours of the morning, as I sit in my room. (I almost said study, since the phrase "a writer's study" comes so readily to mind, but I do not study in my writing room: I write. Occasionally I brood. I also change my clothes there, since that's where my closet is. But I study in a larger room, with more light, where I can dally among my books without the mute, shaming presence of the typewriter.) Sometimes, late at night, when I think about children, I wonder if I will ever father one. If I do, what will happen? These are frightening things to think about, or at least they are to me. I have often wished I could try it out, make all the mistakes I need to, without involving an actual human being. No one deserves to be someone else's experiment. So, my grand strategy: I will make an idea instead. An idea cannot be hurt, cannot lead a ruined life, cannot regret that it was ever brought into existence. An idea-child. I will make one. No. We will make one together.

Another question? Well, go ahead, but I warn you: my biological clock is ticking.

Why "together"? Because, as with men and women, and as with all the living, mating pairs of the world, bonded by their different sexes as much as by their shared species, the sharing of individuality will make a child that is strong.

If I write, "our baby is small and dark and round-cheeked, with green eyes shading to turquoise around the pupils, with hair as black and shiny as a silk kimono," I have begun to make a child—but you have not really done your part. Like the children of the Pharaohs, married brother to sister for marching generations, the breeding strain has not been sufficiently leavened. The children of such unions have hidden, sometimes tragic flaws. If I say instead, "our baby is small, with a face that will someday be beautiful, but is now only an admonition to a parent's love, with eyes faintly peevish and hair as soft as a whisper," I have sacrificed some of the hard edge of realistic description, but I have allowed you to do your part, to add your *genes to mine. The writer's child will now take on a shape even more particular to you—hair dark or fair, as you choose, eyes of any color that seems true at the moment that you read. Thus, I sow, you nurture, and together we will make something that is unique to us two.*

So, let's make our baby. But don't misunderstand—some decisions must be made in the writing. Its sex, for instance: only a fool of a writer could engender and then raise a child while resorting only to indefinite pronouns. That is the stuff of a horror story: "When it was eighteen, it entered college." So we must choose. In fact, you, beloved reader, you must wait this time—as most parents must, at least in this still-primitive age—for the forces of creation (me, in my current lightning-guise) to make this choice for you: boy or girl.

In my room, I have often thought about just this thing. Should my child be a boy or a girl? This is not an easy decision. I understand boys, and so I love them, but I also feel a slight, almost imperceptible contempt for them, like an old salesman watching the pitiable attempts of a young trainee. I have been there. I have done it. (I am, after all, a male writer. I realize that, in the context we have established, this may be deemed a tasteless reminder, especially for male readers uncomfortable with their feminine side. Forgive me. I am feeling revelatory tonight.)

On the other hand, I am afraid of girls. Not, I hasten to say, afraid for my own person: women have been in many ways my closest and deepest companions. But as a man, I am already a little frightened by the capacity of women to hurt the men who care for them, so the awesome and unknown territory of girls and their fathers looms before me like a new country. I feel I could easily become lost in such wild, dark lands. Still, the false courage of authors is upon me. How could I look at myself in the mirror if I would not risk this exploration? And it's only a story, after all—isn't it?

So a girl it will be. We will make a woman-child.

Princess Jessica found the pieces of paper in the garbage can out in the front of the Glass Castle. She was looking for the coopon off a box of Cocoa Pebbles to send away because she forgot to cut it off before the box got thrown out. Princess Jessica found a bunch of paper in there, a long story. She read it all while the King and Queen were out having a Togetherness Night and Jessica was staying home with the Duchess.

And just in case you think that I am Princess Jessica, for your informayshun I'm not. The person writing this is named Jessica too, but she is not a princess and she doesnt live in any castle.

Jessica read the whole story and then she put it back in the garbage can outside the Glass Castle. But Mister George talked to her after the Duchess put the lights out. You shouldnt throw that away, Princess he said. That is a magic story. There is a lot of magic in it and it might help you understand what to hide from.

That is the problem for Princess Jessica. There arnt any hiding places in the Glass Castle because it is all glass. And sometimes when she gets scared by something she wants to go and hide. It used to be okay in the dark with Mister George, because he would talk to her in his skwinchy voice and say not to be afraid, that you could hide in the dark but after a while even the dark did'nt seem like such a good hiding place and Mister George got scared too. So Princess Jessica figures there are better Hiding Places somewhere, Hiding Places that really work. She and Mister George are thinking very hard about where those might be.

Here is more of the story the King of Glass wrote.

This girl child will have hair that curls and eyes that stare and wonder. She will be beautiful, of course—how could our child not be beautiful? We will name her . . . Jessica. Yes, that's a good name, not one of those lighter-than-air names so popular among writers of romances and fairy tales. That's a name a real little girl might have.

But this is a writer's child. We should not wallow in too deep an evocation of reality. We cannot simply allow her to grow up in a mundane ranch-style house in the suburbs, child of workaday parents passing blinkered through their own lives. If I, the writer, and you, the reader, are to experience the full gamut of parental emotions, we must make a world for our little girl. In any case, it's much safer to raise a child in an invented world. Much safer.

Now, stand back. This is where a writer does what a writer does.

"Jessica was a princess and only child. She lived in the Palace of Oblong Crystals, which was located in a small but prosperous kingdom just outside the borders of Elfland."

Good so far?

"Her mother was named Violetta, and was called by her subjects 'The Lady of a Hundred Gardens,' for indeed the Palace of Oblong Crystals had exactly that many gardens, gardens of every shape and kind—hedge gardens, water gardens, rock gardens, winter gardens, every sort of place where things could be arranged and looked at. And that is what Violetta did all day long, wandered from garden to garden speaking in her soft slow voice to the armies of gardeners and workmen and landscapers. Sometimes young Jessica wondered if she herself had somehow been budded in one of the gardens, then gently pruned and brought back to the

palace. It was hard to imagine her mother coming inside for long enough to have a baby.

"*Jessica's father, the king, was named Alexander. He was called by his subjects 'The Lord of the Hundred Windows'—although, unlike the numbering of the gardens, this estimation of the number of windows in the Palace of Oblong Crystals was probably several score too low. But the subjects of the king and queen liked harmony and neatness, as subjects often will, so they bent the facts in order that the fond nicknames should match.*

"*The king had gained his name because many of the palace's windows were made from the strangely shaped crystals that had given the sprawling family home its own unique title. These crystal windows bent the light in strange ways, and at times a person standing before one and staring out across the great circular entranceway, or over Gardens Numbers Forty-seven through Sixty-eight, could see . . . things. Sometimes they appeared to be shadows of the palace and its inhabitants during past or occasionally even future eras, but at other moments the views seemed to be of entirely different places. There was no science to the strange refractory effects, nothing that could be expected and reproduced, and it happened infrequently in any case—the crystal windows generally showed nothing except the prismatically distorted (but otherwise quite ordinary) shapes directly outside. But even that could be fascinating. So the king—having, as kings often do, a great deal of time on his hands—took to spending his days going from window to window in hopes of seeing something rare and uplifting.*

"*One spring afternoon King Alexander stood before the Rosy Bow Window on the second floor. He had been watching the rather stretched and rainbow-colored image of Princess Jessica as she walked across the wide lawn beneath, apparently off to the Mist Garden in search of her mother, when the light streaming through the Rosy Bow Window shifted. The king saw a girl walking across the lawn, but this was not a child of seven but a girl at the doorstep of womanhood, a slender but well-rounded creature with an innocent yet somehow seductive walk. The girl's long hair streamed in the breeze and eddied about her neck and shoulders. As she turned to look up at a bird passing overhead, the king saw the delicate but stirring curve of her breast beneath her dress and was filled with a kind of hunger. A moment later, as his gaze traveled up the arch of her pale neck to her face, he was startled by the familiarity of the girl's face. A moment later, he realized that it was his daughter Jessica, a Jessica grown to nubility. She was beautiful, but there seemed almost a kind of wickedness to her, as though her very existence, her walk, the swing of her hair, her long legs moving beneath the wind-stirred dress, made unwholesome suggestions.*

"*A moment later, the window flickered and the prismatic light returned. He squinted and saw his young daughter striding away on slim but by no means womanly legs, wading through the thick grass toward the Mist Garden.*

"The king went to his bedchamber, shaken."

Jessica doesnt like it when the King of Glass goes into his room, the room that no one can see inside. He makes funny noises in there, clinking things, and sometimes he cries. He has been in the room a lot since he wrote the story. Jessica thinks Mister George might be wrong, that it might be a bad story and not good to keep at all. Jessica sometimes thinks she should burn it in the Duchesses little fire place when she falls asleep after Wheel of Fortune.

Some nights when she is almost asleep herself Jessica hears the Kings footsteps come down the hall going doom doom all funny. He stands in her doorway and just looks. Even though she keeps her eyes shut because she doesnt like the way those kind of footsteps sound, Jessica knows because Mister George tells her later. His eyes are buttons and they never shut.

It is hard to hide in the Glass Castle, he tells her. He says that a lot more lately.

Some nights she wakes up and the King of Glass is sitting on her bed looking at her, touching her hair. He has the funny smell, the closed door smell and he smiles funny too.

One night he was touching her hair really gentle like it might break, and he said kind of wispery Daddys home. Princess Jessica started to cry. She did'nt know why, she just did.

That night, after the King of Glass was gone Mister George said right into Jessicas ear, something must be done and soon. Hiding is not the anser. His raggedy ears made him look really sad, so sad that she started crying again.

Here is some more of the story the King of Glass wrote. There isnt any more. This is all that he threw away.

"Despite this troubling vision, the next day King Alexander found himself standing again before the Rosy Bow Window, admiring the pink-tinted view of the garden, but secretly waiting for something, although he would not or could not admit to himself exactly what it was. However, nothing more interesting than a small squadron of gardeners passed by, and whether the time-refracting qualities of the window had ceased to operate, or he looked upon something that, whatever future

the window displayed, would always be the same—and gardeners certainly seemed an eternal feature of the local landscape—he could not tell. He went to his Private Study, poured himself a glass of frostberry wine, and thought deeply.

"Now, King Alexander had a most secret and important window in his Private Study—the most magical window in the entire palace, a window that only looked out, never in. When he sat and sipped his glass of bittersweet wine, he saw things through that window that no one else could see. And, best of all, since it was a window that only he knew about, and that worked in only one direction, he could watch without being seen. It was the darkest and best secret in all of the Palace of Oblong Crystals, and it belonged to him because he was the king. No one else could be trusted with such a powerful object.

"Queen Violetta had long since stopped coming into the Private Study—she had almost ceased coming into the palace at all, content to spend her days among her peonies and fuchsias, breathing the warm damp air of the Conservatory, or bundled up tight in the windy Farther Hedge Garden. And young Princess Jessica had not been in the room for many years, since it was the place where Alexander thought his deep kingly thoughts and was no place for children.

"He stared into his special, private window, as he sometimes did, and looked at things as they truly were, for that was its greatest power and deepest secret. He saw that Violetta his queen did not care for him, that she was envious of his dreams, that she wished to make him an unimaginative creature of habit and routine as she was. He saw that his subjects did not respect him, that the gardeners snickered when the queen made jokes at his expense, that the footmen and butlers and maids and charwomen all scorned him, even as they stuffed their mouths with the fruits of his largesse.

"As for the queen's mother, to whom he had given a gracious apartment right in the palace—well, the old woman's malice was palpable. She had tried to prevent her daughter from marrying him in the first place, and never lost an opportunity to speak glowingly (and falsely) of Violetta's dead father, holding him up as an example of what Alexander would never be.

"Worst of all, he saw that his own child, the Princess Jessica, was becoming a diminutive version of her mother, the queen. For years she had loved to play games with him, to be lifted and spun in the air like a bird, her hair flying—but now she would not play, and spoke to him angrily when he tried to persuade her. She turned away from him when he tried to express his fatherly love. She rejected him, as Violetta rejected him.

"His Princess Jessica was changing, drifting away from him across a widening sea, on a one-way voyage to a place where he could not go, the Country of Women.

"King Alexander summoned up Jessica's image in his private window and

watched her as she walked across the great palace dining room, a stuffed toy dangling from one hand, her hair an unbrushed tangle across her shoulders.

"*She spent more time talking to her teddy bear than she did talking with him. And was she not too old for such a childish toy? Certainly she was in many other ways already aping her mother in her headlong rush toward womanhood.*

"*The king poured another glass of wine and thought on these, and other, things.*

"*It was late in the afternoon when King Alexander awakened, his head misty, his feet cold. He had drunk a little more of the frostberry wine than he had intended, perhaps. His glass had fallen from his hand and lay in glittering shards on the floor of his study.*

"*As he leaned forward to pick it up, he saw something pale flit across his mirror. Distracted, his hand folded too hastily around the broken stem of his wineglass. He cursed, sucked his fingers, and tasted blood, staring at the magical window.*

"*Framed in the rectangular space was the young woman he had seen before, the one who so much resembled the Princess Jessica. She was bathing herself in one of the garden pools, surrounded by bobbing water lilies. The leaf-filtered afternoon sun made her skin seem glistening marble.*

"*He stared at her pale shoulders and long white neck as she dipped her face to the water, and decided he had been wrong: in truth she bore only the faintest resemblance to Jessica. No, this beautiful young woman had none of that flinty look of Violetta's, the look that Jessica has already begun to assume, for all her young age.*

"*She was like his daughter only in that he admired her, as he had once admired a younger, more tender Queen Violetta. She was like his daughter only in that if she looked at him, he felt sure it would be with respect and love, as Princess Jessica once had. But this graceful girl was untainted, grown full and ripe without souring.*

"*The young woman stood, and water ran down her naked belly and thighs; small splash-circles spread, chasing the larger ripples of her rising. Her breasts were small, but womanly-full, her legs achingly long and slender. As the breeze touched her cold skin she shivered, and his heart seemed to expand with love—and with something bigger, something deeper, darker, and altogether richer.*

"*Unthinkingly, he lifted his fingers toward her image in the window, then stopped in surprise. Blood was running down his hand and onto his wrist.*

"*He paused as an idea came, a wild, willful idea. Blood, wine, solitude—he had all the makings of a powerful magic.*

"*Something in him shriveled at the thought, but his eyes and heart were so full of the pale-skinned, naked girl before him that he swept the doubts away like cobwebs. Here was what he wanted, needed . . . deserved. A girl as beautiful as his wife when he met her, as innocent as his daughter had once been . . . a woman-child who would truly love him.*

"He wiped his hand clean on his trouser leg, then allowed a fresh rill of blood to ooze from the cut along his finger. He reached out to the window and drew a four-sided figure around the girl as she stood in the lily-blanketed pool, penning her in a square of red smears. He drank from the bottle and felt the blood of the berries run down his throat and bathe his thirsty heart. He said words, secret words in his own secret language. What they meant was: 'You are mine. I have created you, and you are mine.'

"The girl framed in the window looked up suddenly, shivering again, although she had almost finished drying herself."

Mister George heard the end of the Kings story because Jessica read it to him out loud. It made him angry and he said some words Jessica did'nt know.

Tipical littery wanna bee he said. No story ark. Everything turns into sell fubsest intro speckshin.

Princess Jessica wrote that down in her jernal because she did'nt know the words and asked him what it meant. Mister George said that it did'nt matter, that style was not the real ishoo.

We must do something, he told her. The beast is rising. We must do something soon.

Jessica said that he was scaring her, and that anyway it was time to go watch Jeopardy with the Duchess.

Leave it to me then Princess, said Mister George. I will do what I can.

That night Jessica took her bath. All the My Little Ponys had fallen in because they were trying to cross the ocean on a Pony migrasion like Jessica saw on the television, except it was'nt ponys on TV but some kind of deers. One of the Ponys got behind her back, lost in the bubbles, and when she found it and turned around, the King of Glass was standing in the doorway. He looked at her for a long time until she said, Daddy go away I am having a bath.

The King said O, so you are too big to have a bath with Daddy in the room and laughed, but it was'nt a nice laugh like he used to. He went to the cabinet and took out a bandaid and wrapped it around his finger. He had a kleenex there, and when he put the bandaid on he threw the kleenex in the toilet. It had blood on it, and this made Jessica more scared because she remembered the story.

Wheres Mommy she asked.

Who the F-word knows, the King said and laughed again. Jessica put her hand on her mouth because of the F-word, but she was mostly scared because she did'nt say it, her father did. Probably out rolling in the delfinnyums or something, he said. Who the F-word cares.

I'll come back later and read you a story he said, then. He came to the edge of the bath and pulled her close and tight. The Ponys all fell in again off the slippery side. He patted her hair and kissed Princess Jessica's mouth. He had the closed door smell real bad and he was breathing loud.

When he took his face away for a second Jessica said really fast I need to say something to Mommy. I have to tell her something about school.

The King stood up and looked at her. His eyes were funny.

I'll come tell you a story later he said and went out.

The Queen of Flowers did'nt come until Princess Jessica was dried off and in her jammies. Ready for bed, thats a good girl, she said.

Why does Daddy go in his room and close the door, the princess asked.

The Queen sat on the bed. I guess he just needs some time to himself she said. Sometimes people need to be by themselves. He is working hard at his writing, you know.

But he smells funny, when hes been in there Jessica said.

Her mother did'nt say anything.

Mister George thinks he might be turning into a monster said Jessica, like in that Werewolf in London movie. He might be changing into a bad thing from being in that room.

The Queen laughed. Is that what Mister George thinks hah? Like in a monster movie, she said. Maybe Mister George should not watch movies like that.

They talked some more but the Queen had to finish her winter garden plan, so she went back downstairs. Princess Jessica thought for a long time about how anyone could see her because of the Glass Castle but it was dark so she couldnt see out at who was watching. Jessica was afraid to fall asleep because she thought that if the King of Glass came to tell his story and she was'nt awake hed be mad, but she held Mister George really tight for a long time and then she got sleepy.

Somebody was talking in her ear for a long time before she finally heard the words wake up Jessica wake up!

She opened her eyes and Mister George was standing up on the end of the bed. Jessica was very surprised because he had never been able to move, only talk.

Why are you moving, she asked.

Get up Jessica, he said. We are going somewhere. We are going to do something.

But I am not allowed to go out of the house at night said Princess Jessica. She was scared to see Mister George walking on the end of the bed. He walked funny too, like his crooked leg was too short.

We are not going out of the house, not really he said in his skwinchy voice and pointed to the closet. We are going there.

Jessica stood up. Like the Lion and the Wardrobe she asked? She did'nt like to think about the Witch part.

See S Loowis, said Mister George and made a grumpy noise. O, Father Seuss, spare me from alligory. Come on Jessica.

She got up and wondered if her Mom and Dad were asleep or if they were awake. Sometimes they had fights all in wispers. She listened but couldn't hear anything. She followed Mister George to the dark closet. He went in it. She went in it too.

But it was'nt a closet on the inside. There was fog and funny way far off noises and it went back a long way. This really is just like the Wardrobe she thought, and wondered if an alligory was anything like an alligator.

After a minute they were in a narrow street. There was a very big round moon in the sky, all tho it was hard to see because there was fog. A bunch of houses were up and down the street, all close together all broken down and old and scary. They were dark except that some of them had yellow lights in the tiptop windows.

I don't like this Jessica said. I want to go back.

It is not a nice place, said Mister George but it is where we have to go. He was walking along in front of her just like a real person, except he was still himself, still very small and his ears were still ragged. It is Rats Alley.

Now Jessica had to not think about alligories and rats both. But why do we have to come to this place she said, where is it?

Rats Alley, I told you he said. But it is less a where than a what. It is where the shades of poetry and sin and sorrow over lap. It was my place once and it is the only path I know to find the Player King.

Another King said Jessica, she did not understand the rest. Is he a friend of the King of Glass?

He is a much more Important King, said Mister George. I hope he will be your friend.

Something was crunching under Jessicas feet. It sounded like candy sticks but when she looked close she saw it was'nt.

Did the alligories get them she asked really quiet, but Mister George did not say anything.

Something came out of one of the dark doors and stepped in front of them. It looked like the Scarecrow of Oz, but it was'nt smiling. It had an even more skwinchy voice then Mister George like the rope hanging around its neck was too tight.

Hello clubfoot, it said. It stood right in the way.

We are seeking an oddyents with the Player King said Mister George. He was trying to be brave but he was very small.

But you have no safe conduck, it said. Why should I let you pass? Its fingers made a creeky noise like the branches outside Jessicas window when it was windy.

Mister George did'nt say anything for a long long time. Jessica wanted to run.

For love of the moon, he said then. For memory. This one is young and still unmarked.

And why should I not take her sweetness the scarecrow said and leaned forward to look at Princess Jessica. Its eyes were painted on and crooked. Perhaps that will make memory stop burning. Perhaps it will blacken the moon and I can forget.

You are not here to forget ezra, said Mister George. We all travel here to remember.

The scarecrow lifted its stick arms wide then stepped back into the shadoe. Go then it said. The voice was far off now. Go. Do not bring any more pieces of the living moon to trouble us in our ecksile.

When they went past the door Jessica heard a sound like hissing. There was wet sawdust all over the ground.

There were eyes and voices in other doorways, but Mister George only said quiet words to them and nothing came out. They went down the street as fast as they could but Mister Georges short legs and crooked walk made them go slower than Jessica wanted.

At last they came to a door, and this one had light in it which made the fog glow in the street beside it. Over the door was a sign with a picture of a bird like a crow and letters that spelled THE BLACK QUILL.

Mister George went inside and Princess Jessica followed him. A thin woman was just inside. She had a tray full of mugs and her eyes were all shadoey even tho they should not. My lord she said. Long time no see. She laughed then.

I was sorry to hear about your eyes Miss Emily he said.

A small loss for great sins she said. I never used them for the truest seeing, in any case. What brings you to visit us after so long.

Tonight is the night of the rovers moon, he said. I have a patishun for the Player King.

He is inside, she said. Watching the show. I will bring you a cup of our best red.

I no longer drink it said Mister George.

My you do take things seeriosly these days don't you, she said. Through there.

Miss Emily went away wisling a slow song, and Princess Jessica and Mister George went down the hall to a big room full of candles. There were benches and tables but they had all been pushed back against the walls. There were lots of people in the room, or at least they looked like people even though some were the wrong shape and lots were wearing masks. Some of them were doing a play and some others were playing fluts and other insterments. The play was about a man who lost his wife and had to go sing for the gray king and queen who found her. Jessica looked at the gray king to see if he was the one Mister George wanted to talk to but he was wearing a big mask that covered his face and he had no arms, so she did not want to look at him any more.

Or whats a heaven for, someone wispered in her ear. Jessica looked up. It was Miss Emily, who smiled again and said Poor Old Rob, then picked up some mugs and went away.

The play stopped a moment later but no one clapped. They all looked toward where Mister George and Jessica stood then they all looked at the far wall. There was someone sitting in the shadoes against the wall who leaned forward. His hair was black and his skin was very white and he had little dots where his eyes should be like when the Duchess turns off the television. Jessica could tell he was a real King but she did not know what place he could be King of.

A brief high ate us, then said the very white man. It will give the ladies time to don their claws. His voice was slow and hollow like talking in a big empty room. So you have come back to see the meenadds feed, young lord?

I come with a patishun, my king, Mister George said, and took a crooked step toward him then got down on his knees. I have had my fill both of the rights of bockus and the claws of women.

The Player King stood up and up and up. He was very tall and Mister George was so small and his ears were so tattery that Jessica wanted to cry for him. Speak then, the king said. What do you want here little house god.

You know my special task my king said Mister George. This innocent is in danger. The one who threttens her calls upon your name to have his way. He trifuls with dream to justify his deed.

The white king looked at Jessica for a long time until she felt all swirly. The princess did'nt understand anything that was going on. She was scared but she was also not scared. The tall man seemed to be too strong and quiet to be a really bad thing.

I have heard him scratching in the walls of my dwelling the Player King said, but he has never been given admittens to my throne room. I have granted him no boon. Are you sure it is not the fact that he considers himself a poet that has offended you little hobbler?

Mister George shook his head. That is of no import he said. I am sworn to redeem where I can, that is my sentence. He is her father. He calls on your name to cloke his deed.

What would you have me do? No crime has been comited no promise breeched, said the tall white man.

I implore you my lord, said Mister George. I was once your faithful servant tho my sins took me to another judge in the end.

What you call sins have little to do with my kingdom, the Player King told him and raised his hand in the air.

But everything to do with mine, Mister George said back very fast. And my duty. At least do not let him hide his deeds behind your mantel. At least make him see for himself what he does. There is some value still in innocents, is there not?

For a long time the tall man did not say anything. Jessica looked around at all the masks all the eyes all the faces in the shadoes. Then she saw that the King was staring at her.

And are you innocent, child he asked. She did not know what to say. I am afraid sometimes she said.

He smiled just a little and said I will think on this. Take her back before the moon sets.

Thank you my lord said Mister George. Your help would mean a small part of my vast det might be repayed. He turned and went to the door and Jessica followed him.

Byrun said the Player King. Byrun hold a moment. Jessica wondered who he was talking to but Mister George stopped.

My lord, he said.

Her name was Ogusta was it not, the tall man asked.

It was my lord said Mister George, then turned to the door again and led the Princess out into the fog. Jessica reached way down and took his paw because she thought he looked very sad.

"*King Alexander was awakened by a touch on his shoulder. Groggy and disoriented, he shifted in his chair and looked at his magic window to see if she had come to him at last. Earlier he had felt her moving closer, felt his spell reach out and enfold her, but he was a little surprised to experience results so swiftly.*

"*But the woman-child was still prisoned behind the window like a butterfly in a glass case, her limbs outstretched in sleep as though she had writhed on the pin before stillness came. She had disarranged her coverings, and her limbs gleamed in the moonlight.*

"*But if it was not his ensorcelled beloved who had touched him . . .*

"*The Lord of the Hundred Windows turned his chair slowly and felt broken glass beneath his shoes. A tall figure stood behind him, dressed all in flowing black, but with a face pale as mortuary marble.*

"*King Alexander started violently. 'Who are you, sir?' he asked. 'How came you to the Palace of Oblong Crystals? What do you want of its master?'*

"*'No mortal can build a palace in the Dreaming and expect to be called "master,"' the figure said. 'That is asking too much. Alexander, you consider yourself a poet, do you not?'*

"*'I write a little . . . but who are you, and how did you come here? This is a private place.'*

"*'If this is a private place, and the dreams you craft here are private, then let them stay that way. If you would re-create them in the waking world, then you must acknowledge the evil that can come of them.'*

"*'I know you,' said the Lord of the Hundred Windows, moving back in his chair. 'I have heard the servants whispering about you. You are the Dark-Eyed One—the old god of this place. Have I done something to offend you? Do you come to punish me?'*

"*'You have done nothing great enough to offend Dream. You have done something that offends another—an old servant of mine. He is sworn to protect innocents from such as you. But, no, I will do nothing to punish you. That is not my charge.'*

"*'Then begone!' King Alexander stood up, filled with the sudden confidence that follows a terror proved unnecessary. 'If you have no power over me, what right do you have to accost me in my secret, private place? What right to interfere in my life, with my loves? She is mine—my creation! I will do with her as I choose. That is my right.'*

"*The shadow-eyed figure seemed to grow. A dark nimbus swirled around him like a cape of mist. He reached out a white hand, then he smiled.*

165

"'I have rights and powers beyond your ken, O would-be poet. But I spoke only the truth. I will not punish you. One thing only will I do, and that is fully within my rights as sovereign over all the lands of dream, and of every hovel and palace therein. I will show you the truth. Look to your beloved secret window and see the reality that even the thickest shadows of Dream cannot hide. See the truth.'

"With those words the apparition swirled like windblown fog and vanished.

"For some time the Lord of the Hundred Windows stood watching the place where the thing had been, fearing that it would reappear. His moment of confidence was long past. His heart beat as swiftly as it had when he had first beheld his beloved. . . .

"His beloved! He turned to the magical window, terrified that his spell would be undone, that her image would be gone forever. To his relief, he saw her sleeping, still as compellingly beautiful as she had ever been, still framed in the possessive spell of his blood. She turned restlessly, arching her neck and exposing for a moment the pale soft shape of her breast. Something shadowy was cradled in her arms . . . a stuffed toy.

"Alexander smiled to see such childlike innocence in the shape of a young woman. But as he watched, the image before him shimmered, then was slowly replaced by one very different.

"The Lord of the Hundred Windows leaned forward, gazing in horrified astonishment at this singular and most important window. His eyes opened wide. His lips parted, but no sound came from his mouth. Thus he sat for a long time, in silence, staring, staring . . . staring."

This is the end of my story, gentle reader. If you feel that you do not understand it, then perhaps I am at fault. But is it the task of a poet to explain all, every allusion, every symbol? Or does he merely sow the seed, and is it not then the reader's responsibility to bear the final issue? Too frequently the blame is cast onto the writer, the poet, when in fact I think it is the ingratitude and sloth of readers which so frequently mars the highest, best truths an author can create.

What happened to the child, you ask? What happened to Princess Jessica? She was a writer's child, and thus only a figment. Together you and I engendered her. Perhaps we were wrong to do so—perhaps to invent a fictitious child to avoid the fear and pain of raising a real one is to murder Time. If so, then I am Time's secret murderer—and you are my accomplice. So take care before you sound any loud alarums.

Whatever the case, the story is finished and the child is dead. All is cast away, a flawed draft that will not see the light of day. Perhaps a writer's child, because she *carries the aspirations of the poet, because she is not of the mundane world, is too per-fect to live. Perhaps there are forces in the world—those who would tyrannize dreams and regulate dreaming—that cannot bear such perfection. If so, then they have won a victory.*

The child is dead. The dream is dead. Do not complain to me that it is not the story you wished. It was the only story I knew.

Thats the last of the story. Princess Jessica put it with the other parts and it is in a box under the bed, but she does'nt read them any more.

Jessica does'nt live in the Glass Castle any more either. The new house is smaller but its not glass. There is a garden which is mostly rocks but her mother says she does'nt feel much like putting in flowers yet. She is tired of flowers.

He was a good man Jessica, her mother says. I know you miss him very much and I do too.

Jessica is not sure that she misses him very much all tho she does some-times. But some other times it feels good that she doesnt have to think about hiding so much. Now it is her mother who makes the crying sounds some-times but she makes them on the couch not in a room with the door closed. Jessica always tells her its okay Mommy but sometimes her mother doesnt believe it.

Jessica tried to talk to Mister George but he does'nt talk any more, not even at night. His ears are still raggedy tho, and he still sleeps next to her in bed. She wishes they could still have talks, but the doctor told her mother once it was just a faze, which means just for a while so maybe everybodys bear stops talking after a while.

Jessicas mother wouldnt let her see what happened to her father but the Duchess, who still lives with them and watches even more television said that he fell and cut himself on a broken wine glass that was on the floor and bleeded and died. When her mother was sleeping that day after the ambal-ance men went away Jessica went to the room and looked at all the blood. It was all in the carpet and wine was there too so there were two colors of red. Thats when she found the rest of the story too, it was beside the tipewriter.

But there was something Jessica did'nt understand quite.

The big mirror over his desk was broken and all the pieces were gone.

Someone must have cleaned them up. In the Glass Castle they always cleaned up the broken stuff and threw it away.

ENDLESS SESTINA

Lawrence Schimel

I love sestinas. (A sestina is a classical verse form, six verses of six lines each, in which the final words recombine according to an obscure formula from stanza to stanza.)

They are not easy to write. (I've written one successful one, and the beginnings of innumerable other ones.)

Here Lawrence Schimel coruscates his way through lust, towards death, in a sestina with sickness and brio.

The sunlight helps to hold delirium
at bay. Seated, warm, I desire
nothing more than my dreams
can provide: escape from death,
from sliding into despair
contemplating my inevitable destiny.

I do not like to call it destiny
for I merely took delight
in the flesh—mine, theirs. While I might now despair
my end, I do not—cannot—regret my desire;
who knew it would lead so nimbly to death?
Warmed by the sun, I sit near the window and dream:

before me on an endless field stands Morpheus,
himself, and I wonder if I am facing my destiny,
a vision of how I will look just before Death
comes to claim me. I must be delirious,
I think, for as gaunt and drained as he looks, I still desire
him. At least a frustrated libido is an easier despair

to handle than one's own death. These days, despair
is such a constant companion, even my dreams
are full of her. The angst of wanting—of needing to be desired—
is inevitable; every boy's unavoidable destiny.
I beg him, "I can show you such delight. . . ."
But Morpheus has other things on his mind than le petit mort.

He is a banshee, foretelling my death
with a keening wail of utter despair.

I shiver at the sound, cold, and know that delirium
and night sweats wrack my body, invading even my daydreams.
I know what I cannot avoid; therefore, call it destiny.
Who am I trying to fool with this desire

for time, for life, for the chance to be desired
again, if only once more before I die?
Before I die! How cruel this untimely fate!
I am so far sunk into despair
I can't even get laid in my own dreams!
But I know this abstinence is only the delirium

invading my dreams. Morpheus, help me fight my destiny.
Let me be desired! I won't give way to despair!
Rage, rage, against the dying of delight!

THE GATE
OF GOLD

Mark Kreighbaum

Mark Kreighbaum is a San Franciscan poet and author. His story and Tad Williams's came in at the same time, like two sides of a coin. Companion tales, perhaps, or bookends.

The doll watched helplessly as Ginny suffered through the nightmare that owned her every time she slept. An immense shadow, reeking of strange smells and sour hate, swung a belt like a snarl of midnight against the skeletal figure of Ginny's mother. The shrieks echoed with agony. The whine of the shadow's belt cracked like lightning against the mother's flesh. Ginny wept, her own screams weak and thready. Ginny's doll hung from the little girl's white-knuckled fist.

He was only a doll, but he tried to hug Ginny, to comfort her. Ginny clasped the doll to her chest with all the force she could manage. She was so small, so frail.

"No no no no. Don't hurt Mommy. Stop it, Daddy. Please. I'll be good. Please." The little girl's voice shattered into sobs. But the nightmare went on, pitiless. The father-monster paid her no heed.

The doll wished it could weep, too. He loved Ginny, though he was only a sliver of the Dreaming, the smallest of small matters in this realm. But he had been thinking and planning. The nightmares couldn't go on. They mustn't. Awake, Ginny didn't consciously know what the dreams told her, but the doll knew how they were scarring her soul and mind.

He knew what he had to do. It meant abandoning Ginny here, though, and he couldn't bear the thought of leaving her alone with no hope. But as she wailed into the darkness and the lightning of satisfied hate fell over and over again, endless, the doll knew it must find the courage to go, to save his friend.

He slipped from Ginny's grasp. She looked down at the doll, her eyes wide with a new fear. In the Dreaming, Ginny's green eyes were transformed into holes of night. He could see all the way down those dark corridors to the pearl of her soul, bleeding, burning.

"Dolly?" She spoke in a terrified whisper.

"I love you, Ginny," said the doll. "Remember."

Then, he turned and ran away into the silver mists before she could say another word and chain him to her side for the rest of the nightmare. He wanted to promise her he would return, but that would be a lie. He was about to violate all the laws of the Dreaming, and he had no illusions about the penalty.

The doll was ancient. He had been the companion to children since the first night brought fear to an innocent's day. Always, he had done his duty, giving comfort, playing games, tumbling and telling tales. He loved all his children. The pain of losing them to older dreams was softened by the new spirits who welcomed him into their small lambent hearts. He had known joy and sorrow both for as long as children dreamed and had never failed his trust. Until now.

He knew many things about the Dreaming that were hidden from his younger kin. Over centuries, he had glimpsed other creatures, some kind, some bitter, observing his children's dreams. The doll took notice, studied them, learned the paths they used to travel in and out, spoke with them if they wished. He had learned about the Dreaming, and its Lord.

Once, he had even felt the cold passage of the Lord of the Dreaming, as he moved on some errand beyond the doll's tiny comprehension. Mere contact with the wake of the Endless brought deeper knowledge of the Dreaming, even to such a speck of illusion as he.

The doll was determined to seek out the Master and demand an end to Ginny's nightmares. Surely, the sculptor who fashioned such love for children out of the stuff of the Dreaming would not deny him. But he was afraid. Afraid. The brush of the Lord's wake had been terrifying. He was less than a spider's web to the storm of the Master. Would such a being even notice a mote like him, much less listen to his plea?

The doll followed a winding path out of Ginny's dream that led sideways out of the imperfect walls of the little girl's imagination. Once beyond Ginny's nightmare, he saw rainbow spheres in countless number filling every space of the silver realm of the Dreaming. They were other dreams, he realized. He was only a doll and could not count above a number he thought of as eleventeen, two pudgy hands full of fingers, but a sudden realization of the immensity around him gave him pause. What he planned was hopeless. The Master would not even notice him, might destroy him with a flicker of thought. And then, what of the generations of children to come? There would be no doll to play with them in their dreams, to make them laugh and grow into dreamers. He wavered. He should go back. Ginny would grow up, lose her need for the doll, and he could go on to another child. He had been the companion to children with nightmares before, some far worse than Ginny's. There would be an end to the pain. He looked back and saw that Ginny's sphere was a dull gray tumor tumbling in the mists. The doll's heart was filled with sorrow and pity. Why did children have to suffer nightmares? It wasn't fair. It wasn't right. He stiffened his tiny form. Let the Lord destroy him. He would be heard.

The Master's home lay at the center of the Dreaming. It was a long way to travel, and he had to finish his journey before Ginny woke. The doll moved with desperate speed through the infinite rainbow spheres.

The palace rose up before him like a black tree. It loomed in the mist as if brooding on incalculable matters. The doll fearfully approached the entrance. An enormous gryphon trained its glittering gaze upon him.

"You are far from your home, little one," the gryphon boomed. The doll could not tell if the gryphon was angry or amused. "You have no business here. Leave now."

The doll felt his courage dissolve. The gryphon was right. He didn't belong here. Some of the strangers who had paused in his children's dreams had told him that the Lord of the Dreaming had guardians who were quick to anger and nearly as powerful as their Master. The doll trembled.

"I . . . I've come to see the Lord Morpheus."

One of the other guardians, the wyvern, gave a throaty chuckle, like the memory of thunder. "I think not," it said.

"Mercy, brothers," murmured the third warden, the hippogriff. "You have traveled in vain, little one. Morpheus is not in residence."

The doll felt the shreds of his courage tatter to whispers. All for nothing. He had failed Ginny.

"Couldn't I please wait? It's very important," he said, timidly.

"Important?" The wyvern laughed. "The Lord of the Dreaming has the care of all reality. You presume greatly, child."

But when it spoke the word "child," the doll felt an answering flare of anger that strengthened his resolve. He was a speck to these beings, true, but he was not nothing. He had cared for children all of his existence, and that had been a very long time, even measured in the millennia counted by such creatures as these.

"I will wait." He tried to say it with some dignity, but it came out as a quaver.

"That would be foolish," said the kindly hippogriff. "Morpheus has passed through the Gate of Gold and his return may be very long in coming."

"The Gate of Gold?"

"There are three gates that rule the Dreaming," said the gryphon. "Surely you know of them."

The doll could tell from the gryphon's tone that it supposed that he did not. But he had listened to many travelers and learned much of the Dreaming.

"Of course. The Gate of Horn is for true dreams. The Gate of Ivory for false." The doll's voice faltered. "But I have never heard of the Gate of Gold."

"Even the Endless must dream," said the hippogriff. "Morpheus bides among the Infinite."

The doll fell silent for some moments. At last, he worked up his courage to speak.

"Tell me how to find the Gate of Gold," he said.

"Why?" asked the gryphon.

The doll could think of no good answer. But as he looked at the gryphon, he saw that it was not angry at him, but rather deeply sad. He had seen such an expression too many times to mistake it. And suddenly he knew. This creature was a child, and the doll had been made to amuse children.

The doll did what he had done for thousands of years. He capered before the gryphon, turning himself into a bright-feathered bird, a colorful dream gryphon, that skirled in the air playing tag with his own feathers. He played games that were old before the first human tamed fire. He flew around and under and behind the great guardian, telling tales of eggs stolen and recovered, singing breakfast songs and cloud rhymes. He played and teased and tickled and tumbled. He used every thing he had ever known or learned. He thought of Ginny, who never laughed anymore, and invented still more games.

And, in the end, the gryphon's immense sadness lifted a fraction, a flicker. It didn't laugh. But it gave a sigh that was not entirely woven of sorrow.

"Indeed," he rumbled. But he turned to his brothers, and they exchanged silent thought. Finally, the gryphon spoke. "Follow the trail of the Master. It will lead you to the Gate."

"Where is the trail?" asked the doll, hardly daring to believe his good fortune.

"It begins there." The gryphon pointed with a claw to a patch of the silver mist that seemed to glitter. "You will feel the mark of his passing, never fear."

"Thank you."

"We give you no gift. Morpheus does not take kindly to unasked-for visitors. And no dream has ever dared disturb him within the Gate of Gold."

The doll bowed. "Even the Lord of the Dreaming shouldn't ignore a child's nightmares."

The guardians said nothing. The doll found the beginning of the trail and felt a chill knife through his being. Following the Master's path might be the end of him. Suddenly, he felt a tug, a light pull back toward Ginny. Her nightmare was almost over. She would be waking soon and he would be sent into sleep. Would he ever have the courage to try again? He thought not. It was now, or never.

He rushed away, down the trail.

"Farewell," whispered the gryphon, fashioned into a dreamless warden who had never known the games of other children. "You were well made."

The journey was hard. The steps of the Lord Morpheus left the doll's entire being cold as ice. He fought the whole way against Ginny's summons. He could hear her faint cries as her nightly torment came close to an end. Grim and frozen, the doll moved against a myriad of silver storms, never slowing his pace.

The Gate of Gold came into view at last. The doll had expected some vast ornate arch, gem-encrusted and shining. Instead, he stood before a simple gold curve, filled with a swirl of ebon.

He paused outside, uncertain and afraid. He could feel the freezing fire from the gate. He knew that if he passed through the arch, he would be destroyed. He called out to the gate. "Lord Morpheus?"

There was no reply.

"Lord Morpheus? If you can hear me, please listen. Children . . . " The doll trailed off. What could he say that would matter to one of the Endless? Surely, the Lord of the Dreaming knew everything he cared to know. Ginny's call was very strong now. He had only moments to decide whether to enter the gate. "Children are the hope of dreams, Lord Morpheus. It's not right to break them with never-ending nightmares. I have seen so many of their dreams. They are always alone. No one cares about the hopes of the young, and they know it. I try to make them laugh, but too often the waking world is empty, and they learn to be empty in dreams. Please help me. I'm just a doll, but I love them."

The only reply was a blast of cold from the gate. A final scream echoed across the Dreaming. Ginny was awakening to the sound of her mother's screams in the waking world.

For the first time in its long life, the doll felt tears break from its glass eyes. He leapt into the Gate of Gold, and the razors of dreaming light ripped through him, severing his being too swiftly for him to even cry out. His last thought was for Ginny, who would be alone again for the rest of her life, and all the children who would never have a doll to play with in their dreams.

Morpheus stood upon a shelf of shadow, looking down on a darkling plain. His glittering eyes, like stars wrapped in black velvet, burned in his pale face. His cloak rippled in a self-created wind. A raven hovered in the air before him.

"I don't get it."

"What is that, Matthew?" murmured Morpheus.

"Well . . . that doll, you know, it's just destroyed itself for nothing. I mean, there isn't any Gate of Gold."

"No," said Morpheus. "There isn't."

"But then . . . well, it was kind of brave," said the raven. "Wasn't it?"

"It was very brave, yes."

"Uh, well, what's gonna happen to Ginny? And her mother and that creep of a father?"

"Those are matters of the waking world, Matthew."

"So, that's it? Geez, it just seems . . . I don't know . . . unfair, like the doll said."

"Does it?" Morpheus fixed his gaze briefly on the raven, who let out a frightened squawk and fell silent.

Morpheus raised a hand as if he were plucking a fruit. The shape of the doll formed in his palm. He whispered something to the manikin and with a gentle toss, the doll vanished into the Dreaming.

"What was that?" asked Matthew.

"I made the doll in the beginning and, as the gryphon said, it was well made." Morpheus drew his cloak closer to his slender frame.

"So, he just starts over? And kids have to have nightmares?"

"Not necessarily." Matthew started to ask another question, but the Lord of the Dreaming quelled him with a glance. "I told the doll that a nightmare belongs to its owner. A brave dream might find a way to chase a nightmare into the sleep of the one who made it."

And with that, Morpheus turned away and headed home. Matthew followed after, in silent thought.

A BONE DRY PLACE

Karen Haber

I met Karen Haber for a few moments at the World Fantasy Convention in New Orleans in 1994, and discovered in meeting her that she was married to Robert Silverberg. The said Bob Silverberg was the first person I interviewed professionally as a journalist, and was (although he doesn't know it) indirectly responsible for the shape of my subsequent journalistic career. And while I wouldn't normally mention people's spouses, loved ones, inamorata, and so forth, in this introductory bit, I thought that warranted some kind of minor commemoration.

This is a tight and punchy story about late nights on the telephone, and saving the world.

Out on the long road beyond burnout, beyond woe, beyond anger, humor, and fear, but mostly beyond hope, is a place some call Desolation Valley. It's a bone dry place for people who are past the rationalizations and recriminations, the acting-out and shutting-in.

The usual therapeutic juju doesn't work here: No happy drugs, sleight of hand, faster-than-light distractions, slam-dunk denials, excuses, or escapes. Only regrets. And yes, those are mandatory.

Some folks just stop by for a visit and get right back on the road going the other way. Others return every year, their reservations prepaid by their parents, grandparents, or somebody else in their gene stream.

Oh, and it's dark. But those who dwell here don't really need light.

Despair, the younger sister of Death, twin of Desire, knows this valley well. She has been here often, stumping along on her short, misshapen legs to sweep up the tag ends of feeling, clutch each shard of a shattered dream, savor the sudden bursts of festering pain.

It's not by choice that she serves. She is one of the Endless, sworn to duty here until the universe ends or her elder sister takes over: Despair doesn't much care which comes first. Until then, she waits. The Endless are patient.

Others were on watch through the long night as well.

The phone, when it rang, was always startling, breaking the midnight hush. The ugly, green-walled home of the Bay Area Crisis Hotline, lit with white-cold fluorescent light. The rooms where the smell of stale coffee and old sweat lingered, mixed with the echoes of old fears. It seemed a place out of time, set apart from dusk to dawn. The rest of the world was asleep, everyone tucked in safely, dreaming sweetly, except for the caller and the volunteer linked by a telephone umbilicus.

182

"Incoming fire," said Bill Rutledge, night shift supervisor, as he watched the red light blink on his phone.

The voice on the other end was a rasping whisper. "My mind was eating itself for breakfast. I decided to wake up."

"It's twelve-thirty in the morning," Bill said. "That's kind of early for breakfast, isn't it?"

A reluctant chuckle. "You guys are good."

"Thanks." Now Bill recognized the voice. It was Zefrem, one of the chronics. He leaned back and ran his hand through his thinning brown hair. "Zefrem, you've called twice today. You know this is the last call you can make until tomorrow."

"Yeah, well, I just wanted to say that I've taken my medication and I'm waiting for it to kick in and I got lonely, so's I called, okay?"

"Sure."

"Okay, well. What are you doing?"

"Talking to you."

"Have I talked to you before?"

"Yes. Many times."

"Oh, good. Bad night?"

"No." Thank God.

Another phone light flashed. Across the room, Rita, the night shift volunteer, gestured frantically for Bill to take the call. She had been on the phone for twenty minutes, working with a Hispanic mother stuck in the city bus station, eight months pregnant, no place to go, no money, no English.

Jesus, Bill thought, *why do they give them our phone number? All the shelters will be filled by now. She might as well stay put in the bus station—at least it's got lights and a bathroom. She can start calling around in the morning, when somebody might have room for her.*

"Listen, Zefrem," he said. "I've got to go. You take care. Somebody will be here tomorrow."

"Yeah, I know. G'night."

Bill switched lines with practiced skill. "Crisis Hotline. How can I help you?"

The voice, when it came, was hesitant, female, low-pitched. "I just don't know anymore. . . ."

"Don't know what?"

A deep breath, a long exhalation. Was she smoking? The pauses could be drug-induced, could be exhaustion or fear. "I just don't know. I just don't, really. I-I can't. I can't do it anymore."

"Are you thinking about killing yourself?"

"Yes. I mean, I think so. I don't know."

"Why don't you tell me about it?" Bill settled in for a long listen. Outside, the fog rolled in, eating the stars.

Across town, in a small cottage near the edge of a deep canyon, Sarah Underhill, student of philosophy, was having a nightmare.

A tigerish noise in the sky. A fervid light brighter than the sun at midday, too bright to see except through black glass, flashing neon against the red silk lining of eyelids. Outside a corona of particles sleeted softly down upon the sleeping city. A thousand souls cried out, briefly. Terrible silence, after.

Sarah came to herself, shivering, her blond hair drenched in sweat. Another god-awful dream. She had struggled with them for weeks, the terrible dreams and visions. She couldn't work, couldn't think. Armageddon was coming, she was certain. But she would outwit it. She could. The pills were in the bathroom. She had prepared for this.

Despair has stood guard over the realms of pain and regret, relishing the agonies of this night. Now she peers into Sarah Underhill's living room, wondering. This one woman, she thinks. This Sarah. Problematical. Something about these nightmares and visions she's having, these dreams, seems wrong. Despair is no expert in dreams, however. She decides to consult her brother, Oneiros, dark lord of the Dreaming Realm.

He does not respond when she grasps his sigil. How typical of him, she thinks, always elsewhere when you need him. Despair—patient and, in her way, faithful—returns to stand watch over Sarah and all the others.

Half a continent away, on a plane not yet inhabited by Despair, men were gathered around a table. Men with hard, serious faces and fanatical light in their eyes. Men who had lost and lost again. They had fingered their scars. They had cursed their enemies. And now they had found a leader and a plan.

They had been talking all night or, rather, they had listened as their leader, the general, talked. A platter in the middle of the table held the remains of a roasted goat. The men ignored it, intent on their leader. It was almost time for them to take action. Yes, it was almost time. They nodded at one another with grim satisfaction.

The addict, whose name was Letisha, sobbed over the phone. "I've already got one kid. What am I going to do with another?"

"Have you considered not having it?" Bill said.

"Sure. You want to tell me how I'm going to pay for an abortion?"

"What about adoption?"

"Abandon another baby? Oh, yeah, right. And who'd want an addict's kid? You tell me that. A black addict's kid?" Letisha sobbed harder.

Bill knew he had no solutions, no answers. And that what Letisha really needed was to get off the junk. But until she did that, she would live minute by minute. And right now, this very minute, what she most needed was another human being to listen and say he was sorry. So he listened.

Rita had finished with her call and was sitting on the threadbare couch, eating cookies and flipping through a tattered three-month-old magazine. She glanced up, caught his eye, rolled hers in sympathy, went back to her magazine.

"I never thought it would be this hard," Letisha said. She choked on the last few words.

"I know. I'm sorry." Bill reminded himself for the thousandth time that he couldn't save everybody, that he had no answers, no solutions. And for perhaps the thousandth time, he hated it.

At 1:30 A.M., Sarah lay in bed waiting for the pills to work, her cat Tito curled against her. Briefly she thought of the cat, with regret.

"I'm sorry, Tito. I'd take you along too, if I could."

And it began, again. The sound. The pain. The sweet purple dark.

The horror.

Cities ignited in flame and exploded, spewing orange dust, and toppled in upon themselves. A maddened cyclone wind swept through the ruins, tossing the luckless survivors into the red ravenous maw of uncontrollable fire. Children screamed as the skin was crisped from their bodies. The scent of roasted flesh was sweet, cloying, nauseating.

The Fenris Wolf loped across the orange clouds. Its fangs were bared and its mouth dripped saliva. It crushed buildings underfoot, trampled all those who would flee before it.

The crust of the earth broke open as the legions of Hades erupted from below in a cacophony of screams and trumpets. The forces of evil rode the land, triumphant, as the universe ended in pain, in unthinkable holocaust. No Golden Age would follow. No rainbow phoenix would come forth, shrug off the ashes, and begin anew. Only scarred and shaken survivors, left to paw through the rubble, to kill for survival. And so the entire ugly killing cycle would continue, red in tooth and claw. No miraculous rebirth, perfect, cleansed, redeemed. No hope. Only blood. Rivers and rivers of it.

Tears and sweat mingled across Sarah's face. "No more," she whispered. "Please."

Despair turns to greet her wide-eyed, wild-haired sister, Delirium. "I was wondering when you'd get here." She nods down at Delirium's companion, the German shepherd named Barnabas. "Watch out for my rats."

The dog manages to look insulted. "I don't do rats."

Delirium brushes her peppermint-striped hair out of her blue and green eyes, peers at the mortal, Sarah, giggles, and says, "She looks so sad. I don't usually get sad ones."

"You're welcome to her," Despair says. "But watch out. She moves in and out of our realms fast."

"They don't, um, they don't usually do that."

Despair shakes her head. "There's something strange here. I really think that Dream should handle this, but you know how he is."

"I do?" Delirium blinks her one blue and one green eye. "Was she, like, was she, you know? Before she took that stuff?"

Despair juts out her square, fanged jaw. "Was she what?"

"Asleep?"

"Of course she was asleep. I was watching her."

"I mean, really? With dreams and everything?"

"Sister, what are you trying to say?"

"I don't know. I never really do."

Barnabas brushes against her leg. *"Sweetums,"* he says. "Do you mean that you think that mortal's tapped into something else? Something that's not dreams? Like prophecy?"

Delirium nods so vigorously that her hair goes swirling up and away from her head. Yellow and green curls tumble into orange pinwheels and blow away on the wind. "I think so. Yes. I do. Yes."

Despair gazes at her sister without speaking. She bends down. Her squat, graceless body seems to melt into itself, slack breasts resting upon raddled knees. She picks up one of her pets, a sleek gray rat, and strokes it thought-fully. "Prophecy? Why would this mortal be granted such a gift? She's no oracle."

"I dunno. Sometimes they catch it, like a bad cold." Delirium's new hair grows in quickly, purple dreadlocks. She twirls a bit of it around her fingers. "Remember Cassandra? Boy, she got a dose. And our nephew, whats-is-name."

"Orpheus," says Barnabas.

"Yeah. Him, too." Delirium pauses, remembering other sadder things. "I don't think he enjoyed it."

Barnabas scratches a flea bite. "They never do."

"No? Oh, I'd like it. At least, I think I would. Our sister, Death, says we know everything anyway. Or anything every way." She pauses. "Umm, what were we talking about?

"The mortal is slipping more firmly into your realm, sister." Despair says, and makes a sign of parting. "Farewell."

Delirium waves but her troll-like sister is already gone, taking her rats with her.

On the bed, Sarah moans softly.

Delirium giggles and wiggles her toes. "This is a nice room," she says. "I like your chair. I like your cat, too. You don't seem to be having a very good time, though."

Barnabas forces his nose against her hand and whines softly. "She gives me the creeps."

"Do you want to go back to my realm?"

"Anyplace else."

"Okay." She smiles as he vanishes. In his wake she scatters a dozen glow-ing purple toadstools and, just for fun, puts miniature yellow pigs on top of them.

The men listened to their leader as he spoke to them of need, of righteous-ness, of redemption by fire. He was strong and proud and upright, shining in their eyes like a small sun. He wore his green paramilitary jacket with its yel-low insignia as proudly as a king's robes. His sharp-billed cap with its scrolls of golden honor sat atop his dark hair like a crown.

The men nodded at their splendid leader, at his words, slapped palms against tabletop and heels against floorboards in appreciation. Fire, yes. Revenge, yes. Death. Redemption. Revenge. Yes, yes, yes. The table and floor rattled and thundered with their approval.

━━━━━

A voice whispered in a long-distance hiss. Sarah's brother, Scott, a scientist, calling from a pay phone near the South Pole. He had been scrambling through the labyrinth of the underground lab, searching for the switch, the food, the light above the exit door.

"Run," he said. "Run, run, run …"

His words broke into sharp pieces in her ears but Sarah could feel his meaning transmitted in pulses over the shining wires and pillowed cables, all the longing and sadness bounced off of satellites and into her brain, once around the auditory canal and home. She's been infected with the twentieth century—love was the vector but the cure was years distant.

"Take care," she said. "I miss you," and many other safe words, safe because he couldn't hear her, because the line was dead. She hung up tenderly. The TV was there, waiting to comfort and understand.

A blue face onscreen said, "Run, run, run …"

The television flared up into flames and melted into a sizzling multi-colored puddle. Sarah didn't care because the entire room was on fire.

She peeled down, pulling off every layer until she reached ground zero, skin, and still couldn't strip off enough, unwind herself, cool down her soul.

Sarah fought up toward wakefulness, slipped, fell back into the flames, the torrent of flames and blood.

"I don't like this one," Delirium says. "Make a different one. Come on, you can do it. Let's have the blue flowers again or the white noise. No, wait. What about blue noise? Or maybe strawberry?"

Sarah is motionless, staring at something that Delirium can't see.

"Stop it," Delirium says. "Stop it. I don't like it anymore. This is real, isn't it? I don't like it." She watches Sarah, fretful now. If only her brother Destruction were here. He would know what to do. But he's long gone. He had been nice to her.

Her other brother? No, not Destiny. The other other one, Dream. He might help. He had helped her before, after she had cried. He was nice, too, sort of.

"Dream! I'm holding your insect face thingamajiggy. You know. Your vigil, um, sigil. Yeah. Anyway, Dream, I need you. Where are you? I know you can hear me. DREAM, ANSWER ME!"

A sound that is not a sound. The movement of air that is scarcely perceived, barely felt. The lord of the dreamworld, her brother, stands before her, dark robes billowing. "You called, my sister?"

"I did?"

Dream, her brother, floats before her, a pale wraith with hair the color of the darkest nightmare and eyes unfathomably deep. A look of irritation crosses his colorless face.

"I did," Delirium says, nodding happily. "See?" She points at the bed, at Sarah. "It's really not my kind of thing, is it?"

"What isn't?"

"Her." Delirium gestures again at the curled lump of Sarah.

"Who is this mortal?"

"Her name's Sarah. Don't you know? I mean, weren't you in charge of her originally? Who gave her all those awful dreams?"

"I may once have given her dreams, sister, but she is unknown to me now."

"You didn't send her the fire and the burning babies and the wolf-thing in the sky?"

"No."

"Well, neither did I."

Dream sighs. "No, I suppose you didn't. Is that all?"

"Dream! Don't you dare leave."

"My sister, I confess I have no idea what you want of me."

"If you'll—just wait a minute, then I'll tell you." Delirium pauses, squinting. She can't remember. But she must. "Um. You're my brother, Dream. Yes, that's right. And I called you. So it must be because of dreams." She smiles, triumphant. "Yes, her dreams."

"I've already told you, sister, she has not been dreaming."

"Then what is it, all this fire and things exploding and cities getting smashed and stuff?"

"Possibly the imaginings of a diseased mind."

"Don't you talk about her that way! She's nice. She's unhappy, and she's trying to die because of all the pictures in her head."

"Then you have called the wrong sibling. You want our elder sister."

"No I don't. And she doesn't, either."

"What exactly is it that you want me to do?"

"Help me find where her pictures are coming from. She took pills and yucky things to get away from them."

"I don't know the source of her discomfort."

"Well, find it. And hurry up."

"And why can't you do it?"

"Because I have to stay here with her. That's my job. But you don't. You can go see Destiny—he likes you best, anyway—or look it up in your library or pond or mirror or lily pad or tea leaves or entrails or . . . "

"Enough! I'll see what I can do."

He thins upon the air. She can see the blue-rose wallpaper on the wall behind him, through him. He is gone. Poof. Dream is like that.

Delirium waves at the empty air and wonders if she should call for Death. Probably not. Her sister is always very, very busy. Sooner or later she would be here anyway. She went everywhere, sooner or later. Better to wait for Dream to come back. Yes. But in the meantime Delirium will do the best she can. She smiles. She has an idea.

"Hey," she whispers to Sarah. "Wake up. Just a little bit." She nudges the telephone with her spangled toe. "Come on. Wake up. You can do it."

The time had come. The leader gave the sign and his followers rose, shook hands, then turned to the piled objects against the wall. Each man took a soft, cloth-wrapped bundle: death swathed in flannel. To them the weight of it against their bellies was sweet, almost as sweet as the weight of a nestling fetus, awaiting birth. But this coming birth would be fiery, bringing death and deliverance. The thought, too, was sweet. The leader reminded them of their quest once more. With tears in their eyes, proud tears, they went out into the night carrying their deadly parcels, secure in their righteousness.

"Brains turned in upon themselves, beating themselves to death," the thin, high voice muttered.

Christ, Bill thought. *It's the Poet. Again.* "Look," he said. "You know the rules. Three calls maximum. This is your fifth today."

"But really, I feel suicidal. . . ."

"No you don't. Read a book or watch TV or something but don't call back here until tomorrow." Bill hung up, immediately regretting his rough treatment of the Poet. He was getting an edge, bad sign. Maybe it was time to take a vacation. But who would fill in here if he were gone? So much need, so few volunteers.

The phone rang.

"Hello? I just took something. At least, I think I did."

Bill sat straight up, all fatigue gone. The woman's voice quavered slightly. This was for real. He could feel it. "What did you take?"

"Little green pills." A yawn. "Some of them."

"Dark green?"

"Pale."

Shit. Probably Valium 20s. That could be bad. Especially if she mixed them. "How many?"

"The whole bottle. And rum. A bottle of that, too."

Definitely bad. He went into major crisis mode, signaling Rita that he had an emergency and to call the police and have them tie in the trace line.

She nodded, signaled back when it was engaged. Fine. Now all he had to do was keep his caller on the line for fifteen minutes.

"Hello?" he said. She sounded woozy. He had to keep her talking. Keep her awake. "Have you vomited?"

"No."

"Can you make yourself vomit?"

"I don't think so."

Don't panic, he thought. *She didn't swallow Drano. It's good old Valium with booze. Takes a while to fully dissolve, get into the bloodstream, and conk her out.* "Did you eat dinner?"

"I think so."

Good. Anything to slow the body's absorption of the poison. "When did you take the pills?"

"I don't know. Maybe an hour ago."

"What's your name?"

"Sarah."

"Sarah, I'm Bill. Why did you take the pills, Sarah?"

"Because the world is coming to an end."

"How do you know?"

"I saw it."

The men separated, all of them taking different cars with untraceable license plates. Some were thinking of the task ahead. Others were thinking of loved ones. A few thought of the parcels, their little clock faces shining green and red and yellow with digital readouts. Tick. Tick. Tick.

Dream, dark lord of the subconscious, has been busy, been many places in the space of time that a mortal lowers and raises an eyelid.

Blink.

His brother Destiny's garden is not a restful place. Nor is Destiny himself a pleasant companion. The visit is brief. Destiny reveals the patterns he sees in his books for Sarah.

"This is not her time, not yet," says Destiny.

"But see, here," Dream replies. "She is tangled here with the destiny lines of these others, these violent men."

Destiny nods. "Sometimes connections cross. At night, late. It happens."

"I see. Thank you, brother."

Blink.

Dream is in the leader's house, the man called the general, listening as the man sits alone at a table and babbles to an imaginary army.

"We will destroy them all. The evil ones must be vanquished. Only then can we make the world safe for our families. We've waited too long. You know what to do. Make them die, make them all die. We must cleanse the world so that our children will be safe."

Dream sees that the man exists in a waking dream state, constantly hallucinating.

"No," says the lord of the Dreaming. "No more. You may dream no longer."

The general's face grows pale and he begins to tremble. His eyes go wide but the light within them falters, dims, fades. His splendid cap tumbles from his head as he crumples like an abandoned puppet, falling into a long, empty sleep which medics will call persistent vegetative syndrome.

Blink.

The general's followers. There are too many to handle at once, dispersed as they are.

Dream returns to find Sarah on the telephone and his sister, Delirium, whispering in her ear.

"Sister," he says. "Why are you interfering?"

Delirium gives him an indignant look. "If I hadn't been supposed to interfere, then I couldn't have, could I? So I must have been supposed to do what I'm doing."

Dream sighs. "Never mind. Listen to me carefully. I need your help in order to prevent many foolish mortals from destroying themselves—and from further polluting the dreams of others."

"You said I was inter— inter—"

"Interfering."

Delirium pouts. "What do you call what you're doing? And you've never asked for my help before."

"It never seemed so peculiarly appropriate."

"Will this stop her bad pictures?"

"I think so."

"Then okay." Delirium takes his outstretched hand. "How was Destiny?"

"The same."

"He always is. Poor Destiny. What do you want me to do?"

"I want you to steal this mortal's pictures and give them to me."

Delirium giggles. "You really want them? But I could give you something much prettier, with hyacinth wings, maybe, or lemon tires. Or you could do it for yourself. Why do you need her pictures?"

"Never mind, Del. Just do it. Please."

"You called me Del." She dimples at him. "Okay, Dream."

She pulls all the ugliness out of Sarah's head, encapsulates it in gossamer bubbles whose curved iridescence masks the horrors within. Gently she tosses each bubble toward her brother.

He catches them in a deep basket made of wind. "Thank you, sister." Laden with nightmares, Dream bows and leaves.

In the time it takes to tell it, he is with the general's men, sitting in the car beside each true believer. In each car Dream raises up one of the shining bubbles and pricks it. Soon his basket is empty. And each one of the general's men knows that he has been betrayed. The general has promised that Armageddon and agony will fall upon the others. He has promised. And lied.

The streets dissolved into rivers of fire and blood. Terrible riders raced beside the general's men, riders in blood-caked armor and horned helmets, on hellish beasts, who pierced their mortal bodies with flaming spears. They fell, screaming, into fiery cauldrons where their skin was burned from their bodies. They writhed in torment, screamed, covered their faces. The luckiest among them died.

"The police and hospitals had a busy night mopping up after a string of strange accidents. Each wreck produced a dead or dying driver and a deactivated bomb. Months later, the bombs led investigators to a silent, unresponsive man lying in a hospital bed in a county ward. Very peculiar. Definitely one for the books.

There was the shriek of brakes, the slam of car doors, and frantic knocking. Sarah raised her head but was too weak to get off the bed.

The front door burst open. Tito scrambled for the safety of the bedroom and, gratefully, Sarah fell into the arms of her rescuers.

One of the blue-coated medics picked up the phone. "Hi," he said. "It's okay. We got here in time."

On the other end, Bill said, "Thank God," and hung up the receiver. He and Rita exchanged high-five slaps of congratulations. He blinked, yawned, stretched. Rescues always made him feel light-headed and spacey. He checked the wall clock. Two hours to go until dawn, until his watch would be over. He shrugged and reached for a cookie.

Sarah sleeps upon the medics' stretcher. Delirium blows the mortal a kiss.

"Take good care of her, Dream," she says. "And come visit me and Barnabas." A kaleidoscope of rainbow colors, and she is gone.

The lord of the Dreaming peers down upon Sarah on her stretcher. "Sleep well," he whispers. "All of your dreams will be sweet." He leaves her dreaming that she is a star twinkling in a blazing, beautiful firmament. In her sleep, Sarah smiles.

Dream is there and then he is not there, and the space where he stood is filled with a strange wind from a bone dry land and a hundred emotions, but not one single regret.

THE WITCH'S HEART

Delia Sherman

Delia Sherman is a real lady. She knows more about things obscure and English than I do, and has written brilliant, stylish stories, and an amazing novel called *The Porcelain Dove*. Sometimes she lives in Boston and sometimes she lives in New York.

This is a beautiful tale of love and madness and heartbreak, hearts and wolves. There's blood running through it, like a strong, intoxicating wine; blood, and desire.

"I have killed."

The girl took two steps into the room and halted nervously, brushing the brindled hair from her eyes to glance at the cocoon of wolf pelts huddled by the fire and then away.

"Are you clean?" A woman's voice, resonant as an oboe, but without emotion.

The girl examined her hands back and front. "Yes," she said.

"Come, then." A long, delicate hand extended from the cocoon of furs and beckoned to the girl, who padded obediently to the woman's side and curled down at her feet.

"I left it at the kitchen door for the cook," said the girl. "It's chewed. I was hungry."

The woman laid her hand on the girl's hair. The girl leaned into the touch. "What was it, Fida? A rabbit?"

"A deer."

"Did you gut it?"

The girl Fida stilled, then shook her head vigorously. The woman's fingers tightened in her hair, gave it a small, sharp tug. "Bad cub," she said.

"Yes." Fida's mouth opened in an embarrassed grin, baring pointed teeth. She began to pant. The woman tweaked her hair again. "I'm hot," said Fida apologetically.

It was no wonder. The room was at blood heat from the fire and seemed hotter still; for it was red as the inside of a heart. Turkey carpets blanketed the floor, crimson hangings muffled walls and bed. The clock on the cherry wood mantel was made of red porphyry. Its hands stood at half past one—whether morning or afternoon was impossible to tell, the windows being both shuttered and curtained.

"I'm hot," said Fida again, and shifted, restless and uncomfortable. "I'm going out."

"You just came in."

"I'm going out again."

The woman withdrew her hand into her furs and shivered. "Of course," she said. "You must do as you please."

In one swift heave, Fida was on her feet and padding to the door. She paused with her hand on the knob. "Will you watch me go?" she asked.

"The moon's full," said the woman.

"I'm going to the Mountain," said Fida.

The figure in the chair went very still. "To the Mountain," she said, laying down her words like porcelain cups. "I will watch you go."

Fida grinned, and was gone.

No need to go to the window immediately, thought the woman. *Just sit a moment longer by the fire while the girl readies herself.* But even as she thought it, she was up, pulling back the curtain, unlatching the heavy wooden shutters, folding one of their panels into the thickness of the stone wall, pushing the casement window open to the night.

It had snowed, snow on deep snow. The clearing between the manor house and the forest was a silver tray polished to brilliance by a full moon riding the Mountain's shoulder. A beautiful night, all black and crystal white, and very, very cold. The chill flooded the woman's lungs, stung her cheeks and her eyes, cut through her layers of wool and fur and velvet as though they were thin silk. She clenched her chattering teeth and endured until a lean pale she-wolf trotted out around the side of the manor and toward the wood, pausing halfway across the clearing to look up at the window.

The woman raised one hand in a bloodless salute; the wolf howled.

As she watched the wolf's shadow lift its pointed chin against the snow, the woman felt time slip. The moonlight fell just as it had a year ago, the night she'd heard a noise outside her bloodred room. An owl, she'd thought at first, or a wolf howling. But when it came again, she thought it was a voice, shouting a word that might have been her name.

She was curious—no one had come near manor or Mountain for more years than she could count—so she had unshuttered the window and looked out. She saw naked trees groping at the edge of a dense wood, snow-draped Mountain brooding beyond, full moon glaring down on the courtyard, and nothing else. But as she shrank back into the room, away from the moon's cold gaze, a wolf had slid across her vision like a shadow.

Two shadows, really. The wolf's shadow was darker than the wolf itself, long and black as a shard of night fallen into the courtyard, stretching out from the wolf's forepaws, shoulders hunched, head tilted curiously, arms splayed just a little too wide for grace: the shadow of a young girl, as human as the wolf was not.

The woman had thrown wide the casement and leaned out into the frigid night.

"Come!"

Her voice rattled the air like a flight of pheasants; the wolf disappeared under the trees before the echo of it faded.

The woman closed the window with stiff, blue fingers and fumbled the shutters and the curtains shut. Then she blew up the fire and crouched beside it to thaw her hands among the darting flames. A young wolf, she thought, still a cub, to judge from the outsize paws and the lean, gangling body. A wolf with a human shadow.

A strange sight. But the woman was a witch, and she had seen strange sights before. A brown man with branching horns and dainty, cloven feet bending gravely above her to offer soup in a silver tureen. A small, sleek woman with apple-seed eyes, who swayed like grass in the wind when she walked. A Lady whose face shone coldly among her dark hair like the moon among clouds, and the Witch's father weeping at her feet. This wolf with a human shadow was not the strangest of them, nor the most unexpected. Once her father's Lady had shown it to her, trotting unsubstantially over the face of the moon. "Tinder," she'd said, and, "A two-edged blade." Then she'd smiled and gone away.

The Witch had not understood the Lady's words at the time, being young and passionate and unacquainted with blades and their uses. But she'd had time to consider them over the long, cold years, and she'd decided they meant that such a wolf was a promise of heat, like tinder, and that fire could burn as well as comfort. Now it was come, she was forewarned. All she need do was bring herself to step out under the moonlight, the starlight, the shadow of the Mountain, and she would be warm.

A flame caught her finger, caressed it to rosy life. She closed her long, dark eyes. "I cannot," she murmured. "I cannot go outside."

"Then you must stay inside." The voice was the Witch's own, and the face to which she raised her eyes. Both voice and face were cast over with a silver brilliance like the moon's.

"You," said the Witch.

"You," agreed the other.

"The hour has come."

"But you can't seize it." The fluting voice was both despairing and mocking. "You're afraid."

The Witch curled herself into the scarlet cushions of her chair and gathered a black shawl around her shoulders. Her visitor laid one arm along the mantel and gazed down at her, smiling slightly. Meeting her eyes, the Witch thought that she saw the moon in them, dead and leering; she shivered, but did not look away.

"I cannot feel fear," she said.

"No," said her visitor. "Nonetheless, you will not go out. Out is too cold, too hard, too bright. You have not been out in years. Besides, it would have pleased your father."

The Witch reached for a cup of tea—peppermint—fragrant and steaming to warm her hands and her cold, empty belly, and found one ready on the table. "What," she said when she had taken a careful sip, "could my father's pleasure have to do with my going out?"

"Very good," approved her twin. "The tea is a nice touch. Haven't you noticed that you never do anything you think would have pleased your father?"

"But breaking the spell would not please him. That was the bargain, wasn't it? That I should live like this forever?"

"That's what I said." The other turned to admire her reflection in the overmantel mirror. "Pretty. I like the earrings. But you should do something new with your hair."

The Witch put her hand to her hair. It poured over her chair like carved and polished wood, deep brown, with a red glint in its depths. "I like it," she said.

"You're afraid to change it," said her visitor. "Your father liked it loose, you know. I remember him saying so."

"I did not call you," said the Witch. "I do not need you. Begone."

"Ungrateful bitch. I was just trying to help."

"I do not need your help."

The other began to laugh, showing small, white teeth that lengthened as she laughed and grew sharp and yellow until they filled all her mouth, and her tongue between them grew long and flat and red, and her laughter slid up into a shuddering howl. And then she was gone, taking the fire with her.

The next night the Witch watched for the wolf in the library from a French door that gave onto the courtyard.

The moon had paced across the sky before the wolf finally appeared, silent as smoke and close enough for the Witch to see the wet gleam of its eyes and its vaporous breath rising. Its shadow on the snow was sharp and clear as a black paper silhouette, blocky and awkwardly configured, yet unmistakably human.

The Witch forced herself to push the door ajar, then her nerve failed her. Shivering, she called:

"Come!"

The wolf started at her voice and loped back into the wood, pausing under the first trees and looking back over its brindled shoulder before taking itself and its shadow to the shelter of the wood.

The Witch ran after it, a step and then another crunching over the pathless snow, carrying her out of the shadow of the manor and into the moonlight. It dazzled her, so that she reeled and lifted both hands to her face and staggered backwards with the snow dragging at her feet like quicksand. Tripping over the threshold, she fell hard upon the library's carpeted floor, where she sat with her fingers pressing hard against her lids until stars appeared in the darkness there, and a milky light like moonrise. Hastily, she opened her eyes. The French doors were closed and shrouded, as they ought to be. But a silver chill was upon her.

In her chamber, she blew up the fire and wrapped herself in the wolf pelt from her bed. Half-expecting the Lady to appear, black-eyed and mocking, she brooded over the fire. The porphyry clock chimed meaningless hours. The flames were scarlet and gold, with coals glowing below them, hot and alive as the sun. One coal was larger than the rest, dull red in the fire's ice-blue heart, drawing her eye until it filled all her vision: a carbuncle encased in faceted crystal. The logs shifted, and the coal flared into whiteness marked with red, like the red mouth in a woman's face—her own face, the Lady's face, salt white, with blind stone eyes turned inward and two lines carved between the brows. The stone eyes twitched and opened on stars in a sky so black that it sucked into itself the soul of anyone gazing upon it. Into its deeps fell the Witch's soul, flying among adamantine knives that pricked her toward the moon, which looked upon her with loving eyes and stretched its bearded lips to engulf her.

The Witch seized one of the adamantine knives. It was all blade. Her hand scattered rubies from her wounded fingers, but she felt no pain as she sliced the star across and across the moon's face, only cold.

"That didn't work the last twenty thousand times you tried it," the Lady remarked. "Can't you try something else?"

The Witch gave a strangled mew, sat upright in the cushioned chair, put her hand out for a glass of wine. Her fingers groped in empty air. "Red wine," she said aloud. "In a golden cup. Set with rubies. Now."

"You must be mad," said the Lady cheerfully. "What you really need is meat. You haven't eaten anything in ages."

"Red wine," said the Witch decidedly, and lifted a brimming goblet to her lips. The wine was warm and fragrant with cinnamon and cloves; it burned in her hands and feet and behind her eyes. She drained the goblet, then dressed herself in a crimson velvet riding dress and little heeled boots lined with wolf fur, wrapped herself in pelisse and shawls, veiled her face against the wind and the cold gaze of the moon and stars. She unbolted the front door, opened it, and stepped outside to wait on the snow while the moon rose over the Mountain, bringing with it the she-wolf and her human shadow.

Seeing the woman, the wolf stopped. The Witch took a step forward. The wolf hesitated, lowered her tail, advanced one paw and then another. Step by slow step, wild-eyed and shivering, wolf and Witch left the safety of manor and forest, approaching the exposed and brilliant center of the clearing, approaching each other. They met. The she-wolf sat on her haunches; the Witch knelt before her and put back the veil, trembling like a bride. "You are Fida," she said. "You are my faithful servant."

The wolf shuddered all over, quick and hard as a death throe, then rolled onto her back and sprawled her back legs, offering the Witch her soft, pink belly. The Witch laid her gloved hand in the furry hollow, stroked upward to the furry chin, and stood.

"Come," she said, and this time the she-wolf obeyed, following at her heel like a well-trained dog back across the clearing through the open door, stopping only to mark the threshold with her scent. She looked about her, with ears pricked curiously, until the Witch closed the door and barred it. The cold, clear scents of pine and game and night and her pack drowned in a hot miasma of dusty wool and woodsmoke. The she-wolf sat down on the Turkey red rug and howled.

The Witch grasped her muzzle in both hands. "I don't like that noise," she said, shaking her gently. "Bad cub."

The wolf drooped her ears and whined; but when the Witch released her, she howled again: a long, panicked ululation.

Cold prickled up the Witch's spine. She needed utter devotion, and here was Fida, scrabbling frantically at the heavy oak door, snuffling at the thread of clean air, telling her that home was on the other side.

Laughter echoed in her ears like a silver bell. "Your father would be very pleased," it rang, mocking.

The Witch stamped her foot. "Bad cub," she shouted, to drown the bell. "Stop that at once and come with me."

The wolf raised her head and fixed her with moonstone eyes. Her nose wrinkled, her lip lifted from her sharp, yellow teeth; she rumbled threateningly. The Witch kicked her sharply in the ribs. She gave one startled yelp; the Witch kicked her again. Whining, the wolf offered her belly as she had in the courtyard. The Witch bent to accept her submission. "Good cub."

The ritual chamber was in the cellar, as far as possible from the open sky and the stars. The stairs leading down to it were cold and smelled of stale earth, like a long-abandoned den. The she-wolf marked them with her scent, and the chamber door and the high stone table that was its only furnishing. In one corner, she discovered a long, lumpy shape covered by a heavy carpet. Her nose pronounced the carpet dusty and the bones beneath it dry and fleshless and long, long dead. She sneezed, then leaped onto the table and sat, ears flicking back and forth, panting anxiously.

She whined when the Witch swept her front paws from under her and flipped her awkwardly on her back, but made no other objection. She even stretched her neck when the Witch put the knife to her underjaw and began to slit her skin away.

The Witch herself had never performed this ritual, but she had watched her father countless times, skinning the pelts from wolves and deer and bears to create servants to wait on him and her. After he died, she had made no more. She needed no servants; she preferred to do things for herself. If she knew absolutely that there would be wood for her fire and bread for her table, it would be so. That was the way of her magic, to work by absolute knowledge. Now, she knew absolutely that the she-wolf would lie still and trustful under her knife, and it was so. She knew she must cut only so deep and no deeper, must cut surely, without hesitation. A moment's doubt would kill the wolf and all the Witch's hopes of warmth. Once she might have doubted. But her father's bargain with the Lady had neatly excised disgust, compassion, and fear, leaving behind nothing but her absolute knowledge and a steady hand upon the knife.

There was no blood. The edges of the pelt were white and dry in the knife's wake, the flesh under it pink and whole and hairless. The pain, the Witch knew, would not be great unless by chance she pierced too deep. As the thought brushed her mind, the knife faltered, leaving a slender, scarlet track just over the breastbone. The she-wolf cried out in a voice neither human nor wolf, and the Witch sucked her breath in hard between her teeth. So easy to slip, to let out life and let in death—the ultimate coldness. Somewhere in the back of her mind a memory stirred, of blood hot on her cold hands, peat brown eyes wide with terror, and a thin, high scream like a dying rabbit's. Annoyed, she began to mutter the ritual aloud, the fluid words drawing the knife with them down the belly to the tail, then sideways between skin and pelt, working the wolf loose from the girl-form beneath.

The ritual took all night, and when the Witch was done, her hands ached with pulling and cutting, her lip bled where she had bitten through it, her eyes and knees twitched and strained. A brindled wolf pelt lay piled at one end of the stone table at the feet of a naked girl.

She wasn't pretty, not as humans measure beauty, being thin-hipped and shallow-breasted, her torso too long for her legs and arms, her hands and feet broad and stumpy, with horny palms and soles. Her hair was brindle gray like her pelt, and stood out in a wild aureole around her sharply planed face. Her nose was long and blunt, and her lips were very thin. Along her breastbone was a scar, red and raised like a whip welt.

"Fida," the Witch called her, and she opened eyes like winter moons. The thin, mobile lips twitched and worked, parted for the long, pink tongue to explore them. She made a tentative huffing noise, sneezed and sat up, eyeing the Witch with her head tilted awkwardly to one side.

"Mistress," she said, her voice rough and deep. She looked down at herself, lifted her hands one by one, licked between her stubby fingers, twisted to examine her altered body. She even tried to smell her crotch, at which the Witch laughed, cracking open the cut on her lip. The wolf-girl's head came up at the sound. Seeing the blood dribbling down the Witch's chin, she licked at it as she would lick the blood from a packmate's jaws. The Witch drew back from the touch of her tongue, hand to mouth, eyes showing white around the starless pupils.

"Bad cub?" the wolf-girl inquired anxiously.

The Witch shook her head slowly, then reached out to tousle the rough, brindled hair. "No," she said. "Good cub."

That day, Fida slept and woke and slept again, curled at the foot of the Witch's bed. When she woke at dusk, the Witch returned her pelt to her so that she could hunt. Following old habit, Fida searched out her pack. But she smelled wrong now—of woodsmoke and hot wool and dust and magic and humanity—and they soon drove her away again. For a little while, she licked her nipped haunches and whined before hunger drove her to hunt alone. She caught a rabbit and ate it, and then caught another to carry home to her new den. The rabbit was a little torn and chewed about the throat and back, but the Witch laughed when Fida laid it at her feet. She picked it up and smoothed the fur matted with blood and saliva, then knelt to caress the wolf's dripping jaws. "Good cub," she said. "I need meat."

"That's what I said." The Lady's voice was smug. Fida growled.

"Be still," said the Witch, and carried the rabbit into the dining room, where she laid it on the dark oak table, seated herself, and looked thoughtfully into the bog-brown eyes of her father's portrait hanging over the sideboard. "Stewed rabbit with dried apricocks and cinnamon," she said, and picked up silver-gilt cutlery. But when she looked down at her first real meal in a hundred years, the rabbit was still whole: laid out on the golden plate she'd imagined for it, mangled and cold.

"Eat," urged a hoarse voice behind her.

"I can't," whispered the Witch. The candle flames reflected in the rabbit's jet-bead eye were chips of diamond, or stars. A broad hand jerked the rabbit off the plate.

"Rabbit *good*," said Fida, and set her teeth to its soft belly to demonstrate. The Lady began to laugh, and the Witch put her hands over her ears and ran down the stairs to the ritual chamber, where the Lady never went.

When she emerged, she tripped over Fida, naked in her girl-shape, stretched out across the threshold.

"Bad cub," she said, and rolled over onto her back.

The Witch lifted her slippered foot and rested it lightly on the girl's hollow belly, at the end of the scar. "Bad cub," she agreed. "Bring me a deer, alive and unharmed, and I'll think you a very good cub indeed."

"Alive?"

"And unhurt."

It took Fida until spring, but she did it in the end, catching the deer in a trap she'd rigged in a shallow cave at the Mountain's tumbled hem. The Witch followed her into the wood to retrieve it, feeling for the first time in centuries the spring of grass and moss and pine needles under her feet, the weave of bark under her hand, the prick of pine scent and decaying leaves in her nose. Fida's shaggy presence at her knee warmed her through; as she led the spell-tamed buck back to the manor, she threw off her heavy shawl and loosened her gown at the neck.

In the front hall, the Lady was waiting for her. "What's this?" she inquired. "Following in Daddy's footsteps?"

"You said I needed meat," said the Witch defensively.

"Did I?" The Lady surveyed the buck. "How obedient of you. Do you intend to eat it alive?"

"I'm going to make a cook out of him." The Witch giggled suddenly. "I think his speciality should be venison stew, don't you?"

The Lady put out her hand to Fida, who advanced stiff-legged and bristling to sniff it. "Clever doggie," she said. Fida began to growl, the hair on her crest rising upright as her lip drew away from her fangs. The Lady snapped slender fingers under her nose. "A two-edged blade," she said, and disappeared.

All that summer of warmth and light and dappled sunshine, the Witch stalked the wood with the wolf padding beside her, silver-gray and graceful through the long evenings. She discovered the joys of the hunt, of blood hot on her hands and coppery on her tongue, and the sweet warmth of Fida's breath on her neck in the black hours between midnight and dawn. Sometimes she slept, and when she slept, she dreamed.

Walking in an ice cave, blue-white and cold as the stars, with one warm spot in the heart of it: a carbuncle in a crystal coffer. The carbuncle was carved in the shape of a human heart, two-lobed, veined delicately with blue. As she approached, it swelled slowly, contracted, and swelled again, warming as its beating strengthened, filling all the crystal cave with blood and heat and life. All save one corner, where a white-faced figure stood, robed in impenetrable black.

So the summer passed and autumn came. The days grew shorter, the nights longer, deeper, brighter with stars, and much, much colder. When the snows came, Fida wandered for a week in her wolf-form, sniffing at old dens and the bones of old kills, howling her frustration to the moon. The moon did not answer her, nor did the Witch, who greeted her return with black silence. Her body was bloodless and white with cold, but she thawed when Fida curled around her in the crimson-hung bed, and closed her eyes and sighed. With her mahogany hair folded across her throat, her unfathomable eyes veiled, her red lips half-open upon her small, sharp teeth, she was like a cub fallen from the teat. Fida nuzzled her neck, smooth and white and hairless, and the Witch turned to her and licked her mouth, petting her shoulders and her soft, shallow breasts. Their legs scissored together, thighs interlaced. Fida whined and nipped at the Witch's lips. The Witch whined too, then scrabbled from Fida's embrace to huddle against the bedpost, shivering and clutching her hair around her like a cloak. There was blood on her lower lip.

"Go away," she told Fida. "I'm cold."

Fida held out her arms. "Let me warm you, then."

The Witch gave a convulsive shudder. "No! No. You're making me cold. Go away."

Fida slipped out of the bed and padded naked to the door.

"Poor doggie," said the Lady.

Fida's eyes narrowed and her lips twitched.

"You don't like me, do you, doggie? Well, I like you. But I like your mistress better." Fida growled, as deep as her human throat would allow. The Lady smiled. "Jealous? I won't touch her, I promise. Now. Run away."

As the door closed behind Fida, the Lady settled herself comfortably in the Witch's cushioned chair. "Lazy girl," she said. "Tsk, tsk. Your father would be so ashamed of you. Don't you want your heart back?"

The Witch searched among the covers for her bed gown. "Of course I want it," she said.

"You're getting fat," said the Lady. "Must be all that venison stew. Or maybe it's love."

The Witch wrapped herself in fur-lined velvet. "I have no heart," she said sulkily. "You have to have a heart to love anything."

"I always thought so, certainly," the Lady agreed. "I don't know why your father was so *surprised* when you killed him. I told him he shouldn't have removed it."

The Witch clutched the bed gown, the fur rough against her icy skin. She was beyond shivering. "You removed it," she said. "That was the bargain."

"It was his bargain. He paid me for it, anyway. Which reminds me. We haven't discussed payment."

"Payment? But there's no bargain between us."

"Yes, there is. I remember it clearly. We discussed it just before you killed your father. You wanted to be free of him and you wanted your heart back. You said you'd give me anything I asked for."

"My heart is still in the Mountain," said the Witch.

"The were-girl can get it for you, if you're afraid to go yourself," the Lady said. "And you've been free of your father for eons. You owe me."

The Witch got out of bed and knelt by the fire. She didn't like being so close to the Lady, but the flames whispered comfort, and she was cold, so cold. "What do you want?" she asked.

"That would be telling, wouldn't it? You just have to be willing to give it to me. Are you willing?"

"I am not your creature," said the Witch.

"Aren't you?" The Lady widened her eyes. "You're mad as a hatter, mad with fear."

"I cannot feel fear," said the Witch.

"You are fear," said the Lady. "Bone to skin, hair to nail, you are made up of fear. Just like your father."

She laughed then, her eyes black and leering and full of stars, her mouth gaping wide on her merriment. The Witch seized the fire irons in icy fingers and slashed them across the Lady's face. The force of the blow sent bright blood spattering over her hand, her face, her gown, and hissing into the fire. The Lady gave a thin, high scream like a dying rabbit's. Her eyes were bright and mocking.

"How many times will you try that?" she said around the fire irons wedged in among teeth and red-stained bone. "It doesn't work. It doesn't work with me. It didn't work with your father. Not that I care; but it does make a mess."

The Witch covered her face with sticky hands. "Go away," she mumbled. "Take anything you want. Anything. Just go away."

"Very well," the Lady said. "I will."

When the Witch unblinded herself, the chair was empty and the blood was gone. So were the fire irons and the fire. The Witch dressed, braided her hair around her head, and called Fida.

Fida had clothed herself in a gown the Witch had imagined for her, loose leaf brown wool made high to the neck and tight to the wrists. She came in shyly and knelt at the Witch's feet, head low, shoulders hunched. The Witch took her by the chin, forced her head up, and looked long into her moonstone eyes.

"Do you love me?" she asked.

"Like hot blood," said Fida, unblinking. "Like the fresh marrow of bones."

"Good. Will you prove it?"

Fida looked puzzled. "I hunt for you. I sleep with you. What more do you want of me?"

The Witch caressed her hairless cheek. "There's a cave at the top of the Mountain," she said. "I want you to go there and bring me back something that I lost a long time ago."

"No," said Fida.

The Witch's hands dropped numbly. "You must."

"I will not. The Mountain is dangerous."

The Witch shivered, little tremors like ripples in still water. "You must, Fida. It's why I made you—to find my heart and bring it back to me, my heart that lies frozen in a cave at the Mountain's peak."

Fida ducked her head stubbornly. "The Mountain belongs to the White Wolves," she said. "They let no living thing pass."

"The Lady set them there to guard my heart from any who would harm me," said the Witch. "You love me. Surely they'll let you by."

"No."

"They're shadows, I tell you. They're for humans to fear, not for a wolf. Not for you."

"I am not afraid. I am not stupid." Fida touched the Witch's knee. "You have power and beauty and endless life. What do you need with a heart?"

"I need a heart," the Witch whispered. "I need *my* heart. I need it to love. I need it to hate. I can feel pain, nothing else. Oh, and cold. I can feel cold."

She began to weep, huddled in her wolf pelt, shuddering with dry, soundless sobs. Fida, reaching up to the blue-white hand, found it cold as snow or death. "You cannot love?" she asked sadly. "You don't love me?"

The Witch stilled. "You warm me," she said at last, and put her fingers to Fida's mouth.

The girl licked them until they were supple and ivory white and held them against her cheek. "I must think," she said.

"You will do it, then?"

"I don't know," said Fida. "I must think."

Sitting still by the open window, the Witch shuddered and wrapped an end of her black shawl around her throat. A year. Four hundred days, or a little less, since she'd first seen Fida; two days since she'd asked her to retrieve her heart from the Mountain. And before that, how long? Ten years? Fifty years? A hundred? What meaning does time have when there is nothing by which to measure it?

Fida had brought time into the Witch's life, marking the hours and days by her presence, by her absence. The Witch felt she had lived a lifetime in that year, two lifetimes in the two days Fida had oscillated restlessly between manor and wood. Now she was gone and the Witch did not know what to think. One moment, she knew, as she knew there would be wine at her hand, that Fida would not return, that the cold centuries would unfold year by year with the Witch at the heart of them, frozen and unchanging. The next moment she knew that Fida would bring her heart to her, awaken her like the Sleeping Beauty, to joy and warmth and peace.

Long after Fida had disappeared into the wood, the Witch sat staring out over the chiaroscuro of snow and forest, watching the shadow of the Mountain nibble at the manor and growing colder and colder until, had she had a heart, it would have stopped beating forever.

In that cold and in that silence, she remembered how lovely she had once found the moon's silver spell cast over Mountain and wood. She remembered loving the stars, and begging her father to teach her the patterns of their celestial dance. Those had been her first lessons in magic, conducted in the observatory her father had built in the manor's attics. They'd had human servants then, and people had come to visit from time to time—men in long black robes and ruffs and woolen caps tied under their spade-shaped beards, men whose skin was like unbleached linen, who smelled like old books. They had talked with her father of the stars, of the Philosopher's Stone that could turn lead into gold and confer eternal life. She'd had a little maid to wait on her, and a little dog to sleep at her feet, and her father had called her his heart's delight. The maid's name was Gretchen. The dog had been Sweetheart. Had she had a name? She must have. But she could not remember it.

The moon was full. Fida trotted up silent, silver glades toward the Mountain, her paws crunching on the frozen snow. She'd been as far as this the night before, to challenge the White Wolves, whose territory began where the trees thinned and the rocks grew thickly together. They'd answered her with growls and bared fangs. She'd fled downhill before them, but she'd learned that they had neither smell nor shadow. Perhaps they were like her mistress's bread, which filled the mouth and left the belly grumbling—shadows of wolves, with only the power that shadows have, to raise the ruff at nothing.

The trees began to dwindle in number and size, bowed by the wind, stunted by the cold, their roots twisted under boulders and down cracks in search of soil and water. Suddenly a wolf appeared, bright as mist in her path, his pack drifting near behind him like snow. Fida bristled and rumbled and cocked her ears forward. The White Wolf stretched his jaws and howled.

Had Fida worn her human form, she would have laughed aloud. No wolf howls at the edge of battle. She shook down her ruff and walked forward to meet him, wary but unafraid. The shadow-wolf howled louder, and his pack echoed him, scattering froth from their jaws like a snowstorm. As Fida approached, their howling grew more frantic, and they themselves more insubstantial, until she walked blindly through a cacophonous mist, following the slope of the ground upward step by step, while around her the White Wolves yammered like terrified puppies.

When the mist stilled, she was almost at the top of the Mountain, her nose against a slit in the rock barely wider than her shoulders. She sniffed deeply, smelled rock and water and something else, something that made her think of a white face and black eyes and sweetly curved red lips. Head warily low, she pushed into the slit and entered the Mountain.

The cave was very cold, colder than a frozen river, and so damp that Fida's bones ached with it. The moonlight crept in behind her, silvering the icy rocks, picking out odd gleams and sparks from the cave's shadowy throat. Slowly the wolf-girl paced into the darkness, her fur bristling.

Ice-rimed rock gave way to a tunnel carved out of blue ice, crazed and clouded like old crystal. At the end of the tunnel, a diamond spark glittered unnaturally, beckoning her forward. The walls breathed an arctic chill that froze her fur into an icy armor and her thoughts into silence, and still she advanced, her pads slipping on the glazy floor toward the ice cave, where the Witch's heart was hidden.

The cave itself was as bright as the tunnel was dark, carved facets of ice reflecting light back and forth to adamantine brilliance. The wolf narrowed her eyes against the glare and padded forward to the center and source of the light.

It was a casket of ice, set with moony jewels and bound with silver bands, fantastically carved and faceted to set off the scarlet heart that rested in its clear depths like an uncut ruby. The air around it shivered with waves of painful cold. The wolf bowed her head and whimpered.

In her blood-hot room, the Witch paced. She knew she must be patient, and yet she could not be still, but strode from hearth to window, from window to hearth, in a fever of restlessness. She wiped irritably at her hairline and her upper lip; her hand came away damp.

The wolf circled the casket, eyeing it as if it were a stag at bay. Her paws and tongue were bleeding and torn from her attack. Her brain was numb with magic and cold. Yet she was hopeful. It seemed a little warmer in the cave than it had been, and the surface of the casket was no longer perfectly flawless. It seemed to her, pacing and watching, that the heart had begun to beat a little, feebly, in time to her stiff-legged strides. Her own heart beat faster.

The Witch stood at the undraped window. Wood and Mountain were mantled in ermine, their image subtly distorted by the rippled window glass. She laid her hands flat against the icy pane. Heat caught in her chest and throat, dragging at each breath. She unbuttoned her woolen bodice and undid her boned lace collar, stroked her chilled hands down her face and neck. It felt nice; not as nice as Fida's coarse fur, damp after a run in the snow or the mist, but nice. She had a sudden image of Fida's head tucked into her shoulder, the brindled hair rough against her skin, the moony eyes hidden. She shivered, but not with cold.

"Well? Are you warm yet?" The Lady's voice was teasing. It was a lovely voice, the Witch thought, resonant as an oboe. Odd she'd never noticed. She turned to it as to a fire.

"I am warmer than I was," she said.

"Good. I hope you like it. Heat's expensive." The Lady was examining herself in the mantel mirror. The Witch saw both reflections, the Lady's and her own, near and distant, side by side. Feature by feature, they were identical: mahogany hair coiled like sleeping snakes around shapely heads, long, slanting eyes, high cheeks, crimson mouths, white throats.

The Witch stepped closer. "Who are you?"

The Lady settled a jeweled pin at her nape. "You," she said.

"No," said the Witch. "You are beautiful and I am not." She took another step. "Your lips are fire and your neck is snow. There are mysteries in the folds of your hair and the curve of your mouth." She was very near now. The two faces, one intent, one detached, watched her hand rise and hover toward the Lady's shoulder.

The Lady stepped aside and turned in one smooth movement. "Do you want to kiss me? There's a price on my kisses."

"Who are you?" asked the Witch again.

"Your father kissed me. He gave all he had for the privilege."

"I will give you everything I have."

"I have that already. You have nothing left to give me. Except everything you might have had. You could give me that."

Fida put off her wolf's pelt as the Witch had taught her, and wrapped it around her shoulders. Gently, she touched one torn finger to the casket, leaving a smear of blood on its clear surface, which slicked and shone for a moment, as if the blood had melted it to liquid. She lifted her finger to her mouth and ripped at the nail with her teeth until blood welled from the wound and dripped onto the casket. A fat crimson drop trembled a moment, cabochon, then collapsed and ran off the casket's side. Where it had been was a tiny pit.

Fida tore at her wrist then, sharp wolf teeth shearing through thin human skin as easily as knives. The resulting stream of blood was strong, pulsing over the icy casket in thick waves that thinned as they sheeted down the sides, melting the facets and the fantastic carving to rose-tinted smoothness, releasing the silver bands and the moony jewels to lie among rocks and pools of ice melt. Her arm grew heavy; she rested her hand on the ice, which burned her fingers, clung to them and to her wrist, freezing her to itself. Still the wound bled sluggishly as Fida knelt by the casket, her pelt slipping from her shoulders, watching her blood soak through the ice toward the Witch's glowing heart.

"Well?" said the Lady. "Is it a deal or isn't it? Your father knew what he wanted, and the last deal we made, you did too." A paper appeared in her hand, one line of small black type printed neatly across the middle and, beneath it, a blotched signature scrawled in brown ink.

"Here it is, in living color," she said. "I help get rid of your father and give you a chance to get your heart back, and you give me your name, your life, and your mind. Signed with your heart's blood, which is a neat trick for someone who doesn't have one."

The Witch reached for the paper; the Lady snatched it away. "Uh-uh," she said. "You'll just have to trust me. Come on, have I ever lied to you?"

"I don't know."

"So you don't," said the Lady cheerfully. "That's the beauty of it. But I always keep my bargains. Just ask your father."

"My father! My father! Why must you always be talking of my father? He's gone."

The Lady looked apologetic. "Well, that's the problem, you see. He isn't. When you cut out his heart, you simply covered him up with a rug and left him in the corner of the ritual chamber." The Witch's eyes shifted away, blank as stones. The Lady smiled and said, "I promised him you'd always be together."

"But what of your promise to me?" the Witch wailed.

"It hasn't been easy, I can tell you. Now. What about that kiss?"

The Witch felt her hair clinging stickily to her cheeks and brow, and lifted her hand to push it back. The movement brushed her loosened gown against her nipples, which hardened. There was sweat trickling down between her breasts, and, beneath the layers of her petticoats, she felt a moist heat between her thighs. The room pulsed around her, quick and hard. She stepped forward, close enough to see the thread of a healing cut on the Lady's lower lip.

Had Fida bitten the Lady, too? She fingered her own mouth, felt the faint ridge Fida's tooth had left there. It hadn't been a bite at all; it had been a kiss. And it had burned her. She recognized the heat now. It was desire for Fida. Fida of the wild smell and the bristly, brindled hair, Fida who never taunted her, Fida who was willing to brave the White Wolves for her. Fida who loved her.

"Yes," said the Lady, "she loves you. She's yours, by her own free gift. As you are mine."

"I am not yours," said the Witch.

"Very well, then; you're not. Save your chilly charms for your little pet, if she returns. She could meet a young dog-wolf on her way back through the wood—winter is mating season for wolves, did you know? And she-wolves are notoriously horny. Or she could run off with your heart, or eat it. You haven't been very kind to her, and she's still a wolf. Everyone knows that wolves are by nature cruel and crafty and mean."

"No," said the Witch. "She'd never do that. Would she?"

"Of course she wouldn't. She'd bring it back, or die trying. Wolves are notoriously faithful. And then you'd be whole again, mistress of your name, your life, and your mind. You'd feel warmth again, and love and fear and desire, and all sorts of other things you've forgotten about. Grief. Remorse. Loneliness. Oh, and you'll grow older. White hairs, some of them growing from your chin, and lines around your eyes and mouth. Loose teeth, droopy breasts. I can't guarantee you'll be able to imagine food and drink and fuel from thin air anymore, either. There are certain kinds of magic only I can give you."

The Witch made a little whimpering noise. Her reflection in the mirror flushed and paled as waves of heat and cold chased one another up her throat and licked her cheeks.

"Ah," said the Lady. "You don't like that, do you?"

"I want my heart," said the Witch. "That was the bargain."

"You can't have both your heart and me," said the Lady.

———

Fida lay white and unmoving in a puddle of pinkish ice melt, her hand cupped protectively around a quivering human heart. The cave was like a cloudy night, dark and close and featureless. In one corner, a shadow flickered black against black and drifted toward the wolf-girl. Shaking long sleeves from its star white hands, it touched her head. Fida's head stirred on her pillowing arm; she opened one eye and sighed. All was well. Her mistress had come to her.

"Good cub?" she whispered.

Her mistress giggled. Fida squinted up at the long face set in the depths of the cowl. No, not her mistress. Like, as a deadly mushroom is like an edible one, but not the same. Her eyes had no white, but were black from lid to lid; and where her mistress smelled of wool and woodsmoke and fear, this woman smelled faintly of peaches. Fida growled.

"Ah, you know me," said the Lady. "Well, never mind. It will be our little secret. You have something that belongs to me, I believe."

Fida closed her hand around the heart. It throbbed and burned in the hollow of her palm like a wound or a living coal.

"Don't be silly," said the Lady. "You can't fight me." Her white face filled the cave, round and unbearably white. "I am everything. I am wiser than heaven and more powerful than a pack leader in his prime. Truth itself is my creature and my slave."

Fida contracted on her sodden pelt, clutching the Witch's heart to rest against her belly, shielding it from the Lady's pitiless eyes with her wide hands and her bony knees.

The Lady's face waned, dwindled to a pale curve of cheek veiled by a drifting wrack of hair. "You can't fight me," she whimpered. "I am nothing. I am more ignorant than dirt and more powerless than a day-old cub. Truth passes through me as though I didn't exist."

Fida closed her eyes. Resting against her belly, the heart pulsed slowly, each beat sending warmth through her, and a trickle of strength.

In the blood-red chamber, the Witch sweated and shivered.

"It's the bitch-girl or me," murmured the Lady, soft as snow falling. "You can't have both. Why are you hesitating? She's an animal, not like you and me. She'll be dead in twenty years or so, just like the rest of them, and who knows whether I'll still want you by then? What do you know about this wolf-girl? How do you know you can trust her? Don't you want to know what she's doing right now?"

The Witch put her hands to her burning forehead, pressed it between them until the pain stopped her. "No. Yes. No. She loves me. I trust her."

"Suit yourself. She might be in trouble, be hurt, even dying. You could help her. But I guess you don't care."

"No! I do care. If she's hurt, I want to see."

The Lady smiled, a feral baring of the teeth. "Very well," she said. "You asked for it." She nodded at the mirror, which clouded and resolved into a dark painting of a naked girl curled on a wolf pelt. The girl was nursing something against her belly. Bending above her was the Witch, her proud face pleading, her hand beseechingly outstretched. The wolf-girl's lips were drawn back, snarling. Her eyes were wild.

"Does she look hurt?" asked the Lady.

"She looks . . . angry."

"Mad as hell," agreed the Lady.

"Why won't she give me the heart?"

"She wants it for herself," said the Lady.

The Witch screamed and, lifting her fists, shattered the vision into a thousand glittering shards. She turned to the Lady, sobbing, the tears hot on her cheeks, bloody hands begging an embrace. "You," she said thickly. "Who are you?"

The Lady opened her arms. "I am whatever you wish me to be," she said. "I am Desire."

But the Witch was still speaking and did not hear her. "You are Love," said the Witch. "You are Family and Home and Safety. You are my Heart."

Then she stepped into the embrace of Desire, which was as cold as the moon, and raised her lips to the lips of Desire, which sucked from her all warmth and hope of warmth. As they kissed, the fire in the hearth burned blue and white as ice, filling the room with a deadly chill. And far below, in the ritual chamber, her father's corpse shuddered and sighed.

In Fida's grasp, the heart throbbed wildly and unevenly, gave a wild, shuddering beat, and was still. Fida cradled it to her, willing it warm again, lifting it to her mouth and licking it. It lay cool and elastic in her fingers, dead meat.

"It's no use," said Desire. "She doesn't love you. She can't love you. She belongs to me."

"But I love her," said Fida passionately. "I love her more than my life."

"Die then," said Desire.

Not long after, Desire took the Witch's heart from between Fida's torn and bloody paws and set it back on the rocky spur where it had reposed for the past three hundred years. She spat upon it and smoothed the spittle into a casket of ice, faceted and fantastically carved, bound in silver bands and set with moony jewels. Then she pulled her cowl up around her face, shook down her long, dark sleeves, and drifted back into the corner.

The Witch sits in her blood-red room, cocooned in wolf pelts. The hands on her porphyry clock stand at half past one—whether morning or after noon is impossible to tell, for the windows are shuttered and curtained. So are the Witch's eyes, lids closed against the ruddy firelight and veiled by the mahogany hair hanging loose over her face. Stone and glass and wood and cloth stand between her and the moon, but she can feel it nonetheless, cold and hungry outside her chamber window, riding above the Mountain where her heart lies frozen in ice. Someday she'll get it back. All she needs is someone who will brave the moon and the Mountain and the Lady's White Wolves, to break the spell and get it for her. Someone who will not betray her. Someone who will love her. A wolf with a human shadow. The Lady has promised.

THE MENDER OF BROKEN DREAMS

Nancy A. Collins

The first time I met Nancy Collins, we were sharing a hotel room. Nancy had to sleep on the floor. It was Steve Bissette's fault, and I tell the story in the afterword to Nancy's anthology, *Nameless Sins*, so you won't hear any more of it here.

Here she gives us a glimpse further into the murky background of The Dreaming.

I am the Mender of Broken Dreams. That is my occupation, my calling, if you will.

I start each day by walking the long halls of the castle, climbing great staircases that curl and wind like the chambers of a nautilus. Every day the halls are different, the stairs head in a different direction, the artwork and furnishings decorating the wings no longer the same.

Some days the door leading to the Restoration Department looks like an ancient vault, sometimes it resembles the yawning, laughing maw of a fun-house clown, other times it is twisted and off kilter, like the lurching door-ways from a German expressionist film.

The Restoration Department is always huge; that much never changes. There are thousands upon thousands of towering shelves that stretch up to the dim ceiling, each shelf divided into cubbyholes of various sizes and shapes, each cubbyhole carefully labeled and marked according to some arcane filing system created while Man picked his neighbors for nits. And in each specially marked cubbyhole there is a box holding the remains of a dream.

My job is to repair the dreams or, should that prove impossible, retool them so they might somehow continue to work. It is an endless task, but immensely rewarding on a personal level. I love my work. It challenges me daily, both artistically and intellectually. I approach each case with the utmost interest and dedication. The repair and restoration of so delicate and ephemeral a thing as a dream is something only a true master craftsman would attempt. And while I blush to sound my own horn, false modesty has no place here. To state it simply: I am the best there is at my craft.

My attendant, Kroll, is waiting for me to arrive, as always. Like many of Lord Morpheus's servants, he is not native to the Dreaming but an emissary from one of the many realms of myth. Kroll claims to be a prince of Nibel-heim, the Land of Dwarves, but with his great shock of orange hair, round little belly and thick features, he looks more troll than dwarf.

I take off my topcoat and drape it over the back of a chair carved to resemble a flying monkey. "Good morning, Kroll."

"Morning, boss. Here's today's schedule," he announces in his *basso profundo* squeak as he hands me a sheaf of computer printouts.

I glance at the columns of serial numbers, nodding my head. "Looks like we have a busy day ahead of us."

"Lucky us," Kroll grunts, and heads over to the motorized cart he uses to traverse the labyrinthine stacks. To aid him in reaching the higher shelves, it comes with a cherry picker.

I do not know how long Kroll has been working in the Restoration Department, but I would hazard a guess that he has been here for a lifetime or two. Occasionally he forgets himself and makes references to my predecessor, the previous Mender. As Kroll starts up the retrieval cart, I unlock the huge freestanding cabinet behind my workbench and take out the tools of my trade: a jeweler's eyepiece, a potting wheel, sculpting tools, a set of soldering irons and glass cutters, a sewing kit, an electron microscope, and far more mundane objects such as C-clamps and drill bits. Just as I've finished laying out my tools, I hear the putt-putt-putt of Kroll's retrieval cart heading in my direction.

Today there are several small and medium-sized boxes, a couple of crates, and what looks to be a rolled-up rug on the cart. I watch Kroll as he unloads a box big enough to hold a freezer unit without breaking a sweat. Although he is the size of a three-year-old child, Kroll's strength is prodigious. Rumor has it that once, while in his cups, he got into a brawl with one of the Aesir while in Valhalla and was forced to flee his myth cycle, which is why he's in Lord Morpheus's service.

I check the serial numbers on the boxes in order to make sure we have the same ones as those listed on the manifest, then open each box to check the contents.

"Hmmm. Lot number 36/92: damaged stained glass. Lot number 87/12BB: frayed tapestry. Lot number 410/ZF: broken mechanical bird-of-paradise."

"I'll get the looms and spinning wheels ready. Let me know what fabrics and dyes you'll be needing."

"Very good, Kroll. And you'd better see to the blast furnace and kiln while you're at it."

I decide to start with the clockwork bird-of-paradise. Mechanical things are always the easiest to fix, even when they have suffered the roughest of handling. I turn the bird-of-paradise over in my hands, admiring the workmanship.

It is made of burnished gold with delicate patterns, chased in silver along its body and with precious stones set in its tail and head. Reality has taken its toll on the thing's beauty, though. Tarnish has corroded the silver and covered the settings with a black goo that turns the rubies and emeralds and pearls into grimy pebbles.

Screwing the jeweler's glass into my right eye, I set myself to repairing its clockwork guts. Within a half hour the dream-machine is whole once more. I hand the bird-of-paradise to Kroll, who produces a burnishing cloth and begins polishing it like a fiendish Aladdin. Soon the clockwork bird looks as good as new—its golden skin reflecting the sunlight that spills in through the high windows like the face of the sun itself.

"Now, let's see if she'll fly," I mutter, holding up the key I found in the box alongside the broken dream. It fits just below the clockwork bird's right wing. I turn the key clockwise, careful not to overwind it. The dream jerks into motion, flapping its wings and tossing back its head to give voice to a joyful burst of clockwork birdsong.

Spreading its gold and silver wings, the bird-of-paradise takes to the air, circling over our heads a few times before flying out the open window in search of its rightful owner.

"What kind of dream do you fancy that was?" Kroll asks, scratching himself with his three-fingered hand.

"Probably one of wealth. It's no doubt going to roost on the bedpost of a peasant farmer somewhere."

I decide to tackle the tapestry next, since matching threads, dyes, and weaves is the most time-consuming of restorations. As I unroll the tapestry, I find myself impressed by its elaborate design and dismayed by the state of its decay.

Brave Persian warriors battle hungry lions and fearsome djinni. An invading army riding war chariots and Soviet tanks is met by heroic soldiers armed with spears and AK-47s, while angry gods and helicopter gunships hover in the war-darkened skies. Some of the images are obscured by bloodstains, while other parts have been damaged by bullets and fire. The tapestry reeks of smoke and gunpowder. Cleaning and restoring it to its former glory will be difficult—I will have to reweave the more damaged sections myself, using more modern materials while utilizing traditional crafts—but the task ahead of me is not impossible.

I clip a small sample from the damaged portion of the dream and slip it under the electron microscope in order better to comprehend the elements necessary to duplicate the weave. Looks to be a mixture of hope, fantasy, romance, pride, and tradition. Not that unusual a blend, really. I jot down notes for Kroll to use for reference as he spins the raw materials into thread.

Satisfied I have the composition correctly identified, I proceed to clean the dream as best I can before placing it on the loom for repair. This is, in fact, far trickier than replacing the damaged portions. If I am not careful and use too much force or too caustic a cleaning agent, I may permanently alter—if not completely eradicate—the elaborate designs worked into it. It requires a steady hand and sure touch to remove the effects of a few centuries of abuse from such a fragile thing as a dream.

By the time Kroll has finished spinning the raw materials into fine thread and dyeing them the proper colors, I have finished cleaning the dream and placed it in the handloom. As I work the treadles and guide the shuttle along its race, the loom's ancient rhythm fills me with the magic of the woof and the weave.

The loom's rhythm is that of the sea. It is the sound of the womb tides each mortal rides before birth. It is the rhythm of bodies as they create life. It is the sound of Making. It is as if I am listening to the beating of a giant's heart, and I allow myself to fall into a trance.

Whiteness. Pungent smells and frightening, bestial sounds that do not come from animals. A memory of pain. Dull, repetitive pain.

The vision is so sharp, so immediate, it startles me from my trance with an audible gasp. My first concern is for the dream I am working on. To my relief, I see that the restoration is a success. While the tapestry will never be mistaken for new, it is once more whole. The colors are a bit faded and the bloodstains are still visible, if one knows where to look, but it does not affect the overall impact. In a way, it serves to enhance the mystique. This is an old dream, but one with many years of use still in it.

Although I am still shaken by my vision, my hands do not tremble as I free the dream from the loom. I lay it out on the floor so I can get a better look at it. Kroll nods his head in admiration.

"Great job. Some of your best work yet, boss."

"Thank you, Kroll. I value your opinion on these matters."

Just then the tapestry flexes itself, like a cat in front of the fireplace. The figures woven into the dream begin moving and making noise. The lions roar, the djinni laugh, the armies clash their swords against their shields, the AK-47s fire celebratory bursts, while the helicopter gunships hum like giant dragonflies.

I nudge the dream with my boot tip. "There you go. You're free to return to your people."

The dream-tapestry wastes no time. It leaps into the air, flapping its outer edges like a manta ray cruising the sandy bottom of a lagoon. Like the bird-of-paradise before it, it slips through the open window and, within seconds, is well on its way home.

I clap my hands together and smile down at my assistant. "What do you say to knocking off for lunch, Kroll?"

"I'd say it's about bloody time."

I like to take my lunch on the window seat, looking out at the wondrous garden below. The garden, like everything else in Lord Morpheus's palace, changes from day to day. Sometimes it is a Japanese meditation garden, complete with elaborate designs raked into the sand, other times it is an English country garden. Once it was a topiary, and I distinctly recall the day it was a cactus grove. On this particular day it is a French garden, like the one at Versailles.

I look down on the neatly manicured grass and the regimented lines of trees and flowering shrubs as I eat my box lunch. The mingled fragrances of orange and cherry blossoms, of rosebushes and honeysuckle in full bloom tickle my nose, erasing the smell of human excrement my vision had summoned so vividly.

As I sip from my thermos of iced tea, I glimpse movement at the corner of my eye. Something dark and yet pale at the same time. Without thinking, I turn my head to look.

That's when I see them—a man and woman, each dressed in clothes black as the space between the stars, each with flesh as white as alabaster. The man is tall, gaunt—almost unhealthily so—outfitted in a long cape. His hair is dark and tousled, as if he has just left his bed.

The woman is shorter, not nearly as thin, wearing jeans and a cutaway tuxedo jacket, an undertaker's mourning derby atop her own unruly mane. The woman is talking, laughing, her hands clapping at some joke. The man looks preoccupied, his features dour. Although he is a stranger to me, there is a haunting familiarity to his features. With a start, I suddenly realize who I am looking at.

It's him.

After all this time—Has it been years? Decades? I cannot remember exactly when it was I became the Mender—I am finally looking upon the face of my master. The face of the Shaping Lord himself: Morpheus, he whom mortals know as Dream.

And if he is Lord Dream, it occurs to me, then the woman with him must be his elder sister, Lady Death.

Even as I think these thoughts, the pale woman turns her gaze from her brother. I glimpse her smile and the sign of the ankh that marks her right eye. Even though she has no way of knowing that I am sitting here, watching her, she smiles in my direction. She is beautiful. Possibly the most beautiful thing I have ever seen, or will ever see. I quickly look away.

Lunchtime is over. Time to get back to work.

I open the next job lot—this time the dream is in the form of a shattered Ming vase, decorated with heavenly storm dragons and good luck bats so stylized they resemble exotic flowers instead of animals. I try to focus on the job at hand, rearranging the broken pieces and mixing the necessary fixative to glue it back together, but I cannot shake the image of Death looking at me and smiling as if I were an old friend she was looking forward to chatting with.

Luckily the shattered dream-vase is not a difficult repair job. I find my mind wandering as I meticulously paste it back together with a brush made from the eyelash of a newborn camel.

Not for the first time, I wonder where it is I come from and go every day. By the time I am aware of my surroundings at the start of the day, I'm already well within the confines of the palace. And, as far as my memory is concerned, the moment I step over the threshold of the Restoration Department at the end of the day, everything goes blank.

I should be able to recall if I go home, relax with a beer, and tell my wife about my day. However, I don't even know if I *have* a home to go back to, much less a wife. I can remember what transpires within the walls of the palace perfectly well—but everything else remains a gray, amorphous mist. I don't even know where or how I came about my prodigious knowledge of the restoration and repair of dreams. It is as if with each working day I am born anew, like Athena leaping from Zeus's brow.

Only once in a while do I have bursts of—I hesitate to call it insight. Visions is a better word. Visions like the one I had earlier. They're always brief, always confusing, and seem to involve pain. Maybe I'm better off not knowing. I keep telling myself that. But I really don't believe it.

The rest of the day passes in a haze. I repair the dream-vase without a hitch, even though my heart is not really in it, and set about repairing a dream in the form of a medieval stained-glass window depicting the martyrdom of St. Sebastian. The saint's face has been eaten away by both man-made and natural forces, leaving the features indistinct. As hard as I try, I cannot replicate the saint's original appearance, so I substitute those of a young actor who died on the street. Aesthetically, it works.

I am surprised when the lights go off, blinking like an owl in the face of strong daylight. Kroll is standing there, his little green felt coat draped over one arm, regarding me oddly.

"Quitting time, boss."

"Oh. Yes. Of course." I get to my feet slowly, moving like an old man with winter in his bones.

Kroll is still watching me, frowning. "Boss—you okay? You seemed, I dunno, a little preoccupied today. You comin' down sick or something?"

"No. I'm fine, Kroll. I was just—thinking."

Kroll shoves his tiny, muscular arms into the sleeves of his coat, pulling peaked cap from his pocket and onto his head. "All that does is lead to trouble, if you ask me."

"Kroll—?"

"May I ask you a question?"

"Go ahead. Shoot."

"Where do you go?"

"Go?"

"You know. After work."

"I go to my quarters in the east wing. That's where most of us who aren't native to the Dreaming end up. I share my space with this pixie gal named Shian. She ain't stuck-up about my kind like those damn faerie-folk Lord Morpheus is so bleedin' fond of."

"She sounds—nice. I'm happy for you, Kroll."

"'S funny, you askin' me that."

"What do you mean?"

"The old Mender, the one before you—used to ask me things like that."

"He did?"

"*She.* The Mender before you was a woman."

"Oh."

"See you tomorrow, boss." With that, Kroll opens the door and disappears into the corridor.

I stare at the door for a long time. It is time to leave. The windows are darkened, the lights are off, the vast cavern of the Restoration Department empty. It is time for me to go home. But to what?

Taking a deep breath, I open the door and prepare to step into the gray nothing that has claimed me every day for as long as I can remember. But, as my foot crosses the threshold, I find myself not in limbo but still in the halls of the palace.

The corridors look different after dark—more sinister and treacherous than during the workday. It's as if the palace can tell that I am not supposed to be here and has altered itself to reflect this. Although I have worked in this place for as long as I can remember, I have rarely strayed beyond the Restoration Department. I know there are countless others in service to the King of Dreams because Kroll is fond of relating palace gossip, and I occasionally catch glimpses of the various courtiers, courtesans, and servants from the windows overlooking the garden. But, during all this time, I have never dealt with anyone but my trollish assistant.

As I round a corner I collide with a tall, gangly figure, knocking him to the ground. To my amazement, it is not a man but an animated scarecrow, its limbs made of wood and draped in a baggy pair of overalls. In place of a head is a pumpkin carved to resemble a jack-o'-lantern, a lit cigarette held between its jagged lips. Next to where it's sprawled is a bucket of soapy water with an industrial string mop stuck in it.

"Hey, buster! Wanna watch were yer goin'?" the scarecrow snaps. "Y'coulda smashed m' noggin', and I just carved it two days ago!"

I help the scarecrow back to its feet. "I-I'm terribly sorry, Mister, uh—?"

"Mervyn. Just Mervyn," says the pumpkinhead, taking a drag on its cigarette. The smoke fills its hollow skull and seeps out through the eyeholes. "I'm the janitor around here. And who might you be? I don't recollect seein' you before. . . ."

"I am the Mender of Broken Dreams."

Mervyn's carved features somehow take on the approximation of surprise. "So *you're* the Mender, eh? I've heard Kroll go on about you! What are you doin' out and about at this hour?"

The words come out before I realize what I'm saying. "I'm looking for Lord Morpheus."

Mervyn's jack-o'-lantern countenance grimaces even more than I thought possible. "Are y'sure y'wanna do that, pal? I mean, the boss is an okay guy, as immortal manifestations of power go, but he's a little, uh, standoffish. Y'just don't go lookin' for him, if y'get m'drift."

"It's very important that I talk to him."

Mervyn shrugs and points down the hallway. "You'll find the throne room down this hall and to the right. At least that's where it was a half hour ago. Nothing's in the same place from day t'day around here anyways, but he's especially fond of movin' the damn throne room every time the mood hits him."

"Thank you, Mervyn! Thank you very much!"

The scarecrow simply shrugs and returns to mopping the polished onyx floor. With every swipe of the mop the floor turns from onyx to sparkling sapphire. "'S'yer funeral, Mac."

The throne room is still where Mervyn said it was. The great doors fashioned of horn, five times the height of a man, carved with the symbols of dreams, are shut. No palace guards stand ready, nor is there any sign of a majordomo or page who could announce me. Timidly, I move to rap on the door, only to have it open before me. From the darkness beyond the threshold there comes a voice, both frightening and familiar. It is a voice from my dreams.

"Enter, Mender. You are very much welcome here."

The doors swing inward, and I step inside the throne room, feeling very small and naked and vulnerable. "L-lord Morpheus?"

The Shaper of Dreams lolls on his throne of horn, watching me with the casual interest a child gives to a shiny-backed beetle. He is still dressed in black, although his clothing is casual to the brink of insult: threadbare jeans, a French-cut T-shirt, and square-toed motorcycle boots.

"You would speak with me, Mender?"

"Y-yes, milord." As I approach the throne I'm astounded at how young he is. Until I look into his eyes. Only there is one reminded that this is the Third Born of the Endless, younger brother to Destiny and Death, a being old beyond human measure. "There is something I must know—something I believe only you can explain."

"And what is your question?"

"What am I?"

The slightest of smiles touches the lips of the Shaper of Dreams. "You have served me well, Mender. Your skill at repairing even the most abused and sullied of dreamstuff is a marvel, even to me. Your work pleases me, Mender. And for that, I shall grant you a boon and answer your question."

"Thank you, milord!"

Morpheus rises from his throne, the shadows pooling about his shoulders to form a cape. "Do not be so quick with your thanks, Mender," he sighs. "Come. Follow me."

Together we walk down a long, dark hallway, toward a distant light. Although Morpheus is slight in build, he radiates the presence of a monarch secure in his power. He glances down at me, his deep-set eyes unreadable.

"Before I answer your question, there is one I would pose; what do *you* think you are, Mender?"

"Since I can never remember where I come from and where I go at the end of my work, I think I must be a dream of some kind. Am I right?"

"Most astute, Mender. You are correct. Does that bother you?"

"What?"

"Being a dream. Does it bother you?"

I frown, rubbing my chin. "I don't know. I guess I should be—I mean, if I'm a dream, that means I'm not real, right?"

Morpheus laughs then, startling me. When he laughs his eyes almost belie their age. "My dear Mender! Surely you, most of all, know that dreams possess a reality all their own! In many cases, they are far more substantial than the dreamers themselves!"

He points a chalk-white finger at a wall, which ripples like water. "Every human born has the keys to my kingdom within them. For many the Dreaming is simply a place to escape the pressures of being mortal. For a handful of poets and madmen it is the land of portents, signs, and inspiration. But for others, it is the one place where true happiness can be found; where beggars ride as kings, the spurned find love, the hungry feast."

The rippling wall steadies, becomes a looking glass. In it a heroically muscled man dressed in a loincloth hacks away at a three-headed dragon.

"The brave warrior you're watching is a computer systems analyst from Passaic, New Jersey," Morpheus informs me. He snaps his fingers and the sword-wielding computer nerd is replaced by a vision of Marilyn Monroe, circa "Diamonds Are a Girl's Best Friend." She is surrounded by a squadron of horny young men clad only in white gloves and formal bow ties, each burdened with bouquets, jewelry cases, heart-shaped chocolate boxes, and rock-hard erections. Marilyn coos and bats her eyes appreciatively at such evidence of lust and adoration. "This dreamer is a preoperative transsexual in Dallas, Texas. There are millions upon millions of other such dream sequences I could show you—all the same, all different. But of all these billions of dreamers, few have spawned dreams substantial enough to become a member of my palace staff. Do you understand what I'm telling you, Mender?"

I feel twin surges of pride and anxiety swell within me. "I-I think so, milord."

Morpheus points to the light at the end of the hallway, now uncomfortably close. "Would the dream like to see the dreamer? I have the power to enter the Waking World when and where I so choose."

We step from the Dreaming into the Waking World side by side, as if traversing dimensional barriers is of no more import than walking into the backyard. And, I guess, for him that might very well be the case.

Whiteness.

My vision from earlier comes rushing back to haunt me, filling my eyes with white glare, clogging my nose with the smell of urine and feces. Instinctively, I shield my face. Gently, Lord Morpheus takes my hands and pulls them away from my face.

The blinding whiteness strobes then fades. I find myself staring at the white walls of what is obviously an institution of some sort, lit by a bare bulb held in a wire cage. The smell of piss and shit comes from the narrow bed against the wall. On the bed, curled in on itself like a giant fetus, is a human.

Morpheus says nothing as I draw closer to the bed, inspecting the creature lying on the mattress. It looks to be a man. No. A boy. Naked except for an adult diaper, the dirty blond hair cropped painfully short. I notice that the sleeper's wrists and ankles are bound to the bed by restraints made from torn sheets. I also notice the bruises along his rib cage and the scars, scabs, and lumps on the back of his head.

"Why is he tied up?"

"He is indifferent to those around him and does not react to pain or recognize true danger. When he is conscious he has a tendency to repetitive physical motion—such as butting his head against the wall. The restraints are for his protection—and the convenience of the nursing staff.

"The boy is autistic." Morpheus's voice is soft and sad. "Something happened to him as he was forming within his mother's womb that affected his cerebellum and limbic system, effectively sealing him away from the reality of the world he was born into. He has lived in a world of his own making since the moment of his birth."

"You mean he's never been awake?"

"I mean that the Dreaming and the Waking World are one and the same for him. He was born into dreams and shall die in them. But the spawn of such a dreamer are not those of the average mortal. Their dreams are far more potent. Far more . . . real.

"All the Menders who have ever served me were born of similar dreamers. The Mender before you was an elderly woman who suffered from Alzheimer's disease. I do not know why it is, but the dreams of damaged minds all possess a genius for repairing that which is broken."

I shake my head in confusion. I cannot take it in. Part of me simply does not want to. "Is *this* what I really am? An incontinent idiot locked inside his own mind?"

"My dear Mender—you may very well ask if *you* are what *he* really is."

"Is there no cure for him, then?" I move to touch the slumbering boy's head, but Morpheus stays my hand. His touch is cold, but not unpleasantly so.

"No. Not in this lifetime. Unless a scientist somewhere in the world outside this horrid room has the strength and inspiration to make a dream come true. Come, let us go. You have seen enough."

As we return to the darkly glowing portal in the middle of the wall, I notice my dreamer's eyes tracking us behind closed lids.

I am the Mender of Broken Dreams.

I take dreams that have been shattered, abused, twisted, and bent by the ravages of harsh reality and repair them as best I can, so they may return to their rightful owners. Restoration work is my calling. My genius, if you will.

I start each day by walking the long halls of the castle of my prince, whom the mortals call Dream. I still have no memories of what I do or where I go before and after work, but it no longer bothers me. I know that I am a dream, and that is enough self-knowledge.

At first Lord Morpheus feared that by revealing the circumstances of my creation, I would go mad—as the Mender before me did, or so I'm told—and try to uncreate myself. But that has not been the case.

I realize that I, unlike the more powerful dreams—the one Lord Morpheus refers to as *tropes* and *archetypes*—am finite. But I do not allow my mortality to worry me. I am determined to make the best use of the time I have allotted to me, whatever that span may be. If I am to find immortality, it will have to be in the souls of those whose dreams I have rescued and returned to them. And perhaps, when the time comes, and a beautiful, pale woman dressed in black comes to embrace a skinny boy with a shaven skull tied to a bed, and escorts him to the place that waits beyond the white walls, perhaps then I will discover if the dream can outlive the dreamer.

AIN'T YOU 'MOST DONE?

Gene Wolfe

Gene Wolfe is one of our finest living authors. He wrote my favorite modern novel (it's called *Peace*), one of my favorite science fiction novels (it's called *The Book of the New Sun*), and he is two books into one of my favorite historical novels (the books are *Soldier of the Mist* and *Soldier of Arete*).

The critic and encyclopedist John Clute described Gene Wolfe as "Sergeant Bilko as Aslan" (by which he meant Phil Silvers and not, of course, Steve Martin).

Here he tells a story of dreams: the ones we have when we sleep, and the ones that power us during the day. Of dreams, and of redemption.

The hot pink dragster had not moved in a minute and a half. It seemed like five; but Benson was careful and accurate in all matters involving time, and it had been one minute and a half. He shifted the transmission into PARK and took his foot off the brake. One and a half minutes— ninety seconds—was a long time. In ninety seconds flat, no more, a skilled man in one of the company's seventeen hundred Magus Muffler and Brake Shops could prep a car for the installation of a new tailpipe, a new exhaust pipe, and a brand-new Magus Muffler—copper, nickel, and chrome plated in successive layers and guaranteed for as long as the customer retained title to the car on which it was installed.

In seven more seconds, the time would be two minutes.

A small carrying case on the rear seat held sixty-four of his favorite compact discs. Benson reached in back for it, got it, and opened it, removing a collection of nineteenth-century sea songs.

The dragster's brake lights faded, and he shifted his car into DRIVE. He had counted on an hour, possibly an hour and a half, at his office before the helicopter that would fly him to the airport arrived. Now he would be lucky to get ten minutes. The dragster crawled forward, and his car with it; when both stopped again, they had traversed perhaps fifty feet.

He returned the transmission to PARK and put the CD into the dashboard player. His back and neck hurt, presumably from the tension induced by this endless delay, and the pain was creeping down both arms. He would have to learn to relax.

Oh, the smartest clipper that you can find,
A-hee, a-ho, ain't you 'most done?
Is the *Marg'ret Evans* of the Blue Cross Line,
So clear the deck and let the bulgine run!
To me hey rig-a-jig in a low-back car,
A-hee, a-ho, ain't you 'most done?

Benson could play that himself, and sing it, too. Play and sing it pretty well, not that anybody cared. He pictured himself seated on the tarred hatch-cover of a transatlantic packet with his guitar on his lap and a villainous black stogie smoldering between thumb and forefinger, ringed by delighted sailors and passengers.

The brake lights of the dragster glowed as obstinately red as ever. Wouldn't that fool kid ever make it easy on himself? Benson let his head loll to one side, then the other, rolling it upon his shoulders.

Oh the *Marg'ret Evans* of the Blue Cross Line,
A-hee, a-ho, ain't you 'most done?
She's never a day behind the times . . .

If things had gone differently, perhaps he, too, would be making CDs and giving concerts, appearing occasionally on TV, consulted by authorities on folk music who would want to know where he had learned this song or that and from whom he had learned it: seamen's songs and rivermen's songs, songs sung by lumberjacks and Civil War soldiers.

With Liza Lee upon my knee, oh!
So clear the track and let the bulgine run!

He was making ten times more than he could possibly have made like that, but money wasn't everything; in fact, once you had food and clothes, a warm place to sleep and a few hundred pocket money, more money meant very little.

One of the dragster's brake lights had gone out, or perhaps the two had flowed together, condensing into a single cyclops light belonging to a newer car. Sweat trickled down Benson's forehead into his eyes. The air-conditioning was already set on MAX, but he moved the fan control up to HIGH, conscious of increased pain under his breastbone where his stomach joined the esophagus. Acid indigestion. He tried to recall what he had eaten for breakfast. Ham? No, the ham had been on Sunday.

When I come home across the sea,
A-hee, a-ho, ain't you 'most done?
It's Liza, will you marry me?
So clear the track and let the bulgine run!

To me hey rig-a-jig in a low-back car,
A-hee, a-ho, ain't you 'most done?

Benson blinked and closed his eyes, after one hundred and twenty-three seconds blinked a second time, aware of weakness and pain. He lay on his back; something had been thrust into both nostrils; the ceiling was off-white and very remote.

Wires clung to him like leeches.

After a time that was neither long nor short so far as he was concerned, a nurse appeared at his side. "You had a close call," she said.

He was not sure what she meant. It seemed best to keep quiet.

"You're awake, aren't you, Mister Benson?" She looked at him more closely. "This is real. You're not dreaming."

He managed to say, "I never dream."

"Really?" She turned to scrutinize what appeared to be an oscilloscope.

"I daydream. Of course." He tried to smile, although he was aware that she was not looking at him. "Much too much, I'm afraid . . . " Talking was no longer worth the effort.

Still not looking at him, but not looking now (he thought) so that she would not have to see his expression, the nurse said, "You've had a heart attack, a bad one. Probably you've already figured that out for yourself."

"It seemed the most likely explanation." Privately, he was relieved. It was better to know the truth, to be sure. People survived heart attacks and lived for years. Decades in some cases.

"But you've come through it." The nurse turned to face him. "You're going to be all right."

"Thank you," he said.

"You're a very important man."

Under the circumstances, that seemed humorous. Smiling took little effort this time.

"We've had all sorts of people phoning and trying to get in to see you."

He could easily imagine what it had been like. He said, "I apologize."

"Oh, it's okay, we're used to it. But for the present, only family members, and no calls. It's for your own good."

She bustled away, stopping in the doorway to ask, "You really don't dream? Ever?"

"No," he murmured. He tried to make his voice stronger, strong enough to carry to her. "Not even when I was a child. I can't imagine what it's like, to tell you the truth."

She regarded him skeptically.

"Like hallucinating, I suppose." He had not thought of this before. "But I've never done that either."

"Everyone dreams, Mister Benson. It's just that sometimes the unconscious mind tells us to forget, cuts us off from it."

I don't, he said, but the words never reached his lips—she had left too fast.

If she was right, he reflected, somewhere in his memory there was a vast reservoir of unremembered dreams; he searched for it, but it was not there.

A touch woke him. The same nurse was bending over his bed. "Mister Benson?"

He blinked. "Would you do me a favor, Nurse? A great favor?"

That surprised her. "Certainly, if I can."

"Call me Tim."

Involuntarily, she glanced at the door. "It says Otis Benson. That's the name we have you down under."

It brought back a book that Michael had liked when Michael was young. Benson told her, "Winnie the Pooh lived in a hollow tree in the woods under the name Sanders." It was easy to smile now. "Or at least, I think it was Sanders."

She smiled, too. "That's right. I read that to my little nephew."

"I," he tried to clear his throat, "on the other hand, have lived under the name Otis Benson. My real name is Timothy Otis Benson. I dropped the Timothy a long time ago."

"I see." As though unsure what to say, she added, "My name's Ruth. You can call me that if you want to, Tim."

"I will, Ruth. My mother called me Tim. Tiny Tim. I'd like to be Tim again."

"I understand. Tim, your daughter's here to see you. I said I'd see if you were strong enough. Are you? We won't let her stay long."

Benson, who had no daughter, said, "Of course I am. Send her in," and watched the doorway with some interest after the nurse had gone.

It was Daisy, and before she came in he had discovered an armless chair of enameled metal beside his bed. As he tried to decide whether the sorrow in her face was genuine he said, "I thought it was you. Won't you sit down?"

She did, knees primly together, hands folded in the lap her salient chest clearly prevented her from seeing. After a second or two, it occurred to him that she was dressed for the office, and he asked her what time it was.

She raised her left hand to consult the diamond-studded watch he had given her. "Seven o'clock."

"In the evening?"

She nodded. "We didn't hear until three—after three. I left when I heard. I left everything in an awful mess, but I left. I told Susan to—to take care of things, and I left. The traffic was terrible."

He said, "I remember." A tall, pale-faced man in black had entered without making a sound. An orderly of some sort, Benson thought, although he did not look like an orderly.

"You were there in your car for more than an hour—this is what they said on the radio—while the traffic crawled around you. I listened while I drove over here, while I was stuck in traffic."

And cried, as Benson saw. Her eyes were red, but it was probably better to pretend he had not noticed. He had always been angry when Daisy cried, never imagining that someday she might cry for him.

"People had been calling on their car phones to complain. They said there was an abandoned car, and finally a tow truck got there, and the driver called an ambulance."

She sighed, and her shoulders slumped. "I guess they drove on the shoulder when they could. That's the way they do, but it still took a long, long time. A terribly long time. Then it was the president and CEO of Magus, Otis Benson. And when I heard I thought, I thought . . . "

"You thought what?" He was genuinely curious, and sensed that she would tell him the truth now.

"I thought, I don't care what anybody says, I'm going, and I'm going to wear black, everything black and a veil." For an instant, her reddened eyes flashed. "Then I thought, nobody will say anything. The loyal secretary coming to the boss's funeral, how nice. Mister Wilson will pat me on the shoulder. I know he will." Her voice rose to a wail. "Oh, Benny! Don't die. Please don't die!"

She should not have called him *Benny* in the presence of the silent man in black, but Benson could not bring himself to rebuke her. "I won't," he said. "I won't." His groping hand found hers.

The prettiest secretary in the company, and when he had reached the top he had taken her, although she was by no means the best secretary or the best typist. She had been a badge, a trophy, letting everybody know that he was in charge, that the board was in his pocket, that what he said went, and there had better be no arguments and no foot-dragging—one trophy among a great many. Susan, who had been his secretary when he was first vice president and sales manager, became his executive assistant at twice her old salary, handling everything tricky, confidential, or sensitive. Daisy had typed a few letters and memos, had brought him coffee and emptied the ashtrays and opened the mail each morning.

And then—

"So I showed them my fake ID that says Daisy Benson," she was saying, "and they let me come up."

He managed to nod. She had that odd old-fashioned streak, worrying about hotels that had ceased to worry about couples fifty years ago, wearing gloves in the lobby or slipping the star sapphire he had given her onto the ring finger of her left hand. Lying in the hospital bed and only half-hearing her, he understood for the first time that she had found satisfaction in that, had liked to think of the sapphire ring as a wedding ring, had fantasized about it. She was still talking, but he interrupted her. "What kind of a ceremony do you want, Daisy?"

"You mean your . . . ?" She stared blankly, the pinkish lids of her wide, bloodshot eyes moving slowly down, and slowly up again. "What?"

"What kind of wedding? You must have thought about it. What kind would you like?"

"We didn't have a real wedding."

For a moment he actually thought that she meant the two of them, that she was reminding him of something he had forgotten.

"Just at the courthouse."

The nurse appeared in the doorway. "You'll have to leave now, Miss Benson."

Reluctantly Daisy rose, letting go of his hand. "At the Consort. Please?"

"All right," he told her. "Soon as I get out of here."

She blew him a kiss from the doorway, and he smiled and shut his eyes. He had wanted to keep Michael's estate safe for him, had wanted to avoid the entanglements of a divorce he had considered only too likely. All of that seemed childish now. Perhaps she really loved him—perhaps she didn't. He loved her, and that was what mattered.

When he opened his eyes again, the tall man in black was standing over him. He had the whitest face Benson had ever seen—so white that he seemed practically transparent. "I'm awake," Benson told him.

"I know you are."

"What is it you want? Do you have to change the bed or something?"

"You have been wronged." The man in black spoke slowly, in a loud whisper. "You would say shortchanged. I have come to set things right."

Benson shut his eyes again. No doubt he was entitled to some hospital amenity that he was not receiving, a TV in his room or an evening snack.

"You have never dreamed."

He had told someone about it not long ago; perhaps it had been this tall man in black. The darkness he saw with his eyes closed was the tall man's black clothing. He had never known it, yet it did not seem strange.

Far off, in a palace beyond the universe, the man in black said, "You will dream now, Timothy Otis Benson, for as long as may be."

He sat up. He had lain down, apparently, on the front seat of his car. Drunk? He hadn't been drunk since college.

Something fell from the seat with a melodious clang, and he bent to pick it up.

It looked like a guitar yet unlike one, too, a tinny affair someone with more skill than sense had made from one of his mufflers and a section of tailpipe, guitarlike but given the S-shaped sound holes of a violin.

Turning it over, he verified that it was in fact (as he had supposed from the first moment he saw it) made from a Magus muffler; Magus's clouded moon was stamped boldly on what was now the back, although the trade name itself, which should have appeared there in capital letters, was missing.

As were the sensuous curves of a real guitar, or for that matter a real violin. This—his questing thumb woke a chord from the five silver strings—was as plain and straight-sided as any prepubescent girl.

How did the song go?

"Little Missy Riddle,
Haul 'em away."

He had meant only to mutter the words, but their old magic overcame him at once; his voice echoed from the windows and the windshield, in some fashion transmuted to mellow gold.

"Little Missy Riddle,
Haul 'em away.
She broke her brand-new fiddle,
Haul 'em away.
Got a hole right up the middle!
Haul 'em away,
To me holly heigh ho!"

Benson grinned as he ducked beneath the Magus-guitar's thin strap. Could you really play this thing?

"Little Missy Taylor,
Haul 'em away.
Said she'd never love a sailor,
Haul 'em away.
She's been harpooned by a whaler!
Haul 'em away,
To me holly heigh ho!"

He had never played, never sung, half so well; moved by innocent vanity, he looked around to see whether anyone had been listening.

Cars, trucks, and buses surrounded him, motionless in the slanting rays of a brighter sun. No brake light glowed crimson now, no exhaust fouled the clear air.

Here in his car that air was warm and musty, and growing warmer. He depressed a switch in the armrest to put down his window, but the glass remained where it was. Turning the key kindled no instrument lights, woke no sleeping tiger in the engine.

He opened the door and got out. Morning was fresh and beautiful, and ghostly in its silence save for the barking of a small dog far off. A jet-black cat with eyes like emeralds blinked at him, spit, and retreated beneath a rusty minivan.

Before and behind him, the sixteen lanes of Interstate 75 stretched as far as he could see, eight north, eight south. Every lane was filled, and every bumper touched another.

He turned back, remembering that he had left his key in the ignition; but he had locked the door behind him, or it had locked itself. There were no keys in the pockets of the worn work pants he wore, no money, no driver's license, no credit cards, and no handkerchief.

"I'm broke and I ain't got a dime,
Everybody gets hard luck sometime."

He had not meant to play, but the low-down blues notes stole out of the Magus-guitar, possessed by a will of their own.

"Mama don't treat your daughter mean,
That's the meanest woman that ever I seen."

The door of a station wagon several cars up the lane swung open and a sleepy-eyed woman in a threadbare housedress got out. Thinking she might be offended, he switched songs.

"Woke up this mornin' with the blues round my bed.
Yep, woke up this mornin' with blues round my bed.
Went to eat breakfast, got blues in my bread."

The woman called, "You hungry?" and started toward him.

"Good mornin', Blues, how d'ye do?
Good mornin', Blues, how d'ye do?
Feelin' good, Partner. How 'bout you?"

Nearer now, the woman repeated, "You hungry?"
Benson shook his head.
"We got a few little somethings left over from last night. The chowchopper come last night."
"I'm really not hungry," Benson told her. "I just hope my singing didn't disturb you."
The woman smiled, and at once the smile made her younger and almost attractive. "I was just layin' there in our car awake, thinkin'. You sure can sing. I never heard nobody on the radio better'n what you are. Not near as good."
"Thank you," Benson said.
"They don' play music much, and ain't good when they do. Maybe you'd play me just one song?"
"If it won't wake people up."
Another car door opened; the man who got out said, "Go ahead. Nobody's goin' to complain."
"A love song," the woman said, and Benson nodded.

"As I was a-walking down Strawberry Lane,
Where the roses grow pretty and fine,
I happened to meet a merry, fair maid,
That would be a lover of mine. . . ."

By the time the song was finished, there were ten or more ragged people around him, some awed, many smiling. Someone shouted, "Another song!" seconded at once by the woman, "Play another one, won't you?"

Benson winked at the nearest man and began it.

"I'm a lonely bush-whacker on the Reed County Line,
I can lick any bastard, yokes one ox o' mine.
If ever I catch him, you bet that I'll try,
I'll lick him with the ox-bow,
Root, hog, or die!

"Git out upon that lonely road,
Crack your whip 'n haul your load,
Whip 'em, boys, and holler,
Yell and cuss 'em 'til you're dry,
It's whack them cattle on, boys.
Root, hog, or die!"

Benson glanced around him. He had fifty listeners now, perhaps a hundred. As he launched into the third verse, he told himself firmly that he should play no more than three songs for them. It was better—far better—to get off stage while you were still welcome, still being applauded with honest enthusiasm. He would count "Strawberry Lane" as the first, this as the second.

"Sing another like that 'un!" a man in the crowd called when he had finished.

Benson shook his head. "There are no more like that."

"Sing a good one," the man he had winked at said. "You know what you got."

"Shenando' " seemed the only possible choice. He began to walk before he finished the first verse, afraid at first that they would follow him, and fearful that they would not.

And when the last was sung, and the last of those who had, had dropped behind him, the Magus-guitar sang still, murmuring the haunting melody of the wooded Eastern river and the cruel, hot, Western flood men had once called the Big Muddy, a mile wide and an inch deep, too thick to drink and too thin to plow, relentlessly rolling to the Gulf of Mexico.

"Where are you goin', Mister?" a boy shouted.

"Moving on," Benson told him, and sang "The Wayfaring Stranger" for him, and then walked on as he had promised.

Where was he going, and where had he been? Once he had sold franchises for a company that was to all intents and purposes a fraud. Bit by bit, he had made the thing real, providing the training that had been promised, upgrading the cheap and sleazy replacement parts, arranging—it had been his one stroke of genius—to sell stock to the franchisees, and welding them, his people, into the force with which he had seized control.

It seemed a very long time ago, something he had worried about once but need worry about no longer. For a moment he paused to study his reflection in the window of a big, black, limolike vehicle, a window cleaner than most.

He looked as he had always supposed himself to look. A tickle from the back of his mind reminded him, for a moment only, that of late he had not looked like that—had been shocked, in fact, each time he saw his own face in a mirror. He turned away, and the tickle ceased.

He was going to marry somebody again, marry a woman he loved, he felt sure, though he could not lay hand to her name at the moment. She would be pleased, whoever she was, to see him looking so young. Or anyway to see him no longer looking old.

"Can you play that thing?" a man much younger than he asked.

Benson nodded. "I'll play you a song, and sing it too, if you'll stroll along with me."

The young man hesitated, then grinned. "One song? That shouldn't be very far. They can't get too mad if you just walk for one song."

"Ah," Benson said, wondering who "they" were.

"'Sides, if you play like most others I've heard, one song ought to be enough. Maybe too much."

"This is the way I play," Benson told him, and his fingers (almost carelessly, it seemed to him) called forth the melody of "Londonderry Air."

"Say," the young man croaked when the last note had faded, "you're good. You're real good." He sounded almost reverent.

"Thank you," Benson said. "It's a good tune, though. So good that some have called it the most beautiful ever written. It's hard to go wrong with a tune like that if you can play it at all."

"You said you'd sing, though. You didn't sing."

"That was before you implied that the way I played one song would be more than enough," Benson explained. "Since it was my playing you'd questioned, I let you hear that. Nothing compels me to sing for people who don't like my music."

"Are you going to sing now?" the young man asked. "I'll come along."

"No," Benson told him, and walked on, a little upset with himself at first, but soon feeling oddly at peace.

He had walked two miles if not more before he understood the feeling. He was at peace because he had been given what, in the depths of his soul, he had always wanted. It was an article of faith with many people that what one wants is never enough when one achieves it.

But that was only because so many—himself included—enjoyed the chase, the struggle, the pursuit of some distant goal. Mountain climbers, when they had at length conquered the peak that had frustrated their efforts for months or years, went looking for more difficult heights. Not because they were insatiable, but because they enjoyed pitting their courage and their skills against Nature.

He had liked pitting himself against Business, had liked being more duplicitous than the crooks, cheating them as they had cheated others, enjoyed beating the corporate politicians at corporate politics—then striking down those who tried to play politics with him.

All that was true; but underneath it, he had longed for this, had longed to be a simple man living among simple people, seeing their faces glow when he sang the old songs. He had been in a hospital; he was quite sure that he remembered that. Someone must have given him this to cure him.

As it had.

The persistent *whick-whick-whick* of a helicopter sounded in the distance. It drew scores of people from cars to look at it, and point, and shout to one another. Benson stopped to look, too, shading his eyes with his hand. It was a big one, as large as the largest military helicopter he had ever seen, but slate blue or blue-gray, not the desert camouflage of the United States Army.

It slowed as it passed overhead, then settled, almost but not quite landing. Men ran to it, queuing up to form a line that soon stretched twenty or thirty yards between the motionless lines of rusty cars and trucks. Benson joined them.

Glancing behind him, he saw hundreds of women and children falling into line in back of the men. A barefoot young woman, a lanky blonde of perhaps seventeen, dashed past him and was admitted to the line by a young man who might profitably have pursued a career in professional football. There was a rumble of complaint, soon stilled.

"Should be eggs today," the man standing behind Benson said happily.

Benson nodded his agreement. Far ahead, flat white boxes about eight inches by eight were being passed out by the crew of the helicopter, together with . . . He strained his eyes.

Men who had been at the front of the line were drifting back now, some eating from the flat boxes they carried, more drinking from clear, squat bottles that were distorted by the pressure of their fingers.

"Hope we get there 'fore the water runs out," the man behind Benson said.

"I'd like a nice drink of water myself," Benson admitted.

"They ought to take as many waters as cracker boxes," the man continued bitterly. "They never do. Water's cheaper, too, only they don't like to bring it."

"It's heavier, I imagine," Benson said.

The man ahead of him turned to stare back at him. "What's that got to do with it? It's just water."

"Weight limits the amount of cargo that a helicopter can carry," Benson explained. "The size of the fuselage is just a matter of convenience, really. Capacity is determined by the power of the engines and the configurations of the rotors."

The man behind him asked, "You from hereabouts?"

"From this city?" For a half a second, Benson considered. "Why, yes, I suppose I am. At least—"

The fist of the man behind him caught him just below the ribs, sending him staggering forward. Something struck the side of his head, and something else, presumably a kick, the side of one knee. He fell, dropping the Magus-guitar. Shod and booted feet attacked him like a flock of birds. He rolled, covering his head with his arms, his legs drawn up to protect his belly.

Someone sprawled on top of him. He gasped and struggled before realizing that the body above his was not that of a new attacker. Overhead, in the lofty space occupied by those who still stood, a woman said, "Don't get him," and a man: "That's enough! Hold on!"

The protecting body vanished. Benson coughed and spit, wondering how badly he had been hurt. There was no blood in his spittle—or if there was, the dust in his eyes kept him from seeing it.

They were still talking above his head. A new voice, a boy's or a very young man's, said, "I guess he didn't know. I ought to have told him." Was that the young man for whom he had played "Londonderry Air"? Benson tried to get to his feet, and succeeded in getting to his knees.

Someone nudged his arm with a booted foot, saying, "You. Get up."

He did, finding that he could stand although his legs were shaky.

"You get back there to the end." It was the hulking young man who had allowed the lanky blonde to join him in line.

Benson nodded, still too dazed to speak. Magically, it seemed, the Magus-guitar was in his hands as before.

"Come on." This was a new young man, short and slight. "You made that out of a muffler, didn't you?"

Benson cleared his throat and spit again.

"I never seen one like that."

He managed to nod. "A replacement muffler." He came very near to adding that it was one of his, one of his company's. He really had made that muffler, in a sense, although not as an instrument.

"You cut those fancy holes with a li'l file? There's a man by us had a file." The young man himself was grasping what seemed to be a hubcap with a dozen wires strung across it, a rude harp or lyre.

Benson contrived to say something suitable.

"It get busted? I'd like to hear it."

Dusting his hands, he spat again. "I owe you a lot more than that." He offered to shake hands, conscious that his own was soiled, but conscious, too, that the one it would be shaking would be soiled at least as badly. "I'm Tim Benson."

The young man's hand was small, but surprisingly hard and muscular. "Aldo Berry. We both of us play, an' we both got names with a *B*."

They had come to the end of the line, the place marked by a bedraggled child who said, "You won't neither get nothin'. Me neither." Her small face was sad and resigned.

"What's your name?" Benson asked her. "You know ours, if you were listening. I'm Tim and he's Aldo. Who are you?"

"B' neice."

"How old are you, B'neice?"

"Ber-nice!"

Benson was so involved with his thoughts that he scarcely heard her. This young man, Aldo, was presumably a musician of some kind; that explained his rushing to the aid of a stranger—the age-old sympathy of one performer for another. And now his rescuer wanted him to play.

Unbidden, his fingers caressed the strings, evoking for perhaps the millionth time since its composition the old Irish melody.

"The minstrel boy to the war is gone,
In the ranks of death you'll find him,
His father's sword he has girded on,
And his wild harp slung behind him. . . ."

Aldo opened his mouth to speak, gulped, stammered, and at last managed to say, "You got to learn me."

Benson sighed. Had he ever been this young? Yes. Yes, of course. He tried to say that he had very little of value to teach anyone—that what he really needed was courage like the boy's own, adding, "You play and sing yourself, don't you? You implied a moment ago that you did."

Aldo nodded hesitantly, accepting a limp slice of bacon from one of the men "The Minstrel Boy" had attracted.

"May I try your instrument? You may try mine, if you like."

The exchange completed, Benson ran his fingertips across Aldo's strings; A-sharp was a shade flat, and he tightened it. Someone handed him a pastry dotted with nutmeats; to free his hands, he gave it to the child.

He had never so much as touched even a modern harp, and he remembered reading somewhere that it was the most difficult of all the stringed instruments; this primitive harp of Aldo's, with its very limited range, should be much easier—more like a mandolin than a modern pedal harp. The question was whether even an approximation of real music could be coaxed from it.

The opening notes of "Shenando'" sounded thin and poor. He would have to reinforce them with their harmonics, plainly, and fill between them like a jazz pianist.

He tried again.

"Oh Shenando' I long to hear you,
Away, you rolling river . . . "

Still pretty bad. He made a third attempt, at first only half-singing the lyric.

"Oh Shenando' I long to hear you,
Away, you rolling river."
Oh Shenando' I long to hear you.
Away, I'm bound away,
Across the wide Missouri . . . "

This time a chance-caught spell among the dancing, tinny notes showed him the river as the composer of that song had seen it, the enchanted gateway to freedom, to adventure and riches, a call stronger than home or honor or any woman. Like the river itself, the song carried everything before it.

"Oh Shenando' I love your daughter,
Roll away, you rolling river.
Oh Shenando' I'm bound to leave her,
Away, I'm bound away,
Across the wide Missouri!"

There were deafening cheers, applause greater than he had ever imagined in his most self-indulgent moments.

Later, as they walked beside a motionless Greyhound bus, Aldo offered him a slab of flatbread. He took it and nibbled tentatively, troubled by the feeling that once he had eaten in this strange place he would become as desperately hungry as the rest of its inhabitants.

"Don't bite down hard," Aldo warned him, " 'less you got good teeth."

Swallowing the morsel he had succeeded in gnawing free, Benson ventured a remark about saliva softening it.

"Or water, if you got a bottle." Aldo appeared troubled; by silence, Benson encouraged him to speak.

"There's the off-road way an' then there's the free way, Tim. We're the freewayers, but you're an off-roader, ain't you? I won't tell."

They talked about that for a time—not about the world beyond Interstate 75, in which Aldo seemed to have very little interest, but about the freewayers, the people like Aldo himself, squatters who lived in their cars waiting for the hand-drawn carts that brought them gasoline, compressed air, and sometimes water, and for the helicopters that brought food and clothing. "It's your clothes," Aldo told him. "Off-roader clothes. You turn them in, Ma'am said, to churches an' things, an' they pick them up an' put them in the slopchopper, an' then throw them down for us."

As Benson tried to grasp the twin horrors of poverty and idleness, Aldo explained, "Ma'am was my ma. Can I tell you 'bout her? You might make a song 'bout her, an' it'd make her proud if she knew."

Benson had tried to write songs of his own many times, never with success. *New folk song*, where he was concerned at least, was an oxymoron, a contradiction in terms. Aldo looked incredulous when he explained that, so Benson asked whether he himself composed the songs he sang.

Aldo nodded, solemn as if they were deciding an issue of life and death. "That's why I'm goin' to the Spaghetti Bowl. I'll get a new one there, but I can't say how I know it. I just do. The songs you sang back there where the chowchopper was? Didn't you make them up?"

Benson shook his head, and spoke (more openly than he ever had to anyone before) of the pleasure folk music had given him, and of his own fruitless efforts to compose folk songs. When he felt that he could stand the pain of self-revelation no longer, he returned the rude harp. "Sing me one of your songs, please, Aldo. A song you made yourself."

"Here's yours," Aldo said, and returned the Magus-guitar. "This's about my ma." He cleared his throat and strummed his rude harp.

> "In all this jam, there's none like Ma'am,
> For playin' nor for singin'.
> She'd drove the land, her an' her band,
> And set the big rooms ringin' . . .

"It's not a very good song," he said when it was finished, "an' that's all the farther I ever got, an' now she's drove out." As though seeing that Benson had not understood him, he added, "Dead, it means."

After that, they talked of Aldo's mother and a sweetheart he seemed not entirely sure was his until he sprinted away to the spot beyond the outer lane where a yellow helicopter was landing.

Benson followed more sedately, wondering what had caused such excitement; the yellow helicopter appeared to be a four-seater, and was certainly too small to carry much cargo.

When he reached the place where it had set down, a tall and professionally personable young woman in a tailored blue jumpsuit was addressing a microphone for the benefit of a video recorder.

Aldo nudged him. "See what she's got, Tim? Ma'am had a thing like that what she's talkin' into, only there wasn't nowhere to plug it in."

Benson nodded, giving most of his attention to the young woman in the blue jumpsuit.

"We're here to look for very special artists we can put on our program," the young woman's amplified voice announced to the crowd. "But it has to be something visual, basically. You have to make things that we can show, or do something we can show you doing. So if there's anyone here like that, I hope that he or she will step forward."

Benson watched Aldo, half-expecting him to volunteer; but he did not.

The young woman in the blue jumpsuit spoke glowingly of the future that she and her station offered, and a voice from the crowd called, "There's somebody back at the chowchopper that sings real good."

"That's you," Aldo whispered.

Nearer now, the young woman pointed to Aldo's rude harp. "What's that you've got? Our other crew discovered a girl last night who had something like that."

Aldo held it up. "Was her name Mar'?"

Mar', Benson remembered, was Aldo's sweetheart. He said, "Sing for them, Aldo. They want to hear you, and so do I."

The young woman in the blue jumpsuit had gotten a grip on Aldo's arm. She drew him nearer the handheld video recorder. Aldo resisted at first, then grinned at her.

"Choppergal, choppergal, dressed so fine,
Got a gal already, an' that gal's mine . . . "

It was a good, rollicking song, and Benson applauded as loudly as anyone when it was done.

"And you, sir," the young woman in the blue jumpsuit said, "what's your name?"

Until two men pushed him forward, Benson believed that she was addressing someone else.

"What's your name?" she repeated.

He did not belong in this nightmarish traffic jam, was not what Aldo would have called a freewayer—or perhaps he was. He had awakened in a stopped car, after all. Would very likely be there now, if he had not locked himself out of it and set off with some vague notion of exploring, of finding someone who would help him retrieve his keys without breaking a window.

"Will you play for us, Tim? We'd like to hear you." He had not been conscious of giving the young woman his name, but perhaps he had. He shook his head.

"Go 'head, Tim," Aldo said. And to the others, "He's so fine! Wait 'til you hear."

He had played "Londonderry Air" only an hour or two ago, and there was a haunting song, "My Gentle Harp," set to the music.

Almost before he knew that he had begun to play, he was concluding the first verse, singing, yet hearing his own voice soar above the crowd as though it were another's. How envious he would have been of that voice, so vibrant with sorrow and majesty, had it not been his own!

"Yet even then, when peace was singing
Her halcyon song o'er land and sea,
Though joy and hope to others bringing,
She only brought new tears to thee."

That was enough, surely—time to retreat into the crowd, to become one of them again. Benson looked at the circle of starved and dirty faces, at the open mouths and awed eyes of a hundred men and women who had never—until now—heard music that touched their souls, and launched into the second verse.

"Then who can ask for notes of pleasure,
My drooping harp, from chords like thine?
Alas, the lark's gay morning measure,
As ill would suit the swan's decline.
Or how shall I, who love, who bless thee,
Invoke thy breath for freedom's strains,
When e'en the wreaths in which I dress thee,
Are sadly mixed, half flowers, half chains?"

Only when the closing notes had ascended to the clear sky from which the yellow helicopter had dropped, did he entirely comprehend how well that old song accorded with the freewayers' plight. Looking at them, he knew that they had known almost as soon as he had begun.

The young woman in the blue jumpsuit, who clearly had not, said, "That was—was just so wonderful, Tim, but won't you play something about this mess? This traffic jam that's kept so many of you here so long? That's what they want to hear, back at our building."

Speaking more to himself than to her, Benson said, "I'd like to go with you. That's been my dream, to sing folk music and be a star. But I don't know any. Only one, actually."

She gave him a professionally charming smile. "Then sing that."

He asked Aldo's permission and received it, then began Aldo's song about his mother, certain that it would mark the end of the opportunity he had so long feared and desired. What dream would remain for him, when this one was gone?

"In all this jam—"

That was what the young woman in the blue jumpsuit wanted, of course: something that actually employed the words *traffic jam*. And whatever its other defects, this did.

"There's none like Ma'am,
For playing or for singing.

She'd drive this land, she and her band,
And set the big rooms ringing."

How had she felt, Aldo's mother, confined to this sixteen-lane hell until death came for her? How had she felt, this no doubt personable, determined, and talented woman whom he would never meet?

"Her face you'd see on your TV,
'Most any day you played it."

Benson struggled to keep the pity he felt from his voice—and, appalled, heard it issue from the Magus-guitar, at once sorrowing and raging.

"She'd like to gone, with me, her son,
But this here jam's delayed it.
Now here we stay, and pray each day . . . "

The last notes died while Benson was still wondering what good those prayers had ever done Ma'am—or her son Aldo, for that matter.

The young woman had his right arm and her cameraman his left. He ducked under a whizzing rotor blade and found himself pushed into a seat behind the two front seats of the yellow helicopter. The door shut, and in a moment the young woman was in the seat beside the pilot, and the cameraman in the seat beside his own. The helicopter rose, seeming almost to float up like a balloon.

Over her shoulder, the young woman said, "I want you for the noon news, Tim. With a little luck we ought to be able to make it." She glanced at her wrist, then back to him. "It's ten-twenty. That's an hour and forty minutes to get you there and get you made up. Should be fine."

The cameraman said, "What about clothes?" It was the first time that Benson had heard him speak.

"I want them to see what he wore in the jam, the first time. Tim, I bet you're wondering when you'll get to live at the Consort-Hilton and do all that shopping I talked about."

He had been wondering no such thing.

"We're going to put you on the eleven o'clock, too. Maybe on the four-thirty if you really go over at noon and nothing big's breaking. After that, we're going to save you for the 'People You Should Meet' show Sunday afternoon—three or four songs and an interview. Today's Grunday, so that'll give you five whole days, and afterward we'll see. It could be longer."

Benson asked, "What day did you say it was?"

The cameraman answered for her. "Grunday."

They were banking, high above the tallest buildings in the city. Far below, obscured by haze, Interstate 75 might well have been locked in any ordinary rush-hour traffic jam.

Benson swallowed, and swallowed again as the helicopter began to descend—far too quickly, it seemed to him. In front, the pilot appeared unconcerned, and the young woman in the blue jumpsuit was whispering into a handheld microphone; on his right, the cameraman was unwrapping a stick of gum.

Benson gripped the armrest and his seat belt. *Grunday.* Where was he? Where in the world was he, anyway?

The yellow helicopter landed with a slight thump on the tarred roof of an office tower, and before he could catch his breath a short, bouncy, round-faced woman with carroty curls opened his door. "I'm Jennifer," she said. "You're Tim? Come on."

He fumbled with the buckle of his safety belt and stooped as he got out. A head shorter than he, Jennifer stood bolt upright, still grinning as she pulled him along. "I've got to take you to your dressing room. It's not far."

What looked like a rooftop shed held an elevator in which the young woman in the blue jumpsuit and the cameraman were already waiting. Its doors closed and it fell from under him the moment Benson entered.

I'm seeing this as a real folksinger would, he thought, a backwoodsman brought to the city like this for the first time—even the familiar is new and terrifying.

His ears popped.

"Here we are," Jennifer announced. Doors slid open, and she and Benson stepped out. "My name's Jennifer, and I'm a page. Did I tell you that?"

Benson gulped and forced himself to say something. "Your name. Jennifer. You told me that up there."

"Well, I'm a page." Jennifer indicated the simple blue frock she wore. "Really I'm a summer intern. I'll get my master's in communications in two years. Come on."

Benson did, trying to recall one of Michael's books in which people were forever saying *come on.* Was he about to meet the Mock Turtle? The Mock Turtle would be reassuringly familiar after all this.

"Anybody who's got one of these blue dresses is a page," Jennifer explained, "except the guys. Guys have blue slacks and blue shirts. Same thing."

"All right."

"Ask us anything. Want a Pepsi? I'll bring it. Here's your dressing room." She opened a narrow green door.

"A glass of ice water," Benson told her as firmly as he could.

"Is that all?"

"A *large* glass of ice water."

"You'll have it in a nanosecond. Only go in your dressing room, okay? And stay there. Makeup will be in. Somebody'll come for you at airtime, probably me."

"All right," he said again, and found himself in a small room containing a couch, a stool, a dressing table, a mirror ringed by lights, and very little else.

He sat down on the couch and looked at the Magus-guitar. He had no memory of having had it on the helicopter whatsoever, yet here it was, still suspended from his neck by its narrow strap. He had carried it and failed to notice it, or it had dematerialized when he finished Aldo's song and rematerialized here. At the moment, those alternatives seemed equally likely.

The door opened, and a young man wearing black slacks, a white shirt, and a deplorable necktie set a tumbler of ice water on the dressing table, saying, "Jenny said you wanted this."

"I did," Benson began. "Thank—"

The door slammed shut.

Shrugging, he picked up the tumbler and began to drink. What had been in the bottles the chowchopper had passed out? Tap water, presumably. Not even cold, since there had been no condensation on the thin plastic.

He sighed, suddenly conscious that he was terribly tired. They would want him to play the song about Aldo's mother; the lyric had stuck in his mind, and the melody was so simple that he had improved it considerably, extemporizing as he played. What about the later broadcasts? They wouldn't want him to repeat the same song, surely.

There was a knock at the door, and he called, "Come in."

Daisy was the makeup girl. A nice touch, Benson thought, and tried to recall to whom he should be grateful.

"It would help if you lie down," she said, and he did.

She opened the large black box she carried and got out a monstrous powder puff. "I'm just going to put a little powder on you, and—" Her other hand dabbed at his cheeks. "A little rouge. Just a touch."

"I'm sunburned, I suppose," he ventured.

"A little white, really."

"Daisy?"

"What is it? Don't purse your lips. You need a lot of color there, too."

"Daisy, don't you know me?"

"Now the powder." It came as a sudden, suffocating cloud; and before it cleared, he heard the door slam.

He got up, went to the door, and looked out. Jennifer had told him to stay in the dressing room, but looking out would do no harm, surely.

Daisy was vanishing around a turn in the corridor, and a very pale but very attractive young woman in a black pantsuit was striding toward him. "Tim? There you are."

An old sea song, "The Bulgine Run," popped into his head, and he played the first few chords for her. "How's this? I'm thinking of doing it on the eleven o'clock news."

She laughed. She had an infectious laugh, and he found that he enjoyed it—that he was drawn to her, in fact.

"Come on," she said, smiling. "Time's up." And then, as they walked down the corridor together, "Would you like to play that thing for me some more? I, like, dig rock stars."

"I was expecting Jennifer," he told her, and was on the point of telling her that she was preferable.

"She's busy right now. What was that song?"

"This?" Benson played the opening bars, and she nodded.

"It's about sailors unloading freight in a railroad yard. You have to know nineteenth-century slang, sailors' slang and railroad slang, to understand everything. They yell to each other and to a girl in what we'd call a taxi, and so on."

The pale young woman in the black pantsuit grinned at him, her teeth flashing in the dimness of the corridor. "I've known lots of sailors and railroad men. I knew Casey Jones."

Benson grinned back. "I'll bet you did."

"Sure, lots," she said. They turned into a new corridor. It was even darker than the last, but there was a light at the end. "Won't you sing it for me? I'd love to hear you."

"All right." He would have one more song ready, and that could only be good.

"Oh the smartest clipper that you can find . . . "

To his surprise, the pale young woman in black joined him on the refrain: *"A-hee, a-ho, ain't you 'most done?"*

VALÓSÁG AND ÉLET

Steven Brust

Steven Brust is a swashbuckling gypsyish individual of Hungarian extraction; a wearer of fine hats; a sipper of fine whiskies; a player of the drum and the doumbek; and a novelist.

He has crept into *Sandman* a couple of times: he can be spotted in The Worlds' End pub in the *Worlds' End* collection, and later, at the Renaissance Festival, in a story called "Sunday Mourning" in *The Wake*.

Steven Brust does not, as he will happily tell you, write short stories. This folk tale is one of the short stories he does not write.

Well, you all talk about *valóság* **and** *élet,* **but I know the** truth about them, and I can prove it to you. If you want me to tell you I will, only you must first buy me a drink so I can wet my whistle.

It came about like this: Once there was a very poor family living in a cottage in the woods. They were so poor that the mother had to knit with cobwebs when she wanted to knit, and the father had to smoke the chimney sweepings when he wanted to smoke. All they had to live on was the milk of one poor old cow.

Now, they had three boys in this family. One day, the oldest one said, "I am going to go out to seek my fortune, so that we won't be poor anymore." You see, he was a good boy, who wanted to provide for his family. So they wished him well, and off he went.

Soon he meets a man who is walking barefoot through the woods. "Greetings, father," says the young man.

"Hello," said the barefoot man. "My name is Valóság. Where are you going and what are you seeking?"

"Why, I am going through the woods, and I am seeking my fortune."

"Well, but what is a fortune?" said the barefoot man.

"A fortune? Oh, it is to live as one dreams of living."

"Is that what you think?" said Valóság. "Then you may have it." And the oldest brother fell down on the spot and began to dream, and nothing and no one could wake him up.

A year and a day after the oldest brother had left, the second brother said, "I am going to go out to seek my fortune, so that we won't be poor anymore." So they wished him well, and off he went. Soon he met a girl with hair as black as a raven's wing.

"Greetings, black-haired girl," he said.

"Hello," said the girl. "My name is Élet. Where are you going and what are you seeking?"

"Why, I am going through the woods, and I am seeking my fortune."

"Well, but what is a fortune?" said the black-haired girl.

"It is what you need never to know hunger or pain."

"Is that what you think?" said Élet. "Then you may have it." And the middle brother fell down dead on the spot.

A year and a day passed. Now, during this time, the youngest brother, whose name was Jáncsi, had been taking care of the cow, and he was always careful to make sure it had as much feed as they could spare, and that it was always kept brushed and its stall was kept clean. And so, when Jáncsi announced that he was going set off to seek his fortune, the cow suddenly spoke. "Be careful, young master, that you do not make the same mistakes your brothers made."

"How are you speaking?" said Jáncsi.

"Well, why shouldn't I speak? Am I not a táltos cow?"

"But what has happened to my brothers?"

"Your oldest brother has met with Valóság, and is dreaming his life away, and your middle brother has met with Élet and is in the land of the dead. You must be careful to avoid the same fate."

"Well, but how can I do that?"

"You must take my horn (in those days, cows had one horn, right in the middle of the head), and you must use it to trap those two so they'll do what you say, then you can get your brothers back and make your fortune."

"But how can I do that?"

"If they try to do something that can't be done, then you can trap their power in the horn."

"But what can I have them do that can't be done?"

"I will tell you this much: everyone dreams of dying, but no one dreams of being dead. And that is all I can say."

And with that, the cow fell silent and would speak no more.

So Jáncsi took the cow's horn and set off through the woods, and soon he met a barefoot man. "Greetings, father," said the young man.

"Hello," said the barefoot man. "My name is Valóság. Where are you going and what are you seeking?"

"I am going through the woods, and I am seeking my fortune."

"Well, but what is a fortune?"

"Who are you to ask me?"

"To find a fortune, you must first visit me, for I hold them all in my keeping."

"Well then, my fortune is my brother, who has been taken by Élet."

"Well, she is just a little farther along this path."

"Then I will go to her. But you must keep me safe."

"How am I to do that?"

"By making a dream of being dead."

"But no one dreams of being dead."

"Then I shall be safe."

So Valóság tried to make a dream about being dead, and Jáncsi took Valóság's power and put it into the horn. Then he quickly ran along the path, and soon met with a girl whose hair was black as a raven's wing.

"Greetings, black-haired girl," he said.

"Hello," said the girl. "My name is Élet. Where are you going and what are you seeking?"

"I am going through the woods, and I am seeking my fortune."

"Well, but what is a fortune?"

"Who are you to ask me?"

"Whatever your fortune is, at the end you bring it to me, for I am the ultimate keeper of all fortunes."

"Well then, my fortune is my brother, who has been taken by Valóság."

"Valóság?" she said. "But surely you passed him in the woods."

"Maybe I did," he said. "But if I am to visit him again, you must protect me."

"How can I do that?"

"By wrapping me in the dream that comes from those who have died."

"But no dreams come from those who have died."

"Then I shall be safe."

So Élet tried to make those who were dead dream, and Jáncsi quickly put her power into his horn. Then he went back down the path, with Élet coming after him. Well, soon enough Valóság and Élet meet, and they just look at each other for a minute, you know, the way you look when you're surprised to see someone, and then Valóság says, "What have you done?" and at the same time, you see, Élet says, "What have you done?" And they look at the young man and they say to him, "What have you done?"

Then Jáncsi says, "Well, you have taken my brothers away from me, so I have taken you two away from the world, and I won't let you go until you have returned my brothers to me and done whatever else I want."

"Well," they said, "and what is that?"

"You must make our fortunes."

"But," they said, "what is a fortune?"

"It is all that my oldest brother has dreamed of while he has been dreaming, and it is the good health that my other brother was looking for before he died."

Having no choice, Valóság and Élet agreed to these terms, and no sooner had Jáncsi given them their power back than up jumped the older brother, and in walked the middle brother, and you can bet they were all glad to see each other!

It took the three of them to carry all of the gold and silver the one brother had been dreaming of, but it wasn't too hard because they all had good health, and so did their mother and father, and the proof is that the buttons on my vest were made out of the very same horn from the táltos cow, and, not only that, but they gave me this fine gold watch because they liked the stories I told them, just as you are going to buy me another drink for the same reason. Now, this all happened many years ago, yet I am certain that if they haven't since died, they are all still alive to this day.

STOPP'T-CLOCK YARD

Susanna Clarke

Several years ago Colin Greenland (whose story opens this volume) sent me a novella by an author he had met at a writer's workshop. It was a wonderful story. The author was Susanna Clarke, who lives in Cambridge and writes like an angel. When I read it, I knew I wanted her to write a story for this book. (She sold that novella to Patrick Neilsen Hayden's anthology *Starlight*.)

The attraction for me of working on this anthology, fraught with strange and unexpected vexations though it has proved, was really the selfish desire to read a Sandman story; something that I have not been able to do until now.

I wish I had written this story. But I'm even more pleased that I got to read it.

In Don Saltero's Coffee-House in Danvers-street Mr. Newbolt was taking coffee with his son.

He said, "It is so long since last I saw you, Richard, I hope you have been well all this time?"

Richard sighed. "Father, I was drowned in the Dutch Wars. I have been dead these fifteen years."

Then Mr. Newbolt saw how cold and white was his face, how cold and white were his hands. "Why, child," he said, "so you were. I remember now. Still I am very glad to see you. Will you not walk home with me? It is scarce five minutes' walk and I daresay you will not mind the rain?"

"Oh, Father," cried Richard, "I cannot come home. I can never come home. Do you not see? This is a dream. It is only a dream."

Then Mr. Newbolt looked around Don Saltero's Coffee-House and saw the strangest people all talking and taking coffee together. "Why, child," he said, "so it is."

Mr. Newbolt woke in the cold and the dark and remembered that he was dying. He had been for forty years England's most famous, most revered astrologer. He had published hundreds of almanacks and made a great deal of money and he had looked into the stars—oh, long, long ago now—and he knew that he must die in this season and in this place. He lay in a clean, sweet bed in an upper room in Friday-street and his old London friends came to pay him visits. "Sir!" they cried. "How are you feeling today?"; and Mr. Newbolt would complain of a coldness in the brain and a heat in the liver, or sometimes, and by way of a change, the other way round. And then they would tell him that all the most gracious planets in heaven were slowly assembling above half-built St. Paul's in time to bid him—their old friend and confidant—a stately farewell.

One friend who visited him at this time was a very famous Jew of Venice and Amsterdam, a most wonderful magician among his own people (who know many clever things). This man was called Trismegistus. He had not heard that Mr. Newbolt was dying and had come to beg Mr. Newbolt's help in some very tremendous astrological or magical business. When he discovered that he had come too late, he signed and wept and smote his own forehead. "Oh," he cried, "all my days I did despise every man's help. I have walked with vanity. This is my punishment and it is just."

Mr. Newbolt looked at him. "Oh, vanity in a fiddlestick, Isaac. I am sure there is no need to be quite so biblical. Let you and I drink some muscatel-wine and we shall soon find someone else to aid you."

So they did as Mr. Newbolt proposed. But, as there was no astrologer or magician in the City of London who had not, at some time or another, ridiculed one or other of them, who had not called one "Impostor" or the other "Juggling Jew," and as they both had an excellent memory for an insult (though they forgot many other things), they had very soon run through every name.

"There's Paramore," said Mr. Newbolt, "and he is cleverer than all of them."

"Paramore? Who is Paramore?"

"Well," said Mr. Newbolt, "I cannot truthfully tell you much good of him, for I never heard any. He is a liar, an adulterer, a gamester, and a drunkard. He has the reputation of an atheist, but he told me once that he professed blasphemy, because he had taken offense at some passages of Scripture and now was angry with God and wish't to plague Him. Like a mosquito that wish't to prick a continent."

"He is not the man I want," said Trismegistus.

"Ha!" cried Mr. Newbolt. "There are women in every parish of the City who thought that John Paramore was not the man they wanted. They soon discovered their mistake. And so did I. For I swore when he first came to me that I would not take him as a pupil, but now, you see, I have taught him all I know. I also swore that I would not lend him money. Still I love the rogue. Do not ask me why. I cannot tell. You must ask for Paramore at a house in Gunpowder-alley—'tis near Shoe-lane—where he owes eight weeks' rent for a little attic about the size and shape of a pantry bin. You must not expect to find him there, but very likely his footman will know where he is."

"He has a footman?" said Trismegistus.

"Of course," said Mr. Newbolt. "He is a gentleman."

So all that day and all the next Isaac Trismegistus trod the City streets and asked a great many people if they knew where John Paramore might be found, but he learned nothing to the purpose and what he did learn only brought him closer to despair. For the City did not think that John Paramore would wish to be troubled with an old Hebrew gentleman just now. The City knew of a certain widow in Clerkenwell with lands and houses and no one could tell what rich commodities, and the City happened to know that this lady—young, virtuous, and beautiful—had lately lost a little boy, a sweet child, who had died of the rickets and the City said that in her misfortune John Paramore was her Mephistopheles who sat in the shadows behind her chair with satirical looks and his long, crooked smile and whispered in her ear and that she prefer'd his comfort to that of honest men and women.

Isaac Trismegistus lived in an old dark house near Creechurch-lane. Like himself the house was a little foreign-looking. Like himself, the house appeared to know that the City was not always kind to strangers, for it had crept into a dusty yard full of shadows and dead leaves, where it hoped to be forgotten. But the Jew and the house differed in one respect, for *he* had not got a great stopp't clock in the middle of his forehead, forever telling the time of a long-dead afternoon.

On the third day after Trismegistus had spoken to Mr. Newbolt a tall, thin, shabby man (who looked nothing at all) knocked on the door of Trismegistus's house. He said that his name was John Paramore and that he had come to learn magic.

"Why?" asked Trismegistus suspiciously. "To catch the women, I suppose?"

Then the thin, shabby man (who had looked nothing at all) smiled a long, thin smile that went up one side of his face and when he did that he looked quite different. He looked what he was—one of the slyest rogues in the City and his sharp, bright eyes had worlds of cleverness in them. "No, sir," he replied with a mix't air of modesty and complacency. "*That* magic I do already have. I hope, sir, that you have not heard any ill report of me? London is a wicked place—an honest man's reputation has no more wear in it than a whore's shoestrings once the City gossips have got hold of it."

Inside the house a great staircase spiraled up into darkness and a cold wind spiraled down. Paramore glanced up and, shivering a little, remarked that it was very quiet. "Why, sir!" he cried suddenly. "You are ill!"

"I? No."

"Indeed you are. You are as pale as wax and your eyes—! You have a fever."

"I have no fever. It is only that I do not sleep." Trismesgistus paused. "I shall die if I do not sleep soon," he said. "But I am afraid to go to sleep. I am afraid of what I might dream."

"Well, sir," said Paramore in a kinder tone, "if you will tell me how I may help you, I shall be glad to do so."

So Trismegistus led Paramore to a room and he taught him two spells. One spell gave Paramore the power to see into another person's dreams, but what the other spell was for Trismegistus did not say. Trismegistus told Paramore to watch his dreams as he slept and if Paramore saw any harm coming to him in his dreams, he was to wake him up.

Trismegistus got into bed and Paramore sat cross-legged on the floor like his Puck, and Paramore said the spell and look't into a little polished crystal.

Trismegistus dreamt that he was in the Venetian Ghetto, in a mean and dusty little courtyard where six old Jews—friends of his—sat silent on battered wooden thrones and one by one each caught fire. Not one of them tried to save himself and all were burnt to ashes. As the old magician watched the smoke and sparks twist into the darkening sky, he saw a recipe for plum cake writ upon one of the stars. It happened that in his dream he had a use for such a thing, and so he went to fetch a ladder to read it better. But all he found was a great fat woman with a moustache made of spiders' legs, that stank of cheese and dirty slops, and who produced, from under her skirts, pairs of rusty scissors, toasting forks, and French tweezers.

Now this Paramore thought was very horrid and so he woke the old man up. But Trismegistus was very cross at being woken and said he had not meant *that* sort of dream at all. He said Paramore should watch for a tall, black castle in an airy place, guarded by a dragon and a griffin and a hippogriff and for a tall, pale man, like a king, all dress't in black with starrey eyes. These, he said, were what he feared more than anything, and he went back to sleep. He slept until morning and neither the castle nor the terrible pale king appear'd.

The next day Paramore paid a visit to Mr. Newbolt.

"The Jew keeps a very odd house, sir," said Paramore. "He says he has no servants."

"Pish! Everyone has servants. Even you, John, have that saucy footman."

"True, but I have been thinking for some time, sir, that I must get rid of Francisco. I must turn him off. I dare not for shame be seen anywhere with him. His clothes are so much better than mine. He was ever a better thief than I."

"I daresay," said Mr. Newbolt (whose thoughts still ran on his old friend), "that it is the loss of his daughter that makes him so solitary and sad. She ran away and married a Christian—a tall, spicy fellow with rogue's eyes and no money—just such another one as yourself, John. Isaac found out their hiding place and visited her in secret and begged her to come home. But she was very proud and would not come, though by that time she knew what sort of a man she had married. Ah, but he was cruel! He gave away her petticoats and ear-rings and candlesticks and spoons to other women. Then one night he came in from his rovings-about and made her get out of bed. 'Why?' she asked, 'Where are we going?' But he bid her be silent. They got into a coach with all that was left of their possessions and they rode away. But he kept looking back, and far away she heard the sound of riders. He made the coach stop and he pull'd her out and took a horse and made her get up behind and they rode on. But he kept looking back and all the while she could hear the sound of rid-ers. They reach'd a black river too deep and too quick to ford and he was almost frantic to know which way to go. She begged him to tell her what he had done. But he bid her be silent and far away she heard the sound of riders. 'Why,' he said, 'you don't want to come along of me and, sure it is, I'll get on faster alone.' So he tumbled her into the quick, black water and she drowned. She had golden hair—a very rare thing for one of her race. Isaac said she put the very sun to shame. But then I thought nothing could compare with my dear Richard's smile, and I daresay there are people in the world who did not find it so very remarkable. What do brokenhearted old men know? Oh, yes, the fair-haired Jewess of Stopp't-Clock Yard, I remember her very well. She had a little daughter—but I have forgot what became of her."

Paramore scratched his long nose and frowned. "But how do you know this, sir?"

"Eh?"

"How do you know what the Jewess said to her husband at the moment of her death?"

"Eh?" Poor Mr. Newbolt grew confus'd and unhappy, as old people do when it is prov'd to them that their wits are duller than they used to be. "Isaac told me," he said. "Why! What is that glinting on your finger, John? Has your widow given you a bright new golden ring?"

"I found it, sir, in the Jew's garden. Caught on a rosebush."

"You should tell him, John. Perhaps he has lost such a thing."

But Mr. Newbolt no longer saw very well. It was not a ring at all, but only two or three golden hairs that Paramore had found, just as he had described, and had wound about his long finger.

She looked, as they do, neither old nor young. Under different circum-stances (*very* different circumstances) he might have thought her beautiful.

In her fine, dark eyes and the curve of her cheek was displayed some Spanish or suchlike Romancy origins, but her skin was rather pale. She wore a severe black robe with a line of tiny buttons that went from throat to hem. A pair of silver spectacles swung on a long silver chain around her neck. She had two pieces of paper. She looked at the piece of paper in her right hand, but it was not what she wanted. She looked at the piece of paper in her left hand and liked it better. She put her spectacles on her nose and read, "The Lord of Dreams and Nightmares, the Prince of Stories, the Monarch of the Sleeping Marches, His Darkness Dream of the Endless." She paused and glanced over the spectacles and no amount of cold, astonished majesty on the part of the person seated on the tall, black throne would ever discompose *her*.

"Well," she said, "*are* you?"

The person seated on the tall, black throne agreed that he was all those terrible things and inquired, a little stiffly, who in the world she might be.

"Doktor Estrella Silberhof. Of Heaven. That is to say the Heaven of the Children of Israel. Secretary-in-Ordinary to the Chamber of Dreams, Visions, Visitations, and Extraordinary Hauntings." She produced a quantity of letters and documents beautifully written in several ancient tongues on best-quality vellum and neatly tied with red silk ribbons, all testifying to the fact of her being who she said she was. "I wrote to you," she said, "on September 30th. And again on October 4th. And again on October 11th. I did not receive a reply. I was forc'd to come myself. I arrived six days ago. I have waited six days for an audience. When I first came to the castle it was not my intention to trouble *you*. I asked to speak to your recorders, secretaries, bailiffs, magistrates, clerks, or any other of your servants bearing such like office or offices. But I was informed that no such persons are employed by you. In the interim . . . "

"I have a librarian. You may speak to him. Good day."

". . . In the interim your servants have attempted to fob me off with a weak-brained librarian, a raven named Jessamy, and a prattling fool of a white rabbit called"—she consulted the piece of paper in her right hand— "Ruthven Roscoe. I am here," she said, "about the Returns."

"The Returns?"

She produced a very large book beautifully bound in the palest tan-colored leather with "Memorials of Returns, September 29th, 1682 (R.C.F.)" stamped in gold letters on the spine. It contained approximately seven million names written in excruciatingly small characters with a number of entirely incomprehensible shorthand symbols by the side of each.

"A record," she explained, "of those occupants of Heaven, those righteous dead, who on the night of September 29th left Paradise to visit the living in dreams. I have marked the place for you to see and underlined the subject's name in green ink. Simply stated, Deborah Trismegistus came from Paradise into the Dreaming on September 29th and did not return. My intention in coming here was quite simple: I wish't to compare our Memorials with your own and to discover into whose dream this young woman went. But I am told that nowhere in this realm are any such records kept."

"Doktor Silberhof, Deborah Trismegistus is not in the Dreame-Countries."

She smiled patiently. "No, I did not think that she was. In *that* case, you know, the person dreaming of her would now have been asleep for thirty-three days."

There was a long silence.

"I'll look into it," he said.

In Isaac Trismegistus's bedchamber in Stopp't-Clock Yard John Paramore sat, yawning his head off and peering without enthusiasm into his polished glass.

"I wonder who it is," he murmured, "that goes creeping about this house?"

A little while later, he glanced into a crop of dusty, moonshiny shadows that clustered thickly in one corner. "And I wonder who it is," he observed, "behind that curtain? With two little mousey feet and ten little mousey toes."

He studied his glass for a while. "And I wonder who it is," he continued thoughtfully, "that stands directly before me, peeping out between those little mouse fingers?" He looked up. "Hello, puss-face. What big eyes you've got."

"Grandfather . . . " she said.

"Grandfather is asleep, sweetheart. He dreams of walking in Paris-Gardens. But who is this that walks beside him, that he cannot help but catch up in his arms, who strokes his beard and who provokes him to so many loving smiles and kisses?" He gave her the glass to hold that she might see herself in it. She did not object to being taken upon his lap.

"How cold are these hands. How cold are these feet. And what," he muttered to himself, "have you got on your arms?"

There were two little black boxes, one tied to each arm, with leather straps wound round and round to keep them on. The first box contained a strip of paper, on which was written, WHAT THINGES ARE GOOD FOR LILY TO

DREAME OF. And underneath was a very long list which began, "Breade & Jam, Treacle of Venice, Sugar'd Chesnuttes & Such Like Sweetes & Tit-bits; Ye Goode Dogge, Pepper . . . " In the other box was another long list entitled, WHAT THINGES LILY MUST *NOT* DREAM OF. This list began, "Our enemie, Kinge Morpheus nor anie of his freinds nor anie of his servants; skeletons & old bones . . . "

As he had never laid eyes on her before, he reasoned that she must have come from one of the mysterious rooms at the top of the house. He waited until she had fallen asleep and then he picked her up and carried her out onto the cold, black staircase.

During the day the wind had brought a quantity of dead leaves into the house and now it was entertaining itself by tumbling them up and down the steps and making a queer rattling music with them.

"And if there are no servants," he mused, "then who cares for thee? Combs thy hair like silk and makes thee smell of apples and lavender?" He climbed a little higher. "Staircases are like the bowels of a house, remarkably like—I wonder I never thought of it before—and this is the windiest, most flatulent house that ever I was in. Were I a physician, I would prescribe it three pills fortis. Kill or cure . . . "

He paused at the last twist of the staircase. "Paramore, Paramore," he muttered, "you are speaking without sense or connection. What in the world is there to fear, man?"

At the very top of the stairs stood the dead Jewess, her golden curls silver in the moonlight. A little draft made the dead leaves spin and eddy about her feet. Another shook the tiny, tear-shaped pearls in her ears, but she moved not at all.

"Faith! You must forgive me, madam, but all these stairs have snatched my breath away. My name is Paramore—another very famous magician. And you, madam—if a man might ask—are you a Ghost or a Dream?"

She sighed. "Are men still such fools? Am I a ghost or a dream? Lord! What manner of fool's question is that? What am I? I am her mother." And she took Lily from Paramore's arms and disappeared through a dark doorway.

Mrs. Beaufort (the widow in whose affairs the City took such a warm interest) lived in Jerusalem-passage in Clerkenwell, a street much patronized by musicians. Whenever Mrs. Beaufort paced the length of her large, well-furnished rooms, weighing the emptiness in her arms where her little boy should have been, or peered into mirrors to discover what a childless lady look'd like, she did so to the accompaniment of the slow, sad music of the German gentleman's *viola da gamba* at number 24 or the melancholy airs of the Scottish harpsichord at number 21.

Late in the afternoon of the following day a servant came to Mrs. Beaufort, saying that Mr. Paramore was below and wished to speak to her at once.

When Paramore entered Mrs. Beaufort looked up from her needlework and frowned. "You have been drinking," she said.

"I? No!"

"Wenching then."

"No, indeed!" he cried, all indignation.

"Something then. There is a kind of riot in your face."

"That is because I am happy."

She turned a corner in the hem she was making before she said in a cold and jealous way, "Well then . . . I am glad for you."

"I am happy because of what I may do for you. Tell me," he said, "what you dream of—at night when you go to bed."

She looked very coldly at him for some moments and then pulled her hand away (he was holding it).

"Oh, I am punished!" she cried. "A hundred, hundred warnings I have had in this very room! But these ears"—and she put up her hands as if to menace the offending ears—"would not heed them! And if, sir, I should hold myself so cheap as to submit to you, should you put it all in a poem afterward?—nail it to a post on Snow-hill for every passing fool to smirk at?"

Paramore threw up his hands and cast his looks about him in his exasperation. "I do not mean *that*!" he cried.

"Indeed? And what should I understand from all this talk of what you may do for me and going to bed?"

He crossed his arms. "There are tears in your eyes—which you do deserve for thinking I am so bad—and I have it in my power now to make you so happy. Only believe that I am better than that and you shall be happier yourself."

She smiled and wept together. "That is no reason . . . " she began.

"Hush . . . Tell me what you dream of."

"Of my baby. Of my little boy."

"Then all is well and I shall cure you of all your griefs. For Morpheus is an idle king, grown dull and foolish from the long years of security. His walls are old and crumbling. His gates are unguarded. His servants are not watchful."

The next day Mrs. Beaufort was seen walking in St. Giles Fields, and at her side was a little boy, with hair that was such a mass of fine curlicues and spirals that it appeared to have been written onto his head in gold and silver ink by a very expensive writing master.

The Librarian (who was in the act of polishing his spectacles with a bit of wool) began to change. It started at the tips of his curious ears, which dissolved into fine sand. If he were at all distress'd by this sudden transformation, then he gave no sign.

The throne room, with a musical swish, became sand and tumbled down. A raven swooping across it crumbled to sand in mid-flight. The whole dreaming world turned to sand. And when it was done, all that remained of the whole world was a quantity of sand in the Dream-king's white cupped palm. Then the Dream-king took a pair of scales that he kept for the purpose and weighed the sand and discovered that, as he suspected, he was five grains short.

"How many?" asked Paramore.

"Five," said Trismegistus. "They stuck to the hem of my daughter's gown when I brought her out of the Dreame-Countries, and, as you see, John, I keep them very safe, for who knows how powerful these five grains may be. . . . Now remember, John—'tis very important—were you and I ever to fall asleep at the same time, then Morpheus might slip into our dreams and reach out and take hold of my Deborah and the little English boy and steal them back. While you sleep I shall say spells and watch over them, and while I sleep you shall do the same."

"But perhaps the Dream-king might care to make a bargain with us, sir? After all, he knows us English magicians, does he not? Our brother-magicians have had dealings with him. I have heard of recipes to make a man have a particular dream."

"He is not a king to deal with," said Trismegistus. "He is a king to spy upon, to cheat, to deceive, and to steal from—and then to fear. You and I, that have spied upon him, cheated, deceived, and stolen from him, must—for a part of every day or night—venture into his realm and how he will wish to abuse us then. So while you sleep I shall watch over you, and while I sleep you shall do the same."

In the weeks that followed Isaac Trismegistus and John Paramore brought many dead people out of dreams, through the broken walls of the Dreame-Countries and into the waking world. They restored children to parents, parents to children, wives to husbands, husbands to wives, sweethearts to each other. Some gentlemen of the City who had insured a ship that had sunk near the Barbadoes (and who had thereby lost a large sum of money) paid Paramore five pounds to bring the captain back to life so that they might relieve their feelings by railing at him.

For the first time in his life Paramore began to make money, but he said that it was not the money he cared for. What he did care for, he said, was that young people should not die. Surely, he said, there were saints enough in Heaven to sing the hymns, and sinners enough in Hell to keep the fires blazing brightly through all Eternity? He had heard tell, he said, that Death was lady. Strange behavior for a lady! To be so very hasty and a-grabbing after every little thing she fancied. It was high time, said John Paramore, that someone taught her better manners.

There was at that time living in Petticoat-lane in Whitechapel a young girl, Jess Kettle, seven years of age with brown eyes and a most impudent grin. . . . But she prick't her thumb on an old gardener's pruning hook (which she never should have touch'd in the first place) and a great fistula grew up until all the thumb was corrupt'd. The surgeon made them tie Jess Kettle fast in a chair with apron strings and laces and he struck off her thumb with a chisel and a mallet. But the Fright and Convulsion was more than she could bear, and it was discover'd that with that blow the surgeon had struck her understanding out of her head and her hair came out and she turned the color of three-day-old milk and she spake no more. But her aunt, Anne Symcotts, walk'd to Stopp't-Clock Yard and asked everyone she met where she would find John Paramore, the sorcerer, and when she found him she went boldly up to him and entreated his help. John Paramore said she had a face like a spoon, but was very brave and clever. John Paramore sent the aunt to sleep and into the Dreame-Countries, where she found Jess Kettle's reason and all her bonny looks *and* her thumb, and she brought them, laughing, out of the Dreame-Countries, right from under the Dream-king's very nose. Or so it was said. And Jess Kettle was her merry self again.

The Duchess of Cleveland's pearls (of which she was uncommonly fond) had all been given to Mr. Newbolt for safekeeping, and to this end he had taken them into a large cabbage field, thinking to hide them there. But the string had broke and the pearls had tumbled in between the leaves of a cabbage and got lodged there. Mr. Newbolt knew the cabbage field well. It had lain behind his father's cottage when Mr. Newbolt had been a child seventy years before in Leicestershire. Now, as he stood looking about him in the utmost fright and perplexity, a large black raven alighted on one of the cabbages and pecked at something inside it. Mr. Newbolt shouted and waved his arms and the bird flew away. But it did not go far, but went and flapped about the shoulders of a tall, pale man who had suddenly appeared.

"Ah, sir!" cried Mr. Newbolt. "For pity's sake, help me! I do not know which cabbage to look into."

"William Newbolt," said the tall, pale man, "you are dreaming."

"Yes, I know," said Mr. Newbolt. "What of it?" And he continued to peer in a desperate sort of way into the cabbages.

"William Newbolt," said the tall, pale man, "do you know me?"

Then Mr. Newbolt looked up and saw the cold, white Leicestershire sky and the cold, white gleam of the man's face. And the one was very like the other and Mr. Newbolt began to wonder if, in fact, they might not be the same thing, and the black winter trees that marked the boundary of the field and the black shadows beneath them so resembled the man's black hair and clothes that it seemed impossible that they should not be made of the same stuff.

"Yes, I know you," said Mr. Newbolt. "You are that scrawny, handsome man—Lord! I have forgot his name!—the writing master that killed a cat belonging to an alderman and in the same evening ran away with the alderman's daughter. Sir, did not Mrs. Behn call you Lysander and write a poem on your beauty?"

The tall man sighed and passed a long white hand through his long black hair.

"Of course he is dead, the writing master," said Mr. Newbolt thoughtfully. "They hanged him. I forget for what. Still perhaps that does not signify now. They say that Morpheus is an idle king. His walls are old and crumbling. His gates are unguarded. His servants are not watchful."

A little rain of bitter sleet fell sharply and suddenly down on Mr. Newbolt alone. Mr. Newbolt looked around, puzzled. The tall man appeared to be so full of wrath that, had Mr. Newbolt had his wits about him, he would have been very much afraid. (Mr. Newbolt knew something of the wrath of great princes, having had in his time cause to speak to three—Charles, the first and second of that name, and Oliver Cromwell). But Mr. Newbolt did not have his wits about him. Mr. Newbolt's wits were all asleep in his bed in Friday-street, and so he only smiled dimly at the tall, majestical person.

"*What* do you say?" asked the tall man.

"Oh," said Mr. Newbolt, wringing a stream of icy water out of his clothes and catching it in a little crystal cup that he had just discovered he had with him, "*I* do not say so. You do not attend properly, sir. Other people say it."

"*Where* do they say it?"

"In the town. It is what is commonly reported in the town."

"*Who* reports it?"

"Everybody. But mostly 'tis the wastrel John Paramore."

The tall man folded his arms and a great wind came up out of nowhere and toss'd all the trees about, as if all the world had been put in a great fright by the tall man's frowning at it. Mr. Newbolt stepped up to the tall man and, catching hold of his long black robe, tugged at it.

"But, sir! Will you not help me look for the Duchess's pearls? She will be horribly angry."

"Aye," said the tall man with satisfaction, "that she will." And he stalked away.

In his place came a hundred fat pigs who ate up all the cabbages and swallowed all the pearls. A hundred men next appeared and slit the throats of the pigs and poured the blood into a hundred basins, then the basins were all taken away to be made into pigs' blood puddings. At that moment someone arrived to say that Mr. Newbolt must make haste—the Duchess was asking for him. When he arrived Her Grace was at dinner with all her cronies. A china dish of pigs' blood pudding was set before each. The Duchess said nothing at all. She only looked at Mr. Newbolt and held up her silver fork and wagged it three times at him. Between its silver prongs, glistening bloodily, was a great white pearl.

"I can explain," said Mr. Newbolt.

At the King's palace of Whitehall a great masque was held, in which Apollo, Mars, Minerva, King Solomon of the Jews, and no end of other great and noble personages were to come upon the stage, wearing golden robes and faces like stars and suns and moons, and make speeches about Charles II and lay their tributes at his feet. A tall, thin actor called Mr. Percival (who when out of costume rather resembled an upturned mop that had just heard something very surprising) was employed to take the part of Morpheus. Just before the performance two gallants came to him with a little pot and said how making speeches was thirsty work and would he like some beer? He, not suspecting any mischief, thanked these kind gentlemen and drank it up.

But it was a purging ale.

The consequence was that when poor Mr. Percival went upon the stage to make his speech (about how Morpheus had long dreamt of such a King as Charles II and how he now bestowed his sleepy blessings on humanity) no one could hear the sound of his words above his farting.

At which the King and all the court laugh't like anything. But those who laugh't loudest were those who had heard of John Paramore and what he did and whom he cheated to do it.

That night the King of England had a dream.

He dreamt that he was paying state visits to other monarchs and had reached a throne room, as vast as Hampstead Heath, where a tall, pale king sat upon a black throne, complaining of the bad behavior of some Englishmen who had lately journeyed through his realm.

The pale king seemed quite in a rage about it. He said it had been the cause of a quarrel between himself and his sister and showed the King of England no end of documents and letters and Memorials he had had from persons he called "High Authorities," accusing the pale king of negligence because of something the Englishmen had done.

The King of England looked at the documents but found they were complicated, so he put them aside for the Duke of Buckingham to read and to tell him what was in them.

"I am not at all surprised at what your Majestie tells me," cried the King of England. "My subjects are the most unruly that ever poor prince was burdened with, and the men of London are the very worst. For years they rent my realm in pieces with bloody civil wars, wicked rebellions and the impudent government of Oliver Cromwell, and when their republican humor was spent they sent me a letter, begging my pardon for cutting off my father's head and asking me to be their king again . . . " (The tall, pale king seemed about to speak, so the King of England hurried on.) ". . . It is their damp, island climate which is chiefly to blame. The cold and the rain chills the guts and the brain and makes men first melancholy and then mad and then ungovernable. Madness is, as everybody knows, the English malady. But I have colonies, you know. A great many in the Indies and the Americas, and I have hopes that, in time, when all the philosophers and preachers and mad rogues have gone there, then nothing but good, obedient subjects will remain. Does your Majestie have colonies?"

No, said the tall, pale king, he had none.

"Then your Majestie should get some. Straightaway." The King of England leaned over and patted the pale king's hand. He was rewarded for this by a very small, very chilly smile.

The pale king asked if it was difficult to make the troublesome subjects go there.

"Oh, no," said the King of England, "they go of their own accord. That is the excellent thing about colonies."

The King of England felt a little sorry for this sad, pale king. He seemed so young, so all alone in his great silent, starlit palace, with no ministers to advise him and no mistresses to comfort him. And besides, thought the King of England—as he took a glass of wine from a little silver tray and glanced up at the person who had brought it to him—his servants are so odd. . . .

Paramore remarked that in the past week nine separate persons had come to him. "Each of these men told me they had dreamt of seeing me hung. Faith! This king pokes about in this person's dream and that person's, but he can get no foothold."

Trismegistus said something in reply, but it so happened that Paramore had that very day resolv'd to learn Hebrew (so that he might read Trismegistus's books of magic), and so he had no time just then to hear what the old man said.

A little later Trismegistus said another thing, but once again Paramore did not listen to him. At the end of two hours Paramore look't up and discovered that Trismegistus was gone from the room, but in leaving it (and this was odd) he had knocked over two stools. Paramore went to look for the old man and found him lying on his bed with his eyes closed.

"Mr. Trismegistus! Ah, sir, you should not have gone to sleep without me! I am your watchman, sir. The constable that preserves the good order of your dreams. Now, what's here?"

Paramore said the spell and looked into the glass. Trismegistus stood before two black doors, each as broad as the world and as high as the heavens. Above them and beyond them was nothing but black wind and dead night and cold stars. These doors (which were more vast than anyone could conceive) began to open. . . . With a sudden scream Paramore flung the glass from him and it rolled away to rest in the dust beneath a broken sixpenny mirror.

"Good morning, your Majestie!" cried Doktor Silberhof, her little silver spectacles dancing on their silver chain as she walked briskly up to the tall black throne. "They tell me that you have some news for me. And not before time."

"The Jewish magician is dead, Doktor Silberhof. He died in his sleep last night."

There was a pause for the Lord of Dreams and Nightmares to look quiet, composed, and full of grandeur, and for Doktor Silberhof to look merely puzzled.

"And that's it, is it?" she asked.

The Lord of Dreams and Nightmares gazed down at her from heights both literal and metaphoric. "Paramore, the pseudo-magician, must sleep soon and when he does . . . "

"But, your Majestie! Suppose that he does not!"

"I shall not suppose any such thing, Doktor Silberhof. The pseudo-magician never yet, in all his life, denied himself any thing that he wish'd for."

"But in the meantime, your Majestie . . . "

"In the meantime, Doktor Silberhof . . . " The Lord of Dreams and Nightmares smiled. "We wait."

Three days later Mr. Newbolt's mother was washing his small, three-year-old hands with a warm, wet cloth. It was a summer's day in Lincolnshire and Mr. Newbolt stood in his mother's cool, shadowy kitchen. Through a bright, hot doorway he saw flowers, herbs, and sleepy, humming bees.

Mr. Newbolt's maid was washing his shriveled, eighty-year-old legs. Mr. Newbolt lay in a bed in a silent, candlelit room in Friday-street. The maid straightened herself and put a hand to her aching back. In the other hand she held a warm, wet cloth.

Mr. Newbolt knew dimly that one washing took place in the Dreame-Countries and one in the waking world, but as to which was which Mr. Newbolt neither knew nor cared.

Mr. Newbolt dreamt that someone with a thin, anxious face came to see him and talked to him for a long while about a matter of great importance.

". . . and so what am I to do, sir?"

"About what, John?" asked Mr. Newbolt.

"King Morpheus," said Paramore.

Mr. Newbolt considered this for a long while and then he said, "You have made him angry, John."

"Yes, I know. But what can I do?"

"Why," said Mr. Newbolt, "nothing that I know of. He talks of broken rules and robberies and insults (I hear him, John, in my dreams). I daresay he will pursue you to the ends of the earth and beyond . . . "

They sat in silence a while longer and then Mr. Newbolt said kindly, "You look a little pale, John. You are not well. Let Mary make you a posset."

Paramore laughed a strange sort of laugh. "No, no, I am quite well."

After this Mr. Newbolt appeared to fall asleep again (always supposing that he could truly have been said to have woken up in the first place), but just as Paramore was at the door, Mr. Newbolt roused. He said, "Were he only like his sister—what a difference that would make! For there never was such a sweet and gentle lady! I hear her footsteps, as she goes about the world. I hear the swish-swish-swish of her silken gown and the jingle-jangle of the silver chain about her neck. Her smile is full of comfort and her eyes are kind and happy! How I long to see her!"

"Who, sir?" asked Paramore, puzzled.

"Why, his sister, John. His sister."

Outside in Friday-street a thin, cold rain was falling. Paramore looked up and saw a rough, country giant of a man walking toward him, wearing a curious hat which covered his eyes and which the man had apparently fashioned for himself out of old paper. Perhaps the man pushed against him, for Paramore (who had not slept all week) suddenly found that he was steadying himself against a wall. Just for a moment Paramore let his head rest against the wall, but as he did so he noticed that inside the red bricks there were tiny grains of golden sand. . . .

There was an orchard walled with rose red brick. Once the walls had been covered with roses, but it was winter now and all that was left was the thorns. There was grass; there were many apple trees. But grass and trees were all wintry now. In the mazy pattern of winter sunlight and blue shadows stood a pale king all dress't in black. His black arms were crossed. The toe of his black boot tapped upon the ground. He raised his head and look't at John Paramore. . . .

Paramore woke with a start. He walked very slowly back to Stopp't-Clock Yard. In that gray rain London seemed no more than the dream of a city and all the people in it ghosts. That evening someone came to Paramore and told him that Ralph Clerrihew (an Islington candlestick-maker whom Isaac had brought back out of dreams four weeks before) had disappeared from the face of the earth.

On the next day (which was Wednesday), at three o'clock in the afternoon, Paramore was descending the staircase in the Jew's house in Stopp't-Clock Yard. At the first step he felt tired to death. At the second step he felt tired to death. At the third step he touched some particularly frail part of the wood and the staircase shuddered, letting fall cobwebs and dirt. Paramore looked up and saw, without surprise, tiny grains of golden sand falling into his face. . . .

The next step was a barren orchard with a pale, smiling king.

In that moment Lord Morpheus stole back a Mortlake laundress—the mother of four little ones. On Thursday, in the time it took for Paramore's eyes to close twice, Lord Morpheus took back a negro seaman and a famous prostitute named Mrs. Aphra Pytchley; on Friday it was a baby and an albino doll-maker from Wapping; and on Saturday a glove-maker and his wife. On Sunday Paramore fell asleep for a full quarter of an hour, but Lord Morpheus took back no one at all. Paramore could only suppose that Morpheus meant it for a joke—to ape a greater divinity by resting on the Sabbath. But in none of Isaac's books was there the least hint that Morpheus knew how to make jokes.

By the following Saturday in all the coffeehouses and taverns in London men vied with each other to tell the most grisly tales of the things that Paramore did to himself to keep himself awake. But even if these tales were true, then they did no good—for by the following Saturday Morpheus had taken back all the revenants but two.

At the house in Stopp't-Clock Yard the dead Jewess went into her father's little closet, where all his books and powders were kept, and found Paramore slumped upon the ground, his head nodding between the pages of an open book.

"Paramore!" she cried. "Get up!"

Paramore got slowly to his feet.

"I never knew a man could look so tired," she said.

"Oh . . . I am not tired. It is this house. It is so dark. It makes a man sleepy."

"Then let us leave it instantly and go elsewhere! Where shall we go?"

"Oh . . . " he began. But somehow he forgot what he wanted to say.

"Paramore!" She took his face between her hands. "I was born in the Ghetto at Venice, where curious people come to look at the Jews. There I have seen great Spanish ladies, all dark and soft and glowing, like sunsets. Paramore, would not you like to see a lady the color of a Spanish garden on a summer's evening?"

Paramore smiled a ghost of his crooked smile as it once had been. "I prefer women the color of English gardens on a winter's afternoon. That is my melancholy English humor."

The dead Jewess laugh't and began to speak of English humors. . . .

There was an orchard walled with rose red brick, where a great multitude of birds had settled in the barren trees—birds of the commonest sorts, blackbirds, mistle thrushes, robins, finches, and wrens. But something made them take fright and all flew away together. The pale king lifted his head and smiled. . . .

"Paramore!" She struck his cheek with the flat of her hand and he started awake. She pushed him against the wall the better to hold him up. "You are every bit as clever as he. How will you fight him? How?"

Paramore's ghostly smile appeared. "I will order all the king's army to lie down . . . " he said.

"Good!" she cried. "We shall lay them all down on Salisbury Plain—even the horses! What then?"

"And then, in an enchanted sleep, the English army shall march on Morpheus's castle and pull him from his throne."

"Yes!" she cried. "Paramore, it is a pity that you and I should have to part so soon."

"Perhaps," said Paramore and reached up and took down a great blue jar from the shelf. He emptied some white powder into a little leather pouch and tucked it inside his shirt.

That night it rained, and all of London's sins were washed away. All the streets were full of water and, once it had stopp't raining, all the water was full of stars. Stars hung above the City and stars hung below and London hung between. John Paramore—onetime astrologer and seducer, self-styled poet and magician, present madman—appeared high up among the stars, upon a roof in Blue Ball Court—laughing and singing and calling on Morpheus to come and fight him. He was very drunk.

Householders from Shoe-lane and Gunpowder-alley got out of their beds and gathered in the street below, with the kind and neighborly intention of seeing John Paramore break his neck and of telling his relations all about it afterward. Some of the bystanders found a strange, thin man with a long, pale face lurking in a doorway and, believing this to be Lord Morpheus, began to pull his hair and kick his shins and roundly to abuse him, until it was discovered that he was not Morpheus at all, but a cheesemonger from Aberdeen.

Later Paramore went walking through the dark City streets, from Holborn to the village of Mile-End and back again, stumbling through the scaffolding of all the half-built City churches, clambering over all the beams and shadows and blocks of Portland stone that waited in Cheapside for Sir Christopher Wren to make them into St. Paul's. He could have told you—if you had cared to know such a thing—the number of Morpheus's eyelashes and described in most minute detail the faint crescent-shaped mark on his cheek an inch below his left eye. For there was nothing left in Paramore's head but Lord Morpheus and he filled it till it was nigh to bursting.

Toward morning London grew colder. The sky was filled with clouds like torn bed sheets and broken mattresses, and a gentle snow began to fall. There was not another soul in all the world.

The snow spotted the red-brick buildings and the piazzas. Lofty statues gazed down on Paramore with something remarkably like pity and the flooded Thames flowed silently between walls of silvery grey Carrara marble.

"Carrara marble?" murmured Paramore in amazement. "Lord, what city is this?"

"Do you not know it?" asked a voice.

"Well, sir, it is London—that much I do know. But she was not so fair and lovely yesterday, I am sure. So many beautiful buildings! So many fine canals—with a pale rose-colored dawn in each and every one! And everything so very geometrical!"

"This is the London that Sir Christopher Wren designed when the old city was burnt up in the Great Fire fifteen years ago but which the King refused to build. So I took Sir Chris's drawings and I built his city here."

"Well, I will not tell him, sir, or he will want paying for it. Faith, sir, those Italians brag and brag, but I doubt they have anything so fair as this."

"A city the color of a winter's afternoon," said the voice thoughtfully.

"And do they want magicians in this city, sir?" asked John Paramore. "I only ask because I find myself a little quiet at the moment."

"Indeed? And why is that?" asked the voice.

"Ah, sir," sighed Paramore. "It sometimes happens that a small man—such as myself—has the misfortune to offend a great prince—how or why he cannot tell. But ever after all his actions miscarry and his life runs all awry."

There was silence for a moment.

Then the voice said—in accents of great bitterness—"For Morpheus is an idle king, grown dull and foolish from the long years of security. His walls are old and crumbling. His gates are unguarded. His servants are not watchful."

Paramore looked up and saw a doorcase surmounted with two figures, splendid but solemn, representing Winter and Autumn. Between the two was the Dream-king, with his black elbow propped up on the Autumn's marble head and his black boot idly resting in Winter's marble bosom and his long, black hair whipp't by the wind.

"Ha!" cried Paramore. "Now this is fortunate. I have lately heard a puzzling rumor that Your Grace has taken it into his head to be angry with me and, since it is my wish always to have Your Grace's good opinion, I have come to make amends."

"Paramore," said Lord Morpheus, "is there no end to your impudence?" Then he said, "I am glad you like my London. I intend you shall stay here for a good long while."

In the empty streets the chill winds (or dreams of winds) eddied and played. Yet the streets were not *quite* empty. Dreams of voices and dreams of sad, tolling bells were carried on the wind, and what looked like ghostly bundles of fluttering, flapping rags.

"What are they?" asked Paramore.

"Old dreams. Tired dreams. Bitter, angry dreams," said Lord Morpheus. "You will come to know them better."

"Your Grace is very kind," murmured Paramore, but he seemed to be thinking of something else. "Ah," he sighed, "if only Your Grace were a woman, then I know that I might make you pity me."

"True, Paramore," said Morpheus. "For so many years you have lived on the kindness of women. But there are none here for you to play your tricks on."

Along the street (which both was and was not Cheapside), came the dead Jewess. She walked slowly, for she had a great way to go and had all the breadth of Dreame-Countries to cross before she would reach Heaven's Marches. In her arms she carried the little Christian boy, the widow's child, Orlando Beaufort. He was not sleeping (for the dead do not sleep) but he had buried his face in her neck and his golden curls were mingling with her own.

Lord Morpheus raised one black eyebrow and smiled at Paramore as if to say: *she* cannot help you. *She* cannot help herself.

Deborah Trismegistus stopped in front of the doorway where Lord Morpheus sat. To Morpheus she said, "I see, sir, that you have mended your walls." And to Paramore she said, "'Tis always disheartening to see a king. They are never so tall as fancy paints them."

But Paramore did not reply.

In the waking world snow falls directly to the ground or is carried on the wind, in accordance with the rules and protocols of the waking world. In Dreame-Countries the snow falls and returns into Morpheus. It melds with his white skin in accordance with the rules and protocols of that world. Morpheus's face glistened with snow. He parted the snow to get a better view of Paramore. For it seemed to Morpheus that something had happened to Paramore—it was as if his soul had fallen away in grains of sand and reappeared the next moment with some strange new quality.

Without warning a lady appeared. She came from the direction of Fridaystreet, for she had just been with Mr. Newbolt. She strode capably through the snow. She wore a black silk gown and something very queer swung from a silver chain about her neck. Her smile was full of comfort and her eyes were kind and happy. She was just as Mr. Newbolt had described.

And the name of this lady was Death.

What happened next can only truly be expressed in metaphors—being, as it is, an exchange between two immortal beings. But let us say for simplicity's sake that a kind of argument took place between Morpheus and his sister, Death. Let us say that both of them claimed John Paramore's soul. Let us say that the argument went on for some time, but that the lady (who was a great deal older and cleverer than her brother, and who had ample proof that Paramore had just died of poison in an alley near Blackfriars) paid not the least attention to her brother's many grievances, and Morpheus was forc'd to yield to her.

Death and John Paramore, the dead Jewess and the dead Christian child went away together, and already John Paramore was beginning to bargain and to plead with Death to be allowed to follow the dead Jewess into her own particular Heaven (". . . For I have often thought, madam, how strangely Jewish I feel in my soul . . . "), and Morpheus heard his sister (a most compassionate and forgiving lady) begin to laugh at Paramore's nonsense.

It was whispered among some of Lord Morpheus's servants and subjects that their lord was displeased: but who among them could say for certain? Those dreams which haunted London that night might well have peered up at Morpheus to discover if he were angry, but they surely came away none the wiser—for there was nothing in his eyes but the black night and the cold stars.

AFTERWORD: DEATH

Tori Amos

I discovered Tori in 1991, when she sent me a tape, through a friend, of the record that would become her album *Little Earthquakes*. We've been fast friends and mutual fans ever since.

This is the introduction she wrote to *Death: The High Cost of Living*.

It's funny but on good days I don't think of her so much.

In fact never. I never just say hi when the sun is on my tongue and my belly's all warm. On bad days I talk to Death constantly, not about suicide because honestly that's not dramatic enough. Most of us love the stage, and suicide is definitely your last performance, and, being addicted to the stage, suicide was never an option—plus people get to look you over and stare at your fatty bits and you can't cross your legs to give that flattering thigh angle and that's depressing.

So we talk.

She says things no one else seems to come up with, like let's have a hot dog, and then it's like nothing's impossible.

She told me once there is a part of her in everyone, though Neil believes I'm more Delirium than Tori, and Death taught me to accept that, you know, wear your butterflies with pride. And when I do accept that, I know Death is somewhere inside of me. She was the kind of girl all the girls wanted to be, I believe, because of her acceptance of "what is." She keeps reminding me there is change in the "what is" but change cannot be made till you accept the "what is."

Like yesterday, all the recording machines were breaking down again. We almost lost a master take and the band leaves tomorrow and we can't do any more music till we resolve this. We're in the middle of nowhere in the desert, and my being wants to go crawl under a cactus and wish it away. Instead, I dyed my hair and she visited me and I started to accept the mess I'm in. I know that mess spelled backwards is ssem, and I felt much better armed with that information. Over the last few hours I've allowed myself to feel defeated, and just like she said, if you allow yourself to feel the way you really feel, maybe you won't be afraid of that feeling anymore.

When you're on your knees you're closer to the ground. Things seem nearer somehow.

If all I can say is I'm not in this swamp, I'm not in this swamp, then there is not a rope in front of me and there is not an alligator behind me and there is not a girl sitting at the edge eating a hot dog, and if I believe that, then dying would be the only answer because then Death couldn't come and say Peachy to me anymore and, after all, she has a brother who believes in hope.

Tori Amos has been playing the piano since she was two years old. She was accepted into the Peabody Conservatory at the age of five. She was kicked out for irreconcilable differences at the age of eleven. Her album *Little Earthquakes* was initially released in the U.K. in January 1992 and worldwide release followed. A 1992 world tour gave Tori a chance to eat lots of good food and play over two-hundred cities worldwide alone at her piano. Since then Tori has released two bestselling more albums, *Under the Pink* in 1994 and *Boys for Pele* in 1996.

Clive Barker established himself as a major voice in the horror field with the publication of his anthologies, the *Book of Blood 1–4*, in the 1980s. Novels such as *Imajica* and *The Damnation Game* and films such as *Hellraiser* and *Nightbreed* only strengthen that claim. The covers and interior artwork of many of Clive's works are drawn and painted by him as well. A novelist, playwright, filmmaker, and artist, Clive Barker qualifies as a true Renaissance Man of the Macabre and the Fantastique.

Steven Brust is the popular author of the Vlad Taltos series, chronicling the adventures of an assassin-for-hire. His most recent works include *The Phoenix Guard* and *500 Years After*.

Brenda W. Clough is the author of four fantasy novels, a novel for young readers, and a number of short stories. Her latest book, *How Like a God*, will be published by Tor Books. She has been reading and collecting comics since she was seven years old.

Susanna Clarke lives in Cambridge, England, where she spends most of her time editing cookbooks and watching people take photographs of food. In her stories, she likes to blend history with magic. She is presently working on a novel set in a nineteenth-century Britain where magic is a respected profession, more or less. Her other stories appear in *Starlight* and *White Swan, Black Raven*.

Nancy A. Collins is the author of *Paint it Black, Walking Wolf, Wild Blood, In the Blood, Tempter,* and *Sunglasses After Dark.* Her collected Sonja Blue Cycle, *Midnight Blue,* was published in omnibus format by White Wolf in early 1995. Nancy is currently working on the comics and screenplay adaptations of *Sunglasses After Dark* and the fourth installment in the Sonja Blue Cycle, *A Dozen Black Roses,* and a romantic dark fantasy called *Angels on Fire.* She currently resides in New York City with her husband, anti-artiste Joe Christ, and their dog, Scrapple.

George Alec Effinger began writing science fiction in 1970 and has published about twenty novels and six collections of short fiction. Beyond his science fiction, Effinger has written two crime novels, *Felicia* and *Shadow Money.* His most recently published novel is *The Exile Kiss,* the third book in the Budayeen series that began with *When Gravity Fails.* He is collaborating with Walter Jon Williams to combine the worlds of *When Gravity Fails* and *Hardwired.*

John M. Ford is the author of eight science fiction and fantasy novels and many pieces of short fiction, including the World Fantasy Award–winning novel *The Dragon Waiting* and the Nebula Award finalist "Fugue State." His stories and poetry have appeared in *Omni, Analog,* the anthology *Masterpieces of Fantasy and Wonder,* and many other publications.

Lisa Goldstein's first book, *The Red Magician,* won the American Book Award for Best Paperback in 1983. Since then she has published six novels, the most recent being *Summer King, Winter Fool,* a short story collection, *Travellers in Magic,* and numerous short stories. Her novels and short stories have been nominated for the Hugo, Nebula, and World Fantasy Awards.

Colin Greenland won all three U.K. science fiction awards in 1990 for *Take Back Plenty.* His other works include: *Death Is No Obstacle,* a book-length interview with Michael Moorcock; *Harm's Way,* a Victorian space opera; the Tabitha Jute trilogy, *Take Back Plenty, Seasons of Plenty,* and *Mother of Plenty*; and a graphic novel with Dave McKean, to be called *Tempesta.*

Karen Haber has been published in several anthologies, among them *After the King*, *The Further Adventures of Batman*, and *Alien Pregnant by Elvis*. She has just finished the last book, *Sister Blood*, in a science fiction trilogy published by DAW Books. Karen is the wife of science fiction author Robert Silverberg, and lives in California.

Barbara Hambly's works are mostly sword-and-sorcery fantasy novels, though she has also written a historical whodunit and novels and novelizations from television shows, notably *Beauty and the Beast* and *Star Trek*. She has also made an excursion into vampire literature with *Those Who Hunt the Night*, and at one time she wrote scripts for animated cartoon shows.

Caitlín R. Kiernan was born in Dublin, Ireland, but has lived most of her life in the southeastern U.S. She holds degrees in philosophy and anthropology, and has worked as a paleontologist, a newspaper columnist, and an exotic dancer. In 1992 she began pursuing fiction writing full-time and has sold stories to a number of magazines and anthologies including *Aberrations*, *Eldritch Tales*, *High Fantastic*, and *The Very Last Book of the Dead*. Her first novel, *The Five of Cups*, was published by Transylvania Press.

Mark Kreighbaum has had stories published in anthologies such as *Enchanted Forests* and *Weird Tales from Shakespeare*. His work has also appeared in numerous small press magazines. His latest novel, a science fiction collaboration with Katherine Kerr called *Palace*, was published in 1996.

Frank McConnell is a professor of English at the University of California at Santa Barbara. He is a literary critic, author of four Harry Garnish detective novels, and the media columnist for *Commonweal* for television, popular culture, comics, and rock 'n' roll. In his undergraduate course, *The History of Storytelling*, Neil Gaiman's *Sandman* has emerged as a major topic of study.

Robert Rodi is the author of *Fag Hag*, *Closet Case*, *What They Did to Princess Paragon*, and *Drag Queen*. His fifth book, *Kept Boy*, is due in November. A longtime comics and fantasy devotee, he had several stories published in the 1980s anthology magazine, *Epic Illustrated*, and was, for many years, a regular critic for *The Comics Journal*. He lives in Chicago with his partner, Jeffrey Smith.

Lawrence Schimel is the editor of a dozen anthologies. His own stories and poems have appeared in over eighty anthologies including: *Weird Tales from Shakespeare, Excalibur,* and *The Random House Treasury of Light Verse,* and in numerous periodicals, including: *The Saturday Evening Post, The Tampa Tribune, Physics Today, The Writer, Modern Short Stories,* and *Cricket.* Twenty-four years old, he lives in Manhattan, where he writes and edits full-time.

Delia Sherman is a teacher and novelist who lives in the Boston area. Her novel, *The Porcelain Dove,* has garnered much critical acclaim. Her short fiction has appeared in many major genre magazines as well.

Will Shetterly is a novelist (*Elsewhere, Cats Have No Lord*) as well as a comic book writer (*Captain Confederacy*). With his wife, author Emma Bull, he has coedited five collections of short stories about the magical city Liavek. He is also the publisher of SteelDragon Press, which produces limited-edition books as well as compact discs and tapes. He and his wife live in Minneapolis.

Tad Williams is a novelist, newspaper journalist, short story author, and writer of television and film screenplays. He produces the interactive television show *Twenty-First Century Vaudeville,* seen in San Francisco and Boston, with his next sights on the U.K. His syndicated radio talk shows, *One Step Beyond* and *Radio Free America,* have focused on controversial subjects such as clandestine intelligence, the drug-and-gun trade, political crimes, and assassinations. After spending most of his life in the San Francisco Bay Area, Tad now resides in London.

Gene Wolfe has written mainstream and young adult novels and many magazine articles, but is best known as a science fiction writer, picking up the Nebula Award (for his novella "The Death of Doctor Island"), the Chicago Foundation for Literature Award (for his novel *Peace*), and the Rhysling Award for SF Poetry (for "The Computer Iterates the Greater Trumps") along the way. His most recent full length works, and particularly his exemplary *Book of the New Sun* series, fall into an entirely different category, merging high technology with an almost Dark Age environment. Meanwhile, his short fiction continues to prove you never know just what to expect from him.

Neil Gaiman has been awarded more Will Eisner Comic Industry Awards than any other creator, took the World Fantasy Award for *The Sandman* #19 (making it the first comic ever to win a prose literary award), and has awards for his comics from England, Finland, Canada, Austria, Spain, and Brazil. His miscellany, *Angels and Visitations*, was nominated for two World Fantasy Awards, and was awarded the International Horror Critics Guild for Best Collection. In addition to *The Sandman* he is the author of such graphic novels as *Signal to Noise, Mr. Punch*, and *Violent Cases*. He cowrote, with Terry Pratchett, *Good Omens*, a funny novel about how the world is going to end and we're all going to die. He just made a six-part TV series for the BBC called *Neverwhere*, and is working on a *Neverwhere* novel. He has just finished his first book for children, *The Day I Swapped My Dad for Two Goldfish*, and was surprised to find himself acting in the BBC Radio adaptation of *Signal to Noise*. The *Sandman* collection *Dream Country* was picked by Waterstones and *The Observer* as one of the ten coolest books of the 1990s. He is 35 years old, and is intimately familiar with jet lag in all its forms.

Edward E. Kramer is a writer and coeditor of *Grails* (nominated for the World Fantasy Award for Best Anthology of 1992), *Confederacy of the Dead, Phobias, Dark Destiny, Elric: Tales of the White Wolf, Excalibur, Tombs, Dark Love, Forbidden Acts*, and many additional works in progress. Ed's original fiction appears in a number of anthologies as well; his first novel, *Killing Time*, is forthcoming from White Wolf. His credits also include over a decade of work as a music critic and photojournalist. A graduate of the Emory University School of Medicine, Ed is a clinical and educational consultant in Atlanta. He is fond of human skulls, exotic snakes, and underground caves.

Martin H. Greenberg has edited more than seven-hundred fiction and nonfiction books. He is also a member of the Board of Advisors of the Sci-Fi Channel and CEO of Tekno-Books, the book packaging division of BIG Entertainment. He has received lifetime achievement awards in both the science fiction and, most recently, the mystery fields.